ELEVEN DAYS

Graham Guy

Also By
GRAHAM GUY

Only Eagles Fly

Savage Skies

ELEVEN DAYS

Graham Guy

DoctorZed
Publishing
www.doctorzed.com

First published 1999.

Second Publication 2013 by DoctorZed Publishing

DoctorZed Publishing books may be ordered through booksellers or by contacting:

DoctorZed Publishing
IDAHO
10 Vista Ave
Skye, South Australia 5072
www.doctorzed.com
61-(0)8 8431-4965

ISBN: 978-0-9875445-5-1 (sc)
ISBN: 978-0-9875445-6-8 (e)

A CIP number for this book is available at the National Library of Australia.

Cover image © Branislav Ostojic | Dreamstime.com

Printed in Australia
DoctorZed Publishing rev. date: 09/09/2013

This is for Eugenie

Author's Note

Eleven Days was born on board a Greyhound Bus in the early hours of the morning half way between Los Angeles and New York in 1977. It was a strange moment. You see, for years I'd been writing song lyrics and was in America trying to find a composer but this time, instead of a lyric bouncing forth from my mind, *Eleven Days* arrived, in its entirety.

How could this be? I don't write books. I write songs. But *Eleven Days* became stronger and stronger to the point where I cut short my overseas trip to return home and write it.

Upon completion, I sent off the manuscript to as many publishers, agents and major stars as I could manage. Then came the rejections. Mind you, I was already very schooled in rejection having put up with it for 10 years with song lyrics I had submitted to various artists and agencies, but I had never experienced anything quite like what came back at me from my first attempt at a novel. So I put it aside.

Two years later I rewrote *Eleven Days* and began the whole process over again. But again, the rejections came back and that's how it was for 20 years. I wrote and rewrote the story 5 times during that period but always with the same result.

Finally, through the generosity of others, it was published and made its way into book stores in 1999. It bounced straight into the No. 1 position, ahead of all things *Star Wars*. *Eleven Days* stayed in the Top 10 for 6 months and to date still remains the biggest selling novel in South Australia by a South Australian Author. There were 5 print runs, 3 x 3000 and 2 x 2000 - a total of 10,000 copies sold.

The journey of *Eleven Days* since it first went into book stores in 1999 has therefore been one of great joy and immense frustration. Despite its local success in Adelaide, it still carried no weight with publishers or agents, nationally or internationally. Like Bryce Courtney's *Power of One* which he used as a doorstop in his house for many years until some bright spark picked it up and said, "Hey, this is great!" - *Eleven Days* is now my doorstop.

Yet even after 36 years, I still believe somewhere, somehow, someone will pick up *Eleven Days* and say, "Hey, this is great!".

I thank you, dear reader, to help make this dream happen.

Graham Guy
Adelaide 2013

"Where your treasure is there will your heart be also."

Matthew 6:21

Chapter 1

Katie McFarlane had tears rolling out of her eyes as she listened to her family's solicitor, Jim Duncan, read the last will and testament of her late parents.

They had died so suddenly. So tragically. *All they wanted was my happiness. Oh God, why didn't you take me instead?* Katie thought, as she felt the emptiness of her world close in on her. She wished an immediate end to 1992. She would face the recession and any misery it brought upon her world in the new year. It couldn't be any worse than this.

It was an overly hot spring day in Adelaide, South Australia. The traffic ambled down King William Street in its usual non-hurried manner, and the dresses worn by the throng of lunchtime office workers gave hint that summer would be arriving early. High up in the Mutual Insurance building, Jim Duncan looked across at Katie.

"Do you think you'll keep the house?"

She withdrew a small lace handkerchief from her Oroton handbag and dried her eyes. "One of the last things my mother gave me," she said, clasping the bag and running her fingers over the catch. Jim Duncan didn't speak.

For a moment Katie sat in silence, with her eyes closed. The roar of a passenger jet caused her momentarily to glance out the window. She caught the reflection of its fuselage as it climbed and disappeared from sight. She felt her stomach twist into a knot and the bitter taste of heartbreak emerge in her mouth. She recalled how the sound of an aeroplane used to give her goosebumps, just from the thought of where it could take her. But that all seemed so long ago.

She began to remember. *Sydney airport*, she thought. *That's when it all started. Six months ago. The day I met him.*

1

* * *

It had been another busy day in the departure lounge of Ansett Australia at Sydney Airport. Being the last weekend of the school holidays, mass confusion reigned - kids, grand-parents, surf boards, baggage, farewell kisses, hurried hugs and pleas of safe returns coming from all directions. Excitement, tears, smiles, depression, loneliness, and anxiety sprang forth as flights were called. Katie McFarlane sat alone. Watching, witnessing, observing all the mayhem. She was a little bemused by it all.

Then her departure was called and she began making her way up the boarding platform into Business Class of the aircraft.

Paul Redman had also been waiting patiently in the Ansett Airline's departure lounge. He now squeezed past Katie as he took up the seat next to her. "Sorry," he apologised, as he overbalanced in her direction.

Katie didn't reply. *Do you mind?* she cursed to herself.

As Paul manoeuvred his briefcase to sit in behind his legs, he offered Katie a slightly embarrassed smile. "Hi."

She ignored him. *Why do I always get the creep who wants to talk?*

As the jet took off, Paul waited until the Fasten-Your-Seat-Belts sign went out and tried again. "Visiting friends?"

Go away, Katie fumed, pretending not to hear, instead taking a magazine from the holder at the rear of the seat in front of her.

Slightly embarrassed at being ignored, Paul gladly accepted the offer of a newspaper from the passing air hostess.

Moments later, tea and coffee was offered. "Coffee, white with one, thank you," Katie answered.

"Sir?"

"The same, thanks."

Ahh, the boy's got a mind of his own, Katie thought. As she tried to pull down the tray from the rear of the seat in front of her, it snagged. Paul moved to help, but Katie cut him off. "I can manage, thank you," she said, momentarily glancing at him. It was the first time she'd actually looked at man and she liked what she saw. *Maybe this guy's not such a creep after all*, she consoled herself, taking a second glance.

Paul cussed under his breath, telling himself he was sitting next to some jumped-up pain in the arse. But the truth of the matter was he resented the rejection of his politeness and it embarrassed him. He sought to hide himself in his newspaper. But as he scanned the newsprint, his mind was fixed firmly on the woman seated next to him. *God, she's wearing Paris too*, as wafts of the perfume flowed across him. Suddenly he became uncomfortable. Fidgety. *Who is this woman?*, he kept asking himself. *So cool, calm and collected. No rings. Immaculately presented and smelling like seventh-heaven.*

"Your coffee madam... and yours sir."

The hostess's voice gave Katie another opportunity to glance at the man next to her. *Tailored suit, Bernard moccasins, striped shirt, plain silk tie. Nice looking too. Slight cleft in the chin. Strong jaw. Seems to have a fierce determination about himself. Omega gold watch. Cufflinks. Probably a rich little mummy's boy. Maybe not. Hard to tell. With hands like that, he obviously doesn't dig ditches. And what's that?* she asked herself, noticing a propeller blade in the buttonhole of his suit jacket. *Oh God, he's a pilot!* Her mind flashed back to her childhood days when flight fascinated her. But as she got older and learned that sometimes aeroplanes crash, she began to fear them. *Why am I thinking like this? I haven't even spoken to the guy. I refuse to speak to him. I wonder if he'll try again? Probably thinks I'm a spoiled brat. What do I care? I'm not interested in him anyway. Much!*

Paul Redman glanced across at Katie McFarlane again. He was about to speak when fear gripped his gut at the prospect of further rejection. *I wonder why she won't talk to me? Probably a mummy's little richie. Maybe not. Her clothes aren't expensive. Very nice tailored skirt and jacket. Maybe Stitches. Certainly not K-Mart and certainly not Carla Zampatti. Footrest shoes. Nice watch. Looks like a Citizen. Complementing bracelets and gold bangles. But what a face? And that perfume. God what a turn-on!*

He sat in silence, twisting uncomfortably in his seat from time to time for the rest of the flight.

* * *

At touchdown in Adelaide, both left the aircraft and went their separate ways. *It's my fault, I should have at least spoken to him*, Katie tried to console herself as she walked into the terminal building, careful to keep Paul within her peripheral vision. *Maybe all is not lost. I don't believe I'm going to do this.*

Paul Redman savoured what drifts of Paris remained in his nostrils while casually, but determinedly, scanning the arrival lounge. He couldn't understand why a sudden surge of panic ran through his body. She hadn't even spoken to him. He felt the blood run to his cheeks, forced to face the inevitable. She had gone. Disbelievingly, he scanned the arrival area, but there was no sign of her. He didn't know whether to feel pain or relief. All she had done was cause him embarrassment. He made his way to the cocktail bar, a little unsteady, a little nonplussed and a little shaken that a anonymous person could have such an effect on him.

"Sir?" greeted the barman.

"Brandy and dry. Make it a double will you, please?"

Paul Redman swallowed half the glass in one mouthful and sat pondering the last couple of hours of his life when a voice from behind smacked him back to the present.

"I'd really like to apologise to you for being rude."

Paul froze like a statue. The barman smiled at Paul, then discreetly turned away. A gentle waft of Paris perfume alerted him. *My God it's her!* He braced himself as he turned to face who he knew was standing arm's length from him. His senses were in turmoil, but he knew above all else he had to create the impression that her presence had no affect on him. He also couldn't resist a pay back. "Well if it's not Miss Independence..."

"I guess I asked for that didn't I? I'm sorry, I knew this wasn't a good idea," she said sheepishly, turning to walk away.

Paul jerked himself from the bar stool and gently took her arm. "Hey, I'm sorry."

She withdrew her arm from Paul's hand. "Look, I just feel a little awkward right now...if you don't mind I'd like to go."

"Don't leave it like this," Paul said. "Can't we try for a take-two?" He hoped she would perceive a note of sincerity in his tone. Slowly she eased off. "OK...take three then?" It got through her defences.

"I'm Katie McFarlane," she said, offering Paul her outstretched hand.

He grasped it firmly. "And I'm Paul Redman."

Gesturing at his glass on the bar, "So, proof or otherwise?"

"Just a mineral water, thank you."

For a moment, an uneasy silence fell between them. Then as one spoke, so did the other. Then silence. Then the same again. They laughed, then repeated the same child-like bungle of words.

"Sorry," Paul said, "your turn."

The barman placed a mineral water in front of Katie. She took a small sip. "So, where's home to Paul Redman?"

"Adelaide."

"Do you normally sit around in airport cocktail bars drinking on your own?"

"This is not a normal day," he told her.

"Bad business meeting?"

"Worse than that."

"Oh really?"

"Uh-huh."

"How worse?"

"Much worse," he added.

"Did you lose your wallet?"

"No."

"Someone steal your car?"

"Worse than that," he said.

"What then?"

Paul smiled inwardly. *I'm enjoying this.* "I've just spent two hours sitting next to the most beautiful woman I've ever seen in my life and she didn't want to know me. How much worse can it get than that?"

"Did you speak to her?"

"Uh-huh."

"What did she say?"

"Nothing."

"Nothing?"

"Nothing!" he repeated.

"Did you try again?"

"Uh-huh."

"And?"

"Nothing."

5

"Nothing, again?"

"No, nothing."

"But if she later apologised, would all be forgiven?"

"Maybe."

"What do you mean, maybe?" she asked.

"Depends."

"On what?"

"On whether she'll let me take her out to dinner."

"Don't be ridiculous."

"I love your perfume."

"I don't wear perfume," she lied.

"Paris, isn't it?"

"I have to go."

"Please don't," Paul said, reaching over to touch the top of her hand.

"This is crazy..."

"What's your star sign?"

"Oh God, this is crazy," Katie laughed.

"Tell me."

"Leo...now I really do have to go."

"Dinner with a Sagittarian could be fun."

"You're a Sagittarian?"

"You know about these things?" Paul queried.

"Everybody reads their stars," Katie laughed. "If they sound good we believe them. If they don't, they're just a lot of nonsense anyway. Besides, aren't Leos and Sagittarians supposed to be the perfect match?" She sipped more from her glass. "God, that's pretty scary."

"You married?" Paul cut in.

"No, are you?"

"No."

"So which one of us is telling lies?"

"Why would you ask that?" he asked.

"Everybody is married these days. There's not a man alive who won't lie if he thinks he can score."

"I'm not lying," Paul said, suddenly serious.

"But you want to score...sorry that wasn't fair."

"What about you. Don't women tell lies?"

6

"This one doesn't."

"So what do you do?"

"I like to keep myself challenged. And you?"

"Ah-ha, a career girl! Me? I'm always spending a hundred thousand dollars on a house," Paul answered with a grin.

"A builder?"

Paul shook his head. Then glancing down at his smooth, well kept hands, she added, "Yes, obviously with hands like that you don't carry bricks. What then?"

"I'm an architect."

Katie looked at her watch. "Now I do have to go. I guess all this didn't turn out so bad after all, did it?"

Paul could feel her slipping away. "Can I call you?" he said, a note of urgency in his tone.

Walking from the cocktail bar, Katie glanced back over her shoulder and smiled.

Paul's arms gestured in despair. "Where?"

"I'm a nurse." Then she was gone.

Paul Redman returned to his double brandy and dry. He reached inside his coat pocket and jerked out his mobile phone. Quickly he dialled information. Then he dialled again. "Ten thousand hospitals in a city," he mumbled. "Oh well, here goes. Oh hi," he said, raising his voice as the receiver was picked up in the Royal Adelaide Hospital, "could you put me through to Katie McFarlane please?"

"One moment sir."

A female voice finally answered after the twentieth ring. "Casualty."

"Oh hi, could you help me find Katie McFarlane please?"

"Sister McFarlane you mean sir."

"Yes of course, Sister McFarlane." He felt a thrill run through his body.

"She's off today sir."

"When will she be in next?"

"Who's calling please?"

"Her brother, it's her brother calling," he lied. *Hope she's bloody well got one.*

"Katie is back at ten o'clock tonight, Mr McFarlane."

7

He pressed the OFF button on his mobile. "Yeeees!" he yelled, throwing his arms in the air, startling other patrons in the cocktail bar.

Paul Redman made his way to the car park, located his red Mercedes and took the long way home. As he drove, he seemed oblivious to all the other traffic and everything else which surrounded him. His mind was in automation, his body removed, his senses half-dimmed by an experience he was still trying to come to terms with.

How is it possible to be totally bowled over by someone who just breezes in and out of your life in a couple of hours. And the mind games. The verbal warfare. Why did she follow me to the bar? Why didn't she speak to me on the plane? Why wouldn't she have dinner with me? Why did she change her mind? She would have to be married. Wouldn't she? How can a woman who looks like she does NOT be married? Must be something wrong with her. Has to be. Yet she's no pushover. Guess I learned that the hard way. Funny isn't it? It's always the plain-janes who get married and have kids. The pretty ones get left till last because eligible blokes just assume they're spoken for. Maybe she fits into that category. Maybe she just gets her kicks like this. To hell with it. I just know I want that woman. I really do want that woman. What a body. And that mouth. I just love that mouth, it says so much...

Smiling inwardly, Katie McFarlane pulled away from the airport toll gate. *I don't believe I just did that,* she thought to herself. *I have never done anything like that in my life before. He must think I'm nothing but a smart mouth. Maybe he likes a woman to be a little forthright.* She laughed out loud at this suggestion of herself. *A little forthright. It's a wonder he didn't tell me to get lost. And all those questions. Hardly gave the poor bloke a straight answer. So he's an architect! You sure can pick 'em can't you girl? He's probably as exciting as watching the grass grow.*

She exited onto the main road and headed west. *Can't take much notice of today though. Mind you, he was quick on his feet. I wasn't too bad either, if I do say so myself. So now what? He's got to be married. Or divorced. Didn't ask him if he had any kids. Wonder if he'll try and find me? No he won't. Oh, he won't bother, will he? Oh well, guess it was fun while it lasted. Will he find me? Why would he? When it's all boiled down, I was downright rude to him. Why didn't I speak when he first got on the plane? That would have been much easier. I wonder if he'll ring? In your dreams, girl, in your dreams. But he did seem quite nice'*

Paul Redman parked the Mercedes in North Terrace in front of Ayers House restaurant, just across the road from the Royal Adelaide Hospital. It had just gone ten p.m. He tapped his fingers against his mobile phone in his breast pocket. He looked back over his shoulder to the front of the hospital, then checked his watch again. Still tapping his fingers on the phone, he again felt that hollow, dry pain grip his stomach. *Will I or won't I?*

He was still contemplating the question he was posing to himself when a single beam from a high-powered torch caught him in the middle of the face.

Chapter 2

'Slick' Bennedict was always a mongrel. Right from school days when he rode in tandem with his awkward gawky mate 'Roly' Patterson.

The gum-chewing, recess-time smokers were the high school girls Slick appealed to. Elvis Presley and Rock 'n' Roll were just beginning to emerge and Slick was quick to move into the slipstream.

Even at fifteen years of age, Slick was given a wide berth by others his own age, as they knew that to mess with him meant you also messed with barrel-chested, buck-toothed Roly, as strong as a bull for a kid his age. Upset Slick and you got the treatment. That meant being lured to the rear of the shelter-shed, grabbed in a bear-hug from behind by Roly then punched almost senseless by Slick. Just before release, the unfortunate victim was warned to forget who did this to them.

Roly, almost on cue, would whip out a comb from his back pocket so Slick could return to the schoolyard in an unruffled state. But you can't fool kids. When Slick and Roly were doing their business, they would stand around in huddles waiting for their bloodied friend to return, cowered and beaten.

The two would then wander over to a group of giggling girls whose faces showed evidence of their first experiences of applying cheap make-up, eye-shadow and pale pink lipstick. Slick knew and quickly recognised the signs. "Go for the chicks with the real short skirts and the pale pink lipstick," he'd tell Roly.

Roly hero-worshipped Slick and Slick knew it. "Why?"

"Cos you can smack 'em round, make their tits bleed...even poke sticks up their arse if you want to. And they really like sucking dicks."

"Yeah!" Roly would say, pleading to be told more.

"Yeah."

"But do you really punch 'em out?"

"Well I don't punch 'em out. I slap 'em round. You get abused and all that shit, but they love it. Especially those bitches with the pale pink lips," he said, gesturing towards a particular group.

"But why do you make their tits bleed?"

"They're only fucking bitches mate, why not? Besides, it gives you a bigger stiff dick."

"Faaark...really?"

Slick Bennedict and Roly Patterson couldn't have been more opposite in appearance and intelligence. Slick was tall and his thin body was exaggerated by his choice to wear stove-pipe, black-studded jeans, pink shirts undone to the chest with the collars turned up, iridescent pink socks and black suede, ripple-soled boots. And by some sheer stroke of good luck, his handsome face had eluded the pimples and acne that plagued most other teenagers. Latherings of Brylcreem ensured his hair was always cast back hard against his scalp, dovetailing at the back. It was how Elvis looked.

This town didn't have an Elvis, but Slick was prepared to ride the bandwagon. He soon realised two things. Elvis's unique look placed him far off mainstream and, secondly, girls just loved that look. If he mimicked Elvis, girls might just swoon after him too. And they did. In their droves. Slick could have any girl he chose. And he chose many. Despite his traits of brutality, such antics only seemed to enhance his reputation. As often as three times a week, Slick would choose another to make the lunchtime sojourn to the rear of the shelter shed. And always with faithful Roly keeping watch.

Slick was only of average intelligence, but he made out he was brighter than most and it worked. Besides, he also knew enough to know that fifteen-year-old girls weren't interested in brainpower. It was the bulge in the pants that mattered and Slick became a master of its use.

Unlike Roly Patterson, who was short, slow of mind and intelligence, almost fat, with a big chest, thick arms, and a round, pimpled, awkward face that sat buck-toothed under a basin haircut. Girls couldn't stand him. He would try to grope at their breasts, then turn and guffaw to Slick when they scorned his attentions.

On a high after the two had meted out their treatment to another often-unsuspecting victim, Slick, on ambling over to a group of girls, would pick one. She'd go coy but would be only too eager to accompany him to the rear of the shelter-shed. Roly would stand guard until the two emerged a few minutes later. Immediately the girl would be converged upon by her giggling mates and they'd walk off in a huddle, their arms around each other.

Roly would smirk at Slick. "Geez mate, how did you go, did you get anything out of her?" Slick would offer a cocky, smart-arsed grin, then excitedly rub a hand into Roly's face. "Smell that boy...what do you reckon?" Roly would get an erection from the thrill enjoyed by his mate.

One particular time, just before school broke up for the second term, a school teacher noticed one of her girl students hand a note to a class mate. She immediately demanded to see the note. It was a message to Slick telling him she had a four inch opening to her vagina and a large laboratory test tube would fit up inside without any problems.

The teacher, horrified at what she'd read, immediately left the classroom and went to the headmaster's office. Equally shocked and outraged, the headmaster demanded both the girl and Slick be brought before him.

As the two stood in the office, the headmaster angrily voiced his disgust and outrage over the note. The girl stood, quivering and trembling with fear, tears rolling down her face, too petrified to speak.

Slick stood eyeball to eyeball with the headmaster, his face expressionless, but with an icy glare which cut the headmaster down like a razor blade. The gutless headmaster backed off and told them that should such an incident be repeated, they would both be expelled.

As they left his office, each was returning to their classrooms when Slick called quietly to the girl. "Come to the back of the shelter-shed."

Horrified, she spun on her heel. "Oh come on Slick, after all that?"

"Two minutes, OK?" he told her, then disappeared from sight.

Slick stood anxiously at the rear of the shed. He didn't have to wait long. Soon the girl appeared.

Slick grabbed her and thrust his mouth against hers and pushed her back against the wall. As he did so, he reached down, lifted her skirt and jammed his fingers up her vagina. He could feel her trembling. "Did you really jam a test tube up there?"

She nodded. "It hurt and I bled, but I wanted to be ready for you anytime you said," she told him.

"How do you know it's four inches long?" She felt the blood rush to her face with embarrassment. "Cause I got mum's tape measure and measured it...it's four and a quarter if you really want to know...come on Slick, we're already in enough trouble...let's go."

"No," he said.

"But Slick, shit babe, do you want to get expelled?"

"I don't care about that, I just want to fuck you."

The girl, now beginning to show visible signs of fear, gave Slick a horrified look. "No Slick, not now, not here. Later."

"No," he said, "now, I want to fuck you now."

As he spoke, his hands had pulled her panties down to her knees. Quickly she unzipped her skirt. It dropped to the ground. She lifted one leg from her panties and stood there, naked from the waist down. "Slick, I'm scared."

He placed a hand across her mouth. "Don't be...I've wanted to do this with you ever since I first saw you."

He quickly unzipped his jeans and in one movement, dropped them with his underpants down to his knees. The girl gasped in delighted fear as she cast her eyes on his erect, hard penis. It was already wet on the end. Slick grabbed her hand and wrapped her fingers around it. "Oh shit!" he exclaimed. But it was too late.

The girl's hand was all that was needed to bring him to a climax. As he stood there cussing, he quickly reached into his jeans pocket and withdrew a handkerchief. "Here," he told her, "use this."

"What now?" she asked, almost fearfully.

"That's it babe," Slick told her, humiliation in his tone.

"But aren't you going to fuck me?"

Slick never approached the girl again, such lack of control and obvious humiliation being too much for his ego. Instead, he chose other easy targets who saw him as a real cool dude riding a push bike with specially constructed, wide handle bars.

With Roly constantly by his side, the two completed their schooling, but with no certificates in education, jobs would be where jobs would be. Whether it be working in road gangs on the local council, working as rouseabouts in shearing sheds or hay carting, where Slick went, Roly went. If you hired Slick, you hired Roly.

The two moved in circles on the wrong side of town, as Slick was always able to score conquests with the poorer, more uneducated types. For years, Roly lived on the promise from Slick that he'd get him a girl, or he could have the ones he didn't want, but when it came down to it, Slick always blamed the girl for backing out. And Roly believed him.

As their teenage years rapidly diminished, the school kids with long memories waiting to get back at him for his schoolyard bullying tactics, still gave him a wide berth. They remembered that to tangle with Slick meant you also tangled with Roly. It wasn't so much that Roly was a good fighter. In fact Roly never punched or hit anyone. It's just that when he wrapped those massive tree trunk arms around you, he became a human vice. There was no escape and you became easy pickings for Slick.

And as Roly approached his twentieth year, he took on the distinct appearance of a wall. The pimples had gone but the chest and arms had become enormous, helped considerably by his insatiable desire to build himself up with what seemed endless sessions of pumping iron.

"Jesus, Roly, you're getting to be the size of a bloody bull...why do you do all this?"

Roly would guffaw his reply. "To attract the sheilas mate."

"Christ you haven't even had your hand on it yet have you?"

The two would laugh it off, as Slick never thought Roly had any other thoughts other than taking joy from his own exploits.

One particular day, the two were sitting in 'Slick's Corner', the area reserved for the two at the local hotel when the sound of a new voice rang in their ears.

"What'll it be fellas?" It was Marjie Green, the new barmaid, and for the first time in his life, Roly decided that even if Slick wanted this one, he wasn't going to get her.

"Two beers luv," Roly replied. "Geez Slick, get a load of that," he said as Marjie made her way down the bar to the beer taps.

"Reckon she might be a bit of a goer?" Slick put in.

"Faaark mate, I gotta have this one."

Slick grinned at him. "Yeah, pig's arse, after me, you'll be next."

Roly's face twisted. "Come on Slick, you always get 'em. Let me have this one," he said.

"Mate, she'll take one look at your bloody arms and chest and reckon your cock's the same size. She'll run a bloody mile. Besides, you're too ugly."

Slick's words cut Roly to the quick. Never before had his friend told him he was ugly. And he resented it. "Don't fucking tell me that," he told Slick.

"Oh come on mate, everyone knows you're ugly. The only reason you hang around with me is because I make you look good."

Roly eased himself off his bar stool and stood face to face with Slick. The size difference between the two was enormous. If Roly wanted, he could have squashed Slick with a fingernail. "If you ever tell me that again, I'll wring your fucking neck...OK? I've got feelings too you know."

Slick tried to laugh it off. But Roly wasn't in a forgiving mood.

Marjie Green returned with two glasses of beer. As she put her hand on some loose change on the counter, Slick placed a finger on her arm. Marjie paused and looked at him. "I haven't seen you here before."

She smiled. "First day, but I do know you're Slick Bennedict."

"Oh piss off...how?"

"It's a girl's business to learn of these things as soon as she hits town." Feeling a rush of blood to his ego, Slick quickly forgot Roly's request to leave this one alone and pursued his next exploit with great vigour.

"So what have you heard?" Slick asked.

"Well I've heard about how you made a fool of yourself once behind the shelter shed...first time was it?" she laughed.

"Oh shit, I don't believe you..."

"But... I'm told you've more than made up for it since."

"You've got great tits."

"What makes you think I've got fuck-me written on each one of 'em?"

"Have you?"

"Room sixteen upstairs...I finish at nine...hi Roly, it is Roly isn't it?"

Marjie Green then left the two and went on serving behind the bar.

"How come she knew my name?" Roly gasped in awe.

"How come she knew mine?"

"You gonna go?" Roly asked.

"What do you reckon?"

"Don't Slick...just this once, let me have a shot..."

"Piss off Roly. She practically asked me for it." Glancing down the bar at her, he rolled his eyes, "Great arse mate. Shit, roll on nine o'clock."

Slick checked his watch. Two hours to fill. Roly never spoke. Slick could see his mate was stewing on not being given a chance at the new barmaid, so he moved to humour him. "Maybe she'll let you have seconds," he laughed.

Roly didn't respond. He sat stone faced staring into the mirror behind the bar. When Marjie returned to fill their glasses, it was Roly who spoke. "Just bring me a bottle of Jack love...and leave the bottle. Slick, you're paying."

"Pig's arse."

Roly spun round at his mate. He rose from his stool and eyeballed him. "You're fucking paying, alright?"

Slick knew how far he could push Roly and for some reason Marjie Green had got under his skin. "OK, I'll bloody pay, alright. Alright?"

Roly didn't respond, instead he half snatched the bottle from Marjie's hand and slammed the neck into a glass. He drank three straight.

"Shit mate, ease up on that bloody stuff, it's about ninety bloody proof. You trying to kill yourself?"

"Fuck off Slick."

A couple of the local lads were hustling up some eight ball teams. "Hey Slick, you wanna game."

"Roly?"

But Roly ignored the question. "Yeah righto, I'm in," Slick called back.

In between shots, Slick would flash a glance at the bar in the hope of catching Marjie's eye. Sometimes he did, sometimes he didn't. But each time their eyes met, Slick felt this next encounter was going to be one to remember.

Roly sometimes caught them looking at each other. But he just continued to sink his thoughts into the bottle of Jack.

The two hours seemed to take forever to pass, and Slick hoped the anticipation of what was to come wouldn't dull his performance come the time. A couple of minutes to nine, Slick wondered if he shouldn't return to the bar to console his mate. When he saw there was only about an inch left in the bottom of the bottle, he decided against it. *Probably collapse in a heap in a minute*, he said to himself.

"Time for one more Slick?"

"No mate, gotta go," he said, noticing Marjie climb the staircase. Roly saw the pair leave and clenched his fist tightly round his glass.

Slick approached room sixteen. He was about to knock when he noticed the door was slightly a-jar. Cautiously he nudged it open.

"What took you so long?"

Slick smiled. "I didn't think nine o'clock was ever gonna get here." Quietly he closed the door and snapped the lock.

Marjie Green was twenty-five. Petite, with dyed blonde hair which hung down by her small breasts. Her blouse was tied around her waist and her black, tight skirt barely covered her lower body. Stilettos gave her much needed extra height and black, fishnet stockings covered her gorgeous legs. When she spoke, her words indicated a degree of education, but her inadequate grammar gave evidence that her working environment didn't pay too much importance on how things were said.

Slick glanced around the room. Floor-to-ceiling cream linen curtains hung from the two windows. A tired, burgundy carpet covered the floor, upon which stood a small dressing table with a wash stand. A gawdy landscape reproduction hung from a cracked frame between an old-fashioned four-poster double bed and a small wardrobe.

Marjie saw him looking. She gestured with an open arm. "Not much, but it's free. Comes with the job."

Slick moved quickly to her and clasped a breast in his hand.

"Shit, you don't mess around do you?"

"Who told you about me?"

"Just talk, you know what small towns are like," Marjie replied.

Slick moved to untie her blouse. "Jesus I need to fuck you."

Marjie smiled and reached up to unbuckle his pants. Frantically the two began to undress each other. As they did, they found themselves by the side of Marjie's bed. Slick wrapped his arms around her and the two fell onto the mattress, their lips and tongues lunging with want and desire. Slick went for her breasts and squeezed.

"I just love little tits."

"Oh fuck, not so hard."

"I like to squeeze little tits too."

He heard her cry out in pain. As she looked down she saw blood oozing from a nipple.

"Jesus Slick, you made it fucking bleed."

Quickly, she spun down the length of his body and thrust his penis into her mouth, sinking her teeth in. Hard.

Slick cried out in pain and brought his arm down with such force his clenched fist knocked Marjie off the bed and across the floor. "Fuck you, you bitch, you fucking bit me."

"And fuck you too Slick, you made my fucking tits bleed...Jesus you hurt me...not to mention whether or not I still have a head left...why the fuck did you have to belt me?"

Slick sprung off the bed and dragged Marjie from the floor back onto the bed. Suddenly he felt more aroused. Suddenly violence was adding more to the thrill, far better than any of that stuff behind the shelter-shed. He pinned Marjie to the bed with his arms and jammed her legs apart with his own. He again searched her mouth with his lips and tongue and again squeezed her tits, taking great joy as he watched the blood ooze through the nipple.

Marjie was trying to cry out in pain, but Slick had his hand across her mouth. Suddenly he got the feeling she was enjoying being roughed up, so he drew back his hand and belted her across the mouth. The blow smashed her lip into her teeth and blood began to trickle down the side of her face.

She tried to wrestle against him, but quickly surrendered when she felt his hard penis pressed into her side. "Oh fuck me Slick, you fucking arsehole...oh shit!...do it!, do it!, do it!"

Roly had drained the last drop of Jack from his bottle and cast his eyes up the staircase.

Ignoring what he still had left to drink, he stumbled from his bar stool and clumsily climbed the stairs. "Room sixteen," he mumbled to himself. "Room sixteen...where the fuck is sixteen?...I'm gonna show that bastard."

As he arrived at the door with the brass numbers one and six screwed to it, he heard a pleading voice which smacked him out of his drunkenness.

"No Slick! No! Oh shit! Slick don't, you're hurting me for Christ's sake!" Then he heard a woman's cry of pain. Roly knew instantly it was Marjie Green.

He took two steps back from the door then, like a raging bull, he lunged forward. The force of the impact splintered the door into a thousand pieces. Roly fought to regain his balance as he sprawled almost at the foot of Marjie's double bed. Slick was laying prone on top of her. Roly saw tears streaming down the young woman's face and blood smeared all over her breasts.

Too startled to move, Slick stared up at his mate. Roly lunged at Slick and grabbed him by the arm and leg and jerked him off Marjie, then flung him hard against a wall. The force of the impact knocked Slick unconscious, but Roly came at him. Again he picked him up and flung him to the floor.

Marjie screamed. "No Roly, Christ you'll kill him...no."

But Roly either didn't hear or chose to ignore her protests. Again he picked up his best friend and slammed him into the floor, all the time screaming abuse at him. "I fucking told you to leave her alone... but no...you had to go and do it didn't you? And you weren't content to fuck her, you had to hurt her." With that Roly leaned back and sunk his boot hard into Slick's rib cage.

Marjie flung herself onto Roly. Panic driven, she pleaded. "Please, no more Roly, he's had enough, can't you see that...you'll kill him... please, leave him alone."

Roly looked at the naked trembling body of Marjie Green and felt himself become aroused. "I've never done it with anyone, and all I wanted was to do it with you. I'm gonna kill the bastard." Roly leaned back to sink his boot into Slick again when Marjie continued her pleas.

"Let me get dressed and we'll go somewhere and you can do it with me OK? But don't hit him anymore."

Roly spat on Slick's naked body as it lay motionless on the floor. "You fucking arsehole," he cussed.

Marjie quickly dressed, then hunted through Slick's trousers for his car keys. "Can you drive?"

"Too fucking pissed love."

"OK... I'll drive."

Marjie, relieved that Roly had decided against inflicting further pain or punishment on his friend, hurried down the stairs, dragging Roly after her. Outside in the car park, Marjie looked around, "OK... which one?"

"The panel van." She opened the passenger door for Roly, then climbed in behind the wheel and sped off into the night.

Roly couldn't believe he was alone with the petite barmaid. His hand reached over, pushed her legs apart and he thrust his fingers into her vagina. "Pull over babe...just fucking pull over will ya?"

Marjie was about four miles out of town when she had to brake suddenly to avoid hitting a cow that had strayed onto the road. The vehicle lurched from side to side as she fought to regain control.

"Faaark, that was close," Roly yelled, amazed at such a near miss.

A short distance later, Marjie swung the vehicle down a dark and deserted laneway. As she drew to a halt, she looked at Roly. "Wanna get in the back?"

As the two climbed into the rear of the vehicle, Roly had Marjie's clothes off quicker than he could open a beer.

"You're too pissed to do it," Marjie jested.

"Yeah, pig's arse," he bellowed, tearing off his trousers.

Marjie's searching hand quickly found Roly and she gasped in disbelief. "Jesus I can't take that...you're like a fucking horse."

"Then just suck me off."

"Christ I couldn't even get it in my mouth."

"So what are we gonna do?"

Marjie rolled over onto her back. "OK big boy, you wanna fuck me, then come on. Come and fuck me."

As he moved his bulk onto her, Marjie nearly puked from the stench of his body odour and breath. Suddenly she became scared. *Shit, what if he dies on top of me, I'll never get the bastard off.*

"I can't find you...where the fuck are you Marjie?"

Fearing she had taken on more than she could handle, Marjie raised her legs back behind her head and reached down. As she grabbed his penis in one hand, she took hold of his testicles in the other. Quickly she made like she was trying to put him inside her, when what she was doing was rubbing him to climax. It happened quicker than she expected. Suddenly Roly was gushing all over her. He was roaring like a bull, as she felt his warm liquid spurt over her arms, her vagina and stomach.

"Oh shit, sorry babe."

Allowing him to take the blame, Marjie knew she had to be careful that he didn't smell a con. "Can you get off me please Roly?"

"Oh fuck, and I still haven't done it," he cussed.

"You wanna wait for awhile?" she asked, hoping he would say yes and then pass out. "Roly?" But it was too late. Roly had already passed out. "Thank Christ for that," she mumbled. She quickly dressed and climbed from the vehicle, checking her watch. Ten thirty. Panic gripped her. *Slick. Christ what about bloody Slick?* She gunned the motor, did a U-turn and sped back along the laneway. Hitting the bitumen, her foot went to the floor as she feared the worse for Slick's condition.

The engine of the panel van was screaming at full revs and the speedo read eighty-five miles per hour when suddenly the life was snuffed out of Marjie Green and Roly Patterson. As Marjie came to the top of a rise, immediately over it and obscured from on-coming view, three cows were standing in the middle of the road. Marjie didn't even have time to brake. The panel van slammed into two of them, rolled three times and smashed roof first into a giant gum tree.

Chapter 3

The sudden shot of light glaring straight into his eyes startled Paul Redman. His fingers froze from tapping on his mobile phone.

"Are you alright sir?" came a voice, "we've noticed you've been here a while."

Paul became a little anxious as he replied, "Fine than..." but his voice trailed off when the torch went out and he saw two police officers standing by his door. "Oh shit! you scared me...yeah I'm fine, just waiting for a friend."

"OK, just checking," one said as they returned to their vehicle and drove off.

Paul checked his watch. "Good God! Have I been here since six?... bloody hell!, four hours, no wonder they stopped." He grabbed his phone and dialled the Royal Adelaide Hospital and asked to be put through to casualty. "Hello, is Sister McFarlane there please?"

On the other end of the line Katie suddenly felt her face go bright red. She turned to shield herself from passing staff.

"Katie, is that you?" Paul asked cautiously, knowing it was but had been taken aback at her coming on the line so quickly. He needed time to think.

"Why that must be Mr McFarlane is it?" a note of sarcasm rang in his ear.

"So they told you?" Paul said.

"Well, seeing as I don't have a brother, of course they told me... where are you?"

"Close by," Paul answered, brightening up a little, relieved she hadn't hung up in his ear.

"I didn't think you'd ring."

"Neither did I."

"Then why did you?"

"Had to find you first."

"OK...now you've rung...what now?"

"Not doing too well am I?" Paul offered in a semi-defeated tone.

"Sorry...how are you?"

"You're all I can think about."

It's what Katie wanted to hear, but not quite so soon. "Thank you for the drink," hardly believing she could give such a nothing response.

"Something is happening here."

"Paul I've only just come on duty, I really have to go."

"What time do you finish?" he quickly put in.

"Six in the morning...now I really have to go."

"Then I'll mee..." but Paul didn't have a chance to finish. Katie had hung up.

* * *

Katie McFarlane had always wanted to be a nurse. As a child, the main game was 'Doctors and Nurses' and she'd often second her parents as unwitting patients. Many times someone would come to the door answered by a 'patient' swathed in bandages, red dye and safety pins.

Katie was the only child born to Sam and Ida McFarlane, with her birth being regarded as something of a miracle. Ida had miscarried on three previous occasions, so when Katie finally made it into the world it wasn't without cost.

Ida nearly died giving birth. The doctors and midwives maintained a bedside vigil until the all-clear was given. During this period, Sam never left the waiting room. After seventy-three hours, the obstetrician finally told him he could go home and sleep, secure in the knowledge Ida would be alright. But the stress of nearly losing his beloved Ida proved too much for Sam. He was ordered off work for a month. But for the first time in his life, being confined to the home didn't bother him. Katie was his constant companion. Ida was unable to breast feed, so it was Sam who made up the formulas, got up for the three a.m. feeds, bathed her, pampered her, gurgled with her, and loved her.

He re-painted her bedroom, hung border prints and dangled mobiles from the ceiling. Everyone in the street and from surrounding neighbourhoods dropped by to see the 'Miracle' baby. Sam's workmates did the same. As the weeks went by, both Sam and Ida regained their strength. Sam returned to his work as a electrical engineer and Ida revelled in the task of doting mother.

The calendar seemed to grow legs as the months rolled into years and, through this incredibly rapid passing of time, Sam and Ida were constantly amazed at the popularity of their daughter. One particular Saturday morning, just after her fifth birthday, Katie went off to shop on an errand. A short time later, her mother, who was in the bedroom, heard the most riotous commotion coming from the kitchen. When Ida McFarlane went to investigate, she discovered seven other children feasting themselves on her freshly made cream puffs and fairy cakes.

"Katie?" she called.

"Hi mum, I just brought a few friends home for awhile," she said in a matter-of-fact manner.

"Have you now," she replied, "is everything alright then?"

"Gee, Mrs Mac, did you make these?" came a question from a mouth totally obscured by a cream puff.

Ida didn't know whether to get angry, scold her daughter, send everyone packing or just ignore it. She chose to ignore it.

But such an experience for Ida was only the beginning. Invariably, Katie would arrive home with 'a few friends' as the McFarlane household in the middle-class suburb of Marion gained a reputation for having the best fairy cakes and cream puffs in the neighbourhood.

It got to the point, as time went on, if their daughter hadn't arrived home with 'A few friends' at least once a week, Ida thought there must be something wrong.

As Katie McFarlane grew into a young woman she carried with her the values, the dignity and the respect for others ensconced in her mind from the teachings of her parents. Puberty arrived with no major problems. Although of continued amazement to Sam was how quickly Katie's breasts began to develop.

"God, she's only twelve," or "God, she's only fourteen, and look at her."

Ida would smile. "It's a pity you never had any sisters dear, and you'd realise how quickly these things happen."

The biggest upheavals through Katie's teenage years centred on disagreements with her father. She wanted her hair long. He wanted it short. Katie wanted her hems short. Sam wanted them long. And on and on the saga went. Year in. Year out. Katie wanted to wear high heels at thirteen. Sam said fifteen. Katie would turn the stereo up. Sam would turn it down. Katie would apply eye shadow. Sam would tell her to go and wash her face. Sam would say be home at eleven. Katie would say midnight. Ida would intervene and they'd split the difference. Katie wanted to go out with boys at fifteen. Sam said sixteen, but she received no help from her mother on this one. Sixteen it was and sixteen it remained.

"And you can aw-gee dad as much as you like," Sam would add.

Birthdays were always cause for celebration, but no celebration was more grand than when Katie turned eighteen and was accepted as a nursing student into the Royal Adelaide Hospital. Sam and Ida McFarlane were just so proud of their daughter. And when Sam handed his daughter the key to the door on her twenty-first birthday, he wept uncontrollably.

"Ladies and gentlemen," he began, "this is our little girl. She kept us waiting for years for her arrival, and when she did take her first breath, all five and a half pounds of her, the doctors called her a miracle baby. And she was our very special miracle girl, because her mother was told she risked her life if she tried to conceive again. You see, what many of you wouldn't know is that Ida miscarried three times before we got Katie. It was the most soul searching decision both of us had ever been faced with. And while we were trying to come to a decision it was made for us when Ida again fell pregnant. My darling Ida knew the risks. I knew the risks. But despite them, there wasn't a moment, not even the slightest hint of a moment, when Ida indicated she would not go through with the fourth pregnancy. God what a woman. When Katie was born, Ida's survival hung in the balance for three days before the all-clear was given. Ladies and gentleman, I tell you this today, not to cause feelings of sympathy towards Ida, but to emphasise to you just how special our daughter is. She has the remarkable gift of being able to endear herself to those she meets and she's had that quality ever since she was a tiny tot. She may be grown up now, but darling, sweet girl, you'll always be our miracle baby, and nobody in this whole wide world will ever love you as much as your mother and I love you. And this is as real as it gets."

* * *

For the first part of her shift at the Royal Adelaide Hospital, Sister Katie McFarlane sat comforting a little girl who had been attacked by a dog. Two people with minor injuries as the result of a car accident also had to be tended to. Another small boy who thought a bottle of glue was milk emulsion had to be admitted to have his stomach pumped. An elderly lady tripped and put her hand onto the hot plate of her stove resulting in second degree burns.

"So much for a quiet day at the office," she told a colleague who was hurrying by.

At one-thirty a.m. a casualty nurse greeted the security officer who had appeared in the section. "Are they for *me*?" she exulted, casting an envious eye over a arrangement of flowers so large it almost obscured the top half of his body.

"Katie actually," he responded.

"Katie!" she exclaimed. "Really? Who are they from?"

"Dunno," he replied, "looks like she's mended some poor sod's broken heart, or else kick-started another one," he added, looking round for her.

"Hardly a bunch of flowers!" came another comment. "They look like the whole shop...cop the orchids."

"Is there a card?"

"Nick off Sally, they're for Katie."

Sally turned on her heel, scanning for the missing sister. "Where are you Katie?" she called. "KATIE?"

Quickly she spotted her and ambled towards her, wiggling her hips and giggling like a ten-year-old. "Guess what *you've* got sister?" she said.

"Oh Sally, sometimes I wonder about you. What are you on about?"

Katie's words were cut short by the security guard standing in front of her with the biggest flower arrangement she'd ever seen in her life. "They're not?" she asked disbelievingly.

"Uh-huh, absolutely."

Katie felt a rush of blood to her cheeks. *Oh God, it's Paul.* She fought to regain herself and focused on the blooms. "Orchids, orchids, orchids, roses, maidenhair fern, and more orchids." Katie leaned over to smell the fragrance.

"Looks like some have about a dozen on the stem. Must have cost the poor bugger a packet," Sally grinned as the security guard handed Katie the long cellophane wrapped package. "Someone's got it bad. Anyone we know? And cop the bow! Well excuse me," she gasped, referring to the massive combination of pink ribbon almost upstaging the arrangement. "Come on, spill the beans. Who is it?"

"You'll never know."

Paul Redman had driven the streets of Adelaide looking for some sign of life, any sign of life, at a florist shop. Checking his watch, his heart sank when he saw it was way past eleven p.m. Suddenly he remembered he had declined an invitation to a ball being held that night at the Hilton Hotel. A shot of adrenalin raced to his brain. "Ah, that's it," he exclaimed, throwing his car into a U-turn.

He rushed to the international hotel. Fortunately, his acquaintance Timothy Cloverdale was the greeter. Timothy saw Paul arrive and was already standing at the driver's side door when he pulled up. "Mr Redman, what a pleasant surprise...going to the ball, sir?"

Paul stepped from his car and put his arm on Timothy's shoulder. "I'm in desperate need of a favour..."

"You know I'll only be too pleased to take care of your car..."

"No, no...the car's not the problem tonight. I'm not going to the ball, but what I do need is the biggest arrangement of flowers you've got."

Timothy's mouth dropped. "But sir, nothing is open at this hour."

"That's right...who's ball is it...what's it in aid of?"

"Er, Singapore Airlines sir." His face lit up. "The room is literally wall-to-wall flowers...and some of them have even been brought in especially from Singapore. You should see the orchids, they are just sensational."

Paul thought for a moment. "Do you happen to know if Sam Godfrey is here. He's the general manager, marketing for South Australia?"

"Indeed sir, I believe he's the M.C."

Paul quickly grabbed a business card from his wallet. "Will you take this to him and ask him if I can have a word?" Paul handed Timothy the card wrapped in a ten dollar note.

"There's no need for that Mr Redman, I'll be glad to."

Moments later, Sam Godfrey, decked out in tie and tails, appeared with a concerned look on his face. "Paul, is something wrong."

Paul Redman explained the situation to his good friend and what he needed.

"Hell, I'll do better than that. Wait here."

Timothy arrived a three minutes later. "Mr Godfrey suggested you should make your way to the restaurant reception area."

Paul headed off as requested and was only just seated when Sam Godfrey arrived with two Singapore Airlines hostesses. Each was carrying a huge vase of flowers. Sam introduced his good friend to the hostesses. They smiled their politeness and Paul stood, momentarily spellbound.

Then one said: "You would like a special bunch of flowers for a very pretty lady, yes?"

Paul smiled. "Thank you, yes."

"We will only take a minute sir."

"Watch this mate," Sam said to Paul. "We had them decorate the ballroom...they can turn a bunch of flowers into an art form."

Before his eyes, Paul Redman watched the two hostesses remove the flowers from the huge vases, lay them flat on a plastic sheet, then masterly interweave them into the most exotic arrangement. The finishing touch was the magic they displayed in turning a pink ribbon into a classic sculpture. They turned and handed Paul Redman the arrangement. He was dumbfounded. He tried to find words of thanks, but nothing would come.

"You like?"

"Oh yes, thank you."

"She must be very special lady, yes?"

Paul nodded. "Jesus Sam, what can I say?"

"Mate, not a problem, loved doing it for you...anyway, who is she?"

"Dunno yet, but hopefully this might help a bit. What do I owe you."

"Mate, that was fun. Buy me lunch sometime."

* * *

It didn't take long for Sally Isaacs to spread the word through the department. Several other casualty staff had now arrived, curious as to who would send such an exotic arrangement of flowers at one-thirty a.m. "Who are they from? Who are they from?" they chorused with great urgency.

Katie's face went bright red, her knees went weak and her hands began to tremble as she plucked the card from the cellophane. Turning her back to hide her self consciousness, she slipped it from the envelope.

I just love the smell of Paris in the morning. I'm in the red car parked opposite. See you at six. Paul.'

"Oh you're mad," she giggled, replacing the card. When she turned round, she faced a throng of inquisitive and inquiring faces.

"Well?" someone asked.

"Well nothing," she responded. "Mind your business and get back to work before I sack all of you," she said.

"Nah nah, na nah nah," said Sally, still giggling.

"And you've got a big mouth," Katie told her.

"Jill," Katie called urgently to her workmate, "I need you now, desperately."

Katie ushered Jill Ashbourne aside. "Have you got your Paris with you, mine's home," she said in a mild panic.

"Well, er, yes..."

"Don't ask," Katie cut in knowing she was about to be hit with forty questions. "Can I just borrow a dab when I knock off...pleeease?"

Jill smiled. "Come with me. Who is this guy?"

"I'm not sure really. I only met him yesterday."

"But look at you. You're all over the place."

"Oh lord, is it that obvious?"

"Sure wish I could find someone who had that effect on me...is he loaded?"

"Poor as a church mouse," she jested, "hey I don't even know that. I just met him, and, well, I just met him...you know."

Jill laughed. "Yeah, sure, you just met him."

Katie knew no matter what she said, Jill wouldn't be convinced. "Keep the bottle," Jill said, "just give it back when you've finished."

"No, no, it's much too expensive, I only need a dab."

Jill placed the bottle of Paris in Katie's hand and wrapped both her own around Katie's wrist. "Give it back to me tomorrow," she smiled, "have fun...now go."

As everyone ambled back to their work stations, Katie again read the card. *I love the smell of Paris in the morning.*

On a hunch, she walked from the main building to the security office at the hospital's entrance. She could see only one car. It was parked in front of Ayers House restaurant. It was a Mercedes Benz.

She spotted the security guard that had delivered the flowers. "What's the colour of that car over there?"

"Oh, maybe red, bit hard to tell in this light...looks like a merc and there's a bloke sitting behind the wheel. Problems?"

"No, no, it's fine, thank you," she replied, turning to make her way back to the casualty department.

* * *

Out on North Terrace, Paul Redman had reclined the front seat of his Mercedes. At three a.m. a police patrol car again drew alongside. It was the same one as before. Again, startled by the flashlight, Paul had to once more reassure the officers everything was alright.

"Waiting for a friend?"

"Waiting for a friend," he told them. As he watched the patrol car draw away, he began to reflect on his own circumstances.

Thirty-five years of age, the best schools, overseas trips, two married sisters and a brother who became a methodist minister. Parents who were liked and respected in the community. The family home in up-market Unley Park, his own in the equally up-market Glenside. Fifteen years service with Archibald Design, one of Adelaide's most respected architectural families. Thirteen as an employee. The last two as the major shareholder. Life was pretty good to Paul Redman.

As he glanced upwards, he caught his own reflection in the rear view mirror which he'd tilted so he could keep an eye on what was happening around him. He noticed his cleft chin and square jaw, and rubbed his hand approvingly across his face.

Yeah, you'll do, he smiled. He surveyed the interior of the Mercedes. *Yep, reckon old grandpa Hardwig would even approve, not that he allowed himself the indulgence of such a luxury vehicle, despite his wealth. The old blighter certainly knew how to make a quid.*

Cecil Hardwig was a struggling industrial manufacturer, getting what he could where he could, when he read an article in a magazine which said, "The person who can come up with a cost effective plastic sticky-tape dispenser would have the world beating a path to his door." So Cecil Hardwig put his mind to it and did just that.

After fourteen prototypes, he was down to his last few pounds, as it was at the time, when the phone rang. The order came from Germany for ten thousand. Within six months he was exporting one hundred thousand. Within six years he was manufacturing and exporting in the millions. The cream on the cake came from his own patented dispenser, which still sold in the millions. Cecil Hardwig died three years ago. In his will he left each of the Redman children two million dollars.

The money was to be invested. Each child was permitted the interest on the money with the capital frozen until each reached the age of forty. In addition to their inheritance, each child also benefited from a trust fund set up when they were born. As Cecil Hardwig's wealth increased, so too did his contributions to the trust funds. This money could be used when each child reached the age of thirty. Paul's parents also inherited two million dollars upon the death of Cecil Hardwig, Paul's grandfather on his mother's side. It was the generosity of his late grandfather which had in effect, set him up for life.

With assistance from his brother and sisters, Paul was able to purchase Archibald Design. A family conference decided that he should be the ninety per cent shareholder with his parents holding the other ten per cent. Paul used part of the trust fund set aside by his grandfather for the purchase and used the rest of the money to buy The Oakdale Country Club at Mildura. Oakdale was a run-down shambles of a once-pristine building that for a time was the local golf clubhouse. But the club had since moved on and part of the course had become a housing estate. His boyhood friend in Renmark, Michael Knight, suggested to Paul he should buy it.

So he flew to Mildura, looked it over, figured it had enormous potential and handed over a cheque there and then. Much to the dismay of his family. After several months of renovations, re-roofing, extensions and a massive upgrading, The Oakdale Country Club was fully operational as a going concern.

Fatigue now began to take hold and Paul closed his eyes. As he drifted in and out, his mind went back over the years. Never a shortage of female companions. Football every weekend in winter, cricket in summer. A six figure income. Some high-performing blue-chip investments. And two million dollars just waiting to be collected in five years time. Archibald Design and The Oakdale Country Club.

But just how good does good get? he wondered. *Maybe all this is not meant for just one man?*

He hated being so fatalistic. Casually, he opened one eye and glanced at the brightly lit hospital entrance in his rear view mirror. He wondered how he had found himself parked in North Terrace when his own bed was not more than ten minutes drive away. He consoled himself with the thought that he didn't want to risk sleeping in and blowing his opportunity.

At around four a.m. he felt himself losing the battle with fatigue, so he reached for his mobile phone and booked a wake-up call. Not that he needed it. A city council street-cleaning truck came along at five-thirty a.m. with its brushes revolving and water jets pumping. Paul cursed as muddy water was splashed across one side of his Mercedes.

Across the street, a paper seller was setting up his stand. A couple of bag ladies passed by, giving a wide berth to the man they could see sitting behind the wheel of the red Mercedes. Then a young man, probably in his twenties, Paul reckoned, toes poking out of his runners and the knees of his jeans torn, came into view. Three earrings in one ear, his filthy hair tied into a pony tail, draped over an unbuttoned, old army great-coat. He leaned down and picked up a cigarette butt, cleaned the filter and lit it. Nervously he checked over each shoulder, then inhaled deeply. His face creased as he reefed the cigarette stub from his mouth. Then he heaved his throat and spat out a large mouthful of gunk onto the street. He rubbed a filthy sleeve past his mouth and walked away.

Paul Redman was transfixed upon the young hobo. *How does a man get himself into that situation? God, don't ever let me get like that*, he said to himself, gripped by the sudden fear of his acquired wealth being swept from him.

He leaned over and took a couple of wipes from a container in the glove compartment. As he wiped his face, he felt the roughness of a twenty four hour growth. He reached for his electric razor and plugged it into the cigarette lighter. After a quick rub over, he combed his hair and tried to combat what was now shaping up as a severe bout of fatigue and stomach nerves.

At five past six a.m. Paul saw Katie walking towards him, carrying the massive arrangement of flowers he'd organised for her. He jolted open his door and stood, watching her approach. When she got to within a few metres, she stopped and looked straight at him. "You've got to be crazy. I don't believe this. I don't believe I am doing this," she said in an even louder tone.

"I've missed you," is all Paul offered. With his gut in such a turmoil, he was grateful he could make any sound at all.

"Thank you for the flowers," Katie said in a more mellowed tone, "they're simply sensational. Where on earth did you get them?"

"Special delivery. Singapore Airlines."

"Oh, of course, at one-thirty in the morning. I guess I asked for that one didn't I?"

If only you knew, Paul smiled to himself. "Are you impressed?"

"Should I be?"

"Depends."

"On what?"

"On whether I've found a short cut to your heart."

"Mr Redman, as wonderful as they are, there are no short cuts to my heart." Katie hoped her expression wouldn't give her away for having told the biggest fib she'd told in years. She was gone. And she knew it. But she still knew she had to be cautious.

Paul walked towards her. Katie held out her hand. Paul held out his, but side-on with his fingers parted, inviting Katie to place her own between his. She did so. As their fingers joined their hands together, he looked at her and ever so softly greeted her, "Good morning Miss McFarlane, you're up early this morning."

For the first time, she found herself really looking closely into Paul's eyes. *God this is so romantic,* she said to herself. She felt Paul squeeze her hand and returned the gesture, ever so lightly, but enough to let him know she was responding. For a moment the two stood looking at each other. The occasional car went past, but neither seemed to notice.

This is moving too quickly. Maybe I should just walk away. Go on, walk away. Walk away! Katie told herself. But she couldn't. And she didn't want to. She was too caught up in the romance of being swept off her feet.

Paul reached up and cupped Katie's face. For the first time he found himself absorbing her in her totality. Shoulder length blonde hair, curled under at the bottom. Deep violet blue eyes which looked like they could turn the tide of the coldest heart. And that face. What a face. If Grace Kelly was perfect, Katie McFarlane would pip her at the post. *But slow down Paul. Slow down old son or you'll lose her. Slow down.*

"Paris in the morning. Wonderful," he said throwing his head and arms in the air, his nose filled with her perfume.

Katie laughed. "I don't know what would be more expensive, buying it or going there."

"Believe me," Paul quipped, "Paris ain't cheap."

"The city or the perfume?"

"Both," he laughed, "And you said you don't wear it."

"I lied."

"Uh-huh."

"But I only wear it on special occasions. It's too expensive for just a plain working girl. I shout myself a bottle a year and use it sparingly."

"You're wearing it now."

"Uh-huh."

"Must be a special occasion."

"I wore it on the plane...that wasn't a special occasion."

"Yes it was."

"Why?"

"You met me."

"And you want me to believe that was special?" Katie put in.

"Trust me! When are you due on again?" he asked wanting to slip away from the subject so as not to give Katie the impression he was crowding her.

"Ten o'clock tonight."

"Can you take a sickie?"

"Never taken one in my life," she answered, mildly shocked at the suggestion.

"Then it's time you did. My office can certainly do without me for a day," he told her, opening the passenger side car door.

As he pulled out into North Terrace and did a U-turn, it was Katie who spoke. "You haven't really rung in sick have you?"

"Not yet, but I'm going to."

"And you've been sitting in your car all night?" she questioned, knowing he had, but still not quite believing it.

Paul offered a sheepish grin. As he swung a right and headed for East Terrace, the lights turned red. When they turned to green, he swung the Mercedes towards Somerton Beach. As the city's buildings went past in a blur, Katie glanced at her surroundings. "It's only a small thing, but where are we going?"

"Paris," he answered, giving Katie a look which told her that any further questions regarding their destination would be treated with a further outrageous answer. *This is going against everything my parents told me. Never get into a car with a stranger. What if he's a rapist? A serial killer?* A pang of fear shot to her stomach, then it was gone. This was dream stuff and she was on the ride of her life. But doubts still tore at her. She looked at Paul, searching his face for reassurance that her instincts hadn't lied to her. At that moment, Paul Redman reached over and held her hand, almost as though he knew she was blaming herself for being so gullible. As she looked at him, he momentarily glanced from the road and into her eyes, a warm smile upon his lips. It was the reassurance she so desperately sought at that moment. *I don't know why, but I just feel so safe with you,* she thought.

The sun had only been up for a short time when Paul and Katie pulled up along the Esplanade at Somerton. Early morning joggers ran along the beach. Anglers were wetting their lines while many others seized the opportunity of a glorious early morning to walk their dogs. Paul pushed a button on the console and let down the electric windows. He closed his eyes for a moment and sat in silence. As the gentle breeze swept in across the ocean and filled the interior of the car, Katie breathed in deeply. The brisk morning air cut into her lungs.

"Isn't that magnificent," she said, "I just love the smell of salt in the sea breeze." Katie watched Paul's eyes focusing on the ocean. If Paul heard what she said, he didn't give any indication. Instead, for a few brief seconds, he seemed to be swept up in the magic of the moment.

Then he said, "Listen to that. Hear the rippling. Hardly a wave. Isn't it wonderful. God I love the sea."

Silence fell between them as they absorbed the magnificent view. The sea that morning was so calm, it looked like a mirror. *It's just so rare to see it like this,* Paul thought. As his eyes panned out to the horizon, he felt a tingling sensation run through his body. *Here I am alone with this gorgeous woman at a location which is nothing short of heaven on a stick.* He desperately wanted to leap from his car and shout so the world could hear: "Look at this woman! Look at the sea! Look at me! Look at everything!" But he remained calm, and Katie McFarlane would never know what will-power he exercised at that moment on that day.

Katie had her head resting against the back of her seat. Her long blonde hair falling loosely around her face and neck. From a particular angle, Paul noticed the sunrise reflecting from her hair like a golden halo. He sat, mesmerised, just looking at her. *God what a tapestry. There's not a camera in the world which could possibly capture such beauty.*

Katie opened her eyes and saw Paul looking at her. She smiled. "Oh wow, this is so wonderful, I could go to sleep."

"You can if you like, or you can drag your toes through the early morning tide."

Katie sat forward. "But my uniform?"

"Just hold it up a little. Come on, you'll love it."

In a matter of seconds, Paul had slipped his shoes and socks off and ducked around the other side of the car to open Katie's door.

"Is it cold?"

"Warm as toast," Paul told her, trying to disguise a slight shiver running through his body.

Katie kicked off her shoes. She gasped as her feet touched the ground. "You lied! It's freezing," she giggled, as she felt the brisk morning air slicing against her skin.

"The tide's out, so we can head down to the beach," Paul said, closing her door.

Katie ran a few steps, dragged her toes through the sand, ran her fingers through her long, flowing, blonde hair and threw her arms in the air. "What a glorious morning. Everybody should do this everyday. No, no. They should pass a law making it compulsory for everyone to do this everyday."

Paul just smiled as he caught up to her. "You've never done this before?"

"A thousand times, but not so early in the morning. I love my bed too much," she answered. Just at that moment, the sun's angle mirrored Katie's reflection straight off the surface of the ocean.

"Don't move," he commanded. "Look down."

As she did, she also saw her own reflection in the surface of the water. "Paul come and stand with me."

Quickly he joined her and placed his arm around her shoulder. Together they both looked down and saw themselves in the surface of the sea. He moved his hand up behind her head and formed his fingers into a V. Katie saw two fingers protruding from the back of her head. "Oh now you've spoiled it." Paul laughed just as a small wave dissolved what had been a perfectly framed shot.

"We didn't make a bad looking couple did we?" Paul commented.

"Well at least one of us looked OK anyway."

"I'm sure you have a totally false impression of me," Katie said.

"I like what I see."

"But you should ask my mum. Don't ask dad though, he's biased."

Suddenly Paul's mood changed to project something of a sombre tone. He took hold of Katie's hand and pressed it to his cheek. "What would you say," he began, "about you and I making this our day. Our once in a lifetime, very, very special day that will last in our memory for a lifetime."

Katie felt a chill of excitement run through her. "But this is all so sudden."

"It is for me too. What do you say? Let's set this one aside. I've never done anything like it before. But right now, right at this moment, nothing is more important to me."

Katie wanted to say yes. She desperately wanted to say yes, but she also knew she was dead-tired after having worked all night. "Paul I wouldn't make it past midday. I'm really very tired. And you must be too. We've both been up all night. Let's walk a little," she suggested.

Silence fell between them. Paul dropped back half a step just to watch Katie dragging her toes through the sand. The sea breeze was tossing her hair and he could tell she was deep in thought. He knew her mind would be racing, just as his was racing, racing with excitement, desire, want. And racing with the sheer delight of being with Katie McFarlane.

She stopped and turned back to him. "What about another day, when we're both not so tired..." She could tell her words were wounding him. She stopped and looked into his eyes. "Paul I don't even know you."

He raised his hands and cupped her face, her hair falling over his wrists. He was almost pleading. "I can't explain this...this thing I feel right now. I just know it feels right. It's as though someone has turned a light on in what was the black hole of my life. Something has happened to me in the past few hours. If it hasn't happened to you as well, OK, we'll put it off."

As they stood together, tiny waves lapped at their ankles. Katie could feel herself beginning to tremble. There was a long pause, then she pulled away from Paul's cupped hands, walked a few steps and looked back at him.

Paul could feel his heart pounding in his chest. He knew her next words would be vital. "Can I make you an offer?"

"Your call."

"Take me back to my car. Let me take a shower and grab a couple of hours sleep and I'll meet you at eleven o'clock."

Paul was ecstatic. "Do you mean it?"

"This whole thing has been a little crazy. Just don't tell my mother..."

Paul moved in close to Katie and held her in his arms. His pulse was racing fast. Katie responded. Seagulls flew by, waves washed over their feet. Gently, he kissed her forehead. She looked up at him as he ran his fingers through her hair. She pulled herself closer into his body as he began to touch the tip of her nose with his tongue and opened her mouth slightly. Paul could sense this was a very precious, very delicate moment. Their lips met. Tentatively. *Do I kiss this girl or don't I?* He waited for Katie to respond. Then he felt her tighten her hold on him.

As they walked a few more steps, arms around each other, dragging their toes through the early morning tide, Paul stopped and kissed Katie again. This time, she did gently pull away. "This girl really must get some sleep now Mr Redman."

"So from eleven o'clock, today is ours."

"All ours," she promised.

Chapter 4

It was a country town, Sunday, summer evening. The local lads of Naracoorte were going around and around the town square in their bought-on-time-stereophonic death-traps, cat-calling what talent had ventured out on to the streets. At the local Ritz cafe, the late-afternoon rush was dropping by for their Cokes and icecreams while two or three groups of two sat drinking cappuccinos.

Slick Bennedict brushed aside the long plastic strips which hung in the doorway and stepped inside. It was a long, thin corridor with a counter one side and a row of squeezie tables and fixed stools on the other. Flashing neons advertised Peters icecream, Cadbury chocolates, Freddo frogs, Coke and Pepsi, with the walls adorned with a shock of other advertising paraphernalia. A long mirror ran the length of the wall behind the counter, obviously to deceive the customer into thinking the place was actually bigger than it was.

Inside the entrance, the icecream fridges with sliding glass tops led into the sandwich bar. The cash register sat towards the centre, then the hamburger and fish and chips area and the cappuccino machine took up the remainder. A handwritten poster hanging from the wall told of the next CWA fete. A Capstan cigarettes painted tin sign hung over the top of the juke box, which took a large area of the end wall of the cafe.

To the local kids, this was their idea of heaven. A bit sleazy, but it was where you could be yourself. It was where clothes didn't matter. Hair styles didn't matter. And lurid suggestions and actions were taken in jest. It was also centrally located, which meant a good passing trade with the locals. But to the kids, the Ritz was a comfort zone. Noisy, unruly but never troublesome. Until now.

Slick Bennedict ambled to the juke box, ignoring the girls serving behind the counter. He withdrew a couple of coins from his pocket, fed the slot and waited for the music. It was his first day out of hospital after a five week admission. He had ben found unconsious by hotel staff after being slammed into the wall and the floor by Roly Patterson, bleeding profusely from the nose, mouth and ears. He remained unconscious for three days, emerging the same afternoon Roly Patterson and Marjie Green were buried. He had suffered a broken nose, black eyes, a bruised ear drum, two broken ribs, bruised kidneys, and a broken collarbone. Visibly, he looked alright but, inside, he was still in great pain. Doctors ordered complete rest. Slick decided he didn't want to stay housebound.

The music had only just begun when Slick felt a hand on his shoulder spin him round. In the split second before a huge right hand smashed into his face, he caught a glimpse of several faces he recognised. Faces of those who had been victims of the Roly Patterson–Slick Bennedict treatment from school days. The blow sent him into the protective glass of the juke box, which shattered into a thousand fragments. The machine died, halting the music. Glass splinters covered Slick as he tried to regain his footing. Immediately he knew his jaw was broken.

"So where's your Roly fucking mate now, you arsehole?" came the words, which he only partly heard, as another thunderbolt caught him on the point of the nose. Slick reeled. The girls serving behind the bar screamed. The groups of two sipping cappuccinos made a hasty retreat to the front of the cafe as a frenzied mob moved in for the kill. As the blows and boots rained down on Slick, a bystander placed himself between Slick, lying dazed and bleeding on the floor, and his attackers.

"What are you fellas trying to do, kill the bugger?" he said in a calm, almost relaxed tone.

The group of five knew this was one man they didn't argue with. It was the bachelor from just outside of town, something of a man mountain they knew as old Gabe Caplin. Not that the old was appropriate, because he was still a relatively young man. But because he never married and lived on his own, he was immediately labeled as 'past it'.

"Piss off Gabe, this's got nothing to do with you," came a demand.

Gabe squared him eye to eye, then looked down at Slick. "That's young Bennedict isn't it?"

"Piss off Gabe, he's had it coming to him for years the mongrel..."

Gabe grinned. The cafe hushed. "He used to hang around with young Patterson didn't he?"

"That's the price."

"So now young Roly's not around, it's open season on his mate."

"Come off it Gabe, he and Roly brutalised heaps of us at school."

Gabe put his arm out to restrain one of the attackers as he tried to move in and hit him again. "Seems to me you've already done enough damage, not to mention the damage you've done to this place...you want to turn out your pockets."

"Fuck off Gabe."

Suddenly the big man's face took on a look that meant negotiations were finalised. "Turn out your pockets boys," he told them, "and whatever you've got in them can go to pay for the damage to the juke box."

One or two began to protest, but they soon realised that to do so would have been meaningless. Cussing and cursing, the group of five emptied their pockets of notes and change. Gabe scooped it up and handed it to one of the girls behind the counter. "Don't know how much it is," he told her, "but when you get that thing fixed, if it's not enough, get onto young McIntosh here, he'll make good the rest, won't you Stevie?" Gabe gestured towards the young lad whom he knew to come from a wealthy home. "And if he doesn't, you tell me, and I'll go and speak with his father...how do you reckon you'd like that Stevie?" Stevie McIntosh stood with his head bowed. He didn't answer. "Stevie?"

"Yeah right."

"OK now you boys just get yourselves out of here."

As Gabe Caplin saw the last of them leave, he leaned down to help Slick Bennedict to his feet. "You're not too good are you son?"

Slick couldn't answer. His face was covered in blood and his jaw was angled awkwardly.

"You better ring the ambulance," he told one of the girls behind the counter. "And as for you young fella, if I were you, I'd be healing up real quick and getting the hell out of this place. Your reputation of how you treat women in this town is downright disgraceful and I've gotta tell you, if I had a daughter and you twisted her tits till they bled, they'd need a front end loader to pick up the pieces after I got through with you.

"What happened to you here today was a pay back from school days. From what I've been told, there's a queue from here to the town hall of blokes who want a piece of you. And that's not to mention the husbands, boyfriends and fathers who want to get hold of you too. So just get out of town...get the hell away from this place because I won't be around to save you next time."

When Gabe saw the ambulance arrive, he walked to the front of the cafe. "He's in here," he told the ambulance officers, stepping out of the entrance to the street.

As he walked towards his vehicle, he watched a few of the locals scurrying to the cafe. He looked back over his shoulder, wondering if Slick Bennedict would take his advice and leave town. He also wondered if he'd learned a lesson about his treatment of women. *I doubt it, I really do. Blokes like that never learn. He'll probably end up in a ditch somewhere, finally brought down by some bugger taking exception to him making a play for his missus. It's a pity that so many others will get hurt as they cross his path. And they will. They surely will. Jokers like him are trouble through and through.*

Chapter 5

Arriving home at her single-fronted bungalow in North Adelaide, Katie McFarlane quickly showered, washed then dried her hair. She felt as though she was running on nervous energy. Her stomach was in knots and a mild panic had gripped her. All the time she found it difficult to come to terms with what was happening to her. She couldn't concentrate. She'd put her keys down, then seconds later not remember what she'd done with them. Then she couldn't remember whether she had given Paul her address. She checked her watch. *Eight-thirty already. In two and a half hours Paul will be here. Must get some sleep.* She picked up the phone to call her mother, then immediately replaced the receiver. Instead she grabbed her alarm clock and set it for ten-thirty, falling into bed. She worried she might be too excited to sleep. But it seemed only moments and the alarm was ringing.

When Paul Redman swung his Mercedes into Katie's street, it no longer carried the muddy remains of the street-sweeper's handiwork. In the hours they had been apart, Paul had washed his car and spent the remaining time on the phone organising the day. Their day. As he pulled up outside Katie's bungalow, he suddenly felt guilty. Like a boy wagging school. Paul Redman wasn't one for taking a sickie and he knew it. *Oh to hell with it.* But the guilt remained.

Inside, Katie was in a blind panic. She hurried round, puffing up the cushions on her two matching deluxe two-seater sofas. In soft, floral tonings with high-padded roll arms, they each had gently arched victorian-style backs and frilled skirts. Katie loved the sofas. Sometimes she imagined they were keeping each other company, like two people, watching the comings and goings of her life. She fussed around. Straightening this, moving that. She pulled the blinds on the picture window, stood back, looked at them, then decided the window looked better when the blinds were rolled up, exactly how they were in the first place.

Carefully she took her two best cups and saucers from her china cabinet and placed them on the kitchen table. She checked the toilet, placed a guest towel in the bathroom, then checked her appearance in the mirror. The cuffs of her white tailor-made slacks sat neatly over her two-tone windsor-blue coloured brogues. Complementing her red- and -white striped lace trimmed blouse, she wore a double-breasted blood-red hunting jacket with double slits at the back. The fall of her hair nestled on a royal blue scarf. Delicate gold chains hung lightly from her wrists, complimenting her manicured nails. She chose little makeup, preferring to remain natural with just a touch of lip gloss.

I guess red and white does suit me, she conceded, trying to convince herself this sudden attack of nerves was entirely unnecessary.

Outside, Paul Redman heard the time pips for the eleven o'clock news, took the keys from the ignition and made his way to Katie's front door. As he did so he noticed lavender bushes on both sides of the entrance to the little gate which led up a short, but defined, pathway to her front door. He imagined sometimes that small children would probably pick the lavender for their mothers.

As he pressed the doorbell, he felt his tongue sticking to the sides of his mouth. Quickly he bit the very tip of it between his front teeth. Immediately, he felt a rush of saliva around his gums. Then he had an urgent need to go to the toilet. The door opened in front of him. He caught the smell of Paris perfume, then he saw her.

"My God, look at *you*."

"And look at you!" she replied, a note of surprise in her voice. For a moment, both stood looking at each other. It was Katie who spoke. "Well," she said, gesturing a welcome with her hand.

As Paul stepped inside Katie's bungalow, his glanced round the rooms. The hall was painted light cream, almost white. Indeed, everything was light cream, including the carpets, which gave a feeling of air and space while still being compact and cosy. Her high-ceilinged, but narrow, hallway was cluttered with black- and -white reproduced photographs, which had a way of blending the past with the present. They were framed by antique wood and preserved beneath glass and consisted mainly of faces of her heritage.

"My beautiful, beautiful grandmother on her wedding day," Katie said, noticing his attention to the photos, "and that's her holding my father when he was a baby. My mother as a little girl. This one was when she was twenty-five."

Paul closely examined Katie's mother. "You certainly weren't adopted were you?" he said, and cast his scrutiny across more framed photographs.

"Often wonder what was going in their lives when those pictures were taken," she said as Paul continued to look. "Don't know who the rest of the people are. Just saw them in second-hand shops and felt drawn to them."

Katie showed him into her main living room.

"Where did you get that?" he asked, noticing her coffee table, formerly an old tea chest.

She laughed. "Found it in an old junk shop when I was a student nurse. Paid a fortune to put a glass top on it and have it restored. Now I couldn't bear to part with it. Doesn't go with anything, but it's a great conversation piece. Especially the period costume dolls on the bottom shelf."

"Oh?" Paul queried.

Again Katie laughed. "Just various holidays over the years. And I remember exactly where I got each one. But come, sit down. Can I get you something. Tea or coffee...something cold?"

"Just a coffee. Black, no sugar. Thank you."

As Katie went into her baltic pine kitchen to put the kettle on, Paul absorbed more of his surroundings. A picture window, spanning two french doors, ran the entire length of the dining and lounge area, separating her courtyard from inside. From there he could view her little, paved garden with herb and flowering terracotta pots strategically placed to capture the precise amount of sunshine for each.

Paul noticed a cherub statue in the centre of the courtyard, impressed with Katie's balancing act between heavy and light, presence and space, clutter and neatness. He saw she had achieved that with the presence of two large dressers which stood proudly against the wall opposite the dining table. He wondered what might be in the drawers, figuring a few well-chosen family heirlooms.

"That's nice," he called, referring to a large antique dining table complete with high-backed chairs and white tasseled cushions. "The dining room setting, I mean."

Katie looked over the benchtop from the kitchen. "Oh? Mum and dad found that for me. I couldn't afford it, so they bought it for me on condition I pay them back."

"Have you?"

Katie laughed. "I'm working on it. Mum's quite convinced I'm going to get away with it. Dear old dad, he's such a pushover."

"Sounds like a nice bloke."

"Love him with my life. Both of them actually. They are such good people. You'll meet them. And mum's a great cook, that's if you like roast dinners and apple pie."

"I love roast dinners and apple pie."

As Katie continued to make the coffee, Paul rose from his chair and walked around the room. "Katie, this is wonderful," he said, focusing on the plants and shrubs in the courtyard as he spoke.

"Architecturally or personally?"

"Both. Indeed both."

"Really?"

"Absolutely. Got a green thumb too I take it?"

"Oh just a few odds and ends to brighten the place up a bit," she called from the kitchen. "Actually, it's dad who has the green thumb. He likes to pop over and fuss about. That rose in the corner across from the cherub is his pride and joy. It's a Chicago Peace. It's supposed to be pink and cream, but this year it seems to be more pink than cream. He strokes it, talks to it. Mum reckons it gets more attention than she does. And she's probably right," she laughed.

"Any brothers and sisters?"

"No, just mum and dad and me. They wanted more but mum couldn't have any." Katie entered the lounge room and stepped out into the courtyard to join Paul. "And what about you?" she asked, handing him his coffee.

"Two sisters and a brother."

"Do you like gardening?" Katie asked, leaning down to run her fingers across the petals of a rose. "Don't answer that," she laughed, looking up at him and seeing an opportunity to jest. "Let me guess. I'd say you're more into chess."

"Chess!" he exclaimed. "Do I look that boring?"

Katie laughed some more. "Well, you know, architecture and all that. I can't imagine you as the outdoorsy type."

Paul took a sip of his coffee, complimented Katie on her choice of crockery and thought to himself, *Just wait and see what I've got in store for you today, lady. Then we'll see who's the outdoorsy type.*

There was still a slight nervousness between the two as they stepped back into the lounge room and sat down opposite each other. Almost as if each was trying to sum up the other.

"So," Katie began. "What about today?" Then her voice took on a tone of insecurity. "Are you sure about all this?"

Paul could sense that even though she had agreed to go along with him, she was still a little apprehensive. He moved from his seat and sat next to her. "What if I was to say that today is the first day of the rest of our lives? I just want it to be a day each of us will remember forever. I know it's quick. I know it's sudden. But I've never been so certain of anything, ever before, in my life."

Katie looked at Paul and put her hands to her face. "This time yesterday I didn't even know you. I guess I'm just a little scared. You see I don't want to wake up in a week's time to discover I've been nothing more than a foolish woman who failed to think-through a situation."

Paul stood to his feet and brought Katie up with him. He took her in his arms. "Please don't fight it. If it wasn't meant to be, I wouldn't be here. Everything, I believe, happens for a reason. Hell, I didn't have to be on that flight. There were many to choose from. You could've lied about where you work and I'd never have found you. I just believe today was meant for us, and by God I'll do everything to keep you safe, protect you and see that it stays in your mind for the rest of your life."

Katie felt her doubts disappear as Paul ever so gently placed his lips upon hers. *You make me feel so secure*, she thought. As they drew apart, Katie ran a finger across his lips. "You'll look a bit sus with lip gloss."

"Oh I dunno, thum blokes wear it," he said with a lisp.

"Somehow you don't look the type." Again she felt a tinge of excitement run up her spine. "Are we going somewhere special for lunch or something? You haven't told me." When he didn't answer, Katie glanced over at him. She couldn't believe a grown man could adopt such a sheepish grin. "Paul Redman, what are you up to?"

"How much time have we got?"

"I'll go back in tomorrow night at ten."

"So you'll take a sickie?"

"I've already rung in...but I don't think anyone believed what I told them."

Inwardly, Paul Redman breathed a sigh of relief. He had gambled on her making such a call. He was very relieved she had.

"Seeing you won't tell me where we're going, am I alright like this?" she said, seeking Paul's approval for her red-and-white outfit.

"If I told you what I really thought, you wouldn't believe me."

"Try me."

"Drop dead sensational. Sweet girl you look simply gorgeous."

At that moment the door bell rang. Katie checked her watch. "I wonder who that could be?" She moved quickly to answer it.

Paul heard the exchange from where he was standing in the lounge room.

"Miss McFarlane?"

"Yes."

"These are for you."

Paul heard Katie give out a joyous shrill.

As she re-entered the room, she was already reading the card attached to yet another arrangement of orchids and roses.

I love the smell of Paris in the morning. May today's memories last a lifetime. Paul.

"Oh Paul, they're just so wonderful. Thank you. Need I ask? Singapore Airlines I guess."

"Special delivery!" Paul lied. What Katie didn't know was that he had again made a call to Sam Godfrey that morning. Sam had then arranged for his secretary to go back to the Hilton and grab the best of what remained of the flower arrangements from the ball and send a sheath to Katie.

"I don't know what to say," she said, her eyes blurring with emotion. "Thank you." Katie went into the kitchen and took a very large vase from a cupboard, filled it with water, then disappeared from sight. A moment later, she said, "Paul, would you like to come down."

Paul followed the voice and soon found himself standing in Katie's bedroom. Sitting on her dressing table were the flowers he sent her at the hospital and this latest delivery. "God they're awesome when you see them like that...aren't they magnificent."

"I've truly never seen orchids like it. And these today look like they've come from the same place as last night's. I don't know who you know Paul Redman, but you can send me flowers like that any time you like. Quite frankly, I'm speechless. This is the stuff of royal weddings."

Paul was chuffed at witnessing Katie's reaction. He went to her. "We really should be going," he told her, placing his arms around her and kissing her on the tip of her nose.

"Will I need a coat?"

"You won't need a coat."

"Not even a clue?" she pleaded.

Paul just smiled and made his way to the front door. Katie followed, and after snapping the deadlock, allowed Paul to take her arm and escort her to his car. "Hungry?" he asked as he started the engine.

"Starving," she said, even though she thought she might be too excited to eat.

"So what do you like?"

"Right now, a cup of tea and a sandwich would be fine." Katie was laughing wildly within herself as she watched the city pass by from inside the highly polished glass of the shiny red Mercedes Benz.

"Can we eat on the run?"

"Sure."

Spotting a corner deli, Paul pulled into the kerb. "Just be a minute," he said, and ducked inside.

As Katie waited, she looked around the inside of his car. The service book in the console told her it was a 300E. Lots of buttons. Stereo system. Mobile phone cradle. *The ash tray's never been used*, she noted with approval. She eyed a gold Parker pen. Even the street directory had its own special leather case. As she moved in the seat she became aware of luxurious lambswool seat covers front and back and lambswool floor mats. She wondered if the highly polished facia panels, gear lever knob and centre-piece for the steering wheel were standard equipment or extras. Either way, she was quite taken with just how stunning it all looked. It seemed only moments before Paul returned with sandwiches and hot drinks.

"Here you go," he told her, handing them to her. "You do this and I'll do the other bit."

As they got underway, Katie juggled the sandwiches and the coffee between the changes of the traffic lights. She noticed they were travelling north on the Main North Road. "Paul this is the road to Sydney for God's sake."

He smiled. "Yes. And Gawler and the Barossa Valley."

"Oh shit, we're going to bloody Sydney aren't we?" Katie began to panic. "Paul I have to be back at work tomorrow night. Besides, we can't spend the night together."

Paul realised Katie was taking everything a bit too much to heart. He glanced over at her. "I promise you will be sleeping in your own bed in your own home tonight."

Katie breathed a sigh of relief, but was bursting with anticipation of what lay ahead. It was only moments later before her questions were answered. Paul slowed down and took a left-hand turn at the sign which read PARAFIELD AIRPORT. Katie's eyes suddenly became large white saucers when she saw rows and rows of light planes.

"Is this what I think it is?" she questioned.

Paul grinned. "Well yes, this is Parafield Airport and what you see are lots and lots of aeroplanes."

"Really? Are we going up in one of those? I hate planes, especially small ones."

"You'll love it," he said, taking for granted Katie didn't really have a fear of flying, rather aeroplanes in general. "Are you scared of heights?"

"No, but I've never been in a light plane. Oh God I'm gonna die."

"You'll be fine," he said, taking hold of her hand. "I know the pilot and he hasn't left anyone up there yet. Nice bloke too." Paul pulled his car into a parking spot. "I'll just be a minute," he told her.

Katie looked around with nervous anticipation. *Oh stop being so stupid!*

Then a feeling of great expectation filled her senses. She wanted to scream out and tell the world how happy she was. But underneath it all, she was scared witless and she knew it.

"All set?" Paul asked when he returned.

"As ready as I'll ever be, I guess." Katie climbed from the vehicle and Paul took her arm as they walked across the tarmac.

"What time does the flight go?" Katie asked, as she hurried to keep up with Paul and he headed towards a group of planes.

"In about ten minutes."

"Which one are we going in?"

Paul kept walking at a rapid pace. "Can't see her yet."

"Where are we going?"

"Ah, there she is," he said, pointing to a Cessna 1-7-2.

"We're going in *that*?"

"Yep. Isn't she magic? Simply love the little darling."

"But it's so tiny," Katie protested, not believing Paul would seriously consider they both take to the air in something so flimsy.

"Wait till you get aboard. She purrs like a kitten," he told her, gently running his hand down the fuselage. "You wanna hop in," he asked, opening the cabin door.

"Don't you think we should wait for the pilot first?"

Then it hit her. She remembered seeing the propeller blade in his button hole on the aeroplane. Then she saw the look on his face.

"Oh shit. I'm looking at him aren't I?"

Chapter 6

Gabe Hutchinson Caplin was forty-three years of age. He was the only child born to Garth and Thelma on a night so cold, nurses at the Naracoorte Hospital ran out of blankets caring for the aged and infirm and had to wrap him in newspaper.

But Gabe's birth did not go well. Thelma was three weeks overdue and thirty-six hours in labour resulting in her being hospitalized for fourteen days after the birth. Because she had had such a difficult labour, doctors told both her and Garth they best leave the business of having babies to someone else.

"You're telling us we can't have any more kids?" Garth asked the doctor, angrily.

"Let me put it this way Mr Caplin. If your wife falls pregnant again, it'll kill her. Sorry to be so blunt, but I take it you wouldn't accept an explanation in any other terms," the doctor replied.

They were devastated. Both were of the opinion that to have only one child was unfair to that child. They discussed adoption, but Garth couldn't accept the idea of being a father to someone else's child. Thelma did her best to change his mind, but Garth would not concede. Often arguments would result from their discussions, but Garth wouldn't be happy just to say his peace and end the subject. Sometimes he'd go for days without even speaking to his wife.

Finally Thelma thought she'd give it one last try. The result was a screaming match which resulted in a two-week silence between them. That was when Thelma promised herself she'd never again raise the subject of adoption. And she didn't. Her family consisted solely of her husband and her son.

Garth and Thelma met when Garth got a job shearing sheep on the farm belonging to Thelma's parents, Wilf and Dorothy Baxter, at Cleve on the South Australian West Coast. It was love at first sight for both of them, despite a four-year age difference.

"Even though I was just a kid, the moment I first set eyes on your father, I never wanted anyone else," she once told Gabe.

In the beginning, and at least for a couple of years, Garth wasn't made overly welcome at Thelma's place. Her parents were land owners, and farmers of that era didn't take too kindly to their daughters having eyes for the hired help. "Particularly bloody shearers. Here today, gone tomorrow and all they do is spend their dough on booze and racehorses," her father would cuss.

Knowing Wilf's attitude to shearers wasn't going to enhance his chances of winning their support, Garth gave the game away and began to work around the district as a casual farmhand. He lived in a boarding house in Cleve so he could be close to Thelma.

"Never work him out," Wilf would say. "Fancy chucking in a good paying job for piece-work. If he thinks he can get to see Thelma more often, he's got another thing coming."

But the occasional visits which Thelma's parents thought were a Saturday night in their home were, in fact, three nights a week behind the haystack.

"Dad said to mum the other day that getting married was becoming a more expensive business these days Garth," Thelma said. "Mum just laughed and said chalk it up to entertainment tax and dad thought that was really funny."

As they became more serious about their relationship and Thelma's parents finally realised they could do nothing to stop it, they gradually began to accept Garth. After four years they married, and decided the best thing was to make a clean break and start their lives afresh.

They decided on Naracoorte. Thelma had remembered learning about the town in the state's southeast during her geography lessons at school. For some reason she always remembered the name and endeavored to learn as much about the place as she could. A rich, rural area with a very good rainfall.

"How good?" Garth asked her.

"About twenty inches, and dad says that's good for about sixteen bags to the acre oat crop and twenty for wheat."

"So what else have you learned about this Naracoorte place?"

"Well it's about seventy-two miles from Robe, which is a really good beach. Actually the hundred of Naracoorte is in the county of Robe. Don't know what it means, but it sounds good. The first residents were people by the name of McIntosh in 1850 and the town was surveyed for the government by a Mr Evans in 1859."

"So does the name Naracoorte actually mean anything or is it just a made-up word?" Garth wanted to know.

"From what I can work out, the Aborigines used to call the place Nanna-coorta. That was back in the 1860s. Nanna-coorta actually means large waterhole."

"How the hell did you find all that out?" Garth asked her, not failing to be impressed.

"I wrote a letter to the government and they wrote back and told me. Pretty smart eh?"

"Well I'll be buggered. You should've asked 'em about Cleve as well."

"I did," she said. "The first landowners were a Doctor McKechnie and his two brothers. They acquired a pastoral lease in 1853. But in 1877 the government resumed control of much of it. Cleve was proclaimed a town in 1879 and named by Governor Jervois."

"Bloody amazing! So you reckon you'd like to live in this Naracoorte place do you?"

"Oh Garth, do you think we could? It just sounds wonderful."

Agreement was reached immediately. Naracoorte it would be.

With the money they'd saved, and a wedding present of five hundred pounds from Thelma's parents, they bought a small farm about twenty-five kilometres from the town.

It totalled eight paddocks and two hundred hectares, three good bores, a dairy, a machinery shed, stables, a two-stand shearing shed and a reasonably comfortable two-bedroomed home. There were also two hundred sheep and two dairy cows.

But times were tough. Garth was forced to take odd jobs around the district with all available money being spent on stock and machinery.

Thelma was desperate for a few things in the house, particularly a washing machine. But it would always be next year.

"Gotta fix the tractor," he'd tell her.

The next year would come and the story would be the same. The implements and the requirements of the farm always took precedence over what Garth regarded as personal comforts. "Fine for you," Thelma would complain, "you don't have to do battle with the washboard, the hand wringer, light the copper and burn your arm every time you do the washing."

Each year she found herself pleading for a machine, any machine, but Garth always found a reason not to get her one.

Things finally came to a head. It was on a day Garth was down the paddock and Thelma caught her little finger in the hand wringer. With no one to call for assistance, she battled for ten minutes to free herself, suffering great pain in the process. After she'd composed herself, she sat down and wrote a letter to her parents telling them of the incident.

Tired of hearing their daughter's continued complaints of not having a washing machine, they wrote back and said if Garth wouldn't buy her one, they would.

When Garth read the letter, he bitched and cursed and carried on like someone had shot up the combine. "By Christ, no one gives a stuff if the bloody tractor breaks down, just as long as you get your bloody washing machine."

Thelma had had enough. "Every year when I ask you, you tell me the same thing. Alright, from now on, I'll wash my own clothes and you can wash yours, and we'll see who gets sick of it first. Let's just see if you are prepared to stand and scrub the grease and grime and blood and God-knows what else out of your pants. Then stand there and try to wind the blasted things through the hand wringer. I'm bloody well fed up with it."

"That's woman's work," he cut back at her.

Thelma felt the hairs on the back of her neck stand on end. "Women's work? Women's work!" she yelled. "Well milking cows, fixing windmills and straining bloody fences is man's work, but do you ever hear me complain? Do you?" Thelma burst into tears and ran to the bedroom.

I'll be buggered. I've never heard her carry on like that before, Garth said to himself. But it shook him up. First he was frustrated. Then angry that his wife should speak to him in that manner. Then he eased off. *Thelma's normally pretty easy going. Wonder what got into her?* He started towards the bedroom but changed his mind. *Better go and buy her a bastard I suppose*, and felt into his pocket for his car keys.

Garth drove to Naracoorte and walked straight into F & F Electrical in Smith Street. He looked around the showroom floor, picked out an engine driven Simpson, handed over a cheque and loaded it on to his utility. He grumbled all the way home of having to go to such expense to appease his wife.

The grumbling continued even when he was unloading the new machine onto the front verandah. Thelma was still in the bedroom. When Garth entered the room, he saw her lying on the bed, so he went and sat down beside her.

"Where have you been?" she murmured, not wanting to look at him. Garth didn't answer. Instead he swept her in his arms and carried her outside onto the verandah.

Thelma's eyes lit up like beacons when she saw the washing machine. "Thank you," she said, "thank you, thank you, thank you."

Content that he had restored peace and quiet around the place, Garth went on with his work. But Thelma was beside herself with excitement. When Garth was out of sight, she stood back and admired the brand new Simpson washing machine. It was light green in colour with a fully enamelled bowl. Thelma ran her fingers over it. "Wonderful. Just wonderful." But her greatest joy was that it also had a mechanical wringer. *No more turning that blasted handle*, she said to herself, recalling the pain she suffered in her little finger. Then, with great gusto, she went to the kitchen. "OK, now it's clean up time."

When Gabe arrived back from the paddock a few hours later, he couldn't believe his eyes. Thelma had strung up three makeshift clothes-lines and all were laden with washing. As he walked over to the lines to get a closer look, he recognised the kitchen and lounge room curtains, many towels, plus sheets and pillowcases. Even the bedspread.

He stepped up onto the verandah and was dusting himself off as Thelma came to greet him.

"Strike me pink woman, is there anything left in the cupboards?"

"Garth it's just wonderful." She ran over to the clothes-line and scooped up a section of a sheet and held it to her face. "Look at these, they've never been so white."

"Unbelievable," he muttered. "Bloody unbelievable."

As times got progressively more difficult, Garth allowed the two front paddocks to be share farmed. The once-a-year wool and harvest cheques were not stretching far enough. Thelma made bread and grew her own vegetables. Once a fortnight, Garth would kill a sheep and share it with Mrs Cropp, their next door neighbour. In return, Mrs Cropp would make Garth and Thelma's clothes for them.

Two years later, when Garth brought Thelma home with little Gabe wrapped in her arms, it was Mrs Cropp who stood at their door to greet them, complete with a wardrobe of booties, bonnets, jackets and pants, all carefully and lovingly hand knitted. All that was known of Mrs Cropp was that she appeared out of nowhere about ten years before and bought a small farm. She was a widow, "Or so they say," Garth would add. She didn't speak of any family and lived alone. She ran a few sheep, milked a couple of cows and went into the town once a week. She also played the piano. Beautifully.

"That's about all anyone knows about her," Thelma would say, when discussing her with Garth.

Mrs Cropp kept to herself, but when the Caplins moved in next door, she greeted their arrival with a hot tub of soup, home baked bread rolls and a hind quarter of sheep. She didn't stay long. Just introduced herself, said her greetings and left. "Now I'm just over there," she said, pointing to her house. "Drop over anytime and I'll put the kettle on."

A week after moving in, Garth and Thelma decided to pay a visit to their kindly neighbour. True to her word, the kettle went on the stove. A half an hour of chitchat followed, when both decided they wouldn't outstay their welcome. As they got up from the kitchen table, Mrs Cropp again loaded up her next-door neighbours with a basket full of home made foodstuffs.

Thelma began to protest when Mrs Cropp interrupted her. "That's my pleasure. It's just comforting to know I have nice neighbours."

As time went by, Mrs Cropp and the Caplins saw each other almost every week. Thelma had a particular liking for the woman, and Mrs Cropp likewise. But as well as they got on, neither asked any personal questions of the other. Mrs Cropp was simply Mrs Cropp. A fine and friendly neighbour.

Chapter 7

Gabe began to grow quickly. The seasons had turned around, which meant Garth didn't have to leave home so often and seek other work around the district.

Mrs Cropp continued to drop by once a week, sometimes twice, because she had taken an incredible fancy to little Gabe. And she always brought him something. A freshly baked biscuit. A piece of chocolate. A ball on a string. Sometimes a balloon if she'd just come back from town. Thelma would scold her for spoiling her son, but she would take no notice. It concerned Mrs Cropp the ever-widening gap between father and son was becoming more noticeable. And she couldn't help but wonder if it was for this reason alone she took pity on the boy. As for mother and son, Gabe and Thelma seemed inseparable.

But it was different with Garth. Sometimes the way Mrs Cropp heard him speak to the boy alarmed her greatly. But she knew better than to intervene. Instead, she would just stand back and observe. *Something's not right here*, she'd say to herself. *Something's just not right.*

As he began to grow, Thelma would watch Gabe trying to perform the duties of a man, something expected of him by his father. When he was often unable to "Lift this", "Hold that" or "Move that over there," Garth's words would cut the boy down. In tears he'd flee to his mother's arms. Thelma would try to soothe him, but inevitably the saga would end up in a slanging match between Garth and Thelma.

One day, Mrs Cropp arrived to hear Garth berating Gabe dreadfully. The boy was unable to carry out his father's directions to move a wheelbarrow he'd just loaded, from the woodheap to the house. The load was too heavy for Gabe to handle and it toppled over. Garth let fly in his unusual manner. The severity of the verbal abuse felled the boy to his haunches, cowering.

Mrs Cropp's jaw dropped in horror as she witnessed a father's treatment of his son. Quickly she went to him.

"Leave him alone Mrs Cropp," Garth ordered.

"But Mr Caplin, he's only a seven-year-old boy. He can't be expected to do what you do."

Garth slammed down the axe he was holding and strode straight up to her, hands on hips, in no mood for advice from outsiders, let alone a woman. "Just don't bloody interfere Mrs Cropp. You are welcome over here anytime, but don't bloody interfere with the way I bring my kid up." Garth then glared at his son. "Now pick this fucking stuff up and get it over to the house. I won't tell you again."

Mrs Cropp was shaken with Garth's outburst. She rubbed her hand across the boy's head and looked at Garth. "I'm sorry Mr Caplin, you'll have no problem with me."

Gabe lifted his tear-filled eyes to see Mrs Cropp walking to her car. As she was about to open the door, he sprang to his feet and ran to her, throwing his arms around her waist.

Thelma, hearing loud voices, had walked out to the verandah to investigate. She stood dumbfounded at how Garth had spoken to their neighbour. When she saw her son run to Mrs Cropp, she was filled with anger. She marched directly at her husband. "How dare you speak to Mrs Cropp like that."

"Piss off Thelma," Garth said and moved over to his son. He grabbed him by the ear. Hard. It made him cry out in pain. "I bloody told you you've got work to do, now bloody well get and do it," he roared, reefing the boy's arms from Mrs Cropp.

Gabe was crying loudly. Thelma was about to intervene when Garth's glare cut her down. The two women looked at each other. Garth stood alone, fuming. Slowly Gabe began replacing the wood in the wheelbarrow. To break the deadlock, Mrs Cropp climbed into her car and drove slowly away.

That poor child, she thought. *What makes a man treat his son like that? Nothing's ever been said, but from one or two comments over the years, I take it*

Thelma can't have any more children. I wonder if that's it? Perhaps he blames her for that and takes his anger out on the boy? As she neared the end of their driveway, Mrs Cropp looked into the rear view mirror just as the wheelbarrow again toppled over as Gabe tried to push it.

For the next three years, Garth's disciplines were enforced even harder on Gabe. He wasn't allowed to participate in any weekend sport with his schoolmates. He wasn't allowed to get to school early for a quick hit of tennis or to kick the football before class began. Even attending a Saturday movie matinee was out of the question. Garth insisted the character of a man was in his ability to work long and hard, no matter what his age.

"Kids your age used to work in coal mines in England. You don't know when you're well off," he'd tell him.

As Garth's attitude towards his son hardened even further, it began to have an effect on his relationship with Thelma. Gabe was Thelma's pride and joy. It tore her apart to see the boy being treated so harshly.

"Let him go into town and play tennis on Saturday," Thelma would plead. Garth would practically ignore her, except to offer up time-worn excuses. "The bottom fence needs fixing. We've got all that wood to bring in. He can help me tail the lambs."

Thelma would remove herself from the conversation and seek solace in the bedroom. She'd allow herself to sob, only if she knew Garth wouldn't discover her tears.

* * *

Three days after Gabe's tenth birthday, Thelma was still deeply depressed and upset. She had wanted to give her son a very special birthday, but she hadn't bargained on the reaction of her husband.

Days before, Thelma and Mrs Cropp had put their heads together and baked his favourite cakes and toffees, complete with hundreds and thousands on top. Mrs Cropp had been into the local school and spoken with Gabe's headmaster to learn who his schoolfriends were. Seven children were invited. Somehow, Garth got wind of it.

How dare they go behind my back and do this! Who the hell do they think they are? I'll bloody show 'em who runs the place around here, just you see if I don't.

On the Saturday morning of the party, Thelma ducked over to Mrs Cropp's place to check all was in readiness. The two were besides themselves with excitement at the prospect of staging a surprise party for Gabe.

Mrs Cropp proudly displayed the trays of toffees and cakes she'd prepared. "And let's not forget his father," she said. "I just know he loves these," she added, showing Thelma a basketful of freshly baked lamingtons.

Thelma's face dropped. "Oh Mrs Cropp!" she said. "I know, I know. I just worry his father's going to hit the roof when he learns we've done this without telling him. Hopefully these will soften him up. You know what they say?" Thelma tried to smile. "The way to a man's heart is through his stomach. I know. I've tried. Unfortunately with my husband, there appears to be a few detour signs along the way."

Mrs Cropp tried to console Thelma. "Don't worry. Just wait till he sees these, he'll come round."

Thelma wasn't convinced. She knew her husband, and suddenly this all seemed a bad idea. The smell of toffees passed her nose and she thought of Gabe. She tried to imagine the look on his face when he saw all his friends turn up. Intuition told her to call the whole thing off. Instead, she decided to continue with the plan. *Maybe Garth will get a kick out of it too,* she hoped.

When Thelma arrived back at the house, it was still two hours before the first guests were due to arrive. As she glanced across to the shed, she saw Garth and Gabe getting into the utility. Her heart sank. Quickly she went to them. Trying to conceal her anxiety, she said, "And just where are you two going?" knowing that once they got down the paddock, they'd be gone for hours.

"Gotta pull the pump up on the windmill," Garth said.

But something told Thelma her husband wasn't being truthful, seeing no tools for the job in the back of the ute. "Well don't forget, it's a very special lunch today for a very special ten year old."

Garth drove away without any further comment to his wife. *Yes it'll be a special bloody day alright.*

"Don't be too long," Thelma called after them as they drove away.

The parents of Gabe's schoolfriends were punctual, right on twelve o'clock. Parents introduced parents to parents. Thelma and Mrs Cropp busied themselves entertaining the children, filling cups with cordial, handing out cakes and toffees. For two hours they kept making excuses for Gabe's absence. With their tummies full of food and soft drinks, the children were beginning to suspect that Gabe wasn't going to show.

"But where is he Mrs Caplin, isn't he coming?" one boy asked.

The parents of the visiting children also began to suspect a no-show and discreetly discussed it amongst themselves, too polite to raise the issue with Thelma.

"I had a feeling this would happen," Thelma told Mrs Cropp, fighting back tears. "The bastard!"

Mrs Cropp felt dreadful. "Thelma I can't imagine why he would do such a thing. I guess I shouldn't have convinced you we should go ahead with it," she said.

Thelma felt she was about two breaths short of bursting into tears. Feeling the gaze of everyone upon her, she decided to act. *How could he humiliate me like this?*, she fumed, and strode towards the shed and climbed aboard the tractor. She cranked up the motor, reversed in a cloud of dust and headed off towards the windmill in the bottom paddock. As she approached, she couldn't see any sign of them. She jerked the vehicle to a standstill and looked out across the paddocks. Way across to the left, she spotted them. She jammed the tractor into gear and started off towards them. She pulled down on the throttle lever, the wind in her face blowing aside her tears of anger.

As she neared them, she saw Garth leaning against the bonnet. She jammed on the brakes and the tractor tore up bits of the paddock as it skidded to a standstill. Garth was leering up at her.

Thelma sprang off the seat and bounced over the top of the huge rear wheel and lunged at Gabe. "How could you? How could you?" she screamed, lashing out at him with both arms. Garth grabbed her by the hair and threw her to the ground. Thelma quickly regained her feet and again launched herself at her husband in a hysterical frenzy.

Again, Garth knocked her to the ground. Gabe, sitting in the cabin of the utility, sprang forward so quickly when he saw what was happening, he cracked his head on the windscreen.

Thelma got to her feet again, this time lashing out at the chest of her husband with closed fists. Garth grabbed Thelma's wrists and held them tightly. "You knew didn't you?" she screamed. "You fucking well knew and you've deliberately done this to us."

"Yeah, I knew," Garth said, sneering. "I saw a couple of invitations." Then he yelled, "Why didn't you ask me? You deliberately deceived me!"

Thelma was floored by the accusation. Garth felt his wife's muscles tension off, so he let go of her wrists. "It was supposed to be a surprise. For both of you," she cried. "It's Gabe's birthday party for Christ's sake, so Mrs Cropp decided we should make it a special day for the two special men in our lives."

"Fuck you Thelma, we don't want any surprises around here. The kid's got work to do. I keep telling you that."

"Come off it Garth. It's our son's birthday. All his friends are up at the house with their parents. Mrs Cropp has gone to a heap of trouble. Not only for Gabe but for you as well."

"No party Thelma. I run this place and don't you forget it. If you want to have a party for the kid, then ask me first, now piss off." Garth again grabbed his wife by the hair and threw her to the ground. Seeing his son's reaction, Garth walked over and grabbed him by the ear, jerked him free of his mother and thrust him towards the vehicle. "Get back in the ute boy," he ordered.

Thelma dragged herself up onto her elbows in a state of shock. She began to shake uncontrollably and cry loudly. Dust and dirt covered her face and clothes. As she wiped her mouth with her arm she felt grit and tears wash into her mouth. She never thought she'd see the day when a man, any man, would do this to her. Let alone her own husband. She tried to speak but the words got choked in her throat. She remembered seeing the utility drive away, leaving her a cowering, blubbering mess on the ground.

Thelma didn't know how long she'd stayed there. Eventually she climbed onto the tractor and drove home. As she pulled into the shed, she looked up to see the place deserted. Everybody had gone. She walked across from the shed and stood staring at the party leftovers. She kicked a couple of empty paper cups lying on the ground. At the end of the table, a small pile of gifts, accompanied by cards left for Gabe, caught her eye.

She picked some of them up and held them against herself, then collapsed onto the ground. No! No! No!" she screamed. As her screams decreased to a whisper, then a whimper, Thelma passed out.

The abusive tones of her husband's voice brought her to her senses, startling her. "What the fuck are you doing here? Get off your arse and clean this shit up. It's bloody tea time too."

Thelma never fully recovered from the shock of how her husband treated her. Thereafter, whenever she spoke or did anything for him, it was with hesitation and nervousness. She had come to fear his temper and avoided, at any cost, the slightest thing which may have set him off.

Even after six months, Garth showed no remorse for his actions, and if anything became more distant from his wife and son. Conversations at meal times were all but non existent, and if Garth did speak, it was only to question, direct or complain. Gabe developed a timidness, almost mouse like, as he picked at his meals.

Thelma found bedtime a nightmare. Garth hadn't been near her for months. Neither as much as touched each other with fingers on skin, let alone anything more deliberate. Thelma dreaded the day Garth would make a move towards her. As she feared, seven months after he knocked her to the ground, he leaned over and placed his hand on her breast. Violently she pulled away. "Don't touch me. Don't ever touch me. Ever. Never again!"

She sat bolt upright in bed and glared at him. She knew too that one blow from his hand would numb her into submission. She waited for it, expecting to be knocked halfway across the room, but it didn't come.

"Well fuck off out of the bed then," he said. "Do you hear me? Get the fuck out of here."

Thelma quickly left the bed, donned her nightgown and grabbed a blanket from the blanket box and left the room. She crept into Gabe's room and climbed into bed with her son. Thelma lay there, her pulse pounding her temples. She feared Garth would come thundering into the room at any moment and haul her back to his bed. But he didn't.

As she lay there, scared and alone, she found it strange to be sleeping in another room. She listened to her son's breathing, which seemed to console her anguish. She raised her hand and stroked his hair. Gabe didn't stir. Being such a narrow, single bed, their torsos touched. Then she wondered about the particular odour emitted by her son. Thelma didn't find it unpleasant.

I guess you'll be a man soon, she thought, realising that puberty wouldn't be all that far off.

Her pulse was still thumping at her temples. She thought of her husband in the next room and a cold shiver ran down her spine. Would he be lying awake soul searching or would he have just rolled over and gone to sleep?

Probably the latter, she told herself.

Thelma felt her stomach twisting into knots and her mouth go dry. She thought she was going to be bilious. She eased herself out of her son's bed and went to the kitchen to get a glass of water. As she stood sipping from the glass, staring out the kitchen window into the moonlit night, she still found it impossible within herself to forgive her husband for his actions.

As the days and weeks and months passed, she would recount both times he knocked her down. Bitterly at first. Then with loathing. Then the fear element would take over. Then she felt she'd been betrayed.

Then, *Maybe he's to be pitied? Maybe he needs help? Lord, don't tell me he blames me for not being able to have any more children. Surely not. After all this time? But he's never said. Of course he wouldn't, would he? Too much male pride. We used to be lovers. We used to be friends, best friends. But now he's so distant and brutal, it frightens me. Please God, show me, guide me. Give me back the man I used to love.'*

Garth and Thelma never again slept in the same bed together.

* * *

Mrs Cropp too felt embarrassed over the birthday fiasco, and her visits to the Caplins became less frequent. *If only I hadn't convinced Thelma everything would be alright. I feel so wretched.*

One afternoon, Thelma called in. "We miss seeing you like we used to," she said.

"I think it's best my dear, just till things blow over a bit. I just feel it was all my fault. If I hadn't..."

Thelma went to her. "Nonsense," she said. "You are not to blame yourself. Maybe Garth just had a bad day," she added, trying to dismiss the subject. "Gabe misses you terribly."

"Oh, and I miss him too. How is the dear?"

"He's fine. His father doesn't let up on him. I shudder to think what's going to happen between those two when he grows up a bit."

There was a note of sadness in her tone and Mrs Cropp could see Thelma was trying to put on a brave face. "And you two. What's going on there?"

"We're estranged. We no longer sleep together and we seldom speak. I can't forgive him for what he did to me."

Mrs Cropp put her arms around her. "Did he hurt you?"

"More than anyone will ever know," she said, now sobbing. "Not physically. A couple of bruises. But it's like he cut my heart out."

"I knew something wasn't right the last time I saw him. I didn't say anything, now I wish I had. The sod of a man. Has he apologised?"

Thelma shook her head.

"What are you going to do?"

Thelma blew her nose and wiped her eyes. "I don't know Mrs Cropp. But don't worry about me. Come and see us soon..."

"Oh now, you just hold on a minute. You can't stay there. You and Gabe move your things over here..."

"Oh no Mrs Cropp," she said, her voice gripped with fear. "The way he is at the moment, he'd hunt us down like dogs."

"But Thelma..."

"No, no please. We'll be OK. Just promise you'll come and visit soon."

Mrs Cropp knew that to persevere would be pointless. Garth was obviously running things his way, with fear the main ingredient. "Alright then," she conceded. "You tell Gab..." Her words were cut short as Thelma stumbled. She reached out and caught her from falling. "Are you alright my dear? Come. Sit down over here. I'll get you a drink of water."

"I'm alright. Just sometimes I get a bit dizzy."

"After what you've been through, it's a wonder you can stand up at all. Have you told Garth?"

She shook her head.

"Have you been to see a doctor about it?" Mrs Cropp asked, handing her a glass of water.

Thelma took a couple of sips. "It's nothing. I'll be alright in a minute. Really."

As she drove away from Mrs Cropp's house, she had only gone a short distance when she turned the vehicle on an angle and stopped. Thelma looked back at her next door neighbour, waved, then continued on her way. Even though it was a nice gesture on Thelma's part, it alarmed her. *I'll go over there tomorrow and check she's alright. This business of dizzy spells bothers me a bit.*

But Mrs Cropp would never see Thelma Caplin again.

Chapter 8

As usual, the school bus dropped Gabe off at the front gate. As he walked home he saw the tractor was missing from the shed, which meant his father wasn't home. *That's great*, he smiled to himself.

He walked inside dumping his school bag on the kitchen floor. "Mum!" he called. "Mum? where are you?" There was no answer. He moved from the kitchen into the lounge room. "Mum?" He figured maybe she was outside, so he went out on the verandah. "Mum, are you there?" he called. Still there was no answer from Thelma. *Surely she's not down the shed?*

He ran outside and across to the building. "Mum?" he called. *That's strange. The ute's here. She didn't say she was going out.* He returned to the house and walked inside. Mildly alarmed his mother was nowhere to be found, he walked up to his bedroom thinking she was probably down the paddock with his father. As he entered his room, he noticed the door to his parents' bedroom was shut. He stared at it for a moment, then knocked gently.

"Mum," he called in a half whisper. "You in there?" There was no reply. Gabe called again, this time his voice a little louder. Still no reply came. Slowly he turned the handle and pushed open the door.

The shock of what he saw chilled him to the bone. Thelma was laying sprawled out on the bed, face down. Gabe screamed. "Mum!" He bolted towards her and cradled her head. "Mum?" He shook her a little. "Mum. Oh shit, mum!" Gabe burst into tears and put his face against hers. It was cold. Her hands were blue. Even at his own tender age he knew there was nothing he could do. She had gone. He wrapped his arms around his mother and cried.

"Don't die mummy, please don't die," he said. Gabe felt his groin go warm. He was weeing his pants and there was nothing he could do to stop it. Gripped by fear and panic, he raced outside. "Dad," he yelled. "Dad?" but there was no answer.

Gabe scrambled into the ute and roared off in search of his father. His gut was in turmoil as he swerved the vehicle across the paddocks in search of Garth. His knew he would probably get a swift right hand to the ear for disobeying his father's strict orders that under no circumstances was he to drive the utility without either him or his permission. Such a threat put the fear of God in him. The sight of his mother forced him to continue. Moments later, he spotted his father and sped across the paddock towards him.

Garth was tending a fly-blown sheep. Still with the sheep between his legs he stood up and, seeing the speed Gabe who was driving, let the sheep go and charged off to meet him.

"You mongrel bastard! I've told you to stay the fuck away from the ute," he roared. Garth grabbed the door handle and was nearly jerked off his feet as Gabe braked hard to a halt. "What did...?" he yelled.

"It's mummy," Gabe blurted out. "She's dead."

The words sliced through Garth like a scythe through wheat. "What?" he yelled.

"I... I just got home from school and... and..."

"Well come on for Christ's sake. What do you mean she's dead?"

Gabe was crying and blubbering so hysterically, Garth found it hard to understand him.

"I... I fo... found he... her in... in the bed... bedroom. S... She was all co... cold and blue."

Garth shoved the boy across the seat of the utility and drove like a madman to the house. He rushed inside to the bedroom. "Oh Jesus Christ!" The sight of his wife's body lying face down reefed his legs out from under him. As he struggled to regain his balance, he lunged forward and thrust her into his arms. Instinctively he knew she had gone. "Oh Thelma," he cried. "Thelma, Thelma, Thelma. Don't leave me. Please don't leave me. I love you. I'm sorry darling. Please don't leave me."

Gabe stood at the door, crying. He heard his father's words to his mother and he was confused. *You seldom spoke to her. All you did was go crook at her. You used to push her to the ground. Why are you saying all these things?* He made up his mind at that moment, he would never forget what he was witnessing. All this seemed like one big lie. *You bastard dad, you rotten bloody bastard. One day I'm gonna make you pay for what you did to her.'*

* * *

For the next four years, Garth and Gabe got by as best they could. They argued and bickered and Garth seldom spared the rod. They resented the very presence of each other. Garth had clamped down even harder on Gabe, making it impossible for him to have any sort of friendships apart from those in the schoolyard. Any offers of help from the neighbours were shunned, but Garth did concede to allow Mrs Cropp to do their washing and ironing.

"Heavens above Mr Caplin, you'll need clean pants and Gabe will need clean clothes for school."

"Only if you let me pay you," he told her.

Mrs Cropp's protests were dismissed only after she agreed to allow Garth to pay her five shillings a week. What Garth didn't know was she also put five shillings of her own with it. Every week she deposited ten shillings into a savings account at the State Savings Bank in Naracoorte. The deposit book was made out to Gabe Caplin with the words 'Gabe's Cropp' written in handwriting just inside the cover. It was her way of telling Gabe that when he turned twenty-one there would at least be one crop to pay a dividend that year.

As the arguing and ill feeling between Garth and Gabe intensified, Gabe swore that one day he was going to knock him over. "Just you wait till I'm as big as you," he cussed one afternoon when again tempers flared. "We'll see then who bosses who around."

Garth's answer was to deliver a backhander so severe, it knocked Gabe flat on his back.

When Gabe wasn't at home, he'd be at Mrs Cropp's. It was as though she had stepped in as the role of mother after Thelma died.

Often when they'd be sharing a cold drink after Gabe had carried out some chores for her, he'd ask her about his mother. Gabe couldn't seem to hear enough about her.

"She just idolised you," she'd tell him. "I like to remember her as being a lovely, pretty lady with a heart of gold. Don't know why your father treated her like he did. She just seemed so gentle and loving."

"I remember what he said to her as he held her that day when I found her in the bedroom," said Gabe. "He was blubbering on about being sorry and all that shit, and I remember at the time thinking how he used to treat her."

"I'm sure he loved your mother Gabe..."

"I heard him tell her that, whatever it was supposed to mean. But I didn't believe it. Not after what he did to her in the paddock that day. Did you ever hear about that?"

Mrs Cropp's gaze dropped to her lap. "Yes dear, your mother told me some of what happened."

"If that's loving somebody, he's got a funny way of showing it." Then out of the blue, as if he'd been storing it in his mind for years, he threw a question directly at her. "What's love? What does it mean?"

Instinctively, she knew the boy desperately wanted an answer. Not just a word or two, but the full-blown explanation. Gabe's eyes had opened wide in anticipation, thinking he was going to hear something very exciting. Something he'd never heard anyone discuss or even talk about. He probably thought love was just a word, much the same as please and thank you. "Heavens above dear, I don't know that I can answer that..."

"Yes you can," he said, pleading.

She pulled up a chair and leaned on the kitchen table. She was about to begin when she paused. She twisted on her chair and tapped her fingers on the table.

"Love," she began, "is something which comes in many forms. We can say I love cream cakes. That's just an expression of adoration. You can say you love your dog. Again, it means you have a fondness for that particular animal. People often say I love this or I love that. It's an expression of affection for a specific thing, object, place or pastime. In all reality it's probably one of the most misused words in our vocabulary. But in the true meaning of the word, the love one person has for another also takes on different forms. The love between a mother and her son is different from the love between a brother and a sister, a boyfriend and a girlfriend, an uncle and an aunt, or a husband and a wife. If you were to say you love me, it would be a different love than what you felt for your mother or what you feel for your father..."

"I don't bloody love that bastard."

"You mightn't think you do, but you do, believe me. To my way of thinking, the true God's meaning of love only comes between a man and a woman when they are husband and wife. Two people who are partners in life. That's when love can make you do crazy things, irrational things, wonderful things, emotive things, and perform great acts of kindness and sacrifice."

Mrs Cropp could see a puzzled look on the boy's face.

"So how will I know if I love someone?"

She smiled. "There's no rules dear, but believe me, you'll know," she said.

Mrs Cropp rose from her chair as she felt her eyes fill with tears. She walked around behind Gabe so he wouldn't see her mop her cheeks.

"One day, it will happen to you. You won't know where. You won't know when. Then out of the blue, you'll feel your knees go weak, your mouth go dry and your stomach will tie itself up into one big knot. If you're really lucky, she'll have the same reaction as you. That's when you'll hear bells ringing." She laughed. "Now don't ask me to explain that, because I can't. You won't be able to sleep. You won't be able to function properly. You'll think about her every waking moment. You'll think about her when you go to bed. She'll be on your mind when you wake up in the morning. You'll be down the paddock and you'll make up an excuse, even only to yourself, to go up to the house, just to ring her up. You won't want anything. All you want to do is hear her voice. You'll even find you dream about her. When it gets sad is when love is mistaken for a crush or a fascination or is one-sided. He or she has feelings for that one person, but that person doesn't respond. Then you have to cut your losses in the understanding he or she wasn't meant for you anyway. Then you'll meet someone else. It may be a gradual getting to know each other, or it may be something that's totally instantaneous.

"And when it happens, nothing else in the world will matter, just as long as you're with that person. And you'll know you love her when she takes priority over absolutely everything else. Whatever decisions you make, you'll make them with her in mind. Every day will be a new day filled with adventure as you get to know each other. Physically and emotionally. You'll want to know everything about her, and she about you. And when you touch each other you experience the most wonderful sensation. Love between a man and a woman is something sacred, something special. No money can buy it, no brains or intelligence can acquire it. It's something free of charge, given at no cost, but all the money in the world can't make it happen if it's simply not there. I guess in some ways it's two hearts joined as one, linked by a common thread of feelings, emotions, care and respect for one another. To me, it is the most valuable thing in the world. Many people spend their lives searching for it. Many die without ever having found it. And that's sad. And there are many who stumble across it and don't realise what they have until it passes them by. Then they spend the rest of their lives trying to recapture what never was, but should've been. And love affects everyone. The rich, the poor, the good people, the bad people. Even the most hardened criminals in our jails have women and children who love them. Oh dear, I'm rambling aren't I...?"

But Gabe hadn't moved a muscle. He was mesmerised and fascinated by the explanation given to just one simple word. "No, no," he said. "That's incredible."

"So there's a very brief overview dear. Since time immemorial authors, poets, writers, songwriters and ordinary people like you and me have been trying to find a simple explanation. I guess there isn't one. That was not short and sweet, but it might give you some idea."

"So you reckon all those things a man should feel about his wife applied to my father?"

"Yes I'm sure they did. But sometimes love can go off the rails when a trust is violated, and it may take time to heal the wounds. Love wounds cut the deepest and take the longest to heal. Sometimes, even a lifetime isn't long enough. That's when you might hear the expression, so and so died of a broken heart."

"Did mum die of a broken heart?"

"Oh no dear. She had a stroke, which means she had a clot which cut off the blood supply to her brain. Hasn't your father told you?"

The boy shook his head. "He just said she had something wrong with her heart. That's all he's ever told me."

Mrs Cropp paused and ran her fingers down the side of his face. *How tragic Garth hasn't seen fit to speak to his son about his mother's death.* Slowly, she continued. "But your mother knew your father loved her. They were just going through a difficult patch as married couples often do. It would have sorted itself out." Mrs Cropp knew this was some sort of acid-test and she just hoped she was convincing enough for Gabe to believe her. She wasn't.

"So if a man loves a lady, he shouldn't hit her should he?"

Mrs Cropp sensed the conversation heading into difficult territory. The last thing she wanted was to come between his mother and his father. Besides, she knew little of their personal lives. She looked for an escape. "They were difficult times dear, can't you forgive him?"

"Bullshit!" Gabe's eyes filled with tears. "He didn't love mum. If he did, he wouldn't have done that to her. If there'd been a gun in the ute that day, I swear I would have shot him."

The boy's comment jolted her. "Gabe, you mustn't talk like that. Don't even think like that. You put any thoughts of guns right out of your mind. The man is your father, Gabe. You mightn't think it now, but the man does love you."

"My father's a bastard Mrs Cropp. I can't wait till I'm old enough to leave home."

"Gabe stop that. Where on earth would you go?"

"I don't know, but what I do know is that I've just about had as much as I can take. Jesus he belts me as quick as looks at me. If you reckon that's love then he's pretty damn confused. Me? I hate the bastard. Simple as that."

Mrs Cropp was concerned that Gabe had adopted such an aggressive and ugly attitude towards his father. It also came as shock to her to learn how often he belted him. "Let me see if I can mend some fences," she told him. "When's your fifteenth birthday?" she asked, knowing full well when it was.

"Oh no, we're not doing that again," he said, recalling the events of five years previous.

"So you're telling me if I have a party here on the night of your fifteenth birthday, you won't come?"

Gabe grinned. "You're amazing! Sure I'll come, but dad probably won't let me."

"Yes he will, because I'll invite him. Now, no more talk of guns, OK?" she said, leaning over to kiss him on the cheek.

* * *

The next morning, Mrs Cropp drove over to the Caplins. Garth had just finished milking the cow and was walking back to the house with a bucket of milk. Gabe was standing at the kitchen sink washing dishes.

"Morning Mr Caplin," she called.

"Mornin'," he grunted.

"Wanted to catch you in case you were going out," she said.

Garth didn't answer as he walked towards her.

Somehow this is not going to be easy, she told herself. "Friday week, I'm having a few people over. Sort of a party. A few drinks. A bit of fun. Would you and Gabe like to come?"

Garth's mind flashed back to the disaster of his son's tenth birthday. It was still a touchy subject with him. To the extent the incident had not been mentioned by anyone in the five years that had followed. It seemed so long ago. Thelma had gone. He personally didn't see a lot of Mrs Cropp, although he knew Gabe did. It didn't please him, but he did allow his son this one excess. He knew he couldn't fill the gap of a mother. Maybe his next door neighbour could. There was little in common with himself and his son. All there seemed to be was constant bickering and argument. Life had become a habit. Work seven days a week. The weekly trip into Naracoorte for supplies. The milking, the shearing, the cropping, the fencing, the hay carting. Nothing but farm duties, month in, month out, year in, year out. He could sense that one morning he'd wake up and his son would be gone. He just hoped it would be sooner rather than later.

He placed the bucket of milk on the ground as he stood close by to Mrs Cropp. "When?"

"Friday week," she repeated.

"That's the kid's birthday isn't it?"

"Is there a problem with that?"

"If you want to give the kid a party, that's up to you."

"So you'll pop over?"

"Maybe, maybe not."

"Will you let Gabe come?" she asked.

Garth glared at her. "It's up to him," he mumbled, leaning down to take hold of the milk bucket's handle.

"So Friday week it is then. While I'm here, do you want me to take some washing back with me?"

"You know where it's kept."

Mrs Cropp collected the washing and placed it on the back seat of her car. As she turned around, she saw Gabe looking at her through the kitchen window. Although Mrs Cropp was very wary of Garth and his temper, she made sure she kept a reasonable distance when they spoke, careful not to show her anxiety. Especially not to Gabe.

"Morning dear," she called and waved, "lovely morning."

Gabe waved back, smiling. Friday week couldn't come quickly enough and when the day of the night finally arrived, he took out his Sunday bests and drove over to Mrs Cropp's.

"You're a bit early," she jested, as he wandered into her kitchen. "What's all that you've got?"

He opened a large paper bag he was carrying and layout his shirt, tie, jacket and trousers on the kitchen table. "Do you think these will be alright for tonight?" he queried.

"The shirt could do with a press." Mrs Cropp saw a look of disappointment run across his face. Then he brightened up when he saw her smile at him. "Just put them over there on the couch, I'll have a look in a moment. So!," she said enthusiastically, "are you all set?"

"Oh yeah, can't wait."

"What's your father had to say?"

"Nothing. He hasn't even mentioned it."

"He might have forgotten."

Gabe smiled. "He'll soon get reminded if he has. What if he chucks a shitty?"

"Oh surely not dear. I think if he was going to do that, I would have seen signs of it last week when I asked him. Besides, he's not to know this is my way of giving you a birthday party."

"Well don't go singing happy birthday to me tonight," a serious and disturbing tone in his voice. "If you do that, he'll probably go off his brain."

"I promise I won't sing happy birthday tonight. Which is why I'm going to sing it to you now. Come with me."

Gabe watched her leave the kitchen into the lounge room. He couldn't recall having taken so much notice of her before. Mrs Cropp was a big woman. probably in her forties, he guessed, but he couldn't quite work out why she only wore the same type of clothes.

He thought she reminded him of a woman he'd once seen in a movie, one of the few he'd ever been allowed to see. It was Ma Kettle, alias Marjorie Main, the Hollywood actress. *Not so much in looks, more in size*, he thought. He seemed to recall Ma being a large lady with big bosoms. But that's where the similarity ended. Mrs Cropp always wore a calf-length, divided skirt with tan leather inserts down the front. A check shirt, always a tan leather waist coat and long, leather boots. Depending on what she was doing, a pair of leather gloves often made up the outfit.

Gabe also began to notice other things about his neighbour. Like the things she surrounded herself with. Her kitchen was open and airy with a large wood stove, a large table in the centre, wooden high-backed chairs, a Charles Hope kerosene refrigerator. Elder Smith's calendar on the wall near the wall-mounted coat hooks and a large, wooden, three-seater settee. Gabe couldn't believe someone living on their own would want so many cupboards. *What the hell does she keep in them? And the pantry as well. Good God!*

Against another wall was what looked like a blackwood sideboard. It appeared to be very old but in superb condition. On its top was a framed photograph of people he didn't know, a set of tea pots and a figurine of a girl in a floral hat sitting on a log of wood. As he entered the lounge room he noticed a piano, again adorned with framed photographs, a big open fire-place, a brass fire-screen, a bellows, a three-piece wide-armed club lounge, and a framed tapestry depicting horses jumping a fallen log, hanging above a crystal cabinet.

Several shelves of the cabinet contained Mrs Cropp's crystal collection. She just assumed people knew about such things. But Gabe didn't. He could recall his mother having a couple of very special shiny glass vases and how she commented from time to time she'd like something in Edinburgh crystal.

Smokey pink-coloured velvet curtains hung from the lounge room window, with centre nets and pull-down blinds completing the combination. In the corner of the room stood a grandfather clock. Gabe loved to visit because, on the hour, the deep sound of the chimes gave him a homely feeling. Across the mantelpiece adorning the fire-place was another shower of ornaments and knick-knacks. A single light hung from flex in the centre of the ceiling, and the carpet, *old but warm*, Gabe thought, gave the room a feeling of prosperity.

Mrs Cropp opened the lid of the upright piano, sat down on the piano stool and began to play. She looked at Gabe. She could tell he was embarrassed. Then she began to sing. "Happy birthday to you. Happy birthday to you. Happy birthday dear Gabe, Happy birthday to you."

Gabe was leaning against the end of the upright. When the song was over, he went to her and hugged her neck. He didn't speak. A solitary tear rolled down his cheek. *If only mum could've heard that.* "Will you play some more?" he asked.

"Of course dear, what would you like to hear?"

Again the boy looked uneasy. "Don't really know what to ask for."

"Let's see now," said Mrs Cropp, thinking for a moment. "Oh I know."

Gabe didn't know how long he stood listening to her play. He only knew he enjoyed it immensely. After a few songs, he looked at his neighbour.

"Where did you come from before you came here?"

Mrs Cropp was caught totally off-guard. She could see the question was innocent enough. It just surprised her that it had taken him so long to ask it.

Mrs Cropp rubbed her eyes with her hands and rose from the piano stool. "No-one's ever asked me that," she replied, matter-of-factly. "Guess they thought if they did, they wouldn't get told anyway."

She went over to the mantelpiece and took hold of a framed photograph. She looked at it for a moment, wiped the glass on the front of herself, then handed it to Gabe.

He glanced at it. "Who's that?"

"That was my husband. We were married on your birthday over twenty years ago," she replied, drawing a handkerchief from her sleeve to dab her eyes.

"You were married once?"

Mrs Cropp nodded, "To the most wonderful man."

"Wh...what happened?"

"His name was Cyril. He was tall and, as you can see, extremely good looking, and we had the most wonderful, eleven, short months together."

"Eleven months! Is that all?" Gabe said.

Mrs Cropp paused to clear her throat and again dab her eyes with her handkerchief. "One day I was helping him feed out, just like you do with your father. We had the trailer loaded with hay on behind the tractor, idling around the paddock feeding the sheep. We lived in Western Australia. Then I don't know what happened. Cyril wasn't watching or maybe he was talking to me and got distracted. But one of the front wheels mounted a large stump and he was thrown off the tractor. He landed directly in front of the left-hand side, rear wheel and was run over by both the tractor and the trailer."

Gabe was flabbergasted. "By his own tractor?"

"By his own bloody tractor! And to make matters even worse, it was in the same week a year earlier his brother died when his tractor hit a tree and split in two." She paused to reflect on how much she should tell the boy. "Seeing the tractor run over Cyril sent me into a blind panic and the damn thing just kept idling across the paddock until it ran into the windmill. There was nothing I could do. There was blood everywhere, because the wheels caught Cyril's head, neck and shoulder. He died in my arms dear. The poor darling died in my arms. I will never forget the sadness in his eyes."

Mrs Cropp walked over to the window. Gabe could see her drying her eyes again.

"D...did he sa...say anything?"

" I don't know how he managed it, but yes, he spoke to me." She turned around to him. "He said, 'Betsy please hold me,' and then he was gone."

Gabe's chin had dropped to his chest, his eyes, saucer-like and tear filled, not knowing which way to look. Then finally, "Is your name Betsy?" he asked in a half whisper.

"Yes darling, my name is Betsy," she sobbed. "Not too many people know that either." She thought for a moment. Then she smiled a little. "You know, Cyril just had this very special way of saying Betsy. It was kind of poetic. Romantic if you like," she said. "Sometimes he'd sort of breathe it, like B-e-t-s-y in a very sexy tone and I would just melt."

Gabe didn't speak, but silently kept urging her to tell him more.

"You would have loved him Gabe, he was such a fine man. After he died there seemed no reason for me to stay, so I left. From then on I just became Mrs Cropp. To everyone."

"When you held him in your arms for the last time, did you feel that wonderful sensation you told me about?" he asked innocently.

"Oh yes dear, then and every other time he either looked at me or touched me. Every day I was with him the feelings we had for each other grew stronger and stronger. It was as though we were one. He was just the most wonderful, wonderful man and I miss him terribly... even after all this time."

"So you really must have loved him."

"More than life itself sometimes. And the funny thing is, I am a great believer in the fact that in life you only ever get one really true shot at happiness. Some people take three or four marriages to find it, but in the end we only have that one shot. I guess I've had mine, as there isn't a soul on earth who could ever replace my Cyril."

"How long after was it before you left?"

"About a year. You see I was pregnant at the time and the shock of the accident caused me to lose my baby... my, you are learning a lot about me today aren't you?"

"You didn't want to tell me?"

Mrs Cropp smiled and again dabbed her tears. "I've never spoken about it before. Maybe it's time."

"You... you lost your baby?"

"Yes Gabe. I was pregnant with our first child. Cyril said he wanted a boy." The memories of her loss caused her to take stock and regain herself. "Cyril's parents, and they're gone now too, were lovely. Despite the fact they were still mourning Stan, they wanted me to stay on the farm. We had five thousand acres over there. But I couldn't. So I sold up and came over here. That was twenty-four years ago. So there, now you know."

"But you should be married, Mrs Cropp."

She moved over and gently stroked his face. "But I am Gabe. Maybe one day you'll understand."

"But it's not fair."

"I'm happy dear. My memories of Cyril will last my lifetime." Again she paused, pondering. "We still have a chat now and again you know," not expecting Gabe to have the slightest understanding of what she was talking about.

"Are you very rich?"

Mrs Cropp laughed out loud. "I suppose so," she told him thoughtfully. "Cyril was a wealthy man and, just before we married, he took out a large life insurance policy against himself in case something should happen. That's funny isn't it?" she said. "He promised to live until he was ninety-nine and eleven months. He got the months right. Just messed up a bit on the years." She took the framed photograph of her late husband and pressed it to her lips, then put it back on the mantelpiece.

* * *

It was a little after eight p.m. when Gabe saw his father swing the headlights of the ute into Mrs Cropp's driveway. As he pulled up Mrs Cropp greeted him, careful not to mention anything of Gabe's birthday. As usual, his father hadn't mentioned his birthday or even given him a gift. *Not since mum died*, Gabe thought. *You've never acknowledged my birthday since mum died. Well fuck you too, see if I care.*

"Well come in, come in," urged Mrs Cropp.

As Garth led the way, Betsy Cropp smiled at Gabe and squeezed his hand. "Today is our secret. OK?" she whispered in his ear. Gabe returned the smile and nodded his head.

Stan and Irene Smythe, the local postmaster and his wife, greeted them as they entered the kitchen. Stan took them into the lounge room. "I think you mostly know everyone," he chirped.

Garth mostly did, except for some couples and some of the children present. Those he did know, he seldom saw from one year through to another. Stan conducted the formalities. "Herb and Dorrie Forrester and their daughter Cecily. Steve and Molly Oswald and their daughter Sandra. And these two little scrubbers over here are the twins, Claire and Janet."

Stan could see Garth was puzzled by the two girls. He laughed. "They belong to Irene when they're good and me when they're bad. Or so she says anyway."

Everybody laughed. It pleased Mrs Cropp. Gabe knew the girls from school but couldn't understand why they had huddled in a group and appeared to be giggling at him behind cupped hands they held to their mouths. It was Molly Oswald who spoke, seeing Gabe's discomfort.

"Don't take any notice of them Gabe, they probably haven't seen you all decked out before. And my word, that is a nice tie."

"Come on Herb, fill some of these glasses," Mrs Cropp piped up.

But still an uneasy silence filled the room. Rumor had spread quickly after Thelma's death that Garth used to knock her about. And in any small, rural environment, such rumors spread quickly. No-one knew exactly, but everyone suspected. It became obvious fairly quickly that no-one in the room particularly liked Garth, rumors or no rumors, and they felt a little uncomfortable in his presence. Mrs Cropp sensed all was not right.

"I think we need a song," she said, moving across to the piano. As the music started, those in the room were drawn to each other and conversation flowed freely. But Garth was left out.

He was standing alone. Gabe stood next to him, trying to ignore the continued giggling of the girls. Irene Smythe broke from her group and went to Garth. "Another drink?" she asked him."

Garth suddenly decided he didn't want to be there. "No thanks, we're leaving. Finish your drink boy."

Gabe was dumbfounded. "But it's only just started" he protested.

"We're leaving, I said, now finish your bloody lemonade."

Dorrie Forrester heard Garth's words and walked over to him. "Don't go Garth, we haven't even had a chance to talk yet."

Garth glared back. "No we haven't have we? And what's more, I don't think anyone in this room has any intentions of it either," he said.

Mrs Cropp continued playing the piano, unaware of the drama going on behind her.

As Gabe hurriedly finished his drink, his father grabbed his arm and strode from the house.

Gabe felt embarrassment like he never knew possible. As the two drove back to their house, he was still too shocked and humiliated to speak. Garth swore and bitched all the way home. "Jesus I knew I shouldn't have been sucked into that. Why the fuck did I bother? Those bloody hypocrites! Don't go yet, we haven't had a chance to talk," he mimicked. "Yeah well fuck 'em I say! fuck 'em!"

Finally Gabe had recovered enough to open his mouth. "Jesus dad, why did you do that?" he asked.

"Fuck 'em boy!, they can go to hell!"

"But I wanted to stay," Gabe replied.

"Yeah, well I wanted to go, so do as you're bloody told!"

Chapter 9

Gabe lay awake for most of the night, churning and burning up inside like he'd been struck down with a fever. He had never been so angry with his father. Five years beforehand he destroyed his tenth birthday party. Now he'd just made sure he didn't enjoy this one.

This has got to stop. This really has to stop. Tomorrow I'm going to see to it that it does.

In the morning, neither spoke over the breakfast table. But Gabe's mind was still in turmoil. *This has gotta come to a head. Now. Right now.* Garth put his boots on and left the house. Gabe followed. He waited till his father was down by the shed when he braced himself for what he knew was going to be the ultimate confrontation. He also knew he was probably about to get the hiding of his life, but something had to give; life with his father had become totally untenable.

"Last night was the biggest mongrel act pulled by the biggest mongrel bastard I've ever met in my life," he yelled.

Garth stopped in his tracks. He turned to confirm his ears weren't lying to him. Gabe was visibly shaking. "You talking to me?"

"Yeah I'm talking to you. You nearly make me puke every time I see you, you selfish brutal bastard," Gabe said, still yelling.

Garth saw red. He burst into the shed and grabbed the stock-whip off the workbench and charged back outside. Gabe froze like a ram before a king brown when he saw his father coming at him, too terrified to move, which allowed the lash an easy and perfect target. Gabe screamed in agony as the leather lace cracked against his rib cage.

"A mongrel act, eh boy?" he yelled, gathering the whip and sending it down on his son a second time. Again Gabe screamed in agony as the lash found its mark.

Again his father drew back the whip. This time Gabe saw it coming and turned his back to try and shield the brunt of the blow, but to no avail. The lash sliced through his shirt and feathered his skin, drawing blood. He howled in agony. Garth yanked back on the whip and lashed out again. This time it caught another area of his back and Gabe fell to the ground, writhing in agony. The force of the blow took his breath away. All the time Garth was roaring like a mad bull. Blow after blow he lay on his son. Gabe tried to get up. Once he nearly made it. But Garth directed the lash at his legs and jerked him over. Gabe clawed along the ground to escape the onslaught. Dirt and dust filled his mouth as spit, saliva and tears covered his face. He had never felt such pain.

Garth continued to lay the lash on Gabe, with each blow mulching his skin a little more. The muscles and veins now bulging on his neck and sweat pouring from his brow. Garth was like a madman. Still the blows came.

Gabe had to do something to stop his father or he would be dead in seconds. After another vicious blow caught the top of his legs and tore through his jeans, he used every ounce of his strength, picked himself up and lunged, stumbling and screaming at his father.

The power of his charge knocked Garth's legs from under him. Frantically Gabe scrambled to his feet and raced into the shed. He went straight for a cupboard on the back wall. He crashed open its doors and snatched the shotgun out of a rack. He spun round with the weapon to see his father coming at him from about twenty feet away.

He jerked back the loading pin of the Browning five-shot semi automatic and released it. A round catapulted into the breech. He pointed the weapon directly at his father.

"YOU TOUCH ME AGAIN AND I'll FUCKING KILL YA!" he screamed.

Garth bulked to a stop, mid stride. "Put the gun down boy or I'll break your bloody neck!"

"Yeah, well you aren't going to break anybody's bloody neck," he said, desperately trying to hold the gun steady. His entire body was erupting violently from within. His hands were slippery. Quickly he glanced at them. They were covered in blood, which was seeping from the wounds in his upper body.

Garth started to move forward. Gabe lifted the weapon a little higher and thrust it in his direction. "I'm fucking telling you, you come near me ever again, ever... and I'll blow your fucking brains out!" Quickly he glanced at his hands again, the sight of his own blood nearly sending him crazy with panic.

Garth stood there, still with the stock whip in his hands. Slowly he began to draw it back, as if setting himself for another lash at his son. "Can't see you doing a lot of damage with a gun that's not even loaded," he said.

"So you want to try me arsehole? Want to fuckin' try me?" Gabe watched as his father started to coil the whip. "Put the whip down!" he screamed.

"You stupid fucking idiot. Do you think I store that bloody thing loaded? Now hand it over," Garth demanded, taking another step.

"One more, you fucking mongrel. Take one more step and your brains will end up on the front seat of the tractor!" Gabe was right on the edge and he knew it. He also knew he was only moments away from collapsing due to his heinous injuries. He felt his body begin to throb. *Jesus, the pain, I don't believe the pain.*

Again Garth stopped. But he wasn't convinced his son wasn't bluffing.

Gabe looked at him. "I said drop the whip. Jesus, you don't believe me do you? You don't fuckin' believe me do you?" he screamed.

Next instant, Gabe pointed the barrel up in the air and pulled the trigger. The blast echoed off the corrugated iron walls of the shed as the shot tore a hole about a foot across through the roof. The recoil sent him backwards.

Garth was stunned. "Shit!"

"Now drop the fuckin' whip!"

Garth obeyed instantly. As it hit the ground, Gabe fired another shot and sent it several feet further away. He then raised the shotgun to his shoulder and pointed it right between his father's eyes. He was now only a few feet away.

"Double-O SG's, arsehole. Pig shot. They make a fucking great hole don't they? And there's still three left and they've all got your name on 'em. Get down on your knees!"

Garth tried to speak but anger and terror choked his voice box.

"Get down on your fuckin' knees!"

Instantly Garth dropped to the ground.

"Look at me. LOOK AT ME!" Gabe screamed. As Garth lifted his head, Gabe rammed the end of the barrel in his mouth. "Forgot about this didn't you? Didn't think I'd have the guts to go for it did you?" Gabe could see the whites of his father's eyes, nearly popping their sockets in raw terror. "A week ago I made myself a promise the next time you lay a hand on me you were gonna die, so I filled the magazine. Are you ready to die arsehole? Are you ready to fuckin' die?"

He knew he'd gone too far to turn back. If he dropped the gun, though, he'd be at the mercy of his father. He needed his father to break. Quickly he jerked the barrel from his mouth and fired another shot as he pressed the barrel against his right ear. Dirt and dust flew as the pellets from the shotgun cartridge hit the ground. Quickly he thrust the barrel hard against his father's forehead.

"Two left bastard. Two left!" Again he jerked the barrel aside, pressed it against Garth's ear and fired.

Garth screamed. More dust and dirt flew. Once more, Gabe thrust the barrel into his father's forehead. "And now there's only one. You ready to fuckin' die?"

Garth vomited, spewing out sick and saliva down the front of himself. Gabe could feel himself getting weaker by the second. Then he began to cry. Still with the end of the barrel jammed against his father's forehead, he blurted, "What the fuck did mum ever do to you for you to treat her like you did? What did she fuckin' do? Did you take the stock-whip to her too you fucking bastard? I oughta blow your mongrel brains out now while I've got the chance!"

"Well you better do it boy, because if I survive this I'm gonna break your fucking neck," Garth replied weakly.

"What the fuck did mum ever do to you?"

Garth couldn't answer.

"You wanted more kids, right? And because she couldn't give 'em to you, you blamed her. You fuckin' blamed her! You're a stinking mongrel bastard! You even knocked her arse over head, and whenver you get the chance you do the same! You fucked up my tenth birthday.

You fucked up last night. You've been belting the shit out of me for years with anything you could get your hands on. Well right now arsehole it's payback time. You're fuckin' dead arsehole. You hear me? There's one left and it's going right into your brains. You're not too fuckin' brave now are you? Where's the whip daddy? You want another go with the whip?"

Gabe was now pressing the end of the shotgun barrel so hard into his father's head, it had broken the skin. Blood began to seep from the wound, but before it rolled down his face it soaked up the gun powder residue which had rubbed off the end of the barrel onto his forehead. If ever a man was a split second away from death, it was Garth Caplin. If he even flinched, Gabe would pull the trigger. He had got past the point of caring about himself. He wanted revenge.

Garth vomited some more, the sick spilling onto his shirt and dirt-covered trousers. He had now urinated in his pants. Gabe saw air bubbles coming from the saliva and vomit oozing from his mouth.

Break you bastard, BREAK! Gabe screamed to himself. He didn't know how much longer he could hold out. He knew it was only fear and adrenalin keeping him on his feet.

"You got any final fuckin' words?" he screamed, jamming the barrel even harder into his father's head.

He could see his words had cut deep and he watched him break with pleasure. It was the truth about Thelma that Garth never wanted to hear. It was the truth he couldn't live with. The words had more impact upon him than the threat of being shot dead. Gabe watched his father roll onto his side, bury his head in his hands and cry like a baby.

As he watched him, Gabe began shaking uncontrollably. He still stood with the shotgun aimed at him. With blood dripping from his fingers, he wanted to do something to help himself, but didn't know if his father was feigning surrender, waiting for him to drop his guard. He stood watching his father, rolling in the dirt, crying hysterically. Slowly he let the gun drop from his shoulder. Still keeping his distance, he reached out and touched his father's shoulder from behind.

Blood from his fingertips soaked into Garth's shirt. He jerked his hand away and shouldered the weapon as his father turned to look at him. It was covered in tear- and vomit-soaked dust, dirt and blood. The smell of urine hung low in the air.

"I'm sorry son," he blurted, "I'm fucking sorry, alright?"

"And you think that makes it alright? Sorry son! How fucking sorry? Do you hear me? How fuckin' sorry?"

"Jesus Christ boy, I'm your bloody father! What do you want from me?"

Gabe swung the barrel of the shotgun and crashed it hard against the side of Garth's head. As he rolled over in the dirt, Gabe jammed his foot into his father's throat and again thrust the end of the barrel into his mouth.

Garth was terror-stricken. His body straightened and went rigid with fear. He snorted and blew saliva around the end of the gun barrel as he tried to breathe. Gabe stood over him, blood from his wounds dripping onto Garth's face. He saw his father glaring up at him as he tightened his finger on the trigger. Garth let out a muffled, howling scream as he braced himself for the blast. Racked with pain, Gabe was now barely able to stand, but he prolonged the agony for his father as long as physically possible. He jerked the barrel from Garth's mouth, deliberately pulling upwards as he did, hoping the brass sight bead on the end of the barrel would catch a front tooth. It did. Garth spun around as the searing pain of a front tooth shattering drove deep into his head.

"AAAHHH!" he screamed, spitting blood and tooth fragments onto the ground. "Fuck you!"

Gabe lunged at him again. "You want to tell me you'll never touch me again or do you want to die. Your fucking choice, but make it now!"

Garth's hands were holding his mouth. Blood and tooth chips squelched through his knuckles as he tried to speak.

"What's it gonna fuckin' be?" Gabe screamed.

"I'll never touch you again," Garth blurted, spitting blood.

"What?"

"I'll never touch you again!"

"And what happens if I drop the gun? What the fuck are you gonna do to me?"

Garth didn't answer. Gabe stumbled around behind his father, and with all the power left in him crashed the barrel of the weapon into his father's head. Garth dropped flat to the ground, senseless.

Gabe's body was screaming in agony. His back, chest and thighs were on fire. Again he felt himself going weak. He fought off the agony and moved over to the stock-whip lying on the ground, hooked his toe in it and kicked it in his father's face. A few feet away, the utility had been reversed into the shed. Still with the shotgun at his shoulder, he backed slowly over to it and checked the keys were in the ignition. He reached in, jerked the gear lever into neutral and turned the key. The engine kicked into life. Gabe, still with the gun pointed at his father, didn't trust the situation enough to lower the weapon.

"You stay the fuck away from me, you hear me? You hear me!"

Garth didn't move.

Gabe was nearly out on his feet. He jerked the door of the ute open. Agonisingly he sat on the edge of the seat and swung himself behind the wheel. He pushed in the clutch, pulled the lever into gear and then turned his attention to the weapon. He held it with one hand and worked the breech pin with the other, ejecting the remaining cartridge. Gabe caught it and threw it on the floor.

He looked over at his father and saw him begin to stir. He then thrust the shotgun into the dirt, slammed the door and roared off in the direction of Mrs Cropp's.

* * *

Betsy Cropp was aghast at the sight of Gabe Caplin's wounds. "My God, did your father do this to you?" she gasped. "Heaven forbid boy, what did he use, the stock-whip?"

Gabe nodded, his face too contorted with pain to speak.

"He did?" she exclaimed, not expecting for a moment that what she said was indeed the truth. "Your father whipped you?"

Gabe had made his way to a chair at Mrs Cropp's table. He sat on the edge, using the table for support.

For a moment she wasn't sure what to do. Gabe couldn't stand anything touching his wounds. Gingerly, Mrs Cropp plucked a strand of his shirt with the nails of her thumb and forefinger to try and look underneath. Gabe cried out. Blood was still oozing from what looked like a tread pattern of welt marks.

"Can you talk?" she asked.

He nodded his head.

"What in God's name happened over there?"

Gabe blurted, blubbered and stammered his way through an explanation, but the biggest problem he had was in stopping Mrs Cropp from calling the police or an ambulance. "But you've been ripped to pieces," she protested. "You must let me get you into the hospital. You need stitches in some of this and lord knows what infections you'll get!"

Again Gabe pleaded with his neighbour.

"But you are in a serious condition. Look at yourself. You need help. Urgent medical help!"

Gabe shook his head.

Finally she agreed to his wishes. "Alright, have it your way. But I'm certainly going to get the doctor to you." She saw Gabe's expression pleading for her not to. "He's a good friend of mine. He's owes me a favor and I'll swear him to secrecy. You must let him look at you."

Gabe was in too much agony to argue. He was about to offer a further protest when he passed out. Mrs Cropp ran to the phone.

Three quarters of an hour later, Doctor Gilbert Hendrickson arrived. He took one look at Gabe and turned to Mrs Cropp. "He really needs to be in a hospital. His father did this to him, you say?" Mrs Cropp nodded. "But the police should be informed..."

"No hospital. No police. Please try and understand Gilbert. And not a word to a soul. Can you help him?"

"Well certainly I can..."

Doctor Hendrickson worked on Gabe for nearly two hours. Finally he washed up and prepared to leave. "You'll need to sit with him for about three days. He'll be in great pain when he wakes up but these should help quite a bit," he said, handing her a small bottle of tablets. "I've stitched him up and taken care of any infection, but we'll need to keep a close eye on him. I'll come by tomorrow and check the bandage."

Gabe was forced to stay in bed for six days as a result of the lashings which tore through his skin. For the first three days, Mrs Cropp barely left his side, warily keeping an eye and an ear out in case his father paid an unexpected visit. This she feared most of all. Soon after Doctor Hendrickson's first visit, she went into her storeroom and took her old Savage double-barrelled, twelve-gauge shotgun from a cupboard. She broke open the breech, snapped it shut then drew back the hammers and pulled the triggers. Satisfied everything was fine, she reached over and grabbed a little bottle of three-in-one oil, squirted a couple of drops on the action, wiped around it with the cloth, then broke open the breech. She dropped two cartridges into the barrels then jerked it shut. She took the gun and placed it just inside the pantry door and within easy reach when she was in the kitchen.

On the morning of the seventh day, Doctor Hendrickson had just left after removing Gabe's stitches when Garth drove up Mrs Cropp's driveway. Gabe, now up and about, saw him arrive.

"I'll go," said Mrs Cropp.

"No, I've got to face him sometime. Just as well be now."

Gabe, unsteady on his feet and still in great pain, slowly walked outside to meet his father. The two glared at each other over a distance of four or five metres.

"It's time you came home," his father uttered.

As Gabe looked at him, he could see where he had ripped out his front tooth and there was still swelling round his mouth. "No way!"

"Well, you can't stay here, you've got work to do," Garth told him.

Gabe laughed. "Jesus, you're amazing. You half fucking killed me and you tell me I've got work to do. Christ I can hardly walk. I've been in bed for six days. I've just had sixty-three stitches out of my back and guts and the only fucking thing you can say is I've got work to do. Well fuck you! You oughta be in bloody jail for what you did to me."

"And so should you."

"Yeah, well you first."

"I said I was sorry didn't I?"

"Only because you had a fucking shotgun jammed in your head and you thought you were gonna die. Forget it, I'm not going back there so you can go on belting the shit out of me."

"I told you no more belting."

"That's today. What about tomorrow or the next day?"

"I've said all I'm going to say. If you want to work on the farm that'll one day be yours, you can't stay here. It's up to you." With those final words, Garth returned to his ute and drove away.

He thought long and hard about what his father told him. *He's never said anything to me before about the farm being mine one day. I'll be buggered.* He slowly returned to the house. He noticed Mrs Cropp had been witnessing the events from her kitchen window. As he glanced across to her pantry, he noticed the shotgun. "I haven't seen that there before," he said.

"Oh, that's always there," she told him, dismissing the subject. "Now what did he say to you?"

"Wants me to come home. Reckons he's gonna give me the farm one day."

"Did he just tell you that?" Gabe nodded. "Well he doesn't have anyone else to leave it to. How do you feel about that?"

"Sooner stay here with you. That's how I feel about that."

"Don't you want to go home?"

"Not while I'm like this."

Three days later, Mrs Cropp saw Gabe tidying up his room.

"Leaving me?" she quizzed.

"Guess I gotta go home sometime," he told her.

"Well you're certainly not walking. Hop in the car and I'll drive you. How do you feel?"

"Still bloody sore. But it looks like I'm healing OK." Gabe moved over to Mrs Cropp and carefully put his arms around her. "Thank you for being my mother," he told her.

* * *

Garth and Gabe developed a testy and distant relationship. Gabe lived in constant fear that one day his father would turn on him. Not to his face. Perhaps when he was sleeping. Which is why every night he made sure he took the shotgun out of the cupboard in the shed and hid it. Garth never knew he did. Before Garth rose every morning, Gabe made sure he'd been down to the shed to replace it. In order for peace to remain, Gabe knew it was imperative he not set his father's temper off. He went to great lengths to make sure he didn't.

Word spread around the district that things were a little strange at the Caplin place, so no-one ever dropped by to say hi and chew the fat. The only contact Gabe had with outsiders were those who called in to see Mrs Cropp when he was there, or those he saw on the weekly shopping trip to Naracoorte. At home, Garth and Gabe each went about their daily activities with very little conversation or interaction. They would help each other, but only when necessary.

Gabe didn't know it, but he had broken his father's spirit. His temper was still there, but it rarely surfaced. The burden he couldn't live with was the memory of how he treated his wife and son. For five years the two men lived semi-reclusive lives. Gabe became withdrawn, unable to drop his guard for fear his father would turn on him. Mrs Cropp tried to get Gabe involved in social activities, but to no avail.

"But Gabe, you're twenty. Soon to be twenty-one. You're now a fully grown man. And look at you. I can't believe how you've grown and filled out. You used to be such a puny little boy. I don't know what you've been eating, but you look like you're all set to break some girl's heart."

But even her attempts to humour Gabe had no effect. Then, one afternoon, Mrs Cropp noticed Gabe coming up the driveway at a time when he never dropped by. He drew the old ute to a halt and casually walked into the kitchen. "This is a surprise," Mrs Cropp greeted him cheerfully. "What are you doing here this hour of the day?"

"Garth's dead," he told her, "found him slumped over the steering wheel of the tractor in the bottom paddock."

Mrs Cropp gasped in horror. "He's dead?"

"Sure is. Must have been there awhile because he's as stiff as a board."

"Oh Gabe, that's terrible. Are you alright?"

Gabe lifted a kettle of boiling water off the stove and filled the tea pot. "Sure. Doesn't bother me too much," he told her.

"But Gabe, he was your father..."

"He was a bastard and a mongrel Aunty Betsy. A right proper bastard and a right proper mongrel. To hell with him!"

"Where is he now?"

"Still down there I guess. I didn't move him. I rang the cops and the ambulance. I'll go back there when I see them go past."

Gabe poured some tea into two cups. He didn't know if he was numb from finding his father dead or relieved. It bothered him there were no feelings of loss or sadness. *Strange*, he thought, *but all I can think about is my mother.* He lifted his eyes to the ceiling of Mrs Cropp's kitchen. *He's gone mum. The bastard's finally gone. He can't hurt either of us anymore.*

Chapter 10

"All set?" Paul Redman asked Katie McFarlane as he completed his final cockpit check.

"Oh gaaawd!" she said, distinctly pale.

"Relax," he said, and smiled reassuringly, "you're going to love it."

Moments later the Cessna one-seven-two was making its way down to the end of runway two-one left. After clearance from the tower, Paul released the brakes, pulled back on the throttle and the small plane accelerated down the tarmac. Katie thrilled at the exhilaration as the wheels locked into the undercarriage shortly after becoming airborne.

"You want to tell me where we're going?" she called over the top of the wind and engine noise.

"Mildura."

She laughed, convinced in her own mind it would be New South Wales. "Not Sydney?"

"Next time," he grinned. "How you doing? Do you like it?"

Katie wasn't sure. She hated flying. Or so she thought. But somehow this was different and she began to lighten up as her fears subsided. For some reason she couldn't explain to herself, she did like it. Perhaps a little too much. "Maybe it's starting to be OK," she answered.

As her fear of flying deserted her, Katie became more at ease when she saw the confidence Paul displayed in handling the aircraft. As she watched and listened to him communicate with the tower, Katie felt herself being turned on by it all. But she wasn't sure which was the stronger force, Paul or the tingling sensation she felt when allowing herself to enjoy the thrill of this first-time experience. She looked at Paul and the two exchanged smiles. He reached over and squeezed her hand, almost on cue.

Why do I think of all this crazy rubbish? she cursed herself. "Why Mildura?"

"There's a new Country Club that opened last weekend. Thought you might like to see it. It's called The Oakdale," he told her, lifting his voice over the top of the engine noise.

"Very big?"

"Huge. Should be there in time for lunch," he grinned. "We should land in about ninety minutes if the weather stays as it is."

"Do you do this often?"

"Fly?"

"Uh-huh."

"Only when I'm accompanied by a pretty girl," he chortled.

"So you're trying to impress me?"

"Wanna do a loop?"

"No, shit," Katie screeched. "Oh God Paul. No Dooooon't."

But it was too late. He had already pulled back on the stick and gone into a steep climb. Katie's face turned white so he immediately eased back on the controls. "Am I impressing you?' he called.

"I hate you!," she yelled back.

"Don't get mad, get even."

"Like what?"

"Learn to fly."

"Go to hell!" Regaining her composure, she dropped her head. "I'm not angry. You just happened to have scared the living daylights out of me." Slowly she began to look up, and when she glanced at Paul Redman the hint of a smile began to emerge. "But I must admit, it did feel good. I want to try it again, now I know what to expect."

Paul laughed. "Some old timers reckon it's better than sex. Wanna lay your seat back?"

"Paul Redman!"

"Joking!" he laughed, pulling back on the controls to put the little plane into a steep climb before breaking off to the left. Katie squealed, the engine roared and both pilot and passenger thrilled in the adrenaline rush of the gravitational forces.

An hour and a half later, Katie McFarlane experienced her first landing in a light aircraft and they were soon making their way to a waiting vehicle. "The girls at work will never believe this," she said, gushing.

Paul smiled as a few more steps saw the rear doors to a brand new Ford Fairlane being opened by the chauffeur. "Right on time too, Mr Redman."

"Hi George, meet Miss Katie McFarlane. Katie, this is George Raisin. He totally spoils me."

George smiled appreciatively as he tipped his cap. "Pleasure indeed Miss McFarlane."

"Oh please," she blushed. "It's Katie, Mr Raisin."

George Raisin looked at her. "If you please maam, then I'll not be a Mister either. It's George."

"Jesus, I'm bloody glad we've got all that out of the way," Paul laughed. "I keep telling him to call me Paul, but he won't listen."

As George Raisin drove Paul and Katie from the airport, Paul wound down his window a fraction to let the breeze blow in his face. A strange feeling of melancholy had overtaken him. *Is this too good to last? Is Katie too good to be true? Is this woman just a fly-by-night fascination?* It had happened before but he chose not to think about it. He looked over at her and smiled. *God I want her. So that's it? It's just bloody lust. No. No. No,* he angrily denied to himself. *It's more than that. In these few short hours I know this is the woman I want to grow old with.*

"So, ever been to Mildura?"

"Mum and dad brought some friends from the U.K. up here for the day last Easter. It's so pretty when all the flowers are out."

Up ahead, a big rooftop balloon came into view. It was multi coloured and, as the vehicle got closer, Katie was able to read the wording: GRAND OPENING ALL WEEK. OAKDALE COUNTRY CLUB. ALL WELCOME.

"Looks like we're here," Paul said.

Katie scanned the sweeping, pebbled driveway leading into what was billboarded as THE OAKDALE COUNTRY ESTATE. She noticed it appeared to be tucked behind a new housing estate, about half a minute's drive off the main Mildura to Adelaide road. Recently planted candle pines had been strategically placed to enhance the grandeur of the club's front entrance.

"The balloon looks very spectacular sir. Wait till you get inside. It's simply stunning," George commented.

As the Fairlane got closer, Katie could see a large gathering of people at the club's entrance. "Who are all those people?"

"They all work for me," he told her.

"Oh shit, Paul," she said, and gulped in disbelief. "You own this?"

"Uh-huh."

As the Fairlane drew to a halt, George Raisin was quick to open Katie's door. As Katie McFarlane climbed from the vehicle, she stepped onto a red carpet. Quickly she noticed a sea of glass supported by steel columns rising to the gable of the roof which formed the front of the structure. Rose beds and manicured lawns led along the footpath right up to the two glass entrance doors. These were ringed with brass and, just above, security cameras whirred. Then she noticed a very special effect, water running continuously down the front window glass for the entire frontage of the building. *Amazing!* she thought.

"Hi folks," Paul greeted his employees. "How would you all like to meet a V.I.P.? and I mean a real V.I.P." Katie could feel herself blushing. Paul moved quickly to put her at ease. "Katie," he began, "This is Peter Lidcombe. He runs the place. And Jill Lawson. She makes sure I don't go bankrupt. And this is our very special Kazumi," Paul continued. "I met Kazumi in Hong Kong last year at a convention. What she served up to us was so magnificent we simply had to have her. So I met with her mum and dad; that's them standing over there by the door," he said, raising his hand to acknowledge them, "sliced through a whole heap of red tape and now we have the best chef in the world working at The Oakdale Country Club. And we love her, don't we people?" he called to the group.

Smiles of approval and laughter greeted Paul's comments as Kazumi stepped forward to offer Katie her hand.

"Madam," she began in broken english, "you are so lucky you know special person like Mr Paul. We did not know Mr Paul know such a pretty and special lady, no. I make you something very special for today lunch, yes?"

"Oh thank you Kazumi," Katie said. "I'm just so overwhelmed by all of this, I don't quite know what to say."

Introductions completed, Paul took Katie's arm and ushered her towards the front doors. Quickly George Raisin was in position to open them. As Katie stepped inside the building she was greeted with the kind of opulence she'd only ever read about in books. Paul could see she was completely taken aback at what lay before her and raised his hand to the group following. They halted and remained silent as Katie tried to absorb her surroundings.

The chandelier hanging from the ceiling immediately over the centre of the foyer was the first thing she noticed. *That's got to be eight feet across. Unbelievable!* Blood-red pure wool carpet went wall-to-wall. A sweeping mahogany reception desk partially filled one wall. Framed Picasso line drawings hung from the wall immediately above a writing bureau which held the visitors book.

"Copies," Paul told her, almost apologetically, noticing Katie had taken a special interest in them. "I'm still trying to get a copy of Guernica, the one he did in 1937." Katie looked puzzled. "Sorry," Paul apologised. "I get a bit carried away with Picasso. You see Picasso hated war and in 1937 he painted what's regarded as his masterpiece. It was inspired by the bombing of the Basque town of Guernica by German war planes."

"So what's so special about the Guernica?"

He thought for a moment.

"Guernica is probably best described as a mass tangle of people and horses crying out in protest at the futility of war. An electric light bulb at the top and towards the left is the symbol offering promise and hope and the whole works is overseen by a rampant bull. I'd love even a small copy of it. Oh well, one day I guess."

She took a couple of steps forward. As her gaze swept across the large, open area of reception, she fixed on two matching antique green-coloured chesterfields. They were placed each side of a brass-bordered, very large glass coffee table. "Love these," she said, caressing the leather with her hand. Katie moved forward and the group followed.

"Casey meet Katie," he said, introducing her to the receptionist seated immediately in front of the trompel'eoil, which tricked the eye into believing she was sitting by a riverbank.

Katie again halted in her stride. A sweeping staircase off to the right.

More paintings of various landscapes and hunting scenes adorned the walls, but she was a touch too far away to tell if they were originals. She walked over to the staircase then turned round to get a reverse view of the reception area. Then she noticed a huge water fountain featuring a matching pair of peacocks with their tails in full bloom. "Isn't that superb," she commented to Paul as she stepped towards it.

"Well that's it so far for the ground floor," he said, "what do you think?"

"What can I say? It's so magnificent, right down to all the balloons, and streamers and glitter. I'm speechless."

"They're only up for the opening week," he told her, raising his eyebrows to the ceiling. "Do you think it's too swankie la-la and all that stuff?"

"Oh lord no! People love to escape for a couple of hours," she answered. "Walk in here and you're walking into another world. I think it's fabulous, absolutely fabulous!"

Paul turned round to face his staff. "OK folks, I won't hold you up any longer. Thank you for making Katie welcome. I'm sure you'll be seeing more of her as time goes by."

The two smiled and started off up the stairs. After a few steps, Katie leaned into his ear and half whispered. "I've just had this really crazy thought."

"Oh?"

"You're not employed by anyone are you? In fact I'll bet you even own your own company!"

"A minor shareholder," he lied. As they reached the top of the stairs, he pointed out the administration offices. "Around that corner is the piano bar. Straight ahead is the main dining room. Down the passageway to the left is the main bar, games room and pokies room."

Kazumi approached. "What time lunch Mr Paul and Miss Katie yes?"

"You're the boss, you say," he answered.

"In twenty minutes alright yes?"

He smiled. "Twenty minutes will be fine. Thank you Kazumi."

The two made their way into the piano bar. Paul introduced Katie to Stephen Ridley, the barman. "So, what'll it be sir, maam?"

Paul looked at Katie. "Oh, er, something light or it'll go straight to my head on an empty stomach."

"Any light?"

"Anything you ask for. Shall we say a light beer and a squash?"

Katie nodded. Paul escorted her out of earshot from the bar. She couldn't help but admire Paul's impeccable taste. Mahogany book cupboards. The same blood-red pure wool carpet, a small chandelier, leather club chairs scattered across the floor in groups of three and four. A highly decorated bar with every conceivable brand of liquor on display. A bottle of Grange Hermitage in a glass display case. Advertising logos, olde-worlde memorabilia. Katie particularly liked a picture hung from a wall depicting a small boy on his three-wheeler bike.

Paul saw her admiring it. "Found it in Burlington Arcade in London. Sort of reminded me of me a bit, so had to have it of course." Katie continued to scan the room. "The oldies are going to love all this, especially this room I think," Paul went on, feeling he was about to be hit with a frenzy of questions. "We reckon it will give them a home away from home feeling, with the touch of added luxury."

Luxury! Katie told herself. *Many people wouldn't have even seen this sort of stuff, let alone have anything like it in their own homes.*

"Some will probably just like to prop," he continued, "and do nothing really. We'd like to have them all in next door playing the poker machines, but at the same time, we understand pokies aren't for everyone. Besides, if we'd have set this place up on what we hoped we'd get from gambling revenue, then the future of Oakdale and the people who work here certainly couldn't be guaranteed. Not that there's any sort of guaranteed longevity in running a club anyway. Everything goes alright while everything goes alright. But if for some reason a few of the locals get a set against you and refuse to come here, pretty soon their negative vibes will spread, the buses will stop coming and the place will be empty. So it's going to be a bit of a tightrope for awhile. We'll have to keep 'em happy. Not let 'em get bored. Keep a buzz going through the place. Always have something going on. Always have that continual lure if I do that, then I get that for nothing."

Katie was impressed. This was the business side to Paul Redman. "And last Saturday was your first day?"

"Officially yes, but we actually began trading as The Oakdale Country Club six weeks ago."

Stephen Ridley arrived with the drinks.

"Toast," he motioned to Katie, raising his glass. She obliged.

"To Oakdale, to you, oh God the whole world. What a great day!"

"And to a safe flight back," she added.

Paul chuckled. "Shall we," he motioned to Katie, offering her a seat. "You've really got a thing about small planes haven't you?"

"Not really. They crash I guess."

"So do cars and trains and trucks and motorbikes."

Katie knew it was pointless carrying on about her light-plane phobia. "So," she said, changing the subject. "Would you like to tell me about all of this?"

"That means I'll be talking about me. I'd sooner talk about you."

"You first."

"OK," he said, grabbing her eyeline and taking a sip from his glass. "Oakdale. Well Oakdale has always been here. At least for thirty to forty years anyway. It used to be the clubrooms for the golf course, part of which is the new housing estate across the road. You may have noticed it as we drove in here."

"My head is in so much of a spin today, it would surprise me if I noticed anything. But yes, I do remember that."

Paul continued. "Then they relocated the golf course and this place was left high and dry. About a year ago, a good friend of mine in Renmark rang and told me it was up for sale and I should buy it."

"A friend?"

"Well he's more than that actually. If I had a brother, it would be him. You'll meet him soon. His name's Michael Knight. We kind of grew up together and have been close mates ever since." Paul paused for a moment, reflecting. "Funny how things turn out isn't it? We both decided early in life that we were going to own a fleet of semi-trailers." He laughed quite loudly. "He became a jeweller and I became a bloody architect. Unbelievable!"

"So you decided to buy the place?"

"They wanted too much for it at first. After about a half-a-dozen trips up here, I was beginning to get frustrated. So just to piss everybody off, I got my secretary at work to ring the owners of the place and set up a midnight meeting. I told her to lie a lot, but do whatever she had to do to get their bums on seats in the office downstairs at midnight. I flew up, all very dramatic, landing around ten thirty. I'd set Michael up as the stooge. I told him to get there at midnight and stall them. Make them wait. So he did that. I walked in at about twenty past and there they were all sitting round the table. I didn't even look at bloody Michael because I thought we'd crack up if our eyes met.

"So all very serious like, I pulled out my cheque book, lay it on the table and looked them all square in the eye. 'Okay. I leave for Hong Kong in six hours. I'll be away for seven weeks.' I wasn't of course, but they didn't know that. You want to sell this place and I want to buy it. I'm prepared to offer you such-and-such right now for the building plus half an acre of land for a car park. Well they huffed and puffed. There were three couples involved, all approaching their mid-fifties. The fellas took exception to the midnight meeting and the new demand of a half an acre for a price ten per cent under my previous offer. The women were drooling as they stared at the cheque book as suddenly they could see a new Mercedes and a few shopping trips there for the taking. Then right on cue, as if we'd pre-planned it, which we hadn't, Michael piped up and said this is Paul's final offer. 'If he walks tonight, he won't be back. And the offer is for cash, right now,' he said. If it had've been up to the blokes, the deal wouldn't have happened. It was the wives. They just wanted to grab the money, and they did. Interestingly, when I wrote out the cheque there and then, I actually had to write out six. One for each of them. And I got my half acre of land too," he laughed.

"If they had've knocked you back, would you have walked away or would you have come back?"

"Oh I'd have come back as often as I needed to. I wanted the place but they didn't know I wanted it as badly as I did."

"Would you have paid more for it?"

"Funny about that. After I had written out the cheques, one of the women said to me on the quiet, "You know we'd have taken a lot less," and she had this really smart-arsed grin on her face.

"So I just looked her straight in the eye and said, "Isn't that amazing, because I was prepared to pay double what I did. Do you reckon she was nice and pissed off over that?"

"Would you have?"

"Not double. Twenty per cent maybe, but no, not double."

"And since then, you've done all this?" Katie said, waving an arm to include the complex.

Paul nodded.

"And Peter? How did you find your general manager?"

"Michael knew of him, so sight-unseen and a phone call later, he had the job."

"You placed that much faith in Michael's judgement?" Katie asked, a surprised tone in her voice.

"Absolutely. Found a few of the others for me as well."

"So you hired your staff, what then?"

"Then we set to with pen, paper and cheque book and transformed the place. The glass on the front came from Czechoslovakia. The carpet from New Zealand. Couldn't get the colour we wanted in Australia. The builders and renovators moved in and bingo. Welcome to The Oakdale Country Club. Mind you, that's a very abbreviated version. There were many headaches, late nights, lengthy phone calls and trips up here to get it to opening night."

"Lunch is served Mr Paul," Kazumi said as she silently approached. Then with great pride. "I too have also prepared something very special for you Miss Katie. You come please, yes."

Paul checked his watch. It was ten past two. "Will we be out of here by three thirty Kazumi?"

Kazumi smiled. "Maybe, maybe not. No leftovers no?" she replied.

"OK, OK, no leftovers." Paul took Katie's arm. "Wait till you taste this girl's cooking. She really is a class act."

The moment Katie set foot inside the dining room, she was struck dumb. One of the bigger tables had been moved to the rear of the room. Forming an arc across it were the words WELCOME MISS KATIE in multi-coloured helium-filled balloons. She knew immediately it was the work of Kazumi.

Tears welled in Katie's eyes as she looked at Paul. "I... I don't know what to say."

She then went to Kazumi and wrapped her arms around her. "That's just the most wonderful gesture. Thank you. Thank you."

It was all too much for Kazumi as well. Tears ran down her cheeks from the sheer joy of Katie's reaction. "You eat now, yes?" she asked.

"We eat now," Katie told her, accepting Paul's offer of a handkerchief. "You're making me feel so special it's as though I've suddenly become royalty," she blubbered.

"Well you sure as hell look like a duchess to me," he told her.

Katie had no sooner sat down opposite Paul and placed her napkin on her lap when Peter Lidcombe piped up, "Make sure you smile when you look at me," he said.

As the two looked up, Peter was standing a few feet away, his Polaroid Instamatic at the ready.

"Heads together please. Paul, come on, move in a little closer. Katie come on, this isn't the bloody gas chamber, this is fun time, come on, come on, come on."

Katie and Paul blinked as the camera flashed before a buzzing noise shot the photo out the bottom. "OK... one more please folks. Heads together. Katie say sex or something will you." She laughed.

"I reckon you might have missed your calling mate," Paul told him. Again the flash went off, the buzzing noise returned and another photograph shot from the bottom of the camera.

Peter collected the two photographs and stood them against the pepper and salt shakers. "It'll only take a minute," he assured them.

Kazumi came to the table. She noticed Paul looking round. Then she guessed. "No menus Mr Paul. Everything is fixed." Kazumi then gestured toward the kitchen and three of her assistants appeared carrying silver trays.

"Mr Paul, Miss Katie, the first tray contains hot Hors d'oeuvres consisting of stuffed artichokes, bananas with bacon, sausage cocktail snaps, hot salmon pastry boats with herbs, spicy beef turnovers, snails with garlic butter and buckwheat crepes. The next tray is Seen Goo Gai Lau To Yan, which is Chinese for chicken and walnuts with straw mushrooms. And the third tray is a Cambodian recipe called Trei Noeung Phkea which means a fish stuffed with dried shrimps. I think you like that Mr Paul, yes?"

"Kazumi, that's wonderful!" Paul said appreciatively. He stood to put his arms around her. "Thank you. For all of this. Thank you. Didn't you do that Trei thingo for me in Hong Kong last year?" Kazumi nodded. "Well I'll be buggered. And you remembered?" Again she nodded. Resuming his seat he looked up at her. "I can't guarantee there'll be no leftovers. It smells absolutely delicious. A banquet for two, right?"

"Oh yes, yes Mr Paul. Miss Katie. She is very special girl!"

Paul looked at Katie and answered. "Yes Kazumi. Miss Katie is indeed a very special girl."

Katie blushed as she felt Paul squeeze her hand. She looked up at Kazumi. "This is just so wonderful."

Kazumi nodded to the kitchen door and instantly, unobtrusively, an assistant appeared. He wiped the ice particles and water off a bottle of Grove Hill 1994 Adelaide Hills Rhine Riesling as he withdrew it from a silver ice bucket and showed Paul the label.

Quickly he glanced at it. "Superb," he said. "Simply superb."

As the attendant half filled two Stuart crystal glasses, Paul looked at Katie as she watched the wine being poured. "Grove Hill's first vineyard was planted in the Adelaide Hills in 1978. The first wine came out eight years later. It's only a small yard, but they sure make a nice drop," he said as he took the smallest of sips.

As Katie began to absorb all the food laid out on the platters, Paul could sense she was a little uneasy. "You okay?" he asked.

"This," she said, opening her hands. "All this...this wonderful food."

Paul breathed a sigh of relief. He chuckled softly. "Don't worry about that. We're not expected to eat a quarter of it. It's just Kazumi's way of saying 'Hey we think you're pretty special. This is our way of saying welcome.' Where she comes from, food is a big deal. So don't worry. It sure as hell won't go to waste. Not around here. But let me warn you. Leave some room for later."

Katie watched as Paul picked up the servers. He sought her agreement with everything he placed on her plate, put it in front of her, raised his glass and said, "Enjoy."

Carefully she worked her way through the sumptuous food, savoring every mouthful. "Paul this is almost indescribable."

"As I said to you, Kazumi's a class act. After she cooked for us in Hong Kong we simply had to have her."

A little later, Kazumi came to the table. "Excuse me Mr Paul, you asked if I could tell you when it's three thirty." Then she saw he had hardly touched his wine.

"Have to fly back to Adelaide in a moment. Can't drink and fly too," he told her. "But I had a couple of sips, thank you it was wonderful."

"Must we leave so soon?" Katie asked.

"Have to be gone by four," he said, "because the next part takes place in Adelaide."

Paul slid Katie's chair back and as they were about to leave the room, she looked back over her shoulder at the balloons which spelled out her name. Katie went to Kazumi and again took her in her arms. "You said you thought I was a special person. Well I happen to think you're pretty special too Kazumi. No-one's ever done anything like this for me before. Ever. Thank you."

Paul was quite touched with the instant rapport and affection between the two women. "I've just got time to give you a quick guided tour before we leave," he told Katie.

Then she heard something which jolted her memory. She stepped away from Kazumi. It was coming from the piano bar.

"Can I have a minute?" she asked.

Paul weakened. "I'll have a word to Peter and come back."

As she listened more intently, Katie picked up the notes of a familiar tune, a long way back in her memory. Following the music, she soon found herself back in the piano bar. Most of the club lounge seats were taken by senior folk, totally enthralled by the music being played by the lady sitting at the keyboard.

Katie moved a little closer, the song filling her with emotion. Goose-bumps climbed up her arms and around her neck. *I haven't heard this in twenty years. Not since grandpa used to play it for me.*

"Excuse me," she whispered to an elderly man who was sitting, listening. "Who is that lady playing the piano?"

"Wouldn't have a clue luv, just someone on the bus trip," came his reply. "Can play a bit though, eh?"

As the song ended, loud and lengthy applause greeted the woman. She stood, faced them and thanked them for their appreciation.

Katie couldn't resist. She walked over to her. "Excuse me," she asked, "but wasn't that the *Double Eagle?*"

"Did you know that one?" she asked. "It's ever so old. Fancy you knowing that!"

"My grandfather used to play it for me. That and another one called *The Black Hawk*. But I think his favorite was the *Double Eagle*. I was only about that high," she said, gesturing knee-high with her hand. "He said it was the German national anthem and he could only play it on the black keys. He used to say the white ones were a waste of time," she laughed.

"Would you like me to play the *Black Hawk* for you?" the woman asked.

Katie was delighted. As the music started, she closed her eyes, remembering. Almost magically, she was sitting in the lounge room of the family home. A big log fire had taken the chill off a cold winter's night. Katie loved this room, especially the family portraits which hung from the walls. She used to stand and look at them and imagine she was talking to them. And they would tell her all about their day. There was an oil of two hunting dogs over the fireplace. A grandfather clock in one corner of the room. *And I can still smell grandpa.* He had that wonderful richness about him which she knew would stay with her forever. A thick wool carpet on the floor. A sideboard decorated with hand-painted plates featuring English wrens. The crystal cabinet with her mother's antique, smoked-glass pickle jar, a family heirloom for four generations. The TV set encased in a walnut cabinet. The Steinway piano. *Oh yes, the piano.*

The piano was a great joy for Katie's maternal grandfather. Whenever he came to visit, invariably laden with gifts for his granddaughter, Katie would always steer him towards the keyboard. The old man would raise its lid, check to make sure the entire family was his audience, and begin to play. The one thing which always puzzled Katie was that he only ever played the black keys. When she'd ask why, he'd smile and tell her the white ones were only for decoration. But there were two songs he loved to play. Both remained vivid in her memory. *The Black Hawk*, the one she was hearing now, and the other one, *The Double Eagle*. Even through the years, if ever she wanted to hear either song, all she had to do was close her eyes, picture her grandfather playing the black keys and back came the music.

She recalled the day after his funeral and how her mother came to her and said, "Your father and I found this amongst poppa's papers," and handed her a piece of paper with a poem written on it. "Darling you were so much the apple of his eye and he obviously wrote this about you. He called it *Old Poppa and Katie*."

When the night was dark, she'd call his name,
He'd stroke her hair and say, "Oh, it's only the rain."
She was five and her name was Katie
And the man she loved was old poppa Ranley.
His face was lined with the wisdom of time,
He'd tell her stories to colour her mind.
Old poppa and Katie were often apart,
Fact is folks say, she was part of his heart.
She would tell him tales of fairies and kings,
Old poppa would listen, "Good gracious, such things!"
She would rub his whiskers and tickle his ear
And tangle the lines of his fishing gear.
But old poppa Ranley would never get cranky,
He'd just smile at Katie and wipe her nose with his hanky.
She knew of the love in that face so lined,
Fact is folks say, they were two of a kind.

And when there were tears, she'd climb on his knee
And appeal quite sadly, "Oh poppa please hold me."
When sorrows were passed and the hurt was healed,
Old poppa and Katie would walk in the field.
She'd hide in a tree, run far, run free,
And old poppa Ranley; he'd just prop by a tree.
But this grand old man didn't seem to mind,
Fact is folks say, they were two of a kind.

And then one day little Katie looked back
At the sound of the eagle when played in black.
On the piano and songs and his grand old chair,
Of the love and care when he'd stroke her hair.
The times of sorrow she saw in his face
And the joys as a child when he stayed over, at her place
Old poppa and Katie were often apart,
But fact is, folks say, life to Katie
Was the smile on the face of old poppa Ranley.

It was the extended applause which brought her back. As she watched the woman at the piano absorb the momentary adulation, she couldn't help feeling a very strong attraction to her. She was a big person, who had the beginnings of arthritis in some of her fingers. *She would have been a looker in her day, though,* Katie thought.

"And I thought I was the only one who played the black keys," she said, a mock disappointment in her voice.

The woman saw tears forming in Katie's eyes. She reached out and cupped her hands around her face. "Seems to me there were a few memories in those old songs?"

Katie nodded, reaching into her handbag for a tissue. "Wonderful, wonderful memories," she answered.

"Would you like to hear the *Double Eagle* again?" she asked.

Katie's face lit up. "Oh would you?"

The woman smiled at her and began to play. Katie leaned on the end of the piano, oblivious to everyone in the room and soaked up the music. She closed her eyes, and once again she was sitting on her old poppa's knee.

When the song ended, Katie couldn't stem the flow of tears. Then she became worried her make-up was being ruined. "Thank you so much for doing that, you really have made such a wonderful day even more memorable."

Katie said goodbye to the woman and walked over to the doorway to join Paul who had been patiently waiting for several minutes. He was now desperate to get to the airport, but didn't have the heart to interrupt what he could see was a very personal moment for Katie.

"We really must be going. Is it OK if I show you the rest of the place next time?"

"So you're not sick of me already?" she asked.

Paul leaned over and kissed her forehead. "Not a chance," he said.

As they made their way down the stairs, Katie looked up to see most of the staff standing at the front door. As they approached, Peter Lidcombe stepped forward from the crowd carrying a very large sheath of flowers. As he handed them to her, he said, "Katie, it's an absolute pleasure to meet you. We are pleased Paul brought you up here today and we'd like you to have these to remember us. Please come back and see us soon."

Katie was totally overwhelmed. "Thank you Peter... all of you."

As they exited, the music of the *Black Hawk* filled her ears. The black keys lady was saying goodbye. George Raisin already had her door open on the Fairlane. "Bye everyone," she called.

George closed the door and the big Ford sped off towards the airport.

Chapter 11

"We can still go up a little higher," Paul told Katie as they headed towards Adelaide at five thousand feet in the Cessna.

"No, no. This is wonderful. Oh I love it," she said. "It's so smooth."

Katie's words were cut short as Paul, hesitantly, reached over and lightly touched her little finger. He need not have been so guarded. Katie turned her hand over and slipped it beneath his fingers. Gently, he took a firm grasp of it, leaned slightly towards her, the hint of a smile upon his lips. "If only you knew the pleasure I get simply from being around you. And right now, I only know I always want to be around you."

"I'm not sure I can describe what's going on inside of me right now," she said.

"How do you mean?"

"What I mean is I'm not sure of exactly what we're dealing with here."

"I know what I think. What do you think?"

Katie paused for a moment. She looked out her side window then back into Paul's eyes. "Now that would be telling, wouldn't it?"

"Wooow!" Paul yelled and instantly pulled back on the joystick of the Cessna sending it into a steep climb before breaking off to the left.

Katie squealed as her stomach came up to meet her. "Oh shit Paul! do you want me to lose my lunch?"

Quickly he levelled the aircraft. "You don't mind if I tell the whole world do you? Sort of whack on the jet stream," he laughed. "Draw a heart in the sky and write 'Katie McFarlane won't say but I reckon I can guess!'"

Katie threw back her hair, and as the afternoon sun shone on its shiny blonde texture, Paul saw the most contented smile fall across her face. From that moment, he knew the ice was broken. No more barriers. No more nervousness.

Paul concentrated on getting them both back safe and sound and for the remainder of the flight neither hardly spoke a word. Periodically, he'd glance across at her, if only to renew the image in his mind of the most beautiful face he'd ever seen in his life. But as controlled and relaxed as he tried to be, inside his gut was in turmoil. He knew what lay ahead for the rest of the evening. At least he thought he did.

When Paul dropped the undercarriage, Katie sat up with a start. "Oh!" she chirped, "Are we home?"

"About to put her down." Moments later, both felt the bump of the wheels on the runway as the tarmac went racing by.

"Oh Paul I'm sorry. I must have nodded off." He was about to answer when a voice from the tower interrupted his train of thought.

"Yes, thank you, all clear," he answered.

The landing completed, he swung the Cessna around and taxied back towards the hangar. Waiting by its huge entrance was a stretch limousine. Katie saw the vehicle from a distance, its driver's side rear door being held open by a man wearing a black suit and a peak cap.

"Oh my God Paul!" she gasped. "What now?"

Paul laughed. "I mentioned to you in Mildura there was more to come," he told her, hardly able to contain himself.

Paul brought the small plane to within a few metres of the waiting limo. The chauffeur came across and opened Katie's door, took her hand and helped her disembark. Paul checked his watch. It was six o'clock. Quickly they climbed into the vehicle and within moments the big white car was heading down the Main North Road towards Adelaide.

Paul reached for the mobile phone in the centre arm rest. It only rang once the other end before it was picked up. "Good evening, this is the Terrace Hotel, can I be of assistance?"

"George?"

"Indeed."

"Paul Redman."

"Good evening sir, I take it you're on your way?"

"Absolutely."

"Everything is in readiness sir, just as you arranged this morning. Shall we say fifteen minutes?"

"Give or take, thanks George." He replaced the handset and rubbed his hands with delight. He looked across at Katie.

"I'm nearly too afraid to ask what that was all about," she said, knowing she wouldn't be told.

Paul didn't respond. Instead, he leaned over the centre armrest and gently kissed her lips. *Fifteen minutes*, he thought to himself. *Plenty of time*. He then crouched forward and removed a large white towel which covered a silver ice bucket, half filled with ice cubes. Placed in it were two champagne glasses and a three-hundred-dollar bottle of 1982 Louis Roederer Cristal Brut.

Paul handed Katie a glass and, as she took a sip, she felt the bubbles tingle the end of her nose. Paul momentarily picked up the bottle to glance at the label. "Isn't that the champagne they used in Agatha Christie's *Murder on the Orient Express*?" she asked, trying to let him know that at least she did know something about the finer things in life.

"Well yes it is. How did you know?"

"I just remember it from the movie," she told him.

"Ever been on the Orient Express?" he asked.

"No. One day," she replied, a serious tone entering her voice. "Paul, for whatever else you've got planned, and from what I've learned of you so far there's obviously something, let me say, really and truly, thank you. If someone had told me forty eight hours ago I would be swept off my feet by this most charming man, flying off to Mildura and drinking Louis Roederer Cristal Brut in a stretched limo, I would have said they were mad. Please believe me when I tell you I'm quite awestruck by all of this. If at times I seem a little hesitant or unsure, then it's because I don't know what to say or, at times, even how to react."

"Darling girl, I'm not doing anything I don't want to do and haven't desperately wanted to do. Before yesterday I had never met anybody with whom I wanted to do it. And if you think you're having fun, oh boy! You want to try it from this side? I'm so happy I could burst."

As the limo travelled down the Main North Road past suburban Blair Athol, Katie noticed a very young girl standing in the middle of the footpath, crying uncontrollably. Quickly she turned her head round to get another look at the child as the limo sped past.

"Did you see that?" she exclaimed, jerking around in her seat.

Her actions startled Paul. "No, what?"

"That little girl! I think she must be lost. Oh Paul can we go back? I think she needs help."

Paul checked his watch. He looked at Katie. He was about to protest but after seeing the look of anxiety upon her face, he knew it would be pointless to do so.

"Can you do a U-ey John?" he called to the chauffeur.

John took the next side street and was able to use a vacant block of land to turn the vehicle around. Slowly he drove back along the Main North Road. Katie sat forward in her seat, straining to see up ahead.

"There she is," she said, "Up there on the right. Oh Paul look at her. Poor darling. Where on earth is her mother? Can you pull over please?"

As the limo drew to a halt, Katie climbed out of the vehicle and crossed the street. The child was no more than four or five years of age. Straggly, unkempt hair, dirty shorts and sneakers. Her little top was almost thread-bare. Katie could tell immediately from the redness of her eyes and the constant stream of tears she had been crying for some time. She knelt down beside her, took her handkerchief from her handbag and began to wipe the child's eyes and push the hair off her face.

"Hello darling," she said softly. "Have you lost your mummy?"

Katie hadn't bargained on the response. The little girl threw her arms around her neck and cried ever harder. As Katie tried to ease her away, the child took an even firmer grip. A few moments later the little girl eased off. "How long have you been here?"

More tears were her only reply.

"Will you tell me your name?"

By now, Paul had joined Katie. "This is absolutely disgraceful. Look at this poor child Paul. Where the hell is her mother?" she said.

Katie returned her attentions to the child. "Darling, we want to try and help you find your mummy. Do you know where you live?"

Tears and a blank stare were the only reply. Katie was becoming disturbed. "What are we going to do Paul? We can't just leave her here!"

Paul looked around at the passing traffic. Nowhere could he see anyone even remotely like they were looking for a child. Again he checked his watch. *Damn,* he cursed silently. *This is really going to throw things out of gear.*

At that moment, an early model Holden sedan pulled up next to the trio. A woman aged in her twenties, wearing sprayed on jeans, a skin tight T shirt and smoking a cigarette stormed over to Katie. "What the fuck are you doing with my kid lady?" she yelled.

On seeing the woman, the child began to scream uncontrollably.

Paul spoke up. "Is this your child?" he asked the woman, a note of arrogance in his tone.

"Who the fuck are you?" she spat.

As Katie again tried to console the child, she noticed red welts on her legs. "Did you do this to her?" she demanded.

A cold, callous sneer came across the woman's face as she flicked her cigarette butt into the gutter and grabbed for the child. But she did not want to leave Katie and clung tightly to her legs. She screamed at the top of her lungs as the woman jerked her free, all the time reaching back for Katie as she was being dragged away.

"Now get in there you little bastard," she said, shoving the child into her car and slamming the door. "And if you bloody well piss off again, I'll smash your fucking head in. And as for you arsehole," she continued, turning her venom onto Paul, "Yeah, that's my fucking kid, alright? Now fuck off and leave us alone!"

As the car sped off down the Main North Road, Paul could see Katie was clearly distressed by what she had witnessed. He withdrew his handkerchief and wiped away the wetness of the little girl's tears from Katie's jacket and held her in his arms. "I don't believe what I've just seen," he told her.

"It makes me angry when I see children treated like that. Did you see the welts on her legs? Women who do that to their kids should be horsewhipped themselves," she said. "Thank you for stopping. I know I shouldn't get involved but sometimes I simply can't help it. I guess I see so much abuse of children in my job, my heart really goes out to them." She looked at him and immediately put the incident behind her. "I promise it won't spoil whatever it is you've got planned," she said.

* * *

The limousine pulled into the Terrace Hotel in Adelaide's North Terrace. Katie McFarlane's lips froze in awe as her door was opened and she stepped from the vehicle onto a specially laid out red carpet. She felt her knees go weak as the soft pile gave way underfoot and the concierge held out his white gloved hand.

"Good evening Miss McFarlane, welcome to the Terrace Hotel. This way please madame."

As the young woman allowed herself to be escorted along the red carpet, panic gripped her. Paul wasn't by her side. She turned her head one way, then the other. As she screwed her head hard over her shoulder, she saw him leaning on the fender of the limo. A broad grin filled his face. "I'll see you in about two hours," he called.

As the concierge walked Katie to the reception desk, he said, "Allow me to introduce you to Mr Talbot Henderson, the general manager of this fine establishment madame. He will take care of you from here."

Katie offered her hand to the general manager. She chose to smile rather than speak. She knew if she tried, the words wouldn't come, so it was left to Talbot Henderson.

"Good evening Miss McFarlane, we do hope your stay with us this evening will be entirely memorable. If you follow me, I'll take you up to your suite."

She now began to feel disctinctly uncomfortable. She didn't like being abandoned by Paul and she didn't like the implications of being checked into a suite by herself. The warning bells of her soul began to ring louder and louder. She was about to call the whole thing off when the lift doors opened and Talbot Henderson spoke.

"Miss McFarlane, Mr Redman has booked the suite until nine p.m. for you. Please feel completely free to use it and all the facilities of this hotel during that time. Mr Redman has asked if you could please be ready to join him when he returns at nine."

Katie checked her watch. It was six forty-five.

"This way please Miss McFarlane," Talbot Henderson said as the lift doors opened on the sixth floor. Moments later he was unlocking the door of the suite. "If you please Miss McFarlane."

The room took her breath away. It was the sheer opulence of five-star super luxury. Placed on the hand-carved mahogany coffee table, situated between twin burgundy-coloured velvet two- seater sofas was a stuart crystal vase filled with five dozen red roses. Luxurious, soft-pile carpet, a small fully stocked bar, TV, stereo, VCR, framed prints on the walls and curtains in the same material as the sofas. As she tried to take in the room and her surroundings, three people entered from the adjoining bedroom.

"Miss McFarlane, this is Monique Delray, fashion co-ordinator for Carla Zampatti on Unley Road, Jacqueline Somerset, principal make-up technician at the Peacock Academy in Pulteney Street and Pixie Hannaford from Eliza's hair and beauty at Burnside. Ladies, allow me to present to you Miss Katie McFarlane."

Katie was dumbfounded. She was scarcely coherent when she asked hesitantly, "Are you sure you have the right person?"

Talbot Henderson smiled. "Miss McFarlane, Mr Redman and his family are dear friends of this establishment. This morning he rang to tell me about a most exciting event in his life. That event of course was his meeting you." Katie was still too stunned to speak. "Mr Redman said he wanted to make today something you would both remember for the rest of your lives." Talbot held out his arm, inviting Katie to accept it. Cautiously, almost unwillingly, she did so. "Allow me," he said and walked her into the bedroom.

Katie threw her hands to her face. Her eyes opened wide and she felt her stomach lodge in the bottom of her throat. Laid out across the king sized bed were three full-length gowns and three after-five dresses. All six were of a different colour and style. All were size eight, with their exact duplicates in size ten hanging in the closet. Next to the dresses were several boxes of evening shoes in various colours and sizes. At the head of the bed were accessories, stockings and lingerie to match each outfit. As Katie tried to take it all in, she saw a big mirror and large hairdryer. On the bench nearby, a complete hair and beauty make-up kit.

"I still don't understand..."

"Mr Redman has arranged for you to choose the outfit to your liking, have your hair done to your choosing and your make-up applied specifically upon your request." Talbot said. "Your bath has been filled and your bath robe is on the end of the bed. I'll bid you farewell for the moment. These three ladies will wait for you in the lounge room. Dinner is at nine madame."

"Dinner?"

Talbot smiled. "This note came with the flowers," he said, handing her a gold-edged, white envelope.

The four helpers left the bedroom and closed the door after them. Still stunned to the point of numbness, she opened the envelope and withdrew the card. A tingling sensation filled her body as her eyes filled with tears.

"Oh Paul," she uttered. It read: *The next time I book this suite, I want to be with you. Have fun in there. See you at nine. Paul.*

Katie flung the card in the air and let out a joyous shrill, then ran and threw herself onto the king sized bed. She scooped up an armful of the new outfits. "Eat your heart out Julia Roberts! Yours was a movie. This is real," she squealed, recalling the bedroom scene in *Pretty Woman.* For a moment she lay on the bed, trying to collect herself. Then she began to get the giggles, which soon became uncontrollable laughter. She scooped up more of the dresses in her arms and buried her face in them. "I don't believe this. I simply don't believe this."

She rose from the bed and fixed her gaze upon the chandelier which hung from the ceiling. She heard her heart pounding in her eardrums. *Please don't let me forget any of this tomorrow,* she prayed.

Carefully she re-lay the dresses and gowns out on the bed. She picked them up singly, held them against herself in front of the mirror, casting a critical eye over each. Then she made her choice. She did the same with the accessories, underwear, lingerie and shoes. Carefully looking, comparing, then choosing. Quickly she stepped out of her clothes, tested the bath water with her toe and hopped in.

A short time later she emerged, clad only in the bathrobe provided. She walked into the lounge room and looked squarely at the three women who were waiting patiently for her.

"OK," she told them. "Who wants to go first?"

* * *

Paul Redman was busier than a fox in a henhouse. The moment he arrived at his house he was on the phone to Talbot Henderson. "How's she doing?"

"Wonderful. I've taken her up to the suite, carried out the introductions and shown her the clothes. Mind you, I think you could have warned her. The poor girl was totally swept off her feet."

"Fantastic! Everything else set to go?"

"Just as you requested," Talbot told him.

"See you soon... and thank you."

"Not at all."

Paul quickly showered, shaved and dried his hair. His mother had already visited during the day and lay his clothes out on the bed. Dinner suit, red bow tie, evening shirt with black onyx buttons, patent leather shoes and black stocking socks. At eight-thirty p.m., he climbed back into the limo for the return trip to the Terrace.

Upon his arrival, he immediately went to the first floor to check all was in readiness. Paul had Talbot seal off the Waterford room, the small, private area leading from the much larger Crystal room on the first floor. The table was set in hallmarked silver cutlery, stuart crystal champagne and wine glasses, wedgwood crockery, solid silver accessories and a huge stuart crystal vase filled with red roses. Seated in the corner of the room were three violinists. Paul spoke to them briefly, then checked with Talbot Henderson they had received their instructions. He looked at his watch. It was ten to nine. "Do you think she'll be ready?" he asked, with enforced calm.

"I'll go and bring her down."

Paul Redman paced the floor of the Waterford room. He felt like an expectant father. Talbot had only been gone two minutes. Beads of perspiration began to form on his forehead. He reached for his handkerchief. Then his palms began to get wet. He rubbed them against his trousers. Again he checked his watch. *Five to nine. Where is she?*

Moments later, the violinists began to play. The song was Chris De Burgh's *Lady in Red*. Paul turned to face the doorway and the sight which greeted him dried his mouth and filled his eyes with tears. Katie had her arm through Talbot Henderson's.

Talbot said, "Mr Redman, may I present Miss Katie McFarlane."

For a second Paul couldn't move. He looked at Katie as she stood motionless. Slowly he came towards her, conscious that his jaw was sitting right on the top of his bow tie. In all his years he had never seen such raw, innocent beauty. As his peripheral vision told him, Katie's entrance had stopped staff and guests in their tracks as they stood to watch. *I know sometimes I get the girl, but right now I certainly have the grand prize.*

"Hello," she said, quietly, softly.

"Now I do believe in fairytales," he told her.

But it wasn't enough. Katie wanted more. "Did I make the right choice?" she asked, releasing herself from Talbot Henderson and doing a spin to show off the gown.

"I'm in love," Paul said.

She laughed, nervously. "Do you really like it?"

"Do that again," Paul said.

As she turned, Paul could see it was the outfit he hoped she would choose. A long, sheer, off-the-shoulder, bright-red gown. So confident was he, he had arranged for the violinists to play *Lady in Red*. But as a back up, in case he was wrong, if she had chosen the blue, the song to be played was *Song Sung Blue* and if it was the yellow, then *Tie A Yellow Ribbon*.

Katie's shoulder-length blonde hair glistened under the lights of the chandelier, adding to the effect of the sheer and stunning line of the gown. She wore no jewellery, carrying only a small gold evening bag that matched her gold Salvatore Ferragamo evening shoes. She also decided on a little make-up. A touch of colour to emphasize her cheekbones, a red lipstick and a smidgen of eye-liner and mascara.

"As I said, I'm in love," he told her again.

"And I'm in love with today. Everything has just been so wonderful." Then for the first time, she noticed the music. Then she saw the roses. She took Paul's hand and went to them and lightly pressed a bloom against her nose and lips. "Oh they're magnificent. Thank you. For these. For the ones you sent to my room. For the last two hours of self indulgence; the girls you had look after me. What can I say? You make me feel like I'm Cinderella."

Paul didn't speak. He opened his arms and she went into them. She felt her eyes begin to fill with tears, totally overwhelmed by the occasion. Paul saw her dilemma and reached for his handkerchief. As she dabbed her eyes, the violinists rose from their seats and formed a half circle around them. Paul tucked his handkerchief into his jacket pocket and began a slow dance with Katie. They moved as one, locked in each other's arms, hoping the moment would last forever.

Talbot Henderson quietly opened the door to the Waterford room, stepped inside and closed it without making a sound. Paul and Katie didn't even know he was there. "If I may dare to interrupt," he said after a while. "Dinner is about to be served."

At that moment the door to the Waterford room opened and four trolleys were wheeled in, each accompanied by two staff. The first contained a large silver tray, laden with an abundance of scallops, oysters, Moreton Bay bugs, king prawns, calamari, smoked salmon, deep-sea perch, and smoked trout. The second, a hind-quarter of beef, rolling on a spit over hot coals. The third, a selection of desserts, cakes, cheese and biscuits, cheesecakes, jellies, trifles and icecreams packed in dry ice. And the fourth, a selection of the very best wines, spirits, ales, champagnes, and soft drinks the Terrace could offer. Including another bottle of 1982 Louis Roederer Cristal Brut.

Talbot Henderson was immensely proud of the presentation. Such occasions were what his life's work had been all about. He knew he didn't have to seek assurances from Paul and Katie. He had served heads of state, governors, the fringes of royalty, and some of the biggest stars in Hollywood. As two waiters pulled back chairs for Paul and Katie, the violinists returned to the corner of the room. Again the music started. After the two made their choice from the first trolley, it was whisked away, quietly and unobtrusively by the two staff.

As Katie made small-talk to Paul over the entree, he noticed she was struggling with the wine list. "I never know what to order either," he said, acknowledging her confusion.

She scoffed. "What about this afternoon. You knew exactly the story behind Grove Hill. You know a lot more than you're letting on!"

"No really," he protested, raising his hands off the table. "I'm certainly no wine expert, although I must confess I do like collecting it."

Katie fixed her eyes upon him. "So how do you know what to collect if you don't know anything about it?"

"Well just from what people tell me," he said, guiltily.

"Oh my God! It's you, isn't it?"

He looked at her, half startled.

"The Redman collection! That's you isn't it? I've read about that. When the Japanese prime minister was here, a feature of the gala dinner and ball were tastings from the Redman collection of prestigious wines."

"Well, not me actually, but my father."

"And you have absolutely nothing to do with it?"

Paul was cornered. He didn't want to frighten Katie off with all this highbrow stuff about wine collecting and the price tags that go with it. He already thought what he had lay on for the day may have been pushing things a little. He tried to skip over the answer to her question.

"It's only a bit of a hobby," he said, not wanting to tell her his father's collection of wines was regarded as one of the finest in the country, if not the most expensive.

"Not sure about that," Katie said, not convinced she was being told the whole story. She returned to the wine list. "I know what I'd like," she said, spotting a name, but speaking before she realised what she had said.

"Tell me."

"No, no," she answered, handing Paul the wine list. "You choose."

He looked at her. He knew instantly what she had chosen, but was too polite to say fearing the expense involved. Paul motioned to the wine waiter. "I think we'll settle on the Louis Roederer." As he spoke, the expression he saw on Katie's face told him that was exactly what she wanted.

Katie asked the waiter for only a light serving of the main course. Paul ordered similarly and chose a 1984 Petaluma Cabernet Sauvignon. As the second trolley was wheeled silently from the Waterford room, Katie rose from her chair and walked over to the violinists. "Thank you for making this such a wonderful evening. Sitting listening to you play is something I'll never forget."

She returned to the table. Immediately the room was filled with classical music. Paul raised his ear to listen. "Did you choose this?" he asked.

"Shhh, it's the only classical one I know."

Paul liked what he heard. "Ah, I know this. It's a, er, it's..."

"Chopin *Nocturne in E Flat*," she said.

"Of course, Chopin."

Katie was totally engrossed in the music. Half way through she looked at Paul. "Dance with me."

Paul took the young woman in his arms. As he held her close to his body, he buried his face in her hair. Again the fragrance of his favorite perfume rose to meet him and he felt himself being stirred. Katie sensed the desire. *If only you knew how much I wanted you*, she thought, pulling herself hard against his hips.

A waiter quietly slipped by and dimmed the chandelier. As they embraced each other on the small dance floor, Paul's hands dropped to Katie's waist. Katie's arms reached up around his neck. He then joined his hands behind her. Gently their bodies rubbed against each other, both knowing what one was doing to the other. "What are you thinking about?" she whispered.

"You." He felt her grip tighten a little. "And you?"

"All those famous lines from love songs, but right now I can't think of any."

Neither remembered much about consuming their main course. They were too engrossed. Too busy being with each other. Both passed on the dessert trolley, opting for coffee and liqueurs. At one thirty a.m., the excitement and events which had packed the day had begun to take their toll. Paul could see Katie was extremely tired. And although he could feel his body was charged with emotion, he also knew he too was ready to drop. He summoned a waiter.

"I think Miss McFarlane and I will make a move. Could you please arrange for her belongings to be brought down from her suite?"

"They're already in the limousine sir, and that's waiting out the front at your convenience."

Talbot Henderson, you're a marvel. "Thank you," he replied.

Katie smiled apologetically. "I'm sorry to fall in a heap like this."

Paul rose from his chair and moved round behind Katie, placing his hands tenderly on each side of her face. "It's OK, after a day like we've just had, we'll probably need another simply to recover."

"Try a week," she replied, raising her hands to his.

Paul assisted Katie from her chair, and as the two got to the door of the Waterford room she turned back to take one last look. *This is such a special moment. So, so special.* "Oh the roses!" she said.

A waiter approached her. "They'll be delivered to your house in the morning Miss McFarlane," he said. "Along with those from your suite."

Paul held out his hand to the waiter and pressed a one hundred dollar note into his palm. "For all of you. Thank you."

The limousine wound it's way around Adelaide streets to finally arrive outside Katie's bungalow. She looked at Paul. "Would you like to come in for a moment?" But he could tell the poor girl was nearly out on her feet and the invitation was more a goodwill gesture than one of a genuine desire to spend more time with him.

"No, no," he said. "You hop straight into bed. I'll call you tomorrow."

"Paul," she began.

He put his fingers on her lips. "I know, I know."

Paul escorted her to the front door. As she opened it, the chauffeur placed a suitcase inside and returned to the vehicle. "You have given me the most wonderful day of my life," he said, and leaned down and kissed her forehead. "You'll be asleep before your head hits the pillow... goodnight sweet girl."

As he turned to leave, "The gown!" she called. "What about the gown?"

"God, you look wonderful in red," he replied.

Chapter 12

Scarfe Olsen was one mean example of brutality on two legs.

Tall and thin, he continued to live and dress from the bygone days of rock and roll. Jet black, slicked-back hair, he was never seen out of his skin-tight black jeans, black shirt and black, ripple-soled desert boots. His real name was Robert, but he never made friends with anyone long enough for them to find out. Friendships to Scarfe were a hindrance, except those he made with women. And they often only lasted as long as they were prepared to put up with his brutality.

Scarfe lived in a one-room in suburban Bowden, a short distance from the Adelaide city centre, but on the opposite end to the scale to the leafy up-market names of Burnside, Wattle Park or Toorak Gardens. He'd lived in semi-squalor for a number of years, surrounded by an old stereo, a stack of rock 'n' roll forty-five discs, a bed, worn-out club lounge, fridge, and stove. When it was working, a TV, but he'd have to kick away any one of a number of things in order to get to it. But Scarfe didn't care. He had a job in the John Shearer machinery factory at Kilkenny, and though he found scraping the lathe marks off new bearings to go into sovereign majestic ploughs a mind-numbing exercise, the weekly pay packet made it worthwhile. That would allow him to go to the pub every night and spend what was left on the horses or the next woman he fancied.

For someone who was of such slight build, he cared little for his own safety and invariably ended up on the business end of a straight right hand. But he won more fights than he lost, purely from adopting dirty tactics. A handful of salt in the eyes. A boot to the testicles. A broken beer bottle jammed against a throat to gain submission. Most of the fights he got mixed up in were over women. Someone else's girlfriend or wife. It was such an incident that earned him the nickname Scarfe.

After another noisy Friday night session in a pub, he got involved in a scrap over a little Italian piece who kept giving him the eye. When he made his move, she became offended and told Scarfe to nick off. When he wouldn't take no for an answer, she told him to fuck off. But Scarfe persisted. The young woman then told him to sit down, she had something for him. Scarfe thought his luck had changed, so he did as she asked. She then stood in front of him, put her hand up her dress, withdrew a tampon from herself and rubbed it in his face. Scarfe flew at her, driving a straight left into her eye socket. "You filthy fucking bitch!" he cussed, spitting and searching around for something to wipe his face. Her boyfriend, down the other end of the bar playing pool, was unaware of the dramas until he saw his girlfriend being knocked rotten over some tables and chairs. Like a bolt of lightning he was on the scene and attacked Scarfe with a billiard cue. Scarfe saw the first blow coming, but couldn't avoid it. By the time his attacker was set to strike for a second time, Scarfe had grabbed him and the two ended up rolling around on the bar room floor.

When bystanders separated them, Scarfe decided to cut his losses and leave. What he didn't bank on was being followed home. He had no sooner placed the key in the front door when he was grabbed from behind. There were four of them: the guy he'd fought with in the pub and his three mates. He was dragged to the ground while the one he had the fight with pissed in his face. He then leaned back and sunk all his force behind a boot to Scarfe's rib cage. Drawing a knife from his pocket, he leaned down and slit Scarfe's throat from ear to ear. Not enough to kill, but enough that he would carry the scar for the rest of his life. In a bid to cover it up, he then wore a black scarfe as part of his daily garb. He tried to find his attackers, but regular crawls through Adelaide's pubs failed to turn up any trace of them.

The knifing incident frightened the living daylights out him for about three months, the time it took for him to fully recover. Gradually he began to return to his old haunts, purely for the purpose of picking up women.

"What is it with you and the chicks man? Every one I talk to tells me you get off on hurting them. Why don't you just screw 'em and leave 'em?" a former casual acquaintance once asked him.

"No fun in that man. You gotta make 'em bleed! Then they beg me to fuck 'em just so I'll stop hurting them."

"That's sick man!"

"Yeah well so are you! Why don't you fuck off and leave me alone!" And so another casual friendship died.

Scarfe prided himself in being able to get pretty well any 'wrong-side-of-the-tracks' woman he wanted. He had some strange quality about him which they couldn't resist. Perhaps a quality that somehow offered greener pastures. But they would soon learn after a half an hour alone with him, greener pastures meant violent sex, bleeding nipples, a punch in the mouth and busted teeth.

Scarfe also got his kicks from dumping them. He was purely a one night stand, and should any of them be masochistic and want a return bout, they were given the customary two word send off.

Then things changed. It was just another Friday night in the pub after work. A young woman, thin, about twenty-eight to thirty, he reckoned, walked into the bar and stood a short distance from him.

"Hi Rowdy," she said, greeting the barman.

"Goodaye luv."

"Give us some change for the cigarette machine will you?"

She handed the barman some notes and took them in change. Scarfe looked her up and down. *Might be a go,* he thought.

Her long, straggly-blonde hair gave the impression she would've once been attractive. As she moved off to the machine, Scarfe's eyes followed her. *Jesus, nice arse.*

Moments later the woman returned and looked at Rowdy.

"Problems?" he asked.

"No bloody B & H."

"Aw shit, I'll see if there's some out the back."

Scarfe put his hand on his own packet and slid them down the bar to her. "Wanna drink?"

"I'll have one of your smokes, but before I say yes to a drink, I've got a kid."

Scarfe shrugged his shoulders.

"You married?" she asked.

"Nup. You?"

The woman scoffed. "That's pretty funny. He pissed off on me. Left me with a kid and nothing to pay the rent."

"How come you're smoking?"

"Got the kid's endowment today. So, is there a drink in this or am I outa here?"

"What do you want it to be?"

"Not some smart-arse looking for a blow job and see ya later."

Scarfe signaled to the bartender and moved down to join the woman. "What'll it be?"

"A double Jack on the rocks."

"You talk pretty tough, what's your name?"

"Lorry."

"Short for Lorraine or what?"

"Just Lorry, OK?"

"OK, I'm Scarfe."

The woman laughed. "Short for what, Capone?"

"Just Scarfe, OK," he told her.

Lorry picked up her drink and sculled it.

"Jesus I haven't paid for it yet!" Scarfe cussed.

"And another," she told Rowdy, dryly, with boredom in her tone. "Any out the back?"

"Sorry luv, right out of 'em," the bartender answered.

"So what's your story, Scarfe?"

"No wife, no kids."

"Bullshit!"

"No fucking wife and no kids."

"Whoooa," Lorry cut in. "Touch a nerve did I?"

"Nope. Never had need of 'em."

"So why do you want to mess with me?"

"Maybe I'd just like to fuck your arse," he told her, annoyed she was endeavoring to smart mouth him.

"I don't take it up the arse," she told him. "But I can handle anything you've got to offer."

"You want to do it now?"

"Two more Jacks and you're on."

"Your place or mine?"

"Certainly not yours. You wanna do it, you do it on my terms in my place."

"What about him?" Scarfe put in, remembering her reference to a husband or partner.

"Oh he's gone, sweetheart. He won't be back. Don't worry. You won't be jumped by some love-struck husband back to claim his wife. He grabbed a sixteen-year-old and shot through three weeks ago."

"So how you paying the rent?"

"Selling stuff. The freezer goes tomorrow. Then I'll continue to try and find a job. The kid's a problem though."

"Boy or girl?"

"Girl. She's out in the car."

Lorry downed another two double Jacks and looked at Scarfe. "You wanna go?"

Scarfe climbed into his old Holden car and followed Lorry to where she lived. She had a third floor flat of small proportions with no real possessions to speak of. Simply the basics.

"What's her name?" he asked as he followed her inside carrying her child.

"Emma."

Lorry went into one of the two bedrooms and lay the child on her bed. Satisfied she was sound asleep, she crept from her room and quietly closed the door. Scarfe walked to the front door, closed it, then turned and belted Lorry so hard in the mouth it sent her sprawling across the lounge room floor. Quickly he was on her and within seconds had ripped her blouse and bra from her body.

"Fuck you!" she screamed.

"Yeah and fuck you too, bitch! You smart-mouthed me in the fucking pub and I don't like being smart-mouthed."

Lorry was about to offer more abuse when Scarfe slammed his fist into her face. He slid off her, undid his pants and thrust his penis into her mouth. Half dazed from the blow, she quickly regained her senses when she felt his hot, throbbing penis touching the back of her throat. Then she felt his hands behind her head, pulling himself hard into her.

Blood was pouring from a deep cut on her lip. As she gagged, Scarfe withdrew, and tore her jeans from her body. He sprang to his feet, swept his arm across the kitchen table scattering cups and saucers and other paraphernalia onto the floor and slammed her onto it face down. As she began to struggle, he jabbed his fist hard into her kidneys. She screamed in agony.

"Don't fucking struggle bitch!" he cussed.

He reefed her legs apart and thrust himself hard into her. Lorry gasped, as though her breath was taken away. Scarfe leaned down and grabbed her tits and squeezed the nipples so hard, the woman was screaming in agony. As he thrust himself in and out, blood oozed onto the table from her cut lip and her nipples. When he climaxed, he squeezed even harder. Lorry had never known such pain. When he finished, Scarfe withdrew, dragged her up by the hair and slammed his fist into her face again. Lorry came to rest, sprawled in a heap and covered in blood and semen, against the legs of the television set.

As she slowly came-to, her glassy eyes tried to focus on her attacker. "You dirty, low-down, sadistic, mongrel bastard. Get the fuck out of here before I call the cops."

Scarfe was sitting in Lorry's three-seater night-and-day, with his leg resting on his knee, smoking a cigarette. He threw her the pack.

"Wanna cigarette?"

Stark naked and in diabolical pain, she gathered what remained of her strength and lunged at Scarfe. He hardly moved. Lorry had telegraphed her actions. He simply reached up and grabbed her by the throat as she came at him. He was squeezing so hard, he was choking her and he knew it. He heard her gurgling and struggling for breath, then threw her to the floor. He walked over to the television set and picked up his packet of cigarettes. He returned to his seat, and looked down at her.

As Lorry struggled for breath, tears came and she began to tremble all over. "Who the fuck are you? Why have you done this to me? What the hell do you want? Are you going to kill me?"

Scarfe laughed. Again he threw his packet of cigarettes at her, along with a handful of notes he pulled from his pocket. "That cover the rent?"

"What do you think I am, a whore?" she screamed. Lorry rubbed the notes in the blood oozing from her lip and nipples and threw it back at him. "Take your fucking blood money and get the hell out of here!" she screamed.

"Go and clean yourself up babe, I'm not going anywhere," he told her calmly.

Now she began to feel scared. What had happened to her now began to sink in. Quickly she scrambled to her feet and dived for the phone.

Scarfe watched her dial a number, then bounced off the couch, pulled a knife from his pocket and held it at her throat. "Put the phone down," he told her.

Lorry was terrified out of her wits. "Jesus Christ, you're fucking mad. You are going to kill me, you mongrel bastard!"

"Here's the story," Scarfe began. "I'm the new man in your life."

Lorry could hear words, but they didn't mean anything. She was wetting herself from the terror of the cold steel blade against her throat.

"Do you hear me? I'm the new man in your life. I will live here. I will pay your rent. I will give you money for the kid and the shopping and you will do as you're told. Do you understand?" Lorry was too terrified to speak. "Do you fucking understand?"

"Yes," she cried.

"If you go to the cops, I will get bail and I will come back and cut your kid's throat. Not yours. Your kid's. OK?"

Lorry nodded.

Suddenly Scarfe felt himself becoming aroused again. He seized a handful of her hair and dragged her to the floor. Still with the knife at her throat, he entered her again.

Lorry was crying hysterically. "Shut your mouth," he demanded. "You shut your mouth!" he cussed, pressing the blade in harder against her throat.

When he was finally spent, Scarfe rolled to one side. Slowly he took the knife away. "Don't fight me babe. If you do, I'll kill your kid. I've decided I want you around and this is where I live from now on. You be here when I get home from work and don't go out unless I tell you." Slowly Scarfe eased himself off the floor and pulled on his pants. "Now get and clean yourself up."

Lorry had gone into convulsions. But Scarfe showed little concern. He picked up his cigarettes from the floor, sat down and lit one. Then he saw Lorry throw up. "You filthy fucking bitch! Get and clean that up too you dirty bastard," he sneered. "And bloody hurry up! It stinks to buggery."

Slowly she began to regain herself. As she tried to get up, she slipped in her own vomit and fell back down.

"I told you to move your arse and clean yourself up."

Lorry didn't answer.

"Move! You want me to fuck you again?"

"Do what you like," she cried, all resistance gone.

Like breaking in a horse, Scarfe smiled to himself. *They struggle a bit for awhile, but it doesn't take 'em long to learn. You're mine now sweetheart, and I'll do with you what I like. It's called the fear element. God I love getting these smart-mouthed bitches and dragging them down to my dirty low level.*

"Give me ten minutes and I will," he told her.

Chapter 13

Katie McFarlane was walking across King William Street from her family solicitor's office to Waymouth Street on her way to the Topham Mall car park when a light plane flying overhead grabbed her attention. A nervous spasm gripped her stomach. Instantly she felt sick. Her heart rocketed into her mouth and she was forced to fight hard to prevent her knees from crumbling beneath her. She hastened her step as best she could. When she reached the footpath, she grabbed hold of the pole supporting the traffic lights. Passers-by took little notice as she fought to regain her composure. She reached for her handkerchief and dabbed at her eyes as she felt the full thrust of raw emotion ravage her body. *I love the smell of Paris in the morning.*

As the buzz of the light plane's engine dissolved in the sounds of the city, Katie McFarlane was again brought back to that magical day. For the second time she heard Paul Redman knocking on her door.

* * *

She'd literally fallen into bed after the most exciting day and night of her life. Totally exhausted from having worked a night shift, flying up to Mildura and back, then being wined and dined at the Terrace. That's apart from being unashamedly spoiled by Paul Redman.

It was midday before she awoke. As she wiped the previous twenty-four hours from her eyes, she found herself looking at the most wonderful red gown, thankful she had had the presence of mind to hang it before falling into bed.

Paul Redman, you wonderful, wonderful man. I love you and I want everything, everything, everything! she laughed, rolling herself over onto her pillow.

Then, *You don't even know him! You simply had a great day. How could you possibly love him? Oh well, back to reality. I wonder if he'll ring? Maybe he's still asleep.*

Katie showered and her hair was still dripping wet when the front door-bell rang. She grabbed her dressing-gown and a towel and quickly threw her hair into a makeshift turban. She peeped through the curtains on her way to the door. *Paul!* she panicked. *He can't see me like this!*

The door bell went again. Fearing if she didn't answer it, he would leave, she went to the door. "Paul?"

"Uh-huh."

"Oh God, I'm just out of the shower. I'm not dressed!"

"Promise I won't look," he told her. She unlatched the door. He was half hidden behind two huge arrangements of flowers. "The Terrace called this morning. Said they tried to deliver them to you, but couldn't get an answer, so I thought I'd do the honour."

Paul edged himself through her doorway.

"Put them on the table, I'll get to them shortly." She could feel his gaze fixed upon her.

"Sorry if I woke you."

"I can't believe I slept for so long."

"I can, you had a big day."

"I don't think I've come down yet. Don't look much like your lady in red now do I?" she said, and blushed. "Oh the gown, I'll get it…"

He moved to take hold of her arm. "It belongs to you," he told her.

"Oh no Paul, I couldn't."

"I fell in love with you yesterday. Besides, there's not a woman in the world who could wear it more gracefully than you."

Katie looked away and tried to avoid giving an answer. "I don't know what to say…"

Katie's words were cut short as Paul gently placed his other hand under her chin, raising her head. He lightly touched her mouth with his own, darting his tongue along the outline of her top lip. Then as if gripped by a lifetime of hunger, he kissed her in a way he'd never kissed a woman before. Katie responded, searching for his tongue. She felt Paul undo the terry-towelling belt she'd loosely tied around her dressing-gown. She did nothing to stop him. He leaned down and swept her into his arms, and still with their lips joined, took her into the bedroom.

As he lay her on her double bed, her gown fell away to the sides, exposing her nakedness. She was still wet from showering. Sliding off the bed to discard his clothing, Paul went to the foot of her bed, leaned down and took hold of her feet. Slowly, he pressed her toes against his lips, then ran his tongue around her big toe. He could hear her breathing intensify as she offered sounds of sheer delight. He slid up between her legs, running his tongue from her ankle to her warmness, absorbing the droplets of water as they rolled off her skin. Katie didn't protest as she felt Paul slide in between her legs and continue to run his tongue over her body all the way to her breasts. Her nipples had become rock hard as Paul's hands found their mark.

Katie began to writhe in anticipation. She placed her hand between Paul's legs and gasped. "Oh Paul, I don't think I can take you. God I want you so much."

"Slowly," he said. "Let's take it slowly, I promise I won't hurt you."

"Oh Paul, please, I want you," Katie pleaded.

Paul moved up Katie's body and entered her. Katie gasped, and threw her head back, then side to side, moaning. "Tell me you're alright?" he whispered, concerned he didn't want to hurt her.

"Oh God, yes, yes, yes!"

They pushed and thrust aggressively against each other and came together in a climax which sapped every ounce of their energy. Finally, bathed in sweat and totally exhausted, Paul rolled off Katie and lay holding her in his arms.

"How am I supposed to go to work after all that?" she asked, kissing him on the nipple.

Paul smiled. "You want to take another sickie?"

"No!," she gasped. "Do you want to get me fired?" She moved her head to the middle of his chest and drew a circle around his navel with her index finger. "Thank you for being so gentle and considerate. Now I'm on cloud nine all over again. I didn't think it was possible to be so happy."

Paul ran his fingers through her still-wet hair, pushing aside her makeshift turban. "How long before you have to be at work?"

"Hours yet," she giggled, rolling on top of him.

* * *

In the days, nights, weeks and weekends that followed, with Paul Redman's persistent determination to win Katie McFarlane's heart forever, the two witnessed their day-to-day lives going from the routine mundane to incredible disarray. Paul could not concentrate at work. His mind was constantly on the woman who had sent his life into a total flap. His place, her place, even the couch at his office. They made love over and over. Lunchtimes, before work, they just wanted to drown in each other's arms.

As she tried to combine her career with her man, Katie's life became equally chaotic. For sixteen magical weeks, the days and nights joined together. Where they met and where they went appeared to be of little consequence, as long as they were together. Restaurants, flights to Oakdale, long drives in the country. Lengthy walks along Somerton beach and long nights in each other's arms made for a bonding that neither believed would change. They would exhaust themselves on the rollercoaster ride of fully charged emotions. Life had become a two-way fairy tale. Neither could believe their good fortune. Neither could believe they had found each other. Such was their all-consuming self-indulgence.

One day Paul Redman's mother rang him at work. "So you haven't left the country?"

"Mother?"

"Well it's nice to know you still remember who I am..."

"Hang on a minute, I was around the the other day."

"The other day just happens to be six weeks ago."

"Come on mum, it's been hardly six weeks?"

"It's been six weeks and last night your father said I should ring and see what's going on."

Paul laughed. "Well her name is Katie. That's what's been going on. She's absolutely sensational. Wait till you meet her."

"So who is she, what's she do, where does she live?"

"Tell you what," he continued. "Her name's Katie McFarlane and we were only talking about this last night. I really do believe I'm going to marry this girl. So we've decided to get both families together on the one day and make it an afternoon of introductions all round. What do you say?"

"Don't you think you should bring her round home first...?"

"No, no. Listen. Let's make it next Saturday at about two o'clock. Katie's parent's house."

"What about your brothers and sisters?"

"Sure, everybody's got to be there. I've got just the place." Paul's conversation with his mother continued at length. He passed on the address of the venue and left it up to his mother to organise the rest of the family. Then, in closing, "I have to fly to Renmark on Saturday morning to have a look at a motel complex we're working on, but I'll be back around one. Plenty of time to get to get back to Adelaide."

Paul called Katie, told her of the plans and asked her if they were acceptable.

"All except one thing."

"Oh?"

"Must you fly? I worry when you're up there on your own."

"I'll be fine. You more than anyone should know that," he said. "Can you organise your side?"

Katie brightened up. "As long as I don't have to wait more than two hours to see you again."

Paul checked his watch. "Will you settle on an hour and a half?"

But Paul Redman had not told his mother or Katie the real reason he was flying to Renmark. His knew the decision would dramatically affect the lives of everyone he held close to him.

* * *

Katie McFarlane was nearing the end of a day shift at the Royal Adelaide Hospital when she heard screams coming from casualty. But they weren't 'I miss my mummy' type screams. These portrayed great pain, even agony. Katie went to investigate.

As she approached, she could see the child was a little girl, probably around four, maybe five, she guessed. Katie spoke to the nurse who was trying to console her. As she kneeled down to the nurse and the child, something sparked her memory. She had seen this child before. Not as a patient. Somewhere else. She looked at her closely. Straggly unkept hair. Dirty shorts and sneakers. Her little top was almost threadbare. By now the child was screaming at the top of her lungs.

"Whatever's the matter?" Katie asked the nurse.

"Her hands sister. Take a look at her hands."

Katie very carefully began to unwrap cotton bandages off the child's hands. This caused even louder screams. As she turned the child's palms up, instantly she began to retch. Fighting to maintain control of herself, she suddenly felt her own body go rigid with anger. "My God!" she exclaimed. "Who did this to her?" Then to the girl, "Darling, darling, come here."

As she reached out her arms to comfort the child, the little girl looked up. Her eyes were swollen into small slits, her grubby face blotches of redness, grime and tear tracks. Instantly, she recognised Katie. Suddenly, Katie remembered.

The little girl lunged at Katie causing the two of them to nearly topple over onto the floor. The nurse attending looked on with dismay. "Do you two know each other?"

Katie smiled an acknowledgment. As the two held onto each other, Katie spoke softly to the child, consoling her, stroking her hair. As she began to settle down Katie spoke to the nurse. "Who brought her in here?"

"Her mother's in the waiting room."

"Darling, will you wait here a moment with nurse Adamson, I'll only be a moment?" Katie handed the girl over to the nurse, turned on her heel and strode to the waiting room. *Who could do this to a child? God, they must be third-degree burns*, she thought angrily.

As she entered the room, she stopped in her tracks, the blood draining from her face. Sitting in the corner was a woman smoking a cigarette, despite the no-smoking signs. She looked to be in her twenties and was dressed in skin tight jeans and a tight fitting T-shirt. *What the fuck are you doing with my kid lady?* It all came back. Aggressively she went to her. "What have you done to your child?"

"Fuck off lady!"

Katie was positive the recognition was mutual. "No I won't fuck off. Not this time. Now what have you done to that child?"

The woman rose from her seat and squashed her cigarette on the floor. "Fuck you nursey, you'll get nothing from me!"

Katie was gripped with rage. "That child's hands have been burned. Grotesquely burned. It looks like they've been pressed onto the hot plate of a stove, now what have you done to her?"

"Piss off!" she scowled.

Katie took a step back. She could see the woman was trembling. Something told her the way she was carrying on, with the arrogance and the language, she was putting up a front. She didn't look the type. She decided to try a different tack.

"Did your husband do this to her?" she asked, with more softness and sympathy. The woman didn't answer. "Look, your child couldn't have done it herself. Doctors will have a dreadful time even restoring any sort of normality to her little hands. Please tell me what happened?"

Before she answered, the doctor entered. "Mrs Downs, I'm Doctor Billings. I take it you're the mother?" The woman nodded. "Emma has suffered third-degree burns to some of her fingers and the palms of her hands. I need to know how this happened," he said in a no-nonsense tone.

The woman still didn't answer.

"Did she fall onto something. A heater. The stove perhaps?"

"Listen, both of you," the woman began, her face contorting with a mixture of fear and anger. "I've got nothing to say to either of you. The kid got burnt OK? If you're going to fix her up, then for Christ sakes do it. Stop coming on to me with all this crap or I'll take her somewhere else."

"I'm afraid it's not as simple as that Mrs Downs," Doctor Billings cut back. "We believe the child has been assaulted and this now becomes a police matter."

"Yeah, well you won't prove nothin'."

"To the contrary Mrs Downs, we can indeed, and for that matter, so can the courts. So perhaps now you might like to enlighten us on exactly what happened to your daughter?"

The woman took another cigarette from her handbag.

"If you don't mind madam," Doctor Billings told her curtly, "we'd prefer that you don't smoke in here. Hospital rules. I'm sure you understand." She flicked the cigarette in his face.

"She was playing in the kitchen, alright? She had a balloon on a string, but she let go of it and it went up to the ceiling. "The string on the thing was too short to grab. I was out of the kitchen, so she dragged a chair over by the stove to try and reach it."

Doctor Billings and Sister Katie McFarlane were listening intently. They weren't convinced.

"She overbalanced," the woman continued, "and her hands went straight onto the hotplate."

"Is that a fact," Doctor Billings said off-handedly. "My dear girl," he continued, "if that had been the case, she would have burnt herself, yes. And quite badly too I suspect. But I put it to you, the injuries she received are consistent with her hands being held onto a hot plate."

She began to weep.

"So, perhaps now, we could have the real story?" The tone in his voice told her his patience had just run out.

Terror turned her face ash grey. Her hands began to shake. As she put them to her face, Katie noticed heavy bruising to her upper arms.

"How did you get those?" she asked. "Fall on the stove too?"

Mrs Downs slumped into a chair and lost total control, crying as neither doctor or nursing sister had ever heard a woman cry before.

"It's Scarfe," she blurted.

"Who's he?" Katie asked.

"He lives with me."

"He's your defacto?" Doctor Billings wanted to know.

The woman nodded.

Nurse Adamson quickly appeared. "The report doctor," she said handing him a folder and quickly leaving. Doctor Billings glanced at it. "So it's Mrs Lorry Downs is it?" She nodded. "So what really happened to Emma?"

She hesitated, then began, "Scarfe was drunk. He's always drunk. But it's not his fault," she added hastily. "Sometimes he just loses it," her voice breaking off into uncontrollable sobbing.

Katie McFarlane said, "He's responsible for the bruising on your arms too, isn't he?"

Lorry Downs gave a slight nod.

"So, Emma, Mrs Downs, what's the story?"

The silence was lengthy. "Scarfe came home," she began, slowly, hesitantly, a tremble in her voice. "He'd been drinking." She pulled some tissues from her bag and cleared her nose. "Emma was playing with her balloon in her room and I had the stove turned on ready for tea. He came in the kitchen and started grabbing at me. I told him he was hurting me but he still kept on. Then he grabbed my tits and squeezed them really hard. I screamed out in pain which brought Emma running into the kitchen. She could see I was in pain, and when I started to cry, she lashed out at Scarfe, yelling at him not to hurt mummy. Scarfe swung his arm and knocked her across the kitchen floor.

"He then began to rant and rave and ripped my blouse off. Emma got up off the floor and ran at him again. I tried to protect her, but he was too strong. Again he knocked her across the kitchen floor. He then dragged me into the bedroom and made me suck his cock while he squeezed my tits so hard, blood oozed out of the nipples. Look!" she cried, and she lifted her T-shirt to show Doctor Billings and Sister McFarlane her blood-stained bra. "He then poured baby oil over my privates and fucked me up the arse. Emma stood at the door screaming and when he'd finished he lashed out and grabbed her and dragged her into the kitchen. When I chased after them both, that's how I got this," she sobbed, pointing to the bruises on her arms. "He then lifted her up, threw her around on his hip and pressed her hands onto the hot plate and held them there..." Lorry Downs could not go on.

"Jesus Christ," Doctor Billings said, stunned.

Katie moved over and put her arms around her. As she looked down, she thought she saw blood stains on Lorry's crotch.

"My God are you bleeding?"

"Probably. I'm ripped to pieces. He used a bottle too."

Doctor Billings suddenly became very angry and frustrated. He moved quickly to the nurses' station. "Nurse, this woman needs to be admitted to surgery right away!" he said.

"Er, Doctor Billings, there's no one available for an hour."

He glared at the woman giving him the message. "Very well, I'll go myself."

"But what about my kid?" Lorry Downs protested to Katie, hearing the directives of Doctor Billings.

Katie moved to comfort her. "She'll be taken care of for now." Katie summoned a nurse. "Will you stay with Mrs Downs please?"

As she turned to leave for the theatre, Lorry reached for Katie's arm. "I'm sorry," she sobbed. "I'm sorry for speaking to you like I did. Scarfe has destroyed everything I own, including my soul. All I have left is my kid."

Katie raised her fingers to the woman's mouth. "Shhhh. Let's get you into theatre first. What I don't understand is why you live with such a cruel, sadistic bastard. For God sakes get rid of him. How long has this been going on?"

"Too bloody long. He was also the one who gave her those red marks on her legs that day on Main North Road."

"It's a wonder you and Emma are not dead."

"Been close a couple of times," she sobbed.

"Then leave! For goodness sakes leave. Go to a shelter or the Salvation Army...somewhere, but leave."

"I...I can't," she blurted. "He said if I did, he'd track me down and cut Emma's throat. Not mine. Hers!"

"This is outrageous! Do you have a family you can turn to?"

"I have no family and Scarfe sees to it I have no friends."

"Do you have a job?"

"Not any more," she said in a voice now scarcely coherent.

"You can't stay in that house. Let me see what I can do."

Lorry Downs grabbed Katie's arms. "Oh God no, please," she pleaded, "you mustn't do that. I have to go back. Please don't do anything. Scarfe would only hunt me down. I must go back. He'll kill Emma if I don't."

Nurse Adamson arrived in the waiting room with a wheelchair to take Lorry Downs to theatre. Katie watched as she was wheeled away, then went back to her daughter. As she kneeled down at her side, again the child clung to her neck.

"Will you let me try and fix your hands?" she asked, tenderly. The little girl clung on even tighter. Katie felt her nod of approval against her neck.

The hot plates had done their worst. Several layers of burnt flesh hung from the child's hands. Katie wondered if she would be scarred for life. She checked her watch. "Darling, you stay here. Nurse Adamson will be back shortly and then we're going to put you to sleep for a little while. OK? Pretty soon we'll have you all brand new again."

Katie fought back tears, hoping she hadn't lied to the little girl.

* * *

It took Doctor Billings two hours in theatre to tend the injuries of Lorry Downs. Surgeons worked for three hours on her daughter. After leaving recovery, both mother and daughter were placed in the same private room. As her shift had finished, Katie McFarlane joined them as they recovered from their anaesthetics.

A short time later, Doctor Billings dropped by. He was joined by one of the plastic surgeons who had saved Emma's hands. She looked at him expectantly.

"We got to her just in time," he smiled, leaning over to caress the child's cheek with the back of his fingers. "Hello sweetheart. You're a very brave little girl."

Katie breathed an enormous sigh of relief.

"And Mrs Downs?" she asked, focusing on Doctor Billings.

"Thirty-seven stitches, inside and out." He looked at Lorry. "If you suffer injuries like this again, I'm afraid you may not survive. It's only by the grace of God you're here now. That damn bottle or whatever the hell it was you said he used had a broken edge. He cut you to pieces. There was only a hair's breadth in distance from you bleeding to death. You, Mrs Downs, will need to stay with us for a few days. And I think your daughter, at least the same."

Katie and the doctors left the room. She shot her eyes to the clock on the wall. It was nearly 4 a.m. *Oh lord*, she panicked, *I've only got a few hours sleep before our families meet and I haven't even been to bed yet.*

Chapter 14

Saturday morning in the McFarlane household was one of great excitement. Sam busied himself mowing the lawn, watering the pot plants, hosing down the cement and setting up tables and chairs at the rear of the house under the covered pergola. A feeling of great anticipation had come over Sam and Ida. Ida had both ovens going in the kitchen and, although Katie was endeavouring to help, she was in such a flap she was only getting in the way. Finally Ida had had enough.

"Go on, shoo, get. Go outside and sit under the tree and read a book or something. You're only hindering your mother."

Katie went to the lounge room, picked up a magazine and sat in her father's favourite chair. Half an hour later, engrossed in thoughts about Paul Redman, a voice startled her.

"You must be Katie? Hi, I'm Paul's brother, Mathew." He then went on to introduce his wife Margaret and children, Josh and Belinda.

Quickly she discarded her magazine and jumped to her feet. "Oh hello, I'm sorry. I was miles away. Nice to meet you all. What time is it?"

Mathew Redman lifted his arm. "Just on one."

"Mathew! Oh, of course, you're the methodist minister. Paul has told me a great deal about you." She crossed the fingers of one hand and held it behind her back. *That's a fib. All he's told me is he has two sisters and a brother who is a minister.* "Thank you for coming at such short notice..."

"Not at all Katie," Mathew beamed.

She could tell she met with his approval, purely from the expression on his face. Margaret was also indulging in a quick summation. When she smiled, Katie knew she had also passed this test.

"We didn't know, but we were told you were rather special. Welcome to the family. I must say you look absolutely stunning." Margaret was wearing long, sheer, white-silk slacks, soft, velvet-look material shoes with a large butterfly bow and a burgundy blouse with wide, pearl beading down the front. Her hair had the most wonderful texture and hine.

"How on earth has my brother been able to convince you he's an honourable man?" Mathew laughed.

"He hasn't yet?" she replied, looking through the lounge window to see if anyone else had arrived.

As she spoke, Paul's two sisters, Heather and Evonne and their husbands Richard and Barry, along with their seven children, pulled into the driveway. Then Paul's parents Jack and Sylvia Redman pulled in behind them.

Katie then made herself known to nearly everyone and, in turn, introduced her parents. Sylvia Redman took the lead. "We're not happy that Paul kept us waiting this long to meet you Katie. Now after having done so, I'd say his father and I are very cross with him indeed."

Katie blushed and offered her hand to Paul's father. "Hello Mr Redman, it's nice to meet you."

Jack Redman ignored Katie's outstretched arm and moved to take her in his arms. Moments later, and at arm's length, he said. "Sweet girl, our home is your home. Don't be a stranger."

As he moved off to mingle, Katie turned to Sylvia Redman. "I wanted to meet you before now, but there always seemed to be something going on."

"Never mind," she smiled. "We're all here now, and that's wonderful."

It could have been a strained situation of strangers meeting strangers. But any apprehensions Katie had of uneasiness occurring were quickly dispersed when she saw how readily she and her parents were accepted into the Redman family circle. She passed the time waiting for Paul by answering all the gee-whiz questions from the children about being a nursing sister in a big city hospital. Katie, though, kept looking at her watch. By one-forty-five, when Paul still hadn't arrived, she began to get a little anxious.

"Relax dear," her mother told her. "He'll be here."

"Well he better not be late. He rang me this morning and said he'd definitely be here by two," she said, looking out to the driveway for signs of his Mercedes.

"It's not two yet, give the man a chance," she replied.

As Katie mingled with Paul's family, she became pre-occupied with the time. Two o'clock came and went. Two thirty, then three o'clock.

"Something's wrong, mum," she said.

Sam McFarlane, seeing his daughter's distress, went to her. He held her close to him and they walked outside together.

At three twenty, Katie could no longer remain under the pergola with everyone else. She went back into the house and sat staring at the phone.

"Why doesn't he ring?" Panic was beginning to grip her as Paul's parents came inside to speak to her. They wanted to know what the last thing was he said to her. She repeated the story she told to her mother. They looked up at the kitchen clock.

Paul's mother raised her hands to her face. "It's been too long Jack. Far, far too long." Jack Redman checked the clock again and moved to console his wife. "If it's that bloody aeroplane..."

"Shhh," Jack said, "Now don't go sounding off. We don't know anything yet. Let's just wait a minute."

Reverend Mathew Redman darted into the kitchen. "I just rang Parafield airport and they say Paul's Mercedes is still in the car park."

"So that's it then," came a comment. "He's probably still stuck in Renmark and can't get to a phone."

"No way!" Katie interjected. "Paul would've rung. He definitely would have rung."

The joyous, happy atmosphere of the occasion had now dissipated as everyone stood around for either Paul to show or the phone to ring. When four o'clock came and there was still no word, Sam McFarlane stole quietly away to the main bedroom. He went in, closed the door and picked up the phone on the bedside table. He dialled police headquarters and asked to speak to the Operations Sergeant.

"Ops, Sergeant Harris."

"Sergeant Harris, my name's Sam McFarlane." Sam went on to explain the situation fully to Sergeant Harris.

He said, "Well sir, at this stage, we have no reports of any aircraft missing, but perhaps if I could have your phone number?"

Sam passed on the number, replaced the receiver and returned to the kitchen. As he entered, everyone's attention was drawn to him. He tried to make light of the situation but a quick summation of all the faces told him everyone feared the worst. "Oh come on folks! He's probably got a flat tyre or something. He'll be here." But no one was convinced, least of all his daughter.

Sam continued. "Look, I've only this minute spoken to the police and they told me there are no reports of any planes missing." Katie grabbed the phone by her side and dialled Paul's home number. She got the answering machine. "Hi, this is coming to you live from five thousand feet. No. I haven't crashed. I'll call you soon. Here comes the beep."

"That's bloody sick Paul! Where the hell are you?" she said into the phone. "You were supposed to be here two hours ago. I'm really pissed off, so just bloody get here." She hung the receiver up, and immediately became aware of the total silence in the room. All attention was upon her. She felt embarrassed. "I'm sorry everyone for saying that," Katie uttered, as the tears started to flow.

Paul's brother went to her. She grabbed her handbag. Tears dripped onto the pages as she flicked through her diary to find Paul's mobile phone number. Quickly she dialled. A recorded message said it was either switched off or out of range. Now she knew something was wrong. Terribly wrong.

"That was his mobile. He's always got it switched on. There's a message on that too."

She felt her stomach winding into a knot. Now Ida started to cry as she began to feel the pain of her daughter. Sam turned and walked outside, wiping his eyes. Jack Redman followed, and put his hand on Sam's shoulder.

"Just wondering whether we shouldn't ring the police again."

The moment the two men stepped back into the kitchen the phone rang. Sam grabbed it a split second before Katie.

"Hello," he said. "Paul, is that you?"

Everyone's face lit up. A moment later, their hopes seemed dashed.

"Yes... Sergeant Harris. Okay... Yes, yes...what have you got?" Then the colour drained out of Sam's face. "Oh Christ!"

"What is it dad?" What is it?" Katie cried. "Is it Paul?"

Sam lowered the phone and said, "There's a plane missing."

Katie screamed. Paul's family rushed to her side.

"Apparently it's a single-engined plane. Air traffic control at Parafield says it lost radio contact with it about twenty minutes before it was due to land."

Ida's heart sank. "Oh my God, then it's Paul?"

"We don't know yet. There's no word of the plane's whereabouts. It may have been forced to land somewhere. We'll just have to sit tight till we hear more. The police will call the moment they know something."

Tears began to flow freely as each person tried to comfort the other. Ida boiled two large containers of water and busied herself getting tea and coffee for everyone. Paul's sisters, fearing the worst, stood with their husband's arms around them, waiting. The children, normally tearing around, also sensed something had gone wrong and sat in silence, also waiting.

Katie withdrew to a corner in the kitchen and sat on a wooden chair with her knees drawn up under her chin. She was stony faced as she glared at the telephone. She felt herself beginning to tremble and she knew it was in fear of what lay ahead.

At five forty the phone rang again, but this time no one wanted to answer it. As it rang, everyone just stared at it, willing it to stop. Finally Sam McFarlane picked up the receiver.

"Hello," he said, cautiously. After a brief conversation with the caller, he turned to Jack Redman. "It's Sergeant Harris. He wants to talk to you."

Sam handed Jack the phone. "Hello, this is Jack Redman," he said, closing his eyes, bracing himself.

Katie lowered her legs to the floor, hoping, praying that Paul was alright, that it wasn't his plane. *Don't let it be you*, she pleaded.

"Mr Redman, this is Sergeant Harris from police operations. Is your son Paul Stanley Redman of twenty seven Hillbank Drive, Glenside?"

"Oh Jesus Christ yes! For God sakes man, get on with it."

"Mr Redman, the Cessna aircraft being flown by your son has

crashed about ninety kilometers north of Gawler. He was the only person in the plane. I'm sorry sir, he did not survive."

The shock was too severe for Jack Redman. He dropped the phone and collapsed onto the floor. Several of the women screamed and rushed to his side. Sam McFarlane grabbed the phone. "Hello, Sergeant Harris? It's Sam McFarlane again, what the hell's going on?"

The policeman repeated what he'd said to Paul's father, and went on, "The person flying the plane has been identified as Paul Redman. He was killed instantly. Apparently the aircraft developed engine trouble and when the pilot tried to land it, the nose wheel clipped the top of a fence causing it to somersault and burst into flames."

"So you're telling me he's been burned to death?"

"That's how it appears sir, yes. Er, was he planning to get married?"

"Yes, probably to my daughter. But how would you know that? We don't even know that. Certainly, she doesn't."

"Apparently a ring with a very large diamond and a white gold wedding ring were found in a strongbox on board the aircraft."

Sam McFarlane was too shocked to speak. He slowly lowered the phone and hung it up. Sam McFarlane went to his daughter and held her in his arms. "My darling, darling girl. I'm so, so sorry. It's Paul sweetheart, he's gone."

Sam held his daughter as she began to whimper uncontrollably. Then Sam broke down as he fought to continue. Paul's family, who were all gathered in the kitchen, stood shocked and statuesque as they heard Sam tell his daughter what happened. "Darling, it looks like he was going to ask you to marry him today, in front of all the family. They found an engagement ring and a wedding ring in a strong box on board the plane."

Katie let out a gut-wrenching scream. Ida ran to her and together with her husband they held their daughter. Jack Redman was partially back on his feet, but for several minutes the McFarlane kitchen was filled with the shock, the tragedy and the trauma of Paul Redman's death. Katie's tears intensified as she poured out her grief. Then she began to shake violently.

Suddenly she screamed, "NO! NO! NO!" and ran through the house and collapsed onto her parents' bed.

Chapter 15

Paul Redman's funeral had been arranged for the Wednesday following the fatal crash. Death and bereavement notices filled more than two broadsheet columns of the Monday *Advertiser*. Media announcements across three states said The Oakdale Country Club would be closed for the week out of respect to its late owner. Despite his parent's request there be no flowers, rather, donations to the Royal Flying Doctor Service, Jack and Sylvia were forced to hire a van to carry them all.

Katie arrived at the Glenside Methodist Church at the same time as Paul's parents. All three converged upon each other to seek solace in each other's embrace. Other family members and friends rallied, including fifty of Katie's workmates. She looked at them in stunned amazement. All wore their nurse uniform. Sally Isaacs handed Katie a single rose. As she did, she threw her arms around her. The rest of her workmates closed in. All were sobbing, some openly crying.

"Hello Sister," Sally cried. "We just wanted you to know we love you and are thinking of you," her voice trailing off with emotion.

Katie was touched. "You are all so wonderful, so amazing, thank you," she said.

Moments later she and her parents moved in unison to the front doors of the church. Reverend Mathew Redman, his wife Margaret and Paul's sisters Heather and Evonne in turn consoled Jack and Sylvia Redman, then turned to Katie and her parents. Katie had dressed herself in everything black. No-one as yet could accept what had happened. Paul's sisters and brothers-in-law stood together as a group, neither able to come to terms with the grief of the occasion.

Outside the wooden entrance stood the entire staff of The Oakdale Country Club. It was Kazumi who spoke.

"Miss Katie, we all loved Mr Paul very much." She paused. Katie saw her bite her bottom lip which was trembling. She dabbed her eyes and looked up at her. "And we just want you to know we also love you very much."

How am I going to get through this? she cried. *Paul. Paul. Paul. What have you done to me?*

As she was about to enter the church, a man dressed in a dark blue uniform and wearing a chauffeur's cap stepped forward and handed her a wreath. As she took it, she withdrew an envelope she had tucked inside her clothing and placed it upon it. Katie dabbed her eyes, cleared her nose and took a deep breath. *I just know I'm not going to handle this,* she told herself.

Off to her left and standing well back in the crowd, she noticed a familiar female face. She focused on it momentarily, was about to walk off, when she looked at the face again. "Just a moment," she whispered to her parents, then went to the woman. As she approached her, she said, "Lorry?"

Lorry Downs handed her a single rose. "I've never had much kindness in my life," she began, her lips and hands trembling. "And until you came along, I barely knew what it meant. You showed me and Emma a kindness neither of us had ever known, and..." The words become stuck in her throat. Katie reached forward and put her fingers on her cheek. "And when I heard you'd lost your man, I just wanted to cut my tongue out for all the dreadful things I'd said to you. I'm sorry, and I'm real sorry God has taken your man and I just wanted to be here today and...and...I don't know why." Her words faded to a whisper and Katie felt her tears running over her fingers.

"How's your daughter?" Katie sobbed. The woman nodded her head. "She...she'll be OK. She keeps asking after you. I didn't have the heart to tell her about this."

"Tell her I'm fine," Katie said. "I'm sorry, but I have to go in now."

"Yes. I didn't even expect to see you, or if you'd remember me."

Katie leaned forward and gently hugged Lorry Downs. "Of course I remembered you. And thank you."

As she entered the church, Doctor Billings from the Royal Adelaide Hospital stepped forward, offered his condolences and stepped back. As he did, Katie noticed he had been joined by several other doctors and specialists she dealt with on a day-to-day basis. She was totally taken aback with their presence.

All the way along the aisle people stepped forward to take her hand and offer her words of comfort. A lot of the folk she didn't know. She assumed they were Paul's friends and in due course would have met them all. When she arrived at the front pew, Katie stepped forward and placed her wreath on Paul's coffin, which was carpeted in blooms. Off to the side she noticed a wreath in the shape of a light plane. The message on the card was partly obscured, but she could make out the word Parafield. She stood for a moment, bowed her head then moved back to sit down between her mother and father. Moments later, Paul's brother, the Reverend Mathew Redman stepped into the pulpit.

How does a man have the strength to bury his own brother? she thought.

Reverend Redman began the service with a hymn, a prayer and a bible reading. He then closed the good book, placed his hands on the lectern in front of himself and leaned forward into the congregation.

"Ladies and gentlemen, friends. Paul was the kind of man every mother wanted for her son. He wasn't the kind of man every man wanted as his brother, specifically me, because he'd never let me win at anything. As boys growing up he would always beat me at snakes and ladders. He could kick the football better than me and he had his first girlfriend three years before I realised boys and girls were supposed to go out together. He could also cook a better barbecue, but he was hopeless at remembering John III: sixteen. But, at the same time, he was no doubt the brother every sister would give their eye-teeth for. Protective, caring, compassionate. He taught his sisters Heather and Evonne how to wrestle, play cards, plant roses, and what to say to their boyfriends on the phone. Richard and Barry, who had the patience and perseverance to put up with my sisters before finally agreeing to say I Do, will certainly attest to that.

"As a son, he was always late for tea, would never pick up his dirty socks, and before he got one of his own, always fibbed to his father about how fast he drove the family car. But that was Paul Redman. My brother." He paused, gripping the sides of the lectern. Slowly he regained his composure.

When he looked up at the congregation, tears were rolling down his cheeks. "You know," he went on, "Paul was such a special person. He was clever. He was a man's man. He was also darn tough. Physically and mentally. He may not have been a big man, but he was very strong and powerful. He was also a man who inspired great loyalty. I loved my brother dearly. But more than that, I liked him. And if you were loved by Paul, you knew you were loved. He was also very spontaneous. He wasn't the type of man to call a meeting to have a meeting. He'd draw a line in the sand. If what he thought was over that line and out of reach and he wanted it badly enough, he'd go for it. Boy would he go for it. Which is why he was so successful. He had enormous belief in himself, and this belief flowed on to others. He used to say to me, 'Don't go into the ministry, come and fly some aeroplanes with me and we'll build an empire.'

"But while we decided to walk different roads, our phone was always connected and we spoke regularly. About four months ago, I detected quite a change in him. A remarkable change in fact. I couldn't quite put my finger on it at the time, but my wife Margaret spotted it in an instant. 'He's in love,' she told me. So I thought about that. I thought long and hard about it.

"Paul was in love and I'm sure, as we're all gathered here today, our hearts and our love go out to that very special person in his life, Katie McFarlane. Katie captured my brother's heart with a love so instant, so real, he used to say to me, 'Mathew, she just takes my breath away.' Our family had yet to meet this young woman, and Paul had arranged for a get together last Saturday. We were so looking forward to it."

Reverend Redman was again forced to stop as the words became lodged in his throat. He drank from a glass of water, dabbed his eyes and continued. "Paul didn't join us last Saturday, and it wasn't until his body was recovered that we learned the real reason why he had flown to Renmark. Not to look over some hare-brained motel complex as he would have us believe. Paul went to Renmark for a very special reason.

Recovered from his aeroplane was a small strongbox. In it were two rings. You see folks, we believe Paul was going to ask Katie to marry him last Saturday." From the pulpit, Reverend Redman looked directly at Katie, who was sitting with her head bowed, constantly dabbing at her eyes and nose with her handkerchief. "Katie," he went on. "Nothing any one of us can say today will heal your grief. But there is not one person here today who is not aware you are a very special person. You would have to be, because my brother loved you, Katie."

She looked up at him.

"Also recovered from the strongbox was a poem Paul wrote. Not many people were aware he had that side to him. I'd like to read to you what it says:

> *I just wanted to tell you how I feel today.*
> *Our hands touched, our lips met*
> *it was only but a moment, probably just a dream,*
> *but I'd never been before you arrived,*
> *so much alive, so filled with inspiration.*

> *And as you took my breath away*
> *I don't recall that living could be so giving*
> *as to allow a moment so priceless,*
> *no famous poet could enhance by licence.*
> *And to the depths of the ocean to the green of the trees*
> *no heart beats faster when the warm of your smile,*
> *reaches out to me.*

> *Such presence and beauty could still the wind, calm any sea*
> *and it strikes like a thunderbolt*
> *with such power*
> *and such honesty*
> *only the strong could not fail to drop on bended knee.*

> *If I lived a thousand summers and wrote a thousand songs*
> *I could never describe the feeling of the moment,*
> *you came along.*

Reverend Redman folded the piece of paper, stepped from the pulpit and walked slowly to Katie. He stood before her, handed it to her and said, "May God be with you."

He then raised his hand to the congregation. "Let us pray..."

Katie gently unfolded the piece of paper as Reverend Redman prayed for the soul of his brother. As his words filled the chapel, Katie's thoughts drifted off. *He must have written that after we spent that day in the country. I remember him saying you take my breath away.*

Her mind raced to recall the moment.

After about two hours of leisurely winding their way through back roads, nooks and crannies, Paul had swung the Mercedes into a deserted bushland area by a creek. He took the travelling rug from the boot, two directors chairs, a picnic basket and began to lay out the cups, plates and wine glasses.

Katie joined him with the flask of tea, sat on the rug and opened the basket. After savoring the wonderfully fine food, and successfully finishing off the last of the gourmet delights, Paul eased himself from the directors chair and stretched out on the rug, delightfully content. Their earlier sessions of love-making that morning had given him a seemingly endless appetite. "Makes you hungry, doesn't it?"

"I was famished," she exclaimed, as she kneeled down and rolled over to rest her head on his chest. A short distance away they could hear the sounds of water rippling across rocks. Two pigeons warbled from a branch overhead.

Paul lifted himself up on one elbow, twisted himself round a little and looked into Katie's eyes. "Did I ever tell you that you absolutely take my breath away. I am so in love with you I never knew it was possible to feel so alive. I don't think if I lived to be ten times a hundred, I would ever be able to find the words of what it feels like to be this close to you."

Paul's words had cut deeply into her. "I can't say I'm in love with you," she began, "because I always believed that to fall in love would take a little more than a couple of months." Turning her head up to look at him, she said, "That's not to say my feet have touched the ground these past ten weeks because they haven't."

"Damn it woman, you've become so much a part of me, I can't

even think straight. I would give everything up for you. I live and breathe every moment of my life for you. If you jumped from the highest building in the world, I'd jump with you. How the hell else am I supposed to tell you I am so fucked up with you I don't even know what day it is."

She knew Paul desperately wanted her to say she was in love with him, but she wouldn't. She couldn't. She knew she was heading that way, but not yet. "Please don't rush me," she pleaded, tenderly, reaching up to kiss his lips.

Paul leaned down and returned her kiss. "I'm sorry babe," he whispered. "I guess I get so wound up with you, I can't bear the thought of there being a tomorrow without you in it."

She put her arms around him. "I think about you all the time too, you know. And I'm the one who has to convince myself that we are real."

It was the sound of the congregation saying "Amen" in unison that brought Katie back. She conceded the briefest of smiles in recalling the happiness of that day. But it was gone. Gone forever. She felt so wretched.

As the pall-bearers lifted Paul's coffin and carried it down the aisle, Katie followed, again supported by the arms of her parents. Still more people moved to console her. One woman in her early thirties said, "Hello, I'm Kaye Godfrey, Paul's secretary."

Katie slightly nodded her head. "Yes, he had spoken of you."

"Paul promised to bring you into the office last Monday..." Kaye couldn't go on.

As Paul's coffin was placed in the hearse, a gust of wind blew a card from a wreath. Reverend Redman saw it happen and picked it up. It was the card Katie had placed on Paul's wreath. As he placed it back, he saw what she had written on it: *Wakin' in the mornin' with you touching my skin, wipin' out the traces of the people and the places that I'd been. Love and forever yours, Katie.'*

He immediately recognised the lines from a Kris Kristofferson song. Paul had sung the praises of the American songwriter so often, he felt as if he knew by heart everything the man had ever written.

Oh Lord, these two people were just so in love, he cried.

Chapter 16

Sam and Ida McFarlane were still immersed in the silence of their own thoughts when the sound of the telephone snapped them back. Sam picked up the phone.

"Jack Redman. Sorry to bother you..."

"No, no, no bother Jack. Ida and I are just sitting round the table... you know, trying to come to terms with all this business."

"Yes, well it's all this business I was wondering if we might have a word about."

"Oh?" Sam queried.

"It's to do with Paul's will. He changed it five days before he died and your daughter is featured quite heavily."

"Katie? Whatever for?"

"Well there's a fair bit to talk about, so Sylvia and I were wondering if you and Ida could drop over and we'll discuss it?"

"But shouldn't you be talking to Katie?"

"Yes, we should, but we understand she's still in a state of shock and something like this might be a bit much for her to handle at this stage, but we'll leave that up to your judgement. Sorry to sound so mysterious Sam, but once you see the tape you'll understand. Can you pop over?"

"The tape?" Sam queried.

"Yes Sam, Paul had a video will."

"Is it legal?" he asked.

"Absolutely."

"Well then, of course we'd be delighted to drop over. Say in an hour?"

"See you then."

Sam and Ida looked at each other. Both knew their daughter should be present. Ida looked in on Katie and saw she had finally dropped off to sleep. Ida's gaze went to Sam. He glanced at Katie, thought for a moment then shook his head. Ida quietly closed the door.

* * *

Sam and Ida McFarlane discussed a number of possibilities of Paul's video on the way to the Redmans. But, most of all, they were mystified why a man who had only known their daughter for a relatively short period of time would consider making an allowance for her at all.

As Sam turned into the Redman's street, Ida's eyes opened wide in awe. "You sure this is right, dear?" noting the opulence and grandeur of the homes passing by. Sam nodded. "This is it, unless there are two Victoria Avenues in Unley Park. Beats the hell out of Plympton doesn't it?" he chuckled.

"I had no idea," Ida added. "Katie never said!"

"Katie probably doesn't even know," Sam said. "I doubt she's even been here."

Sam slowed down, checking the street numbers. "Ah, here we go," he said.

As the headlights lit up the driveway and the facade of the house, Ida gasped. "Oh my lord, would you look at that?"

"Strike me pink Ida, it's a bloody mansion!"

The house was set in magnificent, large, highly maintained, tree-lined grounds, complete with tennis court and swimming pool.

"Oh lord, I really should have put something decent on."

Sam slowly drove down the driveway. Up ahead, he saw Jack Redman waiting at the front door to greet them.

"What a magnificent house. Do we call it a house?" Ida asked as Jack Redman opened her door.

He laughed. "Yes Ida, it's a house. But we just like to think of it as home. We quite like it, but sometimes Sylvia says she thinks it might be a bit big. Evening Sam. Sorry to drag you both out. Come in, come in."

Sylvia Redman walked to the door and greeted them. As Ida stepped inside, her eyes took in a full view of the ground floor of the Redman family home. A solid cedar front door which opened to the entrance foyer, which led to *A maze of rooms*, Ida thought.

A wide, carpeted staircase, soft, salmon pink walls, very expensive, full length curtains in the rooms she could see, and furnishings chosen to blend impeccably with their surroundings. Sylvia gave them a bit of history of the place as they went to the rear of the house. It was built in 1899 and comprised fourteen main rooms, including an entrance foyer, drawing room, dining room, a personal study, pantry, laundry, kitchen with meals area, toilets, and a cellar. Upstairs consisted of seven bedrooms, play rooms, computer rooms, and three bathrooms.

Jack Redman approached. "Come through to the lounge where the video's all set up."

As the four seated themselves in adjoining Moran two-seater sofas, Jack Redman began. "Now this all came as a bit of a shock to us. Paul changed his will five days before he died, but he did it by way of a video, which is what you're about to see. It's all fully legal and above board. A bit unusual, but then again, that was our boy." He pressed the play button, and all four sat, ashen faced, staring at the television set.

"Hi folks," he began. "Now don't cry mum. Mum, stop it. Now dad, you keep a stiff upper lip too old son, this is all very serious business, so I'm not allowed to fool around.

"What you are about to hear is a legal document, live, folks. But it can't be live, because if you're seeing this, it's because I'm dead. Sorry mum. Anyway, because no-one will ever see this, because I'm going to live forever, I could make all sorts of outlandish statements, but I won't. Seriously though, here we go. Hi, my name is Paul Joseph Redman and being of sound mind on this day, the tenth of June in the year nineteen-hundred-and-ninety-two, I hereby declare this to be my last will and testament.

"To my parents, Jack Anthony Redman and Sylvia Marie Redman, I bequeath my house and my ninety per cent shareholding in my company Archibald Design. A ten per cent yearly dividend of the nett being paid equally to my sisters Heather Anne, maiden name Redman, and Evonne Mary, maiden name Redman. The same equal share I bequeath to my brother Mathew Allen Redman." Paul continued to run through his possessions and personal effects, naming specific articles to be left to specific family members. "I also bequeath and in its entirety, The Oakdale Country Club in Mildura to Miss Katie Josephine, maiden name McFarlane. I ask that none of you ever contests this directive. It is my decision to leave her Oakdale as a symbol of my undying love for her. Katie has become my very heart and soul and I love her more than life itself. In addition, and again I stress I don't ever want it to be contested, I leave my entire inheritance to Katie Josephine, maiden name McFarlane.

"As you are all aware, when grandpa Cecil Hardwig died he left each of us one million dollars. As none of you are in need of it, I leave my one million dollar inheritance to Katie and my directive is that she receives this money in five years time, at the same time as the rest of you will be receiving yours. My mother and father of course have already received theirs. In the meantime, Katie is to receive the quarterly interest payments from the investment of that one million dollars. This money is for Katie to do with as she pleases. The Oakdale Country Club is hers to do with as she sees fit. I also bequeath to this most wonderful woman, my beloved Mercedes-Benz car. That is my wish. As I say, no-one will ever get to see this. Well they better not or it'll mean I've gone and left somebody up there, and I ain't gonna do that...bye."

As the video went silent, Sam and Ida, now sitting bolt upright, remained transfixed to the screen. "Well I'll be buggered," Sam said finally.

"Does the rest of your family know about this?" Ida asked.

"They do," Sylvia answered.

"How do they feel about it?" Sam asked.

"We all loved Paul dearly," Sylvia Redman began, withdrawing a lace handkerchief from her sleeve. "If that's what he wanted, then there'll be no argument from us. Obviously it was a shock at first, because none of us knows your daughter. Paul wasn't a child. For him to go to the trouble to commit to video his thoughts on the matter, then he was obviously very serious in his desires to have your daughter by his side for the rest of his life. I think the discovery of the rings in the plane bears witness to that."

Sam and Ida hadn't moved or commented as they allowed Sylvia

Redman to speak. Sylvia paused to dab her eyes and take a sip from her sherry glass.

"In the brief time we had together at your place," she continued, "I think both Jack and I felt an attachment to her. We can't explain it. It's just one of those things. On both our parts from what we've since learned, you didn't even meet our son and we only, ever so briefly, met your daughter. So I suppose what we're asking of you is, how do you think we should break the news of Paul's will to her?"

Sam McFarlane eased himself out of the sofa. "I think this is about the bravest and most noble thing I've ever experienced in my life," he began, trying not to choke on his words. "Obviously Katie's mother and I are shocked beyond comprehension about this. If we are, then certainly Katie would be. I mean the girl has only ever worked for a wage. This business of inheriting a club and a million dollars, Jesus Christ, how's she supposed to handle that? I think if her mother and I could have a few weeks to digest it all ourselves, and when her doctor says she's emotionally strong enough to handle it, we'll tell her." Suddenly a thought struck Sam. "Hang on a minute. I suppose this Oakdale show is going to need her signature?"

"We've looked at that," Jack Redman said. "Peter Lidcombe is the manager and Jill Lawson is the company secretary. They're signatories on the cheque book up there, so I think for the next three or four weeks, they can cover wages and running costs. Certainly Sylvia and I will keep in constant touch. We've also got the business of Archibald Design to clear up as well." Jack Redman paused and rubbed his mouth with his hand. "The rigmarole one has to go through after something like this is unbelievable. As if we don't have enough to contend with in trying to come to terms with all this bloody grief," he said, turning away to disguise his emotions.

Sam and Ida figured it was an appropriate time to to leave.

"Thank you for coming round at such short notice," Sylvia said. "We'll leave it in your hands and expect to hear from you in around three to four weeks then?"

"You will indeed," Sam assured them.

Sam and Ida McFarlane hardly spoke on their way home from the Redmans. Both were too taken-aback to know what to say.

As they pulled into the driveway, Sam broke the silence. "How the hell's she gonna take this?"

Ida sat in the car shaking her head. "I'm just speechless, Sam. All that money. I'm not sure she will accept a penny of it, not if I know our daughter. But one thing's for sure, not a word of this to her until she's well enough to cope."

* * *

Paul Redman's death had a devastating effect on Katie McFarlane. It sliced deep into her soul and cut her down like a razor slicing through silk. She wouldn't eat. Occasionally, she'd accept a cup of tea or coffee after much coaxing from her mother. Sam took his long-service leave to be near his daughter and Ida seldom left the house in case Katie called for her.

"Do you think we should get Dr McNally?" Sam asked, hesitantly. The last time he had raised the subject with Katie, she had flown into a rage.

"No!" she had screamed. "No dad, I won't see him. Just leave me alone. Stop interfering. I don't need a doctor. I need Paul." She then doubled up and, crying hysterically, she blubbered over and over, "I just need Paul, I just need Paul."

That had been a week ago and her condition was getting worse.

"You know how she reacted last time," Ida said.

"Christ Ida, we can't just let her rot away in her room." Sam's words were cut short as the door-bell rang.

Ida answered the front door. "Hello, my name's Michael Knight. We met briefly at the funeral. I'm from Renmark."

"Oh yes of course. Hello Michael, come on in," Ida said, her voice echoing with sadness.

Sam McFarlane entered the lounge room and offered Michael his outstretched hand. "Nice to see you again."

"Sorry to barge in on you like this, but I was wondering if you might tell me where I can find Katie?"

Sam and Ida looked at each other then back to Michael. "Why, she's right here," Ida told him. "Katie's been here since the funeral, but she simply refuses to come out of her room. Hardly eats anything. We were about to call the doctor. We don't know what to do anymore."

"You and Paul friends?" Sam asked.

Michael tried to speak, but choked on his words, tears filling his eyes. He nodded his reply, then said, "Paul and I went right through school together. We did all the stuff. The tennis, the football, the weekends away. The dances. The girlfriends. After we both left school, I went into the family business in Renmark and Paul studied architecture. We stayed good mates. Always keeping in touch. Then about four or five months ago, he met your daughter." He took his handkerchief from his pocket and paused to collect himself. "I never met her during the time they were going out but, right from day one, he told me he was going to marry her come hell or high water." He went to the lounge-room window and looked out at the sky. "Bloody aeroplanes! I used to plead with him. Don't fly the small ones. Jesus, at least get something with two engines, but no, smart-arsed bloody Paul Redman knew better. Nothing was going to happen to him, he'd say."

His words were cut short. "Mum are you there?"

"Excuse me Michael. Yes dear," Ida answered, leaving the lounge-room.

Katie was sitting on her bed. Ida sat next to her and put her arm around her. "You have a visitor."

Katie jerked away from her mother. "I told you I don't want to see anyone," she said with venom.

Ida looked at her daughter despairingly. "Darling, please, it's Michael Knight. Paul's friend. He was a pall-bearer. This whole thing's knocked him rotten."

"What does he want?"

"He's come to see you."

"I told you, no."

Ida rose from the bed and made her way to the door. She looked back at Katie, was going to speak but, instead, left, closing the door after herself. She returned to the lounge-room and was about to tell Michael Knight his efforts to see their daughter were in vain, when she noticed Sam and Michael looking over her shoulder.

Katie had conceded. As Sam looked at Katie, dressed in a crumpled night gown and terry-towelling dressing-gown, she seemed to have aged twenty years in a day. Her hair was straggly, greasy and unkempt. Black rings had formed in the hollowed-out circles of her orbits. She was pale and gaunt and her skin had sallowed.

Katie and Michael momentarily looked at each other, then went into each other's opened arms like two souls who had finally found each other. Slowly the tears came as they stood, united in grief. They wept uncontrollably. Sam and Ida left the room, their own emotions to contend with, returning a few minutes later. Katie had climbed into her father's chair, with her legs curled beneath her. Michael had drawn across a small chair and sat opposite, telling Katie about all the good times he could recall with Paul Redman.

"Was he a good pilot, Michael?" Sam asked.

"From those who knew, Mr Mac, I'm told he was superb. Meticulous in his pre-flight procedures, never took risks, always double-checked everything. Christ knows what caused him to crash, but whatever it was I'll lay you odds-on it wasn't his fault."

"Do you think we'll find out?" Ida wanted to know.

"In time," Michael answered. "Once the Bureau of Air Safety Investigators finalise their reports. Yes, we'll be told."

"And it was you Paul went to Renmark to see on that day wasn't it?" Katie asked.

Michael nodded. He buried his face in his hands. "Jesus Katie, I'm the one who made your rings. I'm the bloody jeweller. It was to be such a big surprise and totally secret.

"This was going to be his big moment. I told him I'd drive down here with them. But he wanted to make a big show in front of the family by asking you to marry him. He reckoned it was going to be such a hoot. And the irony of all this is, I was supposed to have been present as well. The only time I had ever conceded to fly with him in that bloody plane was that day. But I simply was not able to make it. I had to make the presentations at a bloody horse meet. So I couldn't make the trip." Then he looked up at Katie. "I was supposed to have been in the plane with him."

* * *

It was another two days before much movement or conversation started again in the McFarlane household. Michael Knight's visit had taken them by surprise.

Katie continued to mope in her room, oblivious to much that was happeing around her, let alone the outside world. She pulled the phone plug from the wall socket, drew the blinds and, in the semi-darkness of her self imposed confinement, lay down on her bed. She went over and over in her mind the events of the past sixteen weeks with the 'most wonderful man in the world.' Their first meeting. How she thought she'd blown it with her smart mouth. How Paul had sat outside the hospital all night. The flowers. And that incredible day. The black keys lady. The limo. Her first flight in a light plane. Then those that followed. The drives in the country. The hours they just layin each other's arms.

And now it was all gone.

Momentarily she'd feel herself beginning to perk up, then, just as quickly, return to the depths of despair. *Why has this happened to me? I feel so hopeless. So empty. I don't even want to live.* Then her mood swings would take her to Paul and she would lay a venom-ridden trail of anger against him. *You bastard! You rotten bastard! You lied to me. About Renmark. About growing old with me.* More tears would follow, but gradually she felt as though she might be overcoming the raw, gaping cut of grief which had left her so terribly wounded. *And poor mum and dad. How dare I speak to them and treat them like I have. I must apologise. God I must do that. They don't deserve the crap I've been serving up to them. In fact, I'll go and do it now.* Slowly she pulled herself up off her bed and walked down to the kitchen.

"Mum," she called. "Dad." But there was no response. She called again. Still nothing. Then a piece of paper on the kitchen table caught her eye, a note from her parents.

Darling. We've just slipped out for a couple of hours. Didn't want to disturb you. Should be home around five. Love Mum and Dad.'

Katie glanced at the kitchen clock. It was already after six. She felt her heart sink. She tried to make light of it by telling herself they'd just been held up, but deep down she knew something must be wrong. Since Paul's funeral they'd never been out and left her on her own. Her attention went to the driveway. Nothing. She felt a degree of panic. *Maybe I should call the police.*

She reached for the phone then immediately put it down again. *Don't be so damn stupid*, she berated herself.

Still dressed in her nightgown and terry-towelling dressing gown, she made herself a hot drink, then sat at the kitchen table. Again she picked up her mother's note, folded it in halves, and began tapping it on the table. *Where the hell are you?*

A smile fell across her face when she heard the front door bell. Relieved, she moved quickly, thinking they'd left in such a hurry they'd forgotten the house keys. As she opened the front door, her heart leapt into her mouth. Her face drained and her stomach muscles contracted so rapidly she felt her knees bend.

Standing in front of her was a young policeman and an even younger policewoman. "Good evening ma'am, would you be miss Katie McFarlane?"

"Yes," she answered, terrified of what the policeman may say.

"Do you know a Mr Sam McFarlane and a Mrs Ida McFarlane?"

"Oh God, yes, they're my parents! Is something wrong? Has something happened to them?"

"Miss McFarlane, we're sorry to have to inform you, your parents died in a car accident just over two hours ago. Seems they were returning from Gawler when their car was hit by a semi-trailer at the Gepps Cross intersection. It was very quick ma'am. We're so sorry for your loss. If there's anything we..."

Katie McFarlane collapsed at the feet of the police officers and was rushed by ambulance to hospital. She was sedated for twenty-four hours, during which time family solicitor Jim Duncan sat with her. The doctors discharged her on the morning of her parents' funeral, a private ceremony and burial attended by only the closest of friends and colleagues. Katie had to be supported through its entirety by Jim Duncan, who insisted she spend the night at his place.

She stayed in bed for three days, rising on the fourth, only then becoming aware that Jim Duncan had taken a week off work to care for her. He had been around to the family home, picked up some of her belongings, secured the house and returned to his place to be by her side.

Despite her protests, Katie agreed to stay at Jim Duncan's house for another week. On the morning of the ninth day, Katie climbed out of bed and looked at herself in the mirror. She was horrified at what she saw. She felt she had cried so many tears, since losing Paul and her parents, they had formed their own channels on her face. The colour of her skin frightened her, grey, even yellow in places. She licked her index finger and tried to rub the black from under her eyes. It wouldn't budge.

Jesus, what have I done to myself. Snap out of it girl or you're dead meat!'

She then slumped onto a stool and again began to cry. "I can't," she sobbed out loud. "I can't. But I have to. I have to. God if this is grief, I can't take it anymore." She forced herself to stand and again looked at herself in the mirror. She took a deep breath, squared herself and said, "Yeah, well fuck the grief. That's it. Over. Finished."

She dressed, searched around for her car keys, since she knew Jim Duncan had brought her car to his house in case she needed it, then walked out the front door. Katie drove to Somerton Beach, pulled in close to the spot where Paul had on their first date and walked down to sea. She kicked off her shoes then, fully clothed, walked into the water. The ocean was cold and she shivered as it splashed against her. She then dropped into the water and thrashed about, rubbing the salty water into her skin and hair. She didn't know how long she stayed in the water, but when she returned to her car, she looked back across the sea and said to herself, *That's it, no more grief.*

* * *

Katie drove her car from the Topham Mall car park to her bungalow in North Adelaide. Quickly, she unlocked the front door and checked inside to see the removalists had packed everything and taken it away for storage. She was tempted to stand where she and Paul had once stood, and remember. But she didn't. She kept moving because she knew if she stopped the memories would close in on her. She pulled the front door shut and returned to her car, noticing, as she dropped the front-door keys into her handbag, a dog-eared envelope with her name and address on it. She took it out, remembering as she did, it was one of the many cards Paul Redman had sent to her. She opened it and again the words Paul had written placed her back in his arms.

If I could fly to the moon,
I'd take you with me.
If only one rose could bloom,
I'd caress it gently.
But never could its elegance eclipse you.
Not now.
Not tomorrow...
Not even eventually.

"Paul, Paul, my darling Paul," she whispered, feeling her eyes go misty. She replaced the card in the envelope, ran her fingers past her eyes and looked back at the place which generated so many memories.

Katie started the engine and drove to her parents' place. When she pulled into the driveway, she sat for a moment, her head buried in her hands. *I don't want to do this. God I don't want to do this,* she cried out to herself, almost succumbing to her own grief.

Clenching her fists and taking a deep breath, she walked inside. Quickly she packed two suitcases with clothes and other necessities. The last thing Katie picked up was the photograph taken of her and Paul under the helium-filled balloons at The Oakdale Country Club. She looked at it and gently ran the tips of her fingers across Paul's face. She put it in her handbag, snapped the suitcases shut and walked to her car. She threw the suitcases on the back seat, climbed in behind the wheel, turned the key in the ignition and drove away.

"No more grief," she said out loud. "No more Goddamned grief!"

Chapter 17

Gabe Caplin stoked the open fire in the kitchen with a couple of well-chosen pieces of bulloak, pulled his chair in a little and propped his feet up against the woodbox. He cast an envious eye at Joker, his faithful kelpie sheepdog, curled up right in front on a sheepskin rug.

"How come you get the best seat in the house?" he said.

Joker lifted an eye at hearing his master's voice, but didn't bother to stir. For a moment Gabe kept his focus on Joker. He knew he'd be hard-pressed to find a better dog. Even a friend when it came to that. Quick on his feet. Highly intelligent. Knew when it was playtime and when it wasn't. Send him down the paddock to a hundred sheep and he'd do it with no further instructions needed.

Gabe picked up the newspaper and began to flick through the pages, when Joker sat bolt upright. "Don't like the thunder do you?" he smiled. As he continued to read on, Joker began to whine. "Siddown!" he commanded. But the dog ignored him.

Instead, he shot across to the old settee underneath the kitchen window. Then he began to bark. "Siddown, I said. Christ it's only a bit of bloody thunder!" Joker continued to bark and began darting to and from the couch and Gabe. Flashes of lightning lit the kitchen, its thunder filling the night. He lifted his eyes from the paper. "Looks a bad bugger tonight," he said. Still Joker continued to bark. Gabe finally conceded. He flung the newspaper aside and moved to the window. "What the hell's got into..."

Gabe stopped mid sentence when he pushed the curtains aside and looked out the window. "What the bloody hell's that?" he exclaimed.

* * *

Katie had cleared the city fairly quickly. As she wound her way through the Adelaide Hills it pleased her that she was driving away from so much unhappiness. She unwound her window a short distance, and for the first time in weeks she could feel the breeze in her face. Her stomach was still churning and her mind still a tangle of hurt and confusion, but she was pleased with herself that she'd made the effort to leave the city and the hurt behind. Resigning her job wasn't easy. She had formed many friendships, and Sally Isaacs had cried like a baby when she walked from the hospital for the final time. As she sped past the Mount Barker turn-off, she glanced back in her rear-vision mirror. She tried hard not to remember, but she knew this memory would stay with her for a lifetime.

It was the last time she and Paul were together. His memory stayed with her long after the Mount Barker turn-off became a blur in the rear-view mirror. It stayed until a rapid change in the weather quickly brought her back to the present.

The storm came from the north without a warning and the wind blew hard against Katie's small Honda, forcing her to hold the wheel with both hands. She sat forward in her seat to gain better visibility. The vicious, streaked lightning was frighteningly close and the rolls of thunder had developed into ear-shattering blasts. Katie became uneasy.

The last time I was as frightened as this was when I went up in the plane for the first time with Paul, she thought.

Images of her lover flashed through her mind. The words his brother spoke at the funeral service speared through her thoughts. Images of her parents' wrecked car. She didn't want to see the vehicle. Doctor McNally insisted she did. "It will prevent you having doubts later in life," he had assured her.

She drove on.

Now the rain was smacking hard into her windscreen. Visiting the morgue to identify her parents' bodies. Collapsing into Doctor McNally's arms and being comforted by Jim Duncan. Remembering how she vomited when she touched her mother's hand, when all she felt was a crumpled mash under the skin. She began to shake and feel distressed. Suddenly she jerked her hands off the steering wheel for a split second and banged them down.

"Stop it! Stop it! Stop it!" she yelled at herself. "Come on! Snap out of it! No more grief you said. No more grief, so pull yourself together!" Another crack of thunder that split the night was so loud she instantly braked. "Shit! What am I doing? I don't believe this storm!" But try as she did to shake off her feelings of depression, she couldn't.

She pulled over to the side of the road and reached into the glove compartment for a handful of tissues to mop her tears. She took several deep breaths and momentarily watched the storm light the sky. She was jolted back into her seat as streaked lightning dug into the bitumen a few metres from where she had stopped and a thunder bolt cracked right over the roof of her car. *This is unbelievable! And here I am driving to Melbourne through this.* She released her foot on the brake and drove on, still continuing to talk to herself. She wasn't sure if it was one way of ridding her feelings of grief or keeping herself alert. She wondered how far the next town, Naracoorte, was up ahead.

"Surely it can't be too far?" The storm was becoming more intense. She slowed. She glanced at the clock in the console. Eight p.m. "Where are you? Where are you?" she urged, searching for a sign to tell her she was coming into Naracoorte. Moments later it appeared. "Thank God for that!" she sighed with relief. *Now to find a motel. Can't keep going in this.* Straining to see through the rain and the hail, she made out a neon sign in the distance. Her heart sank when it read *Motel. No Vacancy.*

There were others, but all carried the flashing *No Vacancy* message. "Now what the hell am I going to do?" She looked again at the flashing neon. *That's what's happening to my mind,'* she thought. *'Paul just flashes in and out. Mum and dad keep flashing in and out. Doctor McNally said this would happen. Probably for years. Maybe even forever. The flashes may dim with time, but they'll always be there, and sometimes when you least expect them.* "Go away,'"she pleaded. "Please go away."

Katie drove slowly around the streets of Naracoorte looking for somewhere to stay. She reached over and turned on the radio. It crackled into life, but it was so full of static she decided she didn't need the distraction. Her finger was about to push the OFF button when she picked up the end of a commercial.

"...so be sure and cash in on home furnishings right now at Hains Hunkin as we celebrate show week."

So that's it. Everybody's here for the damn show. Better push on I guess. The storm can't last forever. With a bit of luck I'll drive out of it.

Slowly she drove down the main street. High winds were throwing the power lines about like dancing kite-tails, garbage bins were being uplifted and hurled along the footpaths, and tree tops heaved and surged. Again Katie gripped the steering wheel with both hands. Suddenly she was forced to brake hard to avoid a garbage bin dumped on the road a few metres ahead.

"Shit!" she yelled.

At that moment, a flash of vicious, forked lightning lit up the night as bright as day and struck deep into the heart of an old red gum tree. In a split second its high voltage tentacles engulfed the trunk, causing it to drop one of its massive limbs across the intersection fifty metres ahead. Instantaneously, an ear-splitting crack of thunder bashed and rolled its way across the sky. Katie hit the brake pedal. She jolted forward against her seat belt. Her mouth dropped open. "Shit. SHIT!" she yelled. "I've never seen anything like that in my life. Another five seconds and I've have been right underneath it. Shit!" Cautiously, she released the brake and slowly moved off, navigating her way around the smoking, splintered remains of the enormous limb.

Glancing at it as she went by, she continued on her way under the hail- and rain-filled sky. Although she would only discover it later, the fallen limb had obscured the road to Melbourne straight ahead. Instead she veered slightly to the left. On this tributary road she continued her way out of town.

This doesn't look right, she thought, now concerned at the narrowing of the bitumen. *But it must be. I just kept going straight.*

The growing intensity of the storm kept her speed down because the windscreen wipers had become useless against the power of the hail and rain. Again she sat forward, straining to see. Without warning, the bitumen ended and her car thumped and banged as it hit the surface of a pot-holed and corrugated dirt road. The Honda slid from one side of the rain-soaked road to the other forcing Katie to fight hard to keep it under control. She took her foot off the accelerator and the vehicle rolled to a standstill. The torrential rain made it impossible for her to see beyond the reaches of the headlights into the black of the night. Lightning would provide some respite, but not enough to give her an indication of where she was.

Katie drove on, battling the problem of restricted visibility. Frustration and mild panic began to get a grip of her. "Get me out of here!" she yelled.

A heinous lightning-bolt slammed into a giant red gum, followed instantly by a massive crack of thunder. The super-charged streaks of light snaked viciously up its trunk and dropped a forked limb right on top of her car. Katie screamed and tried to avoid being hit by leaning across the seat belt. The Honda car, flattened on one side, stopped dead. Katie was thrust violently forward with the side of her body being caught by the falling limb. The entire left side of the car had been crushed, the roof sliced open as though attacked by a giant can-opener. Her left leg was jammed against the shift selector, forcing the gearbox into neutral. Her right foot was forced under the brake pedal and pressed on the accelerator. The engine was screaming at near-peak revolutions and the headlights pointed aimlessly into the sky.

Then her world went black.

* * *

Gabe Caplin strained his eyes to see into the darkness from his kitchen window. Up on the road running past his front gate, he could make out two lights aimed into the sky.

"Looks like someone's gone arse-up," he said, releasing the curtains and making his way over to the kitchen door. "Better bloody see what's going on. Might be Mrs Cropp, and yet I can't imagine why she'd be out on a night like this. Why would anyone be out on a night like this?" Throwing on his Drizabone, rubber boots and hat, he grabbed his torch and said to Joker, "Come on boy, let's go."

When he stepped off the verandah he glanced at the sky, quickly dropping his face to avoid being hit with the rain and hail. "Christ, what a night!"

The house was about two hundred metres in from the road where the Honda lay crushed beneath the fallen limb. Gabe cursed and cussed for most of the distance as he half-walked and half-ran towards the two light beams. He could hear the screaming of an engine at near-peak revolutions. Joker ran across in front of him causing him to stumble. "What the fuck are you doing? Get out the bloody road, you stupid bastard. Christ I can't see a damn thing."

He kept looking at the headlights aimed into the sky. Finally, he was within a few metres of them. He flashed his torch at where they were coming from. "Jee-SUS, have a look at this!" Gabe again shone his torch up and down the length of the vehicle. Lightning flashed, giving him a momentary all-over view of the wrecked car. It also gave him a clear picture of the driver.

"Shit! Looks like a bloody sheila in there." Quickly he moved to the driver's door and flashed his torch inside the vehicle. More thunder crashed across the sky as the rain bucketed down. Gabe leaned into the cabin and turned the key to cut the engine. He shone the torch on the driver and was immediately gripped by panic.

The woman's left arm was twisted hideously behind her back and blood was oozing from a deep gash in her head. The hail rained down on her exposed and unconscious body. Blood dripping onto shattered glass fragments was immediately washed away.

Joker started to bark. "Siddown!" Gabe yelled. He tried the driver's door. It was jammed. Putting all his weight behind a second attempt, he jerked against the door handle. It opened a fraction. Just enough for him to get his hand in behind the window frame and force it open. He leaned in and put his fingers against Katie's neck. "Thank Christ!" he blurted, feeling a pulse. He saw her seat belt was twisted at an awkward angle. He didn't try to release it. He reached for his pocket knife and sliced through it.

As the belt gave way, Katie's arm dropped down from behind her back. Gabe stuck the torch in his mouth and gingerly took hold of her arm and placed it back in front of her. As he did so, he felt for any broken bones. "Seems alright." Moving his head from side to side, he noticed the car's interior was scattered with her belongings. He grabbed his torch and shone it in her face, then to the roof. "Jesus lady, you haven't got a bloody roof left."

The deep gash on her head bothered him. He grabbed for his handkerchief, then thought better of it. He kicked off a rubber boot, ran his knife blade down the seam of a trouser leg below the knee and cut all around. He tore it off, pulled his boot back on and rolled the piece of material into a bandage. Gently he placed it on her head. As he did so, it rolled off. "Shit!" He picked it up, and placed it back on the wound, but it wouldn't stay there. He jerked his hat from his head and put it over the bandage to keep it in place. "Doesn't look too bloody flash, but it'll do the job. The brim will keep the rain off a bit too."

Shining the torch around further, he saw her leg jammed against the gear selector by a section of splintered timber. He tried to move it but it wouldn't give. He knew he must release her leg because he could tell the circulation had already been cut. "Jesus you're gonna lose that if I don't do something bloody quick." He tore around to the other side of the vehicle and put his shoulder to the limb. Gabe pushed and heaved, but it wouldn't budge. Again he tried, the veins standing out on the side of his neck. Still he couldn't shift it. He felt his heart pounding in his brain. "FAAARK!" he screamed and pushed again. The fallen limb wasn't moving a stitch. He ran back around the vehicle to Katie and edged in beside her. "I've gotta release her leg."

He manoeuvred himself around Katie's limp body so he could reach the gear selector. He grabbed it and jerked as hard as he could, sideways. The upright selector bent over forty-five degrees, allowing Katie's leg to fall away. "Thank Christ for that." Gently he tried to ease her forward. Only one side of her moved. The rain was unbelievably heavy. Gabe kept wiping his face with his arm, but it had little effect. The thunder was so close he felt as though he could touch it as it cracked with an enormous roar. Joker wouldn't shut up despite Gabe's repeated demands. He shone the torch on her upper body. "Bastard! She's trapped under the bloody limb!" He quickly lifted his hat to check the bandage on her head wound. It had stayed in place. He eased himself from inside the vehicle and whipped around to the other side again. Once more he pushed and heaved on the fallen limb. Gabe knew the fallen timber would probably weigh up to a tonne. He felt his hands begin to shake. He had to get the young woman out of there, but how? If he left her and went for help, she may die. He couldn't tell how much weight was actually on her. He couldn't budge the limb. He shone the torch along the vehicle. The front left tyre was already off the rim. The back right-hand side the same. The rear left tyre was still up, although fairly flattened. Gabe thought if he could only buy a couple of centimetres, it may be enough to drag the young woman clear. He reached for his pocket knife, but dropped it in the mud as he tried to open the blade. He frantically shook his hands to try and stop them trembling. He began to panic. He retrieved the knife and tried again. With the blade open, he made sure he had a clear path from the rear tyre to other side of the vehicle. He leaned down and thrust the blade into the tyre. Instantly there was a massive rush of air as the hole blew out and the vehicle slumped, then groaned under the dead weight of the fallen branch.

Gabe scrambled back inside the vehicle, thrust the torch in his mouth and wrapped his arms around Katie and gently pulled. Much to his surprise, the extra centimetres gained were enough. Katie's body slid out from under the limb and Gabe pulled her free of the vehicle. She was still in his arms when there was a bang and a shudder as the fallen limb dropped ten centimetres through the roof of the car, buckling the backrest of the seat like a firm hand on an empty drink can.

"Shit!" he yelled. "You were damn near under that bastard."

Gabe dropped to his knees and carefully placed Katie on the ground. With the rain still teeming, he tore off his Drizabone and covered her with it. He grabbed loose items of clothing in the car, wrung them out and formed a pillow for her head. The right hand rear window of the Honda was still intact, so he popped it out and tore it from its hinges. Quickly he found enough debris to place on either side of her head and rested the glass window on top of it for shelter. *At least it'll keep the bloody rain off your face.*

Gabe knew the young woman was badly injured, but he didn't know how badly. He knew her head wound was also cause for concern, but told himself the diluted blood probably made it look worse than it was.

"Jesus lady I've gotta get you to a hospital and damn quick. Joker, come here boy." Joker shot to Gabe's side. "Here boy. Lay down here. Push yourself into her. Try and keep her a bit warm eh?"

Gabe leaned down and put his dog under his Drizabone, pushing him hard against her body. "Now stay there old boy. You hear me? Stay there now."

Gabe ran back to the shed, oblivious to his drenched condition. The rain hadn't eased for a moment, and still the sky was racked with thunder and laced with lightning. When he climbed into the ute and turned the key, nothing happened. It was stone dead. "Fuck! Of all bloody days!" He spun himself out of the cabin and was half-way to the tractor when he suddenly remembered he had its head off for repairs. He threw his hands wildly into the air. Frantic, he rushed up to the house and grabbed the phone. That was also dead. "Fuck the storm! That bastard tree must have come down over the bloody phone lines!" He raced outside and stood momentarily in the blinding rain. "Jesus, the motor bike! Shit, that's over at Mrs Cropp's. I don't believe this. The ute's stuffed. The tractor's stuffed, the phone's stuffed and the fucking motor bike's not even here. Jesus Christ!"

He ran back to the shed and climbed up onto the tractor. Quickly he dragged the battery from its cradle and hauled it across to the ute. It was too big to fit, so he used some lengths of binder twine to secure it. He turned the key in the ignition and wound and wound and wound. The engine wouldn't fire. Gabe was screaming. "Come on! Come on! Start you bastard! Start!" But it wouldn't. Tears ran down his face and he was gripped by a terror-stricken panic. All he could think of was the young woman whose life may be ebbing away, minute by minute. Mrs Cropp's place was about a kilometre away. Without thinking, he started off in her direction.

Running, walking and stumbling by torchlight across the paddocks, Gabe made it to his neighbour's place fifteen minutes later. By the time he arrived his lungs were screaming for him to stop. *No good going there,'* he thought as he went past Mrs Cropp's house. *'If my phone's out, hers will be too.*

He ran to her shed, kick-started his motor bike and raced towards Kybybolite, a post office, store and railway siding four kilometres away.

Gabe bashed continuously on the door. As the lights came on from inside, he yelled, "Stan, it's Gabe! Is your phone working?"

Stan Smythe came to the door. Gabe blurted out the situation and Stan reached for the phone. Gabe snatched it from him and panicked his predicament down the line.

"We're on our way," the ambulance officer assured him.

"Are you on the bike?" Stan Smythe asked.

"The bloody ute wouldn't go..."

Stan interrupted. "Heavens above Gabe, you can't stay on that thing on a night like this. Leave it here and take the Commodore."

"But I'm wet through!" Gabe protested.

"It'll dry out. Now take the car," he urged, handing Gabe the keys.

"You want me to come with you?"

"Nothing anyone can do now. We'll have to wait till the ambulance gets here. I'll drop this back to you in the morning," he said, climbing into the Commodore. "And thank you."

* * *

"How bad is she?" Gabe asked the ambulance officers.

"Looks like she's been knocked about pretty bad," said one of the officers, trying to make himself heard over the noise of the driving rain and thunder. He paused a moment, shone his torch on the car's wreckage and the vehicle's interior. "How the hell did you get her out of there?"

"That was a bit hard," Gabe said. "I couldn't move the limb, so I let down a tyre. That gave me an inch or two. Just enough to slide her out before the damn thing crashed through the roof."

"Bloody amazing. I reckon this girl owes you her life."

Joker started barking again. "Here boy, come here," Gabe said, cradling Joker's head in his hands. "You did good boy. You did real good," he said softly. "You fellas got a blanket for me dog? Poor bugger's freezin' to death."

"In the back."

Gabe went to the rear of the ambulance and took out two blankets. He wrapped one round Joker and placed him on the front seat of the the Commodore, then wrapped the other around himself. "You did good boy," he again told his dog.

He turned to see the ambulance men placing Katie on a stretcher. They closed the rear doors of their vehicle, one of them riding in the back with her. Gabe followed the driver to the cabin.

"What do you think?" he asked.

"Can't see that she has any major injuries. She's still unconscious, but we'll have her in town shortly. I reckon she'll be alright. Who is she, do you know?"

Gabe shook his head. "No-one from around here."

He watched the ambulance disappear into the rainy darkness, then climbed into the Commodore and swung the vehicle around to focus the headlights on the wreckage. Quickly he drove to his shed. He grabbed a tarpaulin off a bench and drove back to Katie's vehicle. The thunder and lightning had eased and, although he knew his efforts would be all but pointless, he covered the wreck as best he could with the tarp, deciding to return in the morning and salvage the young woman's belongings. Going back to the Commodore, he again tripped over an object which had earlier been caught around his foot. He leaned over to pick it up and saw that it was a woman's handbag. Despite its saturated condition, he could tell it was made from expensive leather. He knew that if he opened it, it would tell him who the woman was. He was tempted to, but he didn't. Instead he put the handbag in the vehicle and drove back to his house.

He wanted to drive straight into Naracoorte, but to do so without a dry change of clothes would be foolish. "How you doing old boy?" he said, patting Joker on the head. "Bloody pretty wasn't she?" Suddenly he felt relieved. The knot in his gut had gone, knowing the young woman was now in safe hands. His gaze went back to the road where the ambulance had disappeared into the night.

I want to be there for her. Don't know why. Don't even know her. But somehow I just want to be there.

He climbed from the Commodore with Joker in his arms and went inside. Still the rain came down. Gabe took his faithful dog over to the few remaining hot coals of the open fire. He threw on a few pieces of kindling to spark them, then grabbed an old towel and went to work on Joker. Moments later, Gabe had him wiped down and wrapped in another blanket and lay on his sheepskin rug.

"There you go old boy, you stay there now. You'll warm up in a minute and be as right as rain in no time. Jesus you're a fucking good dog," he told him, patting his head.

Two hours later, after telling Joker to stay in the car, Gabe Caplin walked into the reception area of the Naracoorte hospital, clutching the young woman's handbag. Receptionist Betty Freeman saw him arrive. "Well Mr Caplin, you've had quite a night, haven't you?"

Gabe looked at her. "Oh?" he queried, not realising word had spread so quickly.

"Already the doctors are saying you saved the young woman's life."

Gabe felt a slight tinge of embarrassment. He walked over to Betty Freeman. "So, how is she?"

She was about to answer when Doctor Mike Harrison entered the reception area.

"Oh Doctor Harrison, this is Mr Caplin. He's the one who rescued the young woman," Betty Freeman said.

Gabe shook hands with the doctor, guardedly. "How is she?"

Doctor Harrison placed his arm around Gabe's shoulder and walked him off down the passageway. "We're not sure yet." Gabe hit the doctor with a cold stare. "Well she's still unconscious," he went on. "Don't know who she is, do you?"

Gabe handed him the handbag he picked up at the scene of the accident. "It's probably in there. It was lying beside her car, but I didn't like to open it. Thought that was more in your line," he said.

"Yes of course Mr Caplin, we'll certainly take care of it."

By now the two had stopped outside a private room. The door was ajar, the lights dimmed. Gabe moved to step inside when Doctor Harrison placed a gentle, restraining hand against his arm. "Just before we go in, let me tell you we've had a good look at her. Apart from being battered and bruised with a fairly sizeable whack on the head, she does appear to be alright. No broken bones we're aware of. Her left thigh is black. So is her left shoulder. The ambulance fellows said you freed her leg then had to let the tyre down or something to free her shoulder?"

Gabe only half heard the question. He was more intent in trying to see through the doorway. "Oh, er, yes, of course, sorry. The bloody storm didn't help matters much."

Doctor Harrison removed his restraining hand and pushed open the door to the private room. Both moved quietly over to the bedside.

"This looks fairly nasty," Doctor Harrison said, carefully pushing her hair back to reveal the wound. "If we stitch it, we'll have to shave it," he whispered. "It's not too deep, more of a heavy graze actually. We've stopped the bleeding. I'm sure it will be alright."

Gabe was transfixed. He began to hear his own heartbeat as he fixed his eyes upon the pretty woman he had saved. He remembered hearing once that if you saved someone's life, then you become responsible for that person. The thought frightened him. Hesitantly, cautiously, Gabe reached out and touched Katie's arm with his fingertips. "She's going to be OK, isn't she doc?"

The doctor glanced at Gabe and immediately felt his concerns. Slowly he ushered him from the room. In the passageway the doctor said, "I think you've been through just as big an ordeal as this young woman. There's nothing anyone of us can do until she regains consciousness. Thank you for bringing in her handbag. I suggest you go home. Get some sleep and ring me in the morning if you'd like to check on her progress."

But Gabe wasn't going to be fobbed off. "I don't want to walk out of here while she's still unconscious," he protested. "If it's all the same to you, I'll just wait in the reception area until she comes round."

Doctor Harrison looked at his watch. "It's very late. Please go on home. The night sister will stay with her and monitor her condition. I only live around the corner and she's been instructed to ring me immediately there's any change."

Gabe stood back from the doctor and glared at him.

"Please Mr Caplin. I can appreciate your concerns. You obviously went a long way tonight towards saving her life. But please, just leave her be for a few hours. Ring me in the morning."

Still Gabe glared at the doctor. Doctor Harrison looked visibly relieved when he saw Gabe back off. "OK," Gabe conceded, "but..."

The rain had stopped and the storm was over when Gabe climbed in behind the wheel of the Commodore. As he drove home, he dropped his hand and wrapped it around Joker's head, now resting on his lap. Approaching the driveway to his farm, he quickly flashed the headlights onto the tarpaulin covering Katie's wrecked car.

"Better get back here at first light and sort this lot out, eh boy?"

He pulled Stan Smythe's vehicle in close to the verandah and went inside. Joker watched as Gabe restarted the fire. When small flames began to flicker, he planted himself firmly on his sheepskin rug. Gabe went through the process of making himself a cup of tea, then came back to the open fire. He sat back in his chair and placed his feet upon the woodbox. As he did so, he glanced up at the old clock on the mantelpiece. The hands were on twenty past three.

Bloody amazing that, he thought. *The day mum died was the day the bloody thing stopped.* Gabe didn't know if it was broken or just needed re-winding. But whatever the reason, because it was his mother's favorite possession, he just let it be.

Chapter 18

"Anyone home?" Sylvia Redman asked her husband. He was standing just outside the front door, looking vacantly into space. She went to him and ran her hand through his arm.

He offered her a grimaced smile. "God, I can't get over the shock of all this," he told her. Sylvia Redman placed her head against her husband's shoulder, the cool, rough finish of Jack's English tweed hunting jacket pressing against her face. There was no need for further conversation. As they stood looking out over their property, each knew the other was overtaken with loss and emptiness.

It was now a week since Sam and Ida McFarlane's funeral. Coming almost immediately upon that of their son, they each were desperately depending on the other to overcome their grief.

"Haven't heard a word from Katie," Jack remarked to his wife. He felt her shake her head against his shoulder. "Do you think she knows?"

"I wouldn't think so," Sylvia answered. "Despite everything that's happened, I'm sure she would have said something."

"Hard to know I guess," Jack said. "I remember Sam and Ida saying they wanted to leave it a little while before they mentioned anything. I just have this dreadful feeling she doesn't know and it'll be us who has to tell her."

"We could tell her solicitor."

"No, no. Wouldn't be right," Jack said. "Has to come from us. And you haven't heard from her?"

"Not a word."

"We'll give it another few days. Poor little blighter. I don't know how you come to terms with losing the three people you love the most in your life. Sure, we lost our Paul, but Katie not only lost him but also her mum and dad." Jack Redman took the handkerchief offered to him by his wife. He dabbed at his eyes. "They reckon God only picks the best blooms for his garden. Well, he must have something of a botanic feast up there right now."

* * *

"Bit of a mongrel, that bastard!" Gabe cussed, rubbing the sleep from his eyes as he stepped out onto the verandah. The sun was just beginning to rise and various shades of orange began to reflect from the surface of scores of water pools created by the overnight deluge. He glanced at the sky. It had cleared and the high winds had gone. "Christ, old Huey did send her down," he said to Joker. "Come on, we better try and get that girl's car down here," he said, lifting the glass from the rain gauge. "Bloody hell, two inches."

Clean shaven and wearing his best shirt and tie, Gabe walked into the Naracoorte hospital soon after seven-thirty. He caught a reflection of himself in a window and stopped. He stepped back and took a second look. *Strike me pink, Gabe Caplin wearing a tie*, he thought. *Aunty Betsy would never believe it.* Then he wondered why he was. He didn't know the young woman. Why should how he looked even rate a mention? But somehow it did. For what he thought was probably the first time in his life, he cared about how someone else would regard his appearance. Then he also realised, he was extremely nervous about meeting her. *Get a bloody hold of yourself. You haven't even met her. Even now you may not get to meet her. What if the doctors say no?*

Gabe was still fielding his own questions when Doctor Harrison emerged from the passageway into the reception area. He was studying a document on a clipboard when he looked up to find Gabe Caplin standing in front of him.

"Oh, Mr Caplin," he said. "You're early. I thought you were going to ring?" Gabe's gaze dropped to his shoes in embarrassment and Doctor Harrison moved over to put his hand on his shoulder. "This place is full of stories about how you dragged her clear moments before that giant limb crushed her car. Anyway, enough of that. Would you like to meet a very grateful lady?"

"Is she awake?" Gabe asked.

"Yes, she regained consciousness around midnight. Her injuries are what I told you about with, thankfully, no additions. She's going to be pretty sore for awhile, so we'll keep her in for a day or two and monitor her condition. Your finding her handbag was a huge help. Her name is Katie McFarlane. She comes from Adelaide. She's actually a nurse and was on her way to Melbourne when she got lost in the storm and took a wrong turn out of Naracoorte. Come and say hello."

Gabe followed Doctor Harrison down the passageway. As he walked, he quickly checked his appearance again with his reflection in the windows. The two men then entered Katie McFarlane's private room. The young woman, with a drip in her arm, had her eyes closed.

"Miss McFarlane," Doctor Harrison whispered.

Katie opened her eyes. "Oh hello. I must have dozed off."

She began to move but Doctor Harrison intervened. "Don't try and sit up. Just lay there quietly, for today at least. I have someone very special for you to meet. I don't know how much you remember of the accident, but this is Gabe Caplin, the man who singlehandedly freed you from the wreckage of your vehicle...in all that rain and hail and thunder and lightning and God knows what else."

Katie's attention moved to Gabe. She could see he was a big man and even in her semi-drowsiness, she could sense his nervousness. She offered her hand and smiled. "Hello. I would just like to say I am very pleased to meet you, Mr Caplin."

"Please, call me Gabe ma'am," he stammered, reaching out to accept Katie's hand. "How do you feel?" Then he cringed at his own question. *You dopey, dumb, fucking idiot. That's got to be the most stupid thing you've ever asked anyone. How the hell do you think she feels?*

Katie looked at him and said, "Let's say I wouldn't be a starter in a half-marathon."

Gabe was reluctant to let go of Katie's hand. It felt so warm. So soft. Enclosed in his own, it felt like that of a child's. But he did let go. "Are you in any pain?"

"Not pain so much as being battered and bruised all over."

Doctor Harrison chipped in. "That you are. It's a miracle you suffered no broken bones or anything other than superficial injuries."

"My car...what's happened to my car?"

Gabe told her the Honda was now a wreck as a result of the accident. He'd taken it to his place, recovered her possessions and as soon as he'd dried them out, he'd bring them in to her.

"Thank...thank you Mr..." Her eyes closed and Katie drifted into a deep sleep.

"The one thing she needs at the moment is complete rest Mr Caplin. I gave her a sedative just before you arrived. That's obviously now had its effect. This time tomorrow, she should be able to get out of bed."

When Gabe arrived back at his farm, Mrs Cropp was already there, hands to her face, aghast as she looked over the remains of a wrecked Honda. "I've been trying to ring, but the phone's out," she called to Gabe. "What on Earth has happened here? Was there someone in there or have you just acquired a wreck for some reason or another? And what's with the shirt and tie? That's not the Gabe Caplin I know."

He tried to ignore the question and went inside to make a pot of tea. Over the kitchen table he detailed the events of the previous several hours.

"So is she going to live?"

"Oh sure," Gabe told her. "That's where I've been this morning."

"Ah-ha, hence the shirt and tie," she said with a slight giggle.

Her comments produced a wry smile from Gabe. *If I live to be a hundred, I will never forget how it felt to hold her hand,* he told himself.

"And you say she's pretty?"

"Just like those women you see in the movies or models wearing those clothes in women's magazines. I remember seeing them in the magazines mum used to buy sometimes."

"She's from Adelaide you say? Certainly someone will be anxious of her whereabouts. Has anyone been contacted?"

"Doctor Harrison. I gave him her handbag. I reckon he'll have already done that."

"So are you going in to see her again? What about her car? And you certainly can't keep all her things here," Mrs Cropp pointed out, seeing the young woman's possessions laid out to dry.

"Whoa, hold on Aunty Betsy," Gabe chipped in. "Yes I will drop in and see her again. But I guess by this time tomorrow, her family will be with her, so I'll just give her a hand to get things fixed up about her car. Reckon that'll be a low-loader job back to Adelaide."

"Certainly looks a mess."

"Oh, it's a total write-off. How she wasn't killed, I'll never know. That bloody limb dropped right on top of her. Another six inches. That's all there was between her living and dying. Unbelievable!"

"So what's on the agenda for today?"

"Better get onto the phone blokes I suppose."

"Yes, well get them to fix mine while they're at it."

Suddenly Gabe had a spring in his step. He busied himself cleaning the place up following the storm and decided it would be of no use making another trip into the hospital that day. He would go in again in the morning.

* * *

At seven-thirty a.m. the following day, Gabe walked through the front doors of the Naracoorte hospital. He saw the sign on the wall: Visiting Hours 3 to 4 p.m. and 7 to 8 p.m. He chose to ignore it. There was no one behind the reception desk, as it was still to open for the day. A night sister, about to come off duty, noticed Gabe sitting in the waiting room.

"You wouldn't be Gabe Caplin would you?" the nurse smiled. "Everyone in the hospital knows how you saved Katie McFarlane." Gabe was about to answer when the nurse continued. "I assume you've come in to see her?"

"Well I was hoping..."

"Of course it's alright," she assured him. "Come on, I'll take you down. She's just had a cup of tea so she may still be sitting up. We had her on a drip for awhile as a precaution, but we've taken that out. She's going to be fine."

The nurse knocked quietly on the door to Katie McFarlane's room and entered. Katie was still sitting up. A look of surprise fell across her face when she saw Gabe enter her room. He was smartly dressed in a rough sort of way. His clothes were clean and pressed but he just looked a little awkward. "Hello Gabe," she said.

For answer, Gabe moved to Katie's bedside and held out his hand. Katie grasped it.

As the nurse left the room, Gabe let go of Katie's hand, looking around the room at three huge vases of flowers. Katie saw him looking at them. They had arrived the day before but there was no card. Katie could only assume they had come from Gabe. She saw him blush a little, a look of uneasiness falling across his face. She thought if she asked him straight out, he may deny it, so she chose a different tact.

"You saved my life. It should be me sending you flowers, not the other way round." Gabe shrugged his shoulders and offered a sheepish grin. "Thank you," said Katie. "They're lovely. "Would you like to sit down?"

"Thank you, er yes, thank you," he muttered, drawing a chair up next to the bed, his attention focused on the floor. More than anything he wanted to look at her, especially as she was now sitting up in bed, and, he assumed, the nurse had shampooed, dried and brushed her long blonde hair until it shone. He could smell her closeness. He froze.

Katie McFarlane looked at Gabe Caplin. It dawned on her that sitting at her bedside was a very humble shy man that through circumstances had found himself in an awkward situation. A man who wasn't used to being around women.

Finally, Gabe plucked the courage to talk to her. "I guess I'm so relieved to see you came through alright," he uttered nervously.

"So how come you found me?"

"You had the accident right outside my front gate. The thunder was unbelievable and when my dog started barking, I thought he was just sounding off at the storm. But he just kept barking and barking and racing across to the kitchen window. Finally I decided to see what all the fuss was about, and that's when I saw your car's headlights pointing into the sky. Where were you going?"

"Melbourne...seems I took a wrong turn."

"Yes, well you certainly did that," he said. "I found your handbag and gave it to Doctor Harrison. Has he informed your family or your husband you're here?"

Katie's eyes dropped and she reached for a tissue as tears began to roll down her face.

"Oh Jesus, I'm sorry m'aam. I didn't mean…"

Katie reached across and touched the top of Gabe's hand. "No, no, don't be. It's just me. I'll be alright in a moment."

Gabe could sense there was something terribly wrong, but he stayed silent, fearing further questions would be too hurtful.

Katie dabbed her eyes and continued, "There's no-one for Doctor Harrison to ring. I no longer have a family. I am an only child. My fiance was killed in a plane crash a few weeks ago. Then my mum and dad were killed in a car smash in Adelaide. The reason I'm stuck out here is that I was on my way to Melbourne to try and start a new life."

Gabe Caplin sat in his chair, stunned from what he'd heard. "Oh my God. You poor, poor girl. You lost everyone?"

Katie nodded. Gabe desperately wanted to hold her in his arms, but self-consciousness and a fear of rejection kept him pinned to his seat. If only he knew what to do. How to react. What to say. Then as though being belted into action by his dead father, he rose from the chair, cradled Katie's head in his arms and held her close to his body. Katie put her arms around his waist and cried. After a seemingly endless stream of tissues, she was finally able to regain herself. She leaned back on her pillows and apologised to Gabe. Cautiously, he reached for her hand.

"After what you've been through, I'd say you've probably got a fair bit more of that to do before those scars start to heal. While I'm here with you, you feel free to rid your soul of that damn grief any way you see fit. You'll not hear any complaints from me. In fact, you'll not ever hear any complaints from anyone."

Katie offered Gabe a tiny smile. "Thank you Mr…Gabe."

"I guess all you want to do now is get the hell out of here and leave Naracoorte as far behind you as you can?"

"I haven't thought that far ahead yet."

The conversation between the two was interrupted by a knock on the door. As they turned to see who it was, Gabe rose from his chair.

"Aunty Betsy?"

Betsy Cropp was dressed in a calf-length, divided skirt with tan leather inserts down the front. A check shirt covered her ample bosom. Her leather waistcoat was the same colour tan as her long, leather boots. Katie looked at the woman and then glanced at Gabe. "My next- door neighbour," he told her. Then to Aunty Betsy: "What are you doing here?"

Mrs Cropp didn't answer. Instead she focused her attention upon the young woman lying in the hospital bed. "Katie?" she asked. "Katie McFarlane?"

"Ye...yes."

Gabe was dumbfounded. His Aunty Betsy *knew* this woman?

Mrs Cropp took a few steps inside the room. By now the two women were closely studying each other. Then Mrs Cropp began to hum a song. It was the Black Hawk and the tune was like a tonic from heaven.

Katie recognised it immediately. Instantly her face lit up and she opened her arms. "The black keys lady!" she said. Mrs Cropp went to her and the two women hugged each other joyously. Then as they drew themselves apart, it was Katie. "The black keys lady...oh this is wonderful. How did you find me? I mean I don't even know your name."

"Betsy Cropp," she said. "And it's lovely to meet you again."

"Will someone tell me what's going on?" Gabe cut in.

"I will dear," said Mrs Cropp, turning back to Katie. "This is so incredible. So what about you? What's all this? And that nice young man. Paul wasn't it? How is he?"

Gabe couldn't understand why, but suddenly he felt the pangs of jealousy, even though Paul must have been the fiance who died. It was then Mrs Cropp's turn to be dumbfounded. Betsy Cropp sat with her face in her hands, scarcely able to believe what Katie was telling her. Gabe leaned over and offered her his handkerchief as she wept openly. In between her own tears and sobbing, Katie enlarged, in greater detail than she did with Gabe, the events in her life which led her to be in the Naracoorte hospital.

"But how could you have even remotely known I was here?'

"Gabe and I have adjoining properties. When he told me about what happened, he spoke at great length and in great detail of this very, very pretty young woman. And the more he told me about you, the more I became curious. So I phoned the hospital. They said it was

Katie McFarlane. I checked my diary. Your name was in there from when I wrote to you. I didn't think there could possibly be two Katie McFarlanes, so I came on in." She reached over and cupped Katie's hands. "And you my dear. What about you? Do you have no one left?"

Katie shook her head. "Well you do now. I don't have a daughter and you don't have a mother. What do you say, Gabe, that we adopt this young woman for the remainder of the time she has to spend in Naracoorte?"

"Oh no," Katie protested. "You can't do that. I can't just walk in and out of your lives. I would feel I was standing in a revolving door. And you would too. Thank you. You are most kind. But I simply couldn't do that. As soon as I'm well I'll return to Adelaide, organise a car and start out for Melbourne all over again…only next time I'll check the map more closely."

"Now Katie McFarlane, you listen to me," Betsy Cropp began, standing back from her chair. "If you think for one moment that either Gabe or myself are going to walk away from you after all you've been through, you've got another thing coming. You need time to recover from this mess you're in. I have a farm, a big house and plenty of wide open spaces. You can have a room to yourself and you can have the run of the place. There's vehicles on the property. You can come and go as you please. So please, let us give you a home, at least for a few short moments anyway?"

Katie looked at Gabe. She saw tears in his eyes at the enormous generosity offered by his neighbour. She looked back at Mrs Cropp. She was standing back from the bed with her hands on her hips. Katie could tell from the look on the woman's face she wasn't going to take 'no' for an answer. She tried to put an age on her, but couldn't. She recalled her playing the piano at The Oakdale Country Club and thought how out-of-character she now looked compared to the woman she remembered sitting at the keyboard. Today it's work as usual. *Mind you she does come across as something of a matriarch.*

Katie pondered the prospect of spending some time at Mrs Cropp's place. Finally she relented. "On one condition. Do you have a piano?"

"I do."

"Then you must play it for me."

Chapter 19

B etsy Cropp spoke with the nurses then had a word to Doctor Harrison, briefing him of the young woman's tragic predicament. He commended her compassion and thoughtfulness in going to her assistance. "But I would ask that she remain in hospital for at least another forty-eight hours." It was now Monday.

Betsy Cropp was overjoyed in seeing the young woman again, but it saddened her that their meeting should have been under such tragic circumstances. *I just knew there was something about her*, she said to herself as she walked to her car in the hospital car park. *They say fate works in funny ways. I wonder why the Lord chose to punish her in this way. Okay, she's had the tragedy. Now it's time for some happiness.*

Betsy Cropp and Gabe Caplin arrived at the Naracoorte hospital shortly after ten a.m. on the Wednesday morning. Gabe had come into town an hour earlier and slipped into Moyles barber shop for a shave, a haircut and a new bottle of 1808 hair-oil.

Betsy Cropp couldn't help herself. "This girl has really got under your skin hasn't she?" she said, noting his appearance. Then she leaned into his ear. "Get rid of the hair oil. Girls today hate hair oil."

Gabe felt his face blossom into a bright red. "Well I could hardly turn up in me bloody work boots could I?"

Betsy smiled. *Lord, Gabe is so gullible. Please don't let him think this girl's smile will lead him into paradise. Gabe Caplin is certainly not the kind of man a girl like Katie McFarlane would have in mind. Besides, what she needs right now is all the love and caring we can possibly give her.*

Katie McFarlane was dressed and waiting for Mrs Cropp. Earlier that morning she had been discharged by Doctor Harrison and asked that she visit him in his surgery in a week's time. Katie rose from her chair when she heard the approaching voices of Mrs Cropp, Gabe Caplin and hospital staff. One of the staff, a nurse, knocked and opened the door. Katie held her arms open and greeted Betsy Cropp warmly. Gabe was speechless. Katie was dressed in blue slacks and a red jumper. She looked sensational.

"Let me look at you," Mrs Cropp said, standing back at arm's length. "Red is certainly your colour. Did I get the size right?"

Katie raised a hand to her mouth. "Mrs Cropp, you shouldn't have. You must let me pay you..."

"Nonsense," she said with a wave of her hand. "You had to have something to wear. By the look of how your things survived the other night, you'll probably need a few more yet. And how are you?"

Katie nodded her head. "I'm very sore and walk with a dreadful limp because of the bruising on my left thigh. Doctor Harrison says I must have complete rest until the weekend at least. You sure you want to do this? I just think I'm going to be a dreadful burden on you."

"Now we won't have you thinking thoughts like that," Mrs Cropp said. "If Doctor Harrison says you must rest, then rest you must. Are we all set then?"

Katie nodded in agreement and lit the room with a smile. "Hello Gabe," she said.

Gabe smiled and nodded. It was all he could think of to do.

"Are you alright to walk Miss McFarlane?" inquired a nurse. "I can get you a wheelchair."

Katie took a couple of steps. "No, I think I'll be alright, thank you."

Gabe seized the moment. He stepped forward, leaned down and carefully swept Katie up into his massive arms before he even had time to think or contemplate what he was doing. Mrs Cropp did a double take, not believing her eyes. When it suddenly dawned on Gabe what he'd done, he felt his knees and hands begin to shake.

Katie let out a joyful, shrill note, as if her breath had been taken away. Gabe smiled at her. "You really must think I'm a totally useless female," she told him in a tone of disgust.

"Oh I don't know. You're probably alright on your day, but it seems you haven't been having too many of them of late," he told her shyly. Gabe turned and carried Katie down the passageway of the hospital.

Suddenly he felt as proud as proud can be. He was carrying the most precious cargo of his entire life, and he was savouring the moment.

* * *

"This is your place?" Katie said, as Mrs Cropp swung her vehicle into her driveway. "It looks fabulous. Have you lived here long?"

"Came here from Western Australia years ago."

"On your own?"

"Yes. On my own. Unfortunately," she said.

Katie depicted a certain emptiness in Mrs Cropp's tone. She wanted to ask more, but decided this was not the time. As Betsy Cropp pulled her car to a standstill, Gabe pulled in alongside.

Katie sat looking out the vehicle's windows. A mob of sheep. A few cows. Over towards the sheds several chooks were scratching the rain-soaked ground.

Gabe came round to Katie's side of the vehicle and opened the door. "Ever been on a farm before?" he asked. Katie shook her head. "You can walk if you like, but the ground's pretty wet. Probably better I carry you."

"Oh Gabe, this is too much."

He leaned into the car and gently wrapped his arms around her and lifted her from the car, being careful not to touch the bruising on her thigh. Mrs Cropp walked on ahead to open up. Once inside, Gabe placed Katie carefully onto a kitchen chair. Mrs Cropp, though, became suddenly fidgety and uneasy. Suddenly Gabe twigged. He walked from the kitchen down the passageway of Mrs Cropp's house and opened the door to the bedroom, the one he knew Katie would sleep. When he looked inside the room, he did a double take. "Holy shit, Aunty Betsy, when did you do this?"

Mrs Cropp stood at the kitchen sink, proud of the room she had redecorated in Katie's honour. "It was finished about two hours ago. The fellows had to work through the night to complete it."

Gabe went back to Katie. "You're not going to believe this. Come and have a look at your room."

Katie slowly rose from her chair and walked carefully, holding on to Gabe's arm. Mrs Cropp followed. When they reached the doorway, Gabe eased his arm away from Katie. Katie gaped at the lavishness of the bedroom.

"Welcome to this house Katie McFarlane. Welcome to this house," Mrs Cropp said.

Katie put her arms around Mrs Cropp's neck. "This is just so, so wonderful. Thank you. I can't imagine why you'd ever want to do this for me. Heavens, we only met briefly."

"You're special Katie. I knew from that first moment I set eyes on you. You were special. Isn't she Gabe?"

"Damn right about that Aunty Betsy."

"Now pop back in there and have a decent look"

Katie did as she was asked. She noticed a combination of lace centre nets and burgundy-coloured, velvet curtains. A brand new crystal-handled brush and comb set sat on the top of a brand new Queen Anne dressing table. Next to it a matching wardrobe, and when Katie opened one door she saw herself in the full-length mirror. When she opened the other she saw several sets of brand new clothes. Jeans, tops, blouses, two jackets, one denim, the other tweed. Two pairs of shoes. She closed the doors, then ran her fingers over the velvet cover on the foot stool. It matched the curtains and blended beautifully with the burgundy-coloured bedspread and cream lace pillowcase. She then kicked off her shoes and dug her toes into the pile of a brand new cream-coloured pure-wool carpet. *Everything is brand new, right down to the silk pyjamas, the bath towel and the slippers*, which were a backless, pink, fluffy number.

Mrs Cropp stepped into the room. Casually, she withdrew the drawer which ran the length of the dressing table, stood back, raised her arm and announced "Da-dah." It was fully stocked with toiletries, haircare and make-up products. "Some things I couldn't get, but most things I could. I had Gabe bring me everything you lost in that line in the accident. Mind you, the Paris was a problem for the local pharmacist till I told him to get on the phone."

"I, I don't quite know what to say, Mrs Cropp. Please forgive me if I tell you I'm a little overwhelmed by it all."

Mrs Cropp smiled. "Oh Katie, it's nothing really. A girl needs her hairbrush. Besides, I've been meaning to trick this room up for years, but kept putting it off. Then when you turned up out of the blue, I thought right, I'm not putting it off any longer. So tell me. Do you like it or is there too much of one thing and not enough of another?"

Katie smiled. "It's perfect. Simply perfect."

Mrs Cropp walked back to the kitchen and called to Gabe. "Will you show Katie the rest of the house, then perhaps we better follow the doctor's orders and let this young lady have some rest."

Katie McFarlane needed no special coaxing to go to bed after she'd had a steaming, hot bath. Mrs Cropp could see she had tired very quickly, and it was only moments before her new house-guest was sound asleep.

"She's really something isn't she?" Gabe said to Mrs Cropp later in the kitchen.

"She's lovely. Just lovely."

"Do you think she'll stay long?"

"I hope a couple of weeks. I guess we'll have to see after that. Now, I suppose I won't be able to keep you away from the place?"

"But I don't know what to say to her."

"Is it because she's beautiful?"

Gabe nodded his head.

"Try and see beyond that. See her for the person she is. I'm dying to get to know her myself. Just treat her as a normal human being. She's not an ornament or a piece of meat to be poked and prodded either. She's been blessed with beauty, but I'm sure if you asked her she'd willingly trade most of it in if it meant she could have avoided losing the three people in her life she cared most about. Think about that. She not only lost the man she was about to marry. She also lost her mother and her father. All in a few short weeks and all in tragic circumstances. And, I can tell you, to lose your parents is one thing, but to lose the man you love is just the most horrible thing. Some women bounce back and love again. Others never get over it."

Gabe saw the look on Mrs Cropp's face and knew she would never get over the loss of her own husband. Although he loved and deeply respected Mrs Cropp, he hoped Katie, at least in this instance, wasn't the same.

"Do you have work to do, or are you going to stick around here and annoy me for the rest of the day?"

"What do you think?"

"That's what I thought. Well I haven't milked the cow today, so you better go and do that. But take off your good clothes first."

Mrs Cropp watched him go. It pleased her to see that Gabe did have something of a glint in his eye after all. She always felt it was there, it just hadn't showed itself. Not that he ever did anything to encourage it. If meeting Katie could at least stir his hormones, he might force himself to actually go into town sometime on his own. Go to a dance. Join a club. Do something, anything, which would bring him into contact with other people, especially women. It had bothered her for years that Gabe never did anything about that part of his life. At one point she thought he might be gay, but after a half-second's consideration, fully dismissed such a thought. He simply couldn't be bothered doing anything about it. Or more to the point, he didn't know how to do anything about it.

Mrs Cropp pondered a little on the Gabe Caplin/Katie McFarlane potential match up then dismissed it from her mind. Right now she was revelling in the joy of having a very special house-guest.

* * *

Jim Duncan buzzed his secretary through the intercom. "Margaret, have you heard from Miss McFarlane?"

"No."

"That's funny. She hasn't rung the office?"

"She certainly hasn't rung in office hours, and there's been no messages on the recorder."

"Perhaps a fax?"

"Nothing there either."

"Yes, well that's really odd. She's been gone a week. There certainly should've been a call by now. Have the Redmans called?"

"No."

"Something doesn't seem right here. Margaret, get Jack Redman on the line for me will you please." Jim Duncan swivelled in his chair and gazed out the office window across King William Street. Casually he reached back with one arm, placed an index finger under a folder and flipped it open. He could see the last correspondence he had from Katie McFarlane. It was what appeared to be a hastily written note signed on the bottom.

> *No more God damned grief Jim. Thank you for being a friend, but I'm out of here. Sell the house, keep an eye on my place. The keys to both are on the kitchen table. You have my power of attorney. Deduct your fees and deposit the rest. I'll call you when I get settled. Regards Katie. P.S. May head to Melbourne.*

Jim Duncan read it a couple of times, as he had done the day before and the day before that. Attached to the note was a receipt from a removalist giving the location of her stored possessions.

"Mr Duncan."

"Yes Margaret?"

"Mr Redman on one."

"Jack. Jim Duncan."

"Hello Jim. Are you wondering what's happened to her too?"

"Well yes. Has she called you?"

"No. Sylvia and I were discussing this a couple of days ago and we thought if there's still no word by Monday, we'd make some calls. Actually the first one would probably have been to you."

"I know she just wanted to put a bit of space between herself and Adelaide but, even with that in mind, it does seem odd she hasn't rung. If not me, then you, surely."

"What do you think?"

"I'll make some more calls and see if I can find out anything. I rang the police this morning and asked about any reports of any major accidents. There was one in Bordertown on the night of the storms, but that was a young fellow from Penola. They said there was another at Naracoorte but didn't have any details. I'll give them another call and let you know if I hear anything."

* * *

Betsy Cropp was up and dressed at six a.m. She'd had a restless night, worrying that Katie would be alright. She found herself constantly getting up, creeping down the passageway and standing close to her. She would listen intently to her breathing then, confident all was well, return to her bed.

She put the kettle on in the kitchen, being particularly careful not to make any loud noise. At six-thirty she went to check again. As she approached Katie's room she could hear muffled sobs. She quickened her pace. As she entered the room, she hooked her toe in the foot stool and dragged it over to Katie's bed. She raised her hand and brushed Katie's hair back from her face.

"Were you having a nightmare my dear?" Katie nodded, her face wet with tears. She dabbed her eyes with the sheet as Mrs Cropp reached for a box of tissues. "You're safe here. No more tragedies. No more pain. OK.? Can I get you something? A cup of tea? You've slept right through. Must have been some fourteen hours." Mrs Cropp smiled. "I was starting to get worried you weren't going to wake up." She continued to stroke Katie's hair and dry her eyes." Can you tell me if you feel alright?"

Katie moved herself and sat up a little. "A cup of tea sounds wonderful...and yes, I think I'm starting to be alright.?"

"Dreams can be such heartbreakers. Do you want to talk about it?"

Katie turned her head to one side. "I can't shake it. And it's always the same thing. Paul used to love flying light planes. I keep dreaming he's coming in to land, misses the strip, and as he flies off into the sky, mum and dad are with him. All I keep seeing is them laughing and joking. That's bizarre Mrs Cropp. It's as though they're really enjoying leaving me behind to pick up the pieces."

Mrs Cropp cupped Katie's face in her hand. "It'll pass. It may take awhile, but put your trust in Father Time. He can be a great healer. And if he doesn't heal, he can at least make human tragedy bearable."

Katie looked at Mrs Cropp and she felt her words were more than those of comfort. They came from the heart and each one appeared to have a bitter-sweet taste of having lived the experience.

Mrs Cropp smiled. "Now what about that cup of tea...and you must be starving?"

"Famished!"

Mrs Cropp cooked her a bowl of porridge, poached some eggs and made a large pot of tea. It pleased her to see the young woman eat well. "That's all good, wholesome country cooking guaranteed to put the colour back into your cheeks and the shine in your hair."

"Thank you," she said. "You are such a good person."

Mrs Cropp was quite chuffed at Katie's remarks. "Well, shower time," she said. "Then, if you feel up to it, we'll go for a walk around the place. You can feed the chooks and I'll introduce you to Stanley. You'll love him."

Mrs Cropp was clearing the table when the phone rang.

"Hello, is that Mrs Betsy Cropp? I'm sorry to be calling you at this hour. I'm ringing from Adelaide..."

"Just a moment please." Mrs Cropp put the receiver on the table and closed the kitchen door.

* * *

After showering, Katie carefully went through the clothes provided by Mrs Cropp and chose a pair of jeans and a long-sleeved, pink, mohair jumper. She dried her hair and forty minutes later walked into the kitchen.

"Now, how would you like to meet Stanley?" Mrs Cropp said.

"I'd love to," she smiled.

"Are you sure you are able to walk alright?"

"I'll have to be careful, but I'll be fine. I think it's best if I start using my leg, especially now that I'm able to."

"Well, you know what's best for yourself, just don't overdo it."

The two women left the house. The sun was up. A gentle breeze rattled the tree tops. A mob of black cockatoos feasted on a patch of Radiata pines a short distance from the house.

"Over there is the shearing shed," Mrs Cropp pointed out. "The stock yards. The dairy. Used to use it once, but now I only have the one milker, so I do her by hand. She's standing over there by the hayshed. Her name's Dolly. She knows I'll be coming over with a bucket and stool shortly. Cagey old devil. I used to put her in the bail when she was younger. Now I just milk her where she stands. But I do declare that sometimes she does try and hide from me."

Katie laughed. "And the chooks?"

"Yes, the chooks. A few geese. Couple of ducks." Mrs Cropp quickened her pace, stepped over to a drum and scooped up half a bucket of oats and handed them to Katie. "Here. Give them these," she said as she continued walking. "If you look over there, just past the chook house, you'll see a couple of peacocks. Remind me and I'll try and get you a tail feather."

Katie was thoroughly enjoying herself as she slowly and cautiously walked with Mrs Cropp. "Do you have any sheep?"

Mrs Cropp laughed. "Hundreds of them. They're down in the bottom paddocks. Should be hundreds more too when they start lambing. Had a huge problem with foxes last year and the year before. Gabe does his best with the shotgun, but there's just too many. Gets darned expensive too. I said to Gabe the other day this year looked like being another bad one for foxes."

By now the two women had made their way to a small shed and holding yard at the rear of the woolshed. "OK," said Mrs Cropp. "Are you ready to meet Stanley?"

"Can't wait," she beamed.

Mrs Cropp opened the door to the shed and walked in. As she did, she grabbed a large dipper and filled it full of oats from a drum. "Good morning sweet boy," she called.

Katie heard the muffled and seemingly contented reply. Then, as if appearing out of nowhere, the handsome head of a massive chestnut Clydesdale stallion appeared from the doorway of his stall. Mrs Cropp wrapped her arm around his head. "Hello boy," she said, stroking it. "Look who's here to meet you." Mrs Cropp handed the dipper of oats to Katie. "Give him these my dear and you'll have a friend for life."

Katie took the dipper and had to hold on tight with both hands as the giant stallion buried his nose into them.

"This is my wonderful, wonderful Stanley. An absolute and total self-indulgence I might add, but what the heck. I bought him as a yearling sixteen years ago for no other reason than I wanted a Clydesdale as a pet. He's so big and gentle. A total sook of course.

Sometimes he follows me around the place all day. And I love it. If I forget to give him his dipper of oats, he unlocks his own gate, comes up to the house and stands by the kitchen window. One day I had to go into Naracoorte early and really did forget to give him his oats. When I got home that night, it was dark, and there he was, still standing at the kitchen window." Mrs Cropp leaned over and kissed him on his nose. "Let me get him out of here and you can have a proper look at him."

Mrs Cropp unbolted the stable door and the big horse made his way outside. Katie stood back and looked him up and down. "I didn't think people kept animals like this as pets. I thought they were work horses."

"As I say, a total self-indulgence."

"Do people actually ride Clydesdales?"

"Not really, but he'll let me get on him. I'll show you." Mrs Cropp picked up an old box and ran her hand over his head, across his mane and down his front leg. "Come on," she coaxed. "Come on...down you come...come on." Stanley moved his weight onto his back legs and dropped to his knees.

Katie giggled.

Mrs Cropp put the box by Stanley's side, stepped onto it, grabbed a handful of mane, and climbed onto his back. "You can see why I need the box," she laughed. The big horse stood up. "That's it," she said to him. "That's a good boy," she said, patting his neck. "You know that's going to cost me another dipper of oats don't you?" she laughed. And to make sure Mrs Cropp didn't forget, Stanley gave her a gentle nudge with his forehead.

Katie McFarlane couldn't believe his cheek. "Oh, excuse me," she said.

Mrs Cropp laughed. "See, I told you he was a sook."

Mrs Cropp got down off the stallion and took Katie to the shearing shed. As the two women walked over to the giant complex, Stanley followed, his head between the two of them as though he was listening to their conversation. Katie found it a little disconcerting being so close to such a massive animal. Mrs Cropp could sense her concern.

"He won't hurt you my dear. He doesn't bite. And one thing he won't do is tread on you. Clydesdales are incredibly light on their feet despite their bulk."

When the two women walked inside the shearing shed, Katie couldn't help but comment on the smell. "What's that?" she exclaimed, turning up her nose.

"Funny isn't it. But I just love it. It's a combination of wee, manure, sweat and lanolin from the wool all mixed into one. You never get sick of it." But Katie wasn't so sure.

Back at the house, Katie was glad to sit down. Her leg had begun to ache, so she sat with it resting on another chair. Mrs Cropp made a cup of tea and, as she was pouring it, told her of the phone call.

"When you were in the shower I received a call from Adelaide. I would have told you at the time, but I wanted to show you around first. It was from a Mr Jack Redman. I take it he must be your Paul's father?"

Katie looked up with a start. "Mr Redman? He called here? Did he say what he wanted?"

"No, except that he and his wife and a Mr Duncan were worried sick about you."

"Oh good heavens! Did you tell them about the accident?"

"Seems the police already had. That's when they became concerned."

"So did you tell them I was in good hands?" she smiled.

"Well yes I did, but Mr Redman said it was vitally important that he and Mr Duncan speak with you."

"Did he say why?"

"He wouldn't elaborate except to ask me if it would be alright if they came down to see you on Monday. I said you were pretty fragile at the moment and would check with you."

Katie shook her head. "Why would they want to drive all this way? You did say I was alright?"

"Certainly I did, but he insisted. What do you want me to do?"

"Oh look, let them come. I don't have a problem with that. I'm sure whatever it is can be solved in a few minutes. Right now I'm ever so grateful to you, and quite frankly I'm revelling in just being here."

Chapter 20

Gabe was on the phone very early the next morning. He'd been pacing the floor half the night in anticipation of spending a few hours alone with Katie McFarlane. The previous evening he had organised to show Katie his property and now he was like an excited schoolboy. He showered and washed his hair, then stood in front of the mirror, combing his hair into different styles, none of which pleased him.

"Be buggered to that!," he finally cursed out loud. "She either likes me as I am or too bloody bad!"

Then he wondered why he was even thinking like that. Katie McFarlane was hardly a prospect. Apart from the generation gap, she was being torn apart by grief. *And chuck in a bloody car smash for good measure*, he thought. But despite it all, Gabe couldn't control the pangs of anticipation that ran through his body. Then he realised he had absolutely no experience in dealing with a young woman on a one-to-one basis.

Mrs Cropp answered the call, trying to stir herself awake as she rubbed the sleep from her eyes. "Gabe, oh Lord! It's only six o'clock, whatever's wrong?"

"I think you better come over," he told her and put the phone down. Fearing the worst Betsy Cropp quickly dressed, checked on Katie, then drove to her neighbour's house. As she pulled up, she saw Gabe and Joker sitting on the verandah.

"Gabe?" she called and quickly went to him. She could tell at a moment's glance he appeared stressed. She quickly looked around. Everything seemed in order. "Whatever's the matter? Are you ill?"

"I'm a bit stuffed!" he told her.

"What do you mean?"

"Well, it's Katie."

Mrs Cropp looked at him inquisitively. "What about her?"

"I have to pick her up today and I don't know what I'm going to say to her."

Mrs Cropp breathed a sigh of relief. "Oh for goodness sakes Gabe, I thought you must have been half dead or something. You dragged me over here because of that?"

"Yeah, well I've been up half the night and quite frankly I'm worried bloody sick."

Mrs Cropp wanted to make light of the situation, but she could see that right now was not the time. She sat on the verandah next to him and patted Joker on the head. "What do you mean, you don't know what to say to her?"

"Well I don't. Christ, Aunty Betsy, I've never been with a woman in my life. And apart from you, my experience with women overall amounts to one big zero. So I'm a bit stuffed in knowing what I'm going to say to her."

Mrs Cropp sighed. "Gabe darling, she's only another person."

"Yeah, pig's arse."

"Now look," she said, steel in her tone, "for goodness sakes forget how she looks. Sure you can't treat her like one of the blokes, but you can treat her as a normal person."

"That's all very fine for you. But what the hell do I talk to her about? I can't talk to her about fixing bloody windmills and fences and tailing lambs can I? And that's about all I know."

Mrs Cropp could see he had a point. She rose from the verandah, walked a few steps, rubbing her chin as she thought. "Well, for starters, don't ask her anything about her past or her sadness. If she wants to tell you, then listen with a sympathetic ear, but don't question her about them. Avoid anything that might be too raw for her to handle at this point in time."

"Should I show her her car?"

"It's funny that. I thought she might have wanted to see it before now, but she hasn't even mentioned it. I was going to, but thought better of it. I'm sure she'll get round to it. So ask her if she wants to see it. Then ask her about herself. Ask her about the work she does. Ask her what sorts of clothes she likes. If she has any hobbies. And be a good listener. Show interest in what she tells you. And don't swear. If you stub your toe or something, don't turn the air blue like I know you can."

Gabe grinned. "Do I invite her inside for a cup of tea?"

"Would you invite me in for a cup of tea?"

"That's different."

"I am a woman too you know, in case you haven't noticed," she said.

Gabe laughed. "You're pretty taken with her too aren't you?"

Mrs Cropp smiled. "In one's life we meet many people. Many turn out to be solid folk, but many more of course turn out to have feet of clay. Look, you have to remember, I hardly know her either. I met her once, very briefly, at a place called The Oakdale Country Club in Mildura. But simply from that one chance meeting, she was someone I felt I had known all my life. Yes, I think this girl is pretty special. But remember too, she's only going to be here for a few days. After she's regained her strength, she'll no doubt test her wings, then she'll be gone. Girls like that don't belong on farms. Accept her being here for what it is. Be a friend to her. Be gentle with her. Who knows? Maybe one day as she goes through life, a chilly wind may alter her path of migration and we'll find her on our doorstep once again."

Gabe could see he had touched a sensitive spot with Mrs Cropp in discussing Katie. He knew she had been taken by her. Only now he realised how much. And it pleased him. He knew his Aunty Betsy was a superb judge of character and he felt her judgement in this case concurred with his own.

"Okay," Mrs Cropp continued, changing her tone. "Now you've got me over here, the least you could do is put the kettle on."

* * *

It was nearly two hours later before she arrived back at her house. It concerned her she'd been gone so long but Gabe had insisted on another forty questions over their cups of tea. When she left, she felt he was more relaxed about picking up Katie McFarlane later that day.

Quickly she went inside to check on Katie. She had awoken a few minutes earlier. She decided not to tell Katie where she'd been, and most certainly not what the topics of discussion were. "Did you sleep well?" she asked

Katie sat up in bed, took a deep breath and stretched her arms. "Must be the country air I think. I didn't wake all night."

"So what do you think you'd like to do today?"

"Gabe's coming over isn't he?"

"Oh yes, of course, later this morning."

"Tell me about him Mrs Cropp."

She smiled. "I've known him since he was a baby. What would you like to know?"

Katie shrugged. "He doesn't appear to be married and I get the feeling he doesn't venture far from home?"

Betsy Cropp laughed. "No Katie, he's not married. He's never been married. In fact, I can tell you he's never even been out with a girl in his life."

"Why on earth not? He seems a very decent sort of man. I'm surprised he wasn't snaffled by someone."

"There were a couple of the local girls who took a shine to him... oh, twenty, maybe even more, years ago, but he wasn't very interested. Seemed content to stay home on the farm. Mind you, when his father was alive he saw to it that Gabe always had work to do when it came to Saturday night. Darn shame really. All the other young folk were going to the pictures or dances or playing sport, but he was never allowed."

Katie wanted to know more. "His mother permitted this?"

Mrs Cropp's expression told Katie she was thinking back. "Well, she didn't have a choice either. What Gabe's father said, went, and that was all there was to it."

"Are they both still alive?"

"No, no. Both died years ago. Mrs Caplin first, then a few years later, Mr Caplin."

"Did you know them very well?"

"Certainly. I was there the day Gabe's mother brought him home from the hospital, forty-four years ago. He was such a gorgeous little fellow. He became totally devoted to her."

"And his dad?"

Mrs Cropp paused. She didn't know how far to go in telling Katie about Garth. She decided to be brief. "Oh, I think they had their problems," she told Katie.

"Father son stuff, or worse than that?"

Mrs Cropp bit her bottom lip, an action not unnoticed by Katie. "Oh, I think you could say it was probably a bit worse than the typical father-son conflict."

Katie felt Mrs Cropp's uneasiness. "I'm sorry. It's none of my business."

"Oh to hell with it," Mrs Cropp blurted out. "It shouldn't be a secret anyway. Gabe's father was a brutal, mongrel bastard Katie. Excuse the French, but there's no other way to put it. The thrashings that boy incurred for absolutely no reason should have seen that man put away. But things are kept quiet in the country. The day Gabe's mother died, it broke his heart. Especially as he was the one who found her. He found his father too. But he didn't cry any tears that day. Ever since then, Gabe has more and more kept to himself. He won't go out anywhere. He comes with me when I go into Naracoorte to do the shopping and that's about it. Oh he's big, a bit gruff. Flies off the handle, but his heart is as big as my farm. I never had a son. But in a way, if ever I had, I would've wanted it to be him."

"I really do find it amazing he's never had a girlfriend."

Betsy Cropp laughed a little. "Now don't go thinking he's gay. In his forty-four years he's never had anyone tickle his fancy. But with you coming to stay, I think he's suddenly realised that this business of having a woman around the place mightn't be such a bad idea."

"Has he told you very much about my accident?"

"He's told me what happened, but he's pretty humble. Certainly others won't hear it from him the way he told me. But I know he's as proud as punch of dragging you clear moments before that giant limb crushed your car."

"Tell me about that? That's all I know."

"Well apparently you were trapped in the car and he couldn't budge you one way or the other. He needed a few extra inches, so he stuck a knife in a tyre. When it blew, it caused the car to drop which lowered you a little. This was all he needed to pull you out. You were no sooner clear of the vehicle and that giant limb totally collapsed and smashed through the roof, flattening your car."

Katie's hands were cupped round her face. Mrs Cropp continued. "You should get him to tell you. It was indeed a night of high drama. The storm was unrelenting. The rain was torrential. He couldn't start his ute. The engine in the tractor was in bits. The phones were out. His motor bike was over here. The poor bloke ran flat out in the dark across the paddocks to my place. He then rode at breakneck speed on his motor bike into the Kybybolite post office. Rang the ambulance. Borrowed the postmaster's car. Had his dog prop up against you to keep you warm...you weren't aware of any of this?"

"Well no, I wasn't!" she gasped. "Good heavens Mrs Cropp, he did all that for me?"

"Well, yes, he did my dear. But that's Gabe. He wouldn't have thought anything of it. You were in trouble and he helped you. That's the sort of man he is."

"I'm stunned. I had no idea. I mean I really had no idea. Oh dear, what should I say to him? How should I thank him?"

"Tell him you'll cook tea for him one night. Mind you, I'll probably hear about it every day for the next year, but that's alright. He'll think he's in seventh heaven."

When Mrs Cropp left the room, Katie sat motionless in her bed, recalling in her mind everything she'd been told. She felt wretched that she hadn't made a fuss over him for all the trouble he had gone to. Then she began to feel a little nervous. Shortly this man who had done so much for her would arrive.

* * *

Gabe Caplin was full of beans when he pulled up outside Betsy Cropp's house. Joker was by his side. He felt he was ready for anything. He bowled headlong into the kitchen as Mrs Cropp was putting away some dishes.

"Hi Aunty Betsy," he chirped, looking around the room.

"And look at you! I don't ever remember you cleaning your work boots before." Gabe offered a sheepish grin. "You'll find her over at the shed. She's feeding the chooks. Now remember what I told you."

"Okay, Okay," he said, leaving the house.

Joker ran on ahead, the sight of a few chooks in the distance too much to resist. Gabe let him go. His pace quickened as he searched around for Katie. As he rounded the corner of the hayshed, she stood only a few yards in front of him. Suddenly everything Betsy Cropp had told him went clean out of his mind. The air of confidence. The spring in his step. The sudden surge of bravery. His stomach came up to meet him and his big, pounding heart thumped in his brain as his legs went to jelly.

"Hello Gabe," Katie greeted him.

All he could do was exhale as her image filled his eyes. Katie McFarlane was drop-dead gorgeous. He always thought a woman had to wear make-up to fully highlight her features. Katie wasn't wearing any. He thought jeans were something for the paddock, not something someone could wear casually and look sensational. And he thought tight-fitting polo-necked jumpers were something a woman wore under a jacket if she didn't have time to iron a blouse. All his preconceived ideas were blown away in an instant with one glance at Betsy Cropp's house guest.

Katie could see how uneasy he was. "How are you. All set to show a city girl a thousand-acre paddock?"

"Er, yes, sure...would you like to go?" *You dopey bastard,* he cussed to himself, *you didn't even say hello. You didn't tell her she looked nice. What the fuck is wrong with you? Talk to her, idiot.* Slowly he regained his composure.

"Aunty Betsy put you to work already has she?"

Katie laughed. "Well I've fed the chooks and patted Stanley."

"So you've met the big fella?"

"Oh yes. Yesterday. Love him."

"Yeah, Aunty Betsy's got a bit of a thing about him. He makes her happy. Be a national bloody day of mourning the day that old bugger dies, I reckon. And it's a bit difficult to know how many years a horse like that will live. Twenty. Twenty-five maybe. I've made arrangements with a Clydesdale stud in the Adelaide Hills that when he does go, there'll be another one here the very next day to take his place. She doesn't know I've done that. But there seems to be some link with her past. She told me once her dad used to drive a team of them."

Now the conversation had begun to flow, Gabe was beginning to feel more at ease. He braced himself. "And I think you look very nice today."

Katie shot her glance at him and saw that he was looking at the ground, blushing profusely. "Oh Gabe, thank you. But I haven't been taking care of myself lately. I wonder though if Mrs Cropp mightn't have prompted you to try and pep me up a bit?"

"Well Aunty Betsy said..." He stopped mid-sentence, halted his stride, looked at her and smiled. "Forget what Aunty Betsy said. That's what I really think. I don't know why it is, but when I see you, I sort of get choked up and can't breathe properly. Then after a while it goes."

"Do you get like that when you are with other women?" Katie asked, careful to not give Gabe the slightest hint that she and Mrs Cropp had been talking.

He laughed awkwardly, not knowing how to answer. If he told Katie the truth, she would think he must be something of a country hick not ever having been out with a woman. If he went the other way, he would have to lie. He didn't want to lie. He didn't think he had a choice.

"Sometimes," he mumbled.

Katie could feel his mood relax a little and after being told by Mrs Cropp of all he did for her, she began to look at him differently. As they ambled back to the house, Katie glanced across at him on several occasions. She didn't think he looked his age. *Forty-one, forty-two maybe. Big hands. Big chest. Big, strong arms. Gee, not an ounce of fat on him. And from what Mrs Cropp has told me, he's obviously as strong as an ox.* She noticed a slight cleft in his chin. Square jaw. Rugged, almost handsome face, but not quite. But certainly not unattractive. A touch of grey at the temples and a few crows-feet. But it was his eyes. *I don't think I've ever noticed a man with such kind eyes*, she thought.

Once back inside, Gabe turned to Mrs Cropp. "We thought we might take a run around the place. Would you like to come?"

"You open your own gates," she jested. "No, no, you go ahead. Perhaps you better check on my ewes and lambs too while you're at it."

"Oh, wonderful. I've never seen baby lambs in their natural state," Katie said.

Mrs Cropp smiled as she watched the two of them leave the house. Gabe opened Katie's door, Joker hopped in after her and moments later they drove away.

Now I wonder what these people from Adelaide want? she thought.

* * *

The Holden utility was full of rust and full of dust. An old travel rug was stretched across the front bench seat. Katie figured the car itself was probably once cream in colour, but that must have been some while ago. It was now a distinctive off-white, brought about by neglect, too many winters and, going by the cracked and torn vinyl dashboard, far, far too many summers. Parts of the floor had rusted through leaving gaping holes and Katie could see where Gabe had attempted to cover them with old bits and pieces of rubber matting. The glove-box door was jammed tight with a piece of red-and-white cardboard. Katie could make out the lettering: *Twelve Gge. No. Four.* She wondered what it meant. Jammed up against the windscreen were a couple of packets of Thibenzole sheep drench, an unopened tin box containing rubber rings for tailing lambs, plus an assortment of chocolate and lolly wrappings. On the floor she noticed a pair of shears, the blades held together with thick twine, the remains of an old canvas waterbag and a clutter of tools including wire strainers, bolt cutters, a pipe wrench and an abundance of string.

Behind her on the parcel shelf, lying covered in dust was an old rifle and a packet of bullets. It was Gabe's single-shot twenty-two calibre Lithgow. As she craned her neck to glance into the rear of the utility, she couldn't believe her eyes. Drums of grease, a forty-four gallon drum of fuel, grease guns, windmill parts, fence posts, a tool box and *Lord knows what else*, she thought.

"So, how do you think you'd like to be a country girl?" Gabe asked Katie as he swung his vehicle from Mrs Cropp's driveway and headed towards his own place.

"Hard to say. I'm loving being here. It's making me forget. And right now I need to forget. I don't know. I think it would get very lonely. Does it get lonely Gabe?"

Gabe was fixed on the road ahead. It was a question he had never really asked himself. It was a question that had never before even been considered. Farm life was farm life. Seven days a week. Night and day. Fix this. Fix that. Bring the sheep in. Order the drench. Plough the paddocks. Reap the crops. Hope like hell the price of wool stays up. Cart the hay. With Katie McFarlane in the car, suddenly he realised farm life was as lonely as blazes.

"It's not something I've ever really thought about," he told her. "I guess if you're born and raised on the land, that's all you know, and for the sake of not knowing any different, you just sort of plod along."

"So no burning desires to go out and see the world?"

Gabe shook his head. He'd never been asked anything about that before either. "Sometimes I look at the travel section in the paper and there's things in there like Disneyland, Las Vegas, Victoria Falls, The Rocky Mountains." He attempted a laugh, but Katie sensed it was hollow. "Hell I wouldn't know what to do if I went there. Besides, I can't imagine going to those sorts of places on my own. Good God, I haven't even been to Robe and that's only seventy-two miles away."

Katie smiled, but she felt sad for him. She got the feeling that even though Gabe was a little blasé about it, he wasn't comfortable in making such admissions. She felt him ease his foot off the accelerator and bring his vehicle to a halt. She watched him peering through the windscreen. "Do you want to see where it happened?"

Katie's thoughts flashed back to the accident. "I guess we're pretty close to the spot are we?"

"Do you remember anything about driving along this road?"

Katie shook her head. "Not really. It was pitch black. The thunder and lightning I guess. And the rain. I remember the rain and that's it."

Gabe drove on a little further and stopped again. "Just up there," he pointed.

Katie looked through the windscreen and noticed wheel tracks veering off the main road. Gabe proceeded another fifty metres then stopped again. He got out of the car and went around to Katie's door. As he opened it, Joker hopped out and Gabe assisted Katie. For a few moments the two of them looked at the scene. Deeply gouged car tracks and drag marks. A carpet of debris made up of tree remnants and the sawn-up remains of a giant limb.

"This is what fell on my car?"

Gabe nodded his head. "Must weigh a tonne. I had to get the chainsaw so I could clear it off the road."

Katie stared disbelievingly at the massive lump of timber. "How on earth did I ever survive that?"

"Someone was watching over you I think. Amazing isn't it?"

"But it's gigantic. How on earth did you ever get me out?"

Gabe felt flushed with pride. "Just did I guess," he shrugged.

Katie walked slowly over to Gabe and put her arms around his waist and reached up to kiss him on the cheek. "Thank you. I think you are simply amazing."

Gabe felt the tinglings of emotions within himself he never knew existed. He didn't say anything. He couldn't. There were no words. He felt his eyes water a little as Katie's closeness swept him away.

When Katie released her arms from Gabe's waist, she was a little taken aback at the hardness of his body. Subconsciously, she compared it to Paul's and couldn't believe the difference. Paul was a much younger man with a degree of athleticism about him. His body was firm and taut. But Gabe's was different. Years of toiling and lifting on the farm had created a skin and muscle texture which was pure strength. Gabe also smelled different. Apart from the freshness of his just having showered, she depicted a certain aroma which didn't come from a cologne bottle. She couldn't determine quite what it was, but it wasn't something she found unattractive.

Gabe walked a few paces. "Your car stopped about here," he told her. "When I got you out, it was bucketing down, so I put my raincoat over you, told Joker here to lie close to you, then went for help."

Katie leaned down to Joker who was wagging his tail ten to the dozen. "So you're the one who kept me warm," she said, cupping his head affectionately in her hands. "I think you're wonderful too," she said, pressing his head against her cheek.

"So there it is. I've cleaned it up a bit, but I've gotta tell you, things were a bloody mess up here. You want to see your car?"

Katie grimaced. "I guess so. I've been dreading this moment."

"Maybe it's best you don't?"

Katie walked back to the car. "After seeing that tree and listening to what you told me, there's probably not much of it left!"

"Well I can tell you, you can't tow it. I had to drag it down to the shed. Actually, it's been crushed pretty well beyond recognition."

"Would you mind if I didn't see it? I think I'd prefer to remember my little Honda the way it was."

"I've put a tarp over it, so you won't see it if you don't want to. Was it insured?" Katie nodded. "Okay, I'll get onto the insurance mob and get them to come and collect it. I've taken out everything that was in it. That's all inside. Should pretty well have all dried out by now."

Gabe climbed in behind the wheel and drove down to his house. "Well this is it. Home sweet home," he told her. "It's not much," he went on, "but it keeps the rain off."

Katie looked around. She thought houses like this only existed in history books. She could see it was old and tired. She doubted if it had ever seen a paint brush or that Gabe had ever walked around with a hammer and a nail to carry out the smallest of maintenance jobs. But she wasn't concerned. She also felt that, apart from Mrs Cropp, she was probably the only other person to ever go there.

"And you've lived here all your life?"

"Never been off the place," he told her, getting out of the vehicle. "I reckon to avoid getting bogged down in some of those back paddocks, we better go on the tractor."

"Is there room to sit?"

"There is on my old girl. She's an old Case which means there's plenty of room around the driver's seat. I only put the head back on her yesterday, so I hope she goes."

Gabe walked off to the shed and climbed onto his tractor. Katie heard the sound of the tractor's engine burst into life and, a few seconds later, Gabe was making his way towards her. "Do you reckon you can climb up here?" he called over the top of the engine noise, indicating how she should get aboard. He leaned back in his seat and offered her his hand. "Careful you don't skin your knees on something!" He had folded an old blanket and placed it on the battery cover, which was attached to the vehicle's rear mudguard, opposite where he sat. Katie found her way to the crammed position, tucking her legs in under herself as best she could so they wouldn't be in Gabe's road as he worked the foot controls.

"All set?" he asked.

Katie nodded, a flush of exhilaration on her face.

Then he called to Joker. "Get up here!" Katie wasn't sure how the dog managed to do it, but he scrambled up the rear of the tractor and jumped into Gabe's lap.

"Have I stolen his seat?" Katie called, trying to compete with the engine noise.

"He'll be right. Sometimes he sits where you've got your legs, but mostly he's not happy unless he's driving the bloody thing."

Being on board a tractor was a whole new experience for Katie McFarlane. As the big machine moved off, she was surprised to see how far she was off the ground. As she felt around for some hand-holds, a large smile fell across her face. "Oh wow! I've never done this before," she called.

"You want to have a look over the paddocks before we go round up the sheep?"

Katie nodded as she turned her face into the wind and closed her eyes. For the next hour, Gabe drove the big Case tractor all over his farm. Katie loved every minute of it and told him so. Especially an area which had a creek running through it. Lining its banks were massive red gums.

"There's bigger ones over at Aunty Betsy's," he told her, killing the engine. "I'll show you later."

"They're so big, so majestic. Is that the right word? It's hard to believe people actually cut them down isn't it?"

Gabe was a little taken aback by the comments. He opened his mouth to speak, but thought better of it. He knew the comments were simply those of a naïve city girl who happened to like trees. But at the same time he realised city folk would have a different perspective. "You don't think they should be cut down?"

"Well I know there wouldn't be a lot of houses and tables and chairs and firewood if we didn't, but there has to be a better way."

Gabe was annoyed with himself for selling her short. "Like what?"

Katie thought for a moment. "Like planting another one in its place so that in a hundred years time, our grandkids will be able to admire them too." Katie looked at him, sensing conflict. "You don't agree?"

Gabe decided to let it ride. "Like to see the ewes and lambs?"

"That's a cop out!" she came back at him.

Their eyes met. "Hey, I'm not going to cut it down. This one or for that matter, any of them. But you'll find it pretty hard convincing cockies to leave trees like this in their paddocks, or even replace them if they chop them down. Trees like this suck all the nutrients from the soil leaving nothing for their crops. If you've got thirty or forty big red gums in a paddock, you're not going to get much of a yield. Not only that, you can't get in close to them with the tractor and plough because of their root structure, so in effect you're also losing a lot of acreage."

"I guess I just like trees," she told him forlornly.

"Tell you what," he said, endeavoring to brighten her up. "As long as I'm around, no one will ever lay a hand on these red gums, Okay? So that means if I've got about fifty years to fill in, that'll be plenty of time for your grandkids to come and see them. That's a farmer's promise to you, so you know it's good. Now, would you like to see the ewes and lambs?"

As they headed towards the bottom end of his farm, a mob of about six hundred ewes came into focus. Overnight, many had dropped their lambs. As Gabe dropped the vehicle to an idle, he scanned the mob. Several ewes were down and in the process of lambing, while several more were standing by the dead remains of their off-spring. Gabe cussed.

"Bloody mongrel bastards! Bloody mongrel bastards! Jesus Christ!"

Katie became alarmed. "Are they all dead?" she asked, not believing she was seeing so many lifeless patches of white.

"Yeah they're dead!" he told her in a tone which suggested he'd seen it all a hundred times before. "Foxes. Bloody foxes." He brought the tractor to a standstill, lifted Joker off his lap, put him on the big mudguard and stood on his seat. He began to count out loud. "Two, five, ten, twelve, fifteen. Jesus Katie the bastards got about fifteen and that's from what I can see up here."

Katie looked at the carcass of one which was close by the tractor. "So why don't they eat them if they kill them?"

"Because they're vicious, mongrel bastards. They kill for the sake of it. Eat the heart and lungs and go onto the next one. Looks like I better run the spotlight round tonight." He stepped down from the seat and drove deeper into the paddock. Katie saw he had spotted a ewe off in the distance. About six crows were picking at its head. He throttled the engine and headed towards it. The crows flew off immediately and seconds later Gabe was by its side. He cussed again.

"Hop off boy," he said to Joker and went to the tool box of the tractor and took out a long-bladed knife. "Don't look Katie," he said.

"What are you going to do?"

"I'll tell you shortly. Look away."

Gabe walked over to the ewe and cut its throat. He walked back to the tractor, pulled a rag from the toolbox and wiped the blade. "You saw those crows didn't you?" Katie nodded. "They're the other mongrel bastards. Sometimes sheep get down on their side and can't get up. If you don't spot them, the dopey buggers will die there, and yet all they have to do is roll over and they could get up on their feet. But they don't. The crows spot their plight, see them as easy pickings, then converge on them and pick their eyes out."

Katie gasped. "While they're still alive?"

"Yep. That's what they did with this one. So you have to kill them. Actually this one's got a lamb somewhere. See the afterbirth?" he told her, scanning around. About sixty yards away, Gabe spotted a lamb on its own. "That'd be him over there. Go fetch him, Joker."

Joker bounded away and Katie watched as Gabe's dog herded the lamb back to Gabe. Katie saw him reach for an axe he had fixed to the rear of the tractor. "So what happens to that little fellow?"

"You can't do much for them either. Other ewes won't take them. You have to knock them on the head."

Katie was horrified. "You're not going to kill it are you?"

"Don't look!" Gabe told her again. Joker cleverly brought the small animal closer to his master. In an instant Gabe bolted a few steps and grabbed hold of it.

"Oh no Gabe, please don't kill it," she blurted, hurrying to climb down from the tractor. She quickly went to Gabe as he was cradling the orphaned lamb in his arms. "Can I hold him?"

Gabe was stunned by Katie's reaction. Knocking such animals on the head had always been the accepted thing on a farm. Now he was being challenged.

"Oh look at him," Katie said, putting her face against its head. "What a marvellous smell! Do all newborn lambs smell like this?"

"You can't take the bloody thing to Melbourne."

"Oh Gabe, and you can't kill it either. Look at the poor little darling. Is it a boy or a girl?"

Gabe lifted up its tail. "It's a girl, not that it'll make any difference."

"Can't we take it home?"

"And do what?"

"Couldn't we feed it and raise it?...pleeeease," she pleaded.

Gabe knew it went against all his better judgment. "Yeah, but hang on. You'll be gone in a few days. Who's going to look after it then?"

"Pleeease," she went on, offering Gabe a look of such sorrow it destroyed all his defenses. She too was very aware she was laying on the feminine charm.

"Christ Katie! If I take a pet lamb over to Aunty Betsy's she'll ring me bloody neck."

"No, I mean you. Won't you look after her? What if I send you some money to feed her?"

Gabe was down for the count and he knew it. There wasn't a snowball's chance in hell he could refuse Katie. "But there's probably going to be others as well!," he protested. "You want me to keep them all?"

Katie didn't say anything, content to nestle her face against the orphaned lamb. Gabe only had to see the look she gave him to know her answer.

"Well bugger me!' he cussed.

And there were more. By the time they had finished going around all six hundred sheep, there were four orphaned lambs. They couldn't be carried on the tractor, so Gabe put them in the corner of a paddock where two fences joined. He called his dog over, leaned down and put his arms around him.

"You stay with them boy, okay? You stay here now. We'll go back and get the ute."

Joker did. When Gabe and Katie returned half an hour later, Joker still had four baby lambs under his care. After going around Mrs Cropp's ewes and lambs, Gabe and Katie turned up a further two. Back at Gabe's house, the big man leaned against his utility and looked in on the newly acquired orphans. "Okay, now what are you going to do?"

Katie joined him. "What would you normally do?"

Gabe knew only too well what was involved in keeping pet lambs. Three feeds a day out of a bottle with a baby's teat. He would have to go over to Mrs Cropp's to get the milk and if she didn't have enough, make up the rest from powder. It had been thirty five years since he'd bothered with pet lambs. But if that's what Katie wanted, he was only too pleased to oblige.

Gabe left the lambs in the back of the utility and made his way to the shed. In no time at all he had constructed a small holding-pen from wire netting off-cuts and a dozen or so iron droppers. He put the lambs in the pen and spoke to Katie. "Any ideas about some warm milk, a baby's bottle and a teat?"

Katie glanced over at him, her eyes taking on a sadness which Gabe didn't enjoy. He moved quickly to remedy the situation. "Aunty Betsy's got all that stuff. Okay? And don't go bloody sending any cheques from Melbourne."

"But..."

"No cheques alright? Christ, I'll look after the damn things for you. Don't worry about it."

"Well I can do it while I'm here," she offered.

Gabe laughed. "No, no, I'll do it. When they're big enough and can fend for themselves, I'll put them back in the paddock."

Katie moved towards Gabe, put her hands around one of his massive arms and rested her head against it. "Thank you," she murmured. "I couldn't stand the thought of you killing these poor little things just because they lost their mother."

Katie's touch rendered him as helpless as the lambs he was looking after. A faint waft of her perfume filled his nose. His eyes clouded a little and his skin became peppered with goosebumps. Katie lifted her head and their eyes met. Probably for a moment longer than they should have. Katie's, out of gratitude; Gabe's, because he was too powerless to do anything about it.

* * *

The bleating seemed to go on all night. Even though Gabe closed all the doors in the house, the cries of the six orphaned lambs penetrated walls, windows and doors. No sooner would he drop off to sleep and he'd be awake again. At first light, he got up, made himself some breakfast and began to organise the milk bottles. Suddenly, he was struck with an idea.

"Come on boy," he said to Joker. "Can't wait for this."

Minutes later he arrived outside Mrs Cropp's house. The sun was creeping over the horizon. Next instant, two enormous blasts shattered the early morning's silence. Hundreds of white cockatoos scrambled into the air from the nearby pine trees, screeching and squawking their disapproval to such a rude awakening. Numerous other birds from surrounding trees were also panicked into flight. Joker stood next to Gabe, frantically wagging his tail. He knew that normally such a noise meant he'd soon be out after a rabbit or a fox. But on this particular occasion, neither would be the quarry. Another blast shattered the quiet Sunday morning. Mrs Cropp appeared at the front door in her dressing gown. When she looked out, she saw Gabe leaning against the bonnet of his utility wearing the biggest grin she'd seen in years. He was holding a twelve-gauge shotgun.

"What on earth's going on?" she demanded.

"Morning Aunty Betsy," he called to her. "Where's that city sheila?" He put the shotgun on the front seat and walked to the house.

"What on earth are you doing?" Mrs Cropp asked.

"She's got work to do," he replied, heading for the kitchen. "Those bloody lambs have kept me awake all night. If I couldn't get any sleep, there's no reason why she should either. Is she up?"

"Keep your voice down dear, she'd still be asleep."

Gabe laughed, "Well I better let off another couple."

"Don't you dare!" Mrs Cropp said.

He was filling the kettle when they heard a voice from the passageway.

"Gabe?" It was Katie, still in her pyjamas and dressing gown. "What's all the noise?"

"Well, good morning Miss McFarlane," he piped.

"What are you doing here? It's still er, midnight."

Gabe put the kettle on the stove, added some kindling and opened the vents in the flue to produce some quick heat. He looked at Katie. Even with the sleep still in her eyes and a brush still to find her hair, she still looked divine.

Mrs Cropp went to Katie and put her arm around her. "You hop back into bed. Gabe's just being silly."

"Hang on Aunty Betsy!" He focused on Katie. "You know all those lambs we've got up in the shed? You're gonna feed them."

"Oh Gabe, don't be ridiculous. She should still be in bed," Mrs Cropp cut in.

Gabe ignored the comment. "So you better get dressed, because there's milk to be warmed up, bottles to be filled."

Katie's attention went to Mrs Cropp, then to Gabe and back to Mrs Cropp.

"Have you ever fed pet lambs before?" Mrs Cropp asked.

"No."

"Do you feel alright?"

Katie nodded and offered a smile.

"Then I guess it's time you learned," Mrs Cropp told her.

Katie shot a glance at Gabe. "Two minutes," she said.

Driving back to Gabe's farm, Katie, with Joker at her feet, asked, "Does it take very long?"

"Depends on how good you are at getting them to drink from a bottle," Gabe smirked.

"Why do I think it's not going to be easy?"

"Tell you what," he went on. "I'll bet after your first experience, you'll never want to have pet lambs again."

"It can't be that bad!"

"We'll see."

"Was that you who came over last night? I had only been in bed a few minutes when I heard a car and voices in the kitchen."

"Aunty Betsy helped me get some milk and milk powder made up. Scrimmaged around and found some bottles and a teat."

"Did you go spotlighting?"

"Went out for a couple of hours at midnight. Got a couple of rabbits for Joker. Seven foxes. Big buggers too!"

Katie could see the justification in killing the foxes but she couldn't help but think there had to be an alternative. She consoled herself in thinking this was the way of farm life, and probably had been for centuries. *But I still don't have to like it. Then again, I like even less what they do to poor little lambs.*

Gabe pulled up outside his house. It wasn't long before the milk and the milk formulas had been warmed and the two made their way to the shed. Katie was struck at the constant bleating.

"Been that way all night," he told her.

"Are they hungry or are they missing their mothers?"

"Bit of both I guess." At the wire-netting enclosure, Gabe told her, "You'll need to hop in there and catch them one at a time and get them to take the bottle."

Katie saw the wry grin on his face. "You don't think I can, do you?"

Gabe giggled. As Katie began to climb over the wire netting, she paused. "I think I'm caught." The material on the inside of her trouser leg had snagged. Katie had one leg on one side of the wire netting and the other on the other side, straddling it.

"Now what are you gonna do?" he asked.

"Oooh," she cursed, trying to free herself.

"I'll lift you off and you can start again. Put your arms around my neck." Gabe reached and lifted her, the snag freeing itself as he did so. He revelled in the opportunity to again get close to Katie; and for the moment it lasted, Katie enjoyed being wrapped in his powerful arms. It offered her a sense of security. Something she was desperately crying out for.

Now inside the small pen, she slowly approached the lambs who had bunched together in a corner. Quickly she grabbed one and stood there holding it. She glanced at Gabe, and he knew instantly she didn't have the faintest idea of what to do next. He turned on his heel, picked up a bale of hay and tossed it into the pen.

"Sit on that," he told her. "Put the lamb between your legs, keep hold of its head and put the teat in its mouth."

Katie sat on the bale of hay but, as she was trying to put the lamb in between her legs, it slipped her grasp and sprang free. Quickly she headed for the group of six and again grabbed one. But again, as she tried to put it between her legs, the same thing happened. Gabe stood outside the enclosure, suppressing a massive belly laugh, but not sufficiently well enough that Katie didn't spot it.

"Alright smartie-pants, you do it," she said.

Gabe couldn't contain himself any longer and laughed loud and long. More determined, Katie again went through her routine. Again, the lamb slipped her grasp. Gabe finally relented. He climbed into the enclosure. Quickly, he grabbed a lamb, sat on the edge of the bale of hay and clamped his thighs around it. "Okay, hand me a bottle."

Gabe poked his little finger into the lamb's mouth. As it began to suckle, he eased the teat on the bottle into its mouth and withdrew his finger. Within moments, its tail started to wag and it began to bunt the bottle. Katie giggled.

"Look at the tail! And why is it bunting the bottle?"

"Thinks it's his mother. They reckon by doing that they're gonna get more to drink. They all do it. Here, you take over."

Katie sat next to Gabe on the bale of hay and he transferred the small animal over to her. "Keep your legs tight in against him, then he won't get away. Get them to suck your finger first, then slide the teat in, in its place. You won't get 'em to suck otherwise!"

Katie held the bottle but nearly lost it several times as the little lamb bunted and bunted and bunted. The faster the tail wriggled, the harder the other end bunted. Katie gave out shrieks of delight. Finally the bottle was empty. Gabe mounted the wire- netting enclosure as Katie caught another lamb and the same process repeated itself. After four had been fed, she said to Gabe, "How will we know which ones have been fed and which ones haven't?"

He pointed to the lambs. "Look at their tummies. That'll give you some idea."

"I see what you mean. They look like they're going to burst."

Finally the bleating stopped, all the milk was gone and Katie climbed from the enclosure. She was overjoyed at her accomplishments. "I had to have some help, but I did do it didn't I? I really did it. Even got them sucking my finger."

Gabe smiled. "Yes Miss McFarlane, you did indeed."

"So how often do they have to be fed?"

Gabe scratched the back of his head. "Where will you be in about four hours?"

"Oh Lord! Gee I'm sorry. But we couldn't have left them to die. Could we?"

"Let's say you must have got me at a weak moment."

"Oh you don't mean that."

Gabe looked at her. He did mean it. But he also knew that no matter whatever it was that this woman would ask him to do, he would. Already he was dreading the moment when he knew she would leave.

As they started walking from the shed to the house, Katie spotted a large tarpaulin. She paused to look more closely. "Is that it?" she asked, a tinge of sadness in her tone, as though pre-empting Gabe's answer.

"You don't need to see it," he told her.

Katie accepted Gabe's assurance and continued her walk back to the house.

* * *

Over lunch at Mrs Cropp's house, Katie was full of enthusiasm and conversation about feeding the lambs. Mrs Cropp listened intently, taking great consolation in being able to provide some sunshine in the young woman's life.

As she served up sago plum pudding and icecream, Gabe put a question to Katie. "So you have visitors tomorrow?"

Katie nodded. "Just some special friends from Adelaide," she said, not wanting to enlarge. "I'm sure they won't be here long."

Gabe could sense she didn't want to talk about it. "I'll ring your insurance mob in the morning and get your car sorted out."

Katie didn't answer. Instead, she offered him a grateful smile of acknowledgment. Gabe wiped the dishes despite protests from Katie, then decided to go back to his own place.

"Will you be back later?" Katie wanted to know.

"Absolutely. I'm not feeding those lambs on my own."

Just on dusk, Gabe arrived back at Mrs Cropp's. "I know, I know, feed time," Katie told him, matter-of-factly.

"You want to come over Aunty Betsy?"

Ten minutes later, Mrs Cropp sat on a bale of hay watching Gabe and Katie feed the lambs. It thrilled her to see such an activity. *People really don't do this anymore*, she thought sadly.

"Aren't they gorgeous?" Katie said, pushing her face into the wool around the neck of one. "They smell wonderful."

"I've always liked the smell of them," Mrs Cropp agreed. "You'll miss all of this won't you?"

Katie looked at her. "It's another world all of this, isn't it?"

"That it is," Mrs Cropp nodded. "That it is. So you were serious when you said you'd never fed baby lambs before?"

"Good heavens yes. I've never been on a farm before. Thank you for bringing me here."

To Gabe and Mrs Cropp, there seemed a certain finality in how they heard Katie's words. Neither of them wanted to face the fact that it wouldn't be too long and she'd be leaving.

Chapter 21

Gabe sensed a change of mood had come over Katie McFarlane. She had suddenly become quiet. Perhaps the effects of the accident were finally starting to take their toll. Mrs Cropp sensed it too. She caught Gabe's eye, and lightly shook her head. Gabe knew it meant Mrs Cropp thought Katie wanted to be alone. He offered no protest.

On the drive back to Mrs Cropp's house, Katie didn't speak. Inside she was bursting with gratitude for the kindness shown to her by Gabe and the woman driving the car. But she knew such moments of farm life she had experienced would soon end and she'd have to leave. She wondered if she would ever see these people again. She made a promise to herself she would. Tomorrow Gabe would contact her insurance company about her car. Then there were the people coming down from Adelaide.

When the two women walked inside, Katie went into the lounge room, curled up in a big armchair, arched her arm and rested her head in her hand. Moments later she found herself looking at a framed photograph on the mantelpiece. As she concentrated more closely on it, she felt the man in the photo was staring straight back at her. She moved her head a little, but still the eyes followed her. Curiosity got the better of her, so she moved to take a closer look. As she approached the mantelpiece, still his eyes came straight back at her. From a distance of a couple of feet she could see its black-and-white texture had taken on the sepia tinge of old age.

Katie heard Mrs Cropp enter the room. "What a nice-looking man. Who is it?" she asked.

"That's my man Katie. You see I too have had a sadness, but mine of course was long, long ago."

"Oh I'm sorry..."

Mrs Cropp waved aside her apology. "No, no, it's alright. That's my Cyril. We were married for eleven glorious months," she told Katie, looking affectionately at the photograph. "Killed himself on his damn tractor...oh, over forty years ago now."

But Katie could tell from the look on her face that, if pressed, she would know to the day, exactly how long ago it was. Katie put her arms around her. "And you only had him for eleven months?" She now stepped closer to the photograph. "What was his name?"

"Cyril. Darling, wonderful Cyril. I guess in life you only get one shot at it...many people wouldn't agree I guess, but if it really is the bells and whistles, heaven knows, nothing or anyone could ever replace it. Certainly Cyril had that effect on me. And I think I had that effect on him. And when he was taken, my whole world fell apart. I think I was numb for ten years. Certainly, I only ever went through the motions of living. His loss left such a hole in my heart. The hole's still there, but Father Time has had his way I guess." As she spoke, she opened a drawer from a cupboard and withdrew a leather-bound box. It was velvet lined and contained a photo album. Mrs Cropp handed it to Katie. "I've never even shown this to Gabe," she told her.

Katie opened the album and began to turn the pages featuring black-and-white snaps of Cyril and Betsy Cropp. A few pages in she came across a wedding card. She looked to Mrs Cropp, who nodded her approval to open it. It was from Cyril to his wife on their wedding day. He chose to write his own verse.

> *To my dearest darling Betsy,*
> *If I owned every spoken word*
> *I'd give them all away*
> *Except the three I need to say*
> *I love you.*
> *Forever yours, Cyril XXX.'*

Katie was visibly touched by the sentiment and reached for a tissue to dab her eyes.

"After something like that, there was no question we were soul mates and anyone else could only ever be second best. I decided I didn't want that and have lived on my own ever since."

Katie closed the photo album and replaced it in the the leather box.

"But enough of me," said Mrs Cropp. "Will you tell me about you? Tell me what happened to you? When we met, you seemed so happy."

Katie took a few steps across the lounge-room floor. She inhaled deeply. "The man you met with me at the club that day was Paul Redman," she began. "We were going to be married. On the day he was to propose to me, he was killed in a plane crash."

"Oh Katie..."

Katie raised her arm. "No, no, now that I've started, let me go on. He had his friend in Renmark make my wedding and engagement rings. And Paul being Paul, he had to make the big impression. He had arranged for both our families to be together on this particular day. He used to fly his own plane and, while we were all together, word came through he'd crashed." Katie could hold back no longer and the tears began to flow. "He used to write little poems for me too. Oh God, I miss him..." Her words dissolved into a faint whisper and she was unable to continue. Mrs Cropp went to her. The two women held onto each other. "And..and just like that big hole you felt inside your heart is exactly like the huge, gaping hole that's in mine."

Silence fell between them for a brief period allowing Katie to regain control. "After we buried Paul, my mum and dad were killed in a car smash. So that did it for me. After a while, I'd had enough of this grief business and decided to start a new life. You see, I work as a nurse and I was on my way to Melbourne to try and get a job. Then this happened."

Mrs Cropp had made her way to one of her lounge chairs. It was as though she was stricken with heart pain. "Oh Lord, Katie, and here we are taking you around paddocks and goodness knows what else..."

Katie smiled. "Oh don't apologise for that. Right now, you and Gabe are the most wonderful thing that's happened in my life and I thank God you came to see me in hospital. As for bringing me out here, I don't know how I could ever thank you. And Gabe. I think he'll always be my hero. I mean what can you say about a man who saves your life? From the small amount of time we've spent together he's been so gentle and compassionate I do believe what you told me. His heart is as big as this farm. I mean he hasn't had to try and accommodate me. He must surely have more to do than explain about gum trees and pet lambs. But he has been so giving. And so have you. The clothes. The room. Mrs Cropp, I don't know what to say. Please let me pay you something."

Mrs Cropp rose to her feet and almost scolded Katie. "You will do nothing of the kind. Now you listen to me. Neither Gabe Caplin or Betsy Cropp have done anything we didn't choose to do. And something else too. When you leave here, and I have to tell you Gabe and I are dreading the moment, your room will stay your room. It will always be made up should you ever wish to return. Now there'll be nothing more said on the matter. I just happen to think you are a very special person. I knew it from the first time I met you. It saddens my heart you have suffered so much in your short life. I know all about that, as I've told you. And while you're in this house, I will do my darndest to see that sadness stays the hell away from you."

Katie too had grown very fond of Mrs Cropp. She hoped she had sufficient strength of character to live up to the highly held opinions Mrs Cropp had of her. "You take my breath away with your generosity," Katie cried, wiping away her tears as she continued to move around the lounge room. She'd sit for a moment. Then she'd walk a few steps. Look out a window. Then she went to the piano and opened its lid. With one finger, she lightly touched one key, then another. She looked at Mrs Cropp through clouded, tear-filled eyes.

Mrs Cropp nodded. "Are you sure?"

Katie nodded and a few moments later the sounds of a very familiar song filled the room. Katie again curled herself into a lounge chair as the memories of Paul Redman and The Oakdale Country Club came flooding back.

Later that night, as she lay in bed with the sounds of the Black Hawk still fresh in her mind, she tried to put into perspective all the things that had happened to her in such a short space of time. She had met Paul and lost him. She had lost her parents. She wondered if she'd ever see The Oakdale Country Club again. And for that matter, any of Paul's extended family? The staff at the Royal Adelaide? Will she find a job in Melbourne? Tomorrow's meeting with her solicitor and Paul's parents.

I must keep coming back here to see Mrs Cropp. And Gabe. God that man's as solid as a rock. So different to Paul. Then she was confused as to why she would want to even compare the two. *I wonder what he really thinks of me? In fact he's so different from any man I've ever met. I certainly don't find it any imposition to be around him.* But underpinning all her thoughts was the gut-wrenching grief of having lost Paul Redman and her parents. Right now what she needed was time, and she knew it. Time to re-focus. Time to regain her self-control. Time to forget.

But Mrs Cropp said she had never gotten over her Cyril. Oh Lord, you know I love Paul. Is that what you want for me too? I do so want to love Lord. And I do so want to be loved. Tell me Lord? Tell me what you want from me?

* * *

Gabe couldn't sleep. It wasn't the lambs that kept him awake. It was Katie McFarlane. He could still smell the fragrance of her perfume. He tried to savour it, but gradually it began to fade. So he climbed out of bed, grabbed the torch and headed outside to his utility. He went to the passenger side, opened the door, and a smile fell across his face. *That's it*, he thought, as he put his head in the cabin around the area where Katie had sat.

Satisfied she was still 'with' him, he went back to bed. He wondered why he'd left it so late in life and never bothered to pursue an interest in women. *Didn't see too many who looked like her I guess. And those who displayed a bit of promise were quickly snapped up.* He wondered too, what would become of Katie McFarlane after she left. If he'd ever see her again. If Mrs Cropp would ever see her again. *Probably not*, he thought. *Probably not.* And it saddened him. But he also realised the truth in Mrs Cropp's statement that women like her don't belong on farms.

He also tried to come to terms with why he was so affected by her presence. The more he thought about her, the more he desired to be with her. But he also came to the realisation that Katie McFarlane would only be a brief interlude in his life. He didn't know how he'd react when she actually left. In fact he refused to even think about it.

Right now, she would be lying in bed over at his Aunty Betsy's place and, in a few hours time, he would once again be with her.

* * *

Monday morning Betsy Cropp rose early. She wanted to get all her chores out of the way before Katie's visitors arrived from Adelaide. Besides, having guests gave her an excuse to display her very best china and linen. By the time Katie showered and dressed, Mrs Cropp had already set the dining-room table. The aroma of freshly baked scones filtered its way through the house, enticing her to the kitchen. Two trays of brown topped delights caught her eye. She stood admiring them and leaned over to get a closer smell.

"The butter's in the fridge," Mrs Cropp told her.

Katie needed no encouragement. She quickly buttered a scone and rolled her eyes in sheer delight at the first bite. "Oh wow! Mmmm, they are scrumptious," she said, walking into the lounge room. When she saw the setting on the dining table, her eyes widened in total surprise. "Oh you shouldn't have..."

"Nonsense. I enjoy getting out the good stuff. It's pretty rare these days that I do, so it was a good excuse."

Katie stood back admiring Mrs Cropp's finest possessions. The lace tablecloth, the Wedgwood tea and coffee service, a very large platter filled with savories. She had also added every conceivable extra to the tea and coffee service, including sweet bowls were filled with chocolates, other smaller dishes and a large bread-plate.

"Do you think they'll be on time?" queried Mrs Cropp.

Katie nodded. "Early if anything."

* * *

Gabe Caplin was also up early. Katie's presence had given him added purpose in his life, though he knew it to be only temporary. Up until the day she arrived, the last thing on his mind would have been rescuing and taking care of orphaned lambs. Now he was revelling in the task. Even while he was warming the milk on the stove, he ducked across to his old ute, opened the passenger door and smelled the interior of the vehicle.

Good, it's still there, he thought, absorbing as much as he could of what remained of Katie McFarlane's presence. He desperately wanted to see her, but his thoughts went back to how she was the day before. With the last of the lambs now with a full belly, he wandered back to the house and sat on the verandah. Joker sensed his melancholy mood and pushed his head under his arm.

"What do you reckon boy? Want to see her again? Yeah, yeah, I know. Me too. But it's probably best if we stay away today. I got the feeling yesterday she wanted to be on her own for awhile. Besides, she's got some people coming to see her. No, no, we'll stay put today. We'll go and see her tomorrow."

* * *

As it happened, Gabe saw Katie a lot sooner than he thought. Just after lunch he took a frantic call from Mrs Cropp that Katie had fled the house in total distress. The last she saw of her was going through the gate adjoining their properties. Gabe immediately set off in search. Five minutes later, he could tell the vehicle in the distance belonged to Betsy Cropp. Panic gripped his gut and he floored the throttle in his ute. Quickly he came upon the vehicle, but there was no one in it. He reefed open the door.

"Katie!" he called. "Katie!" he called again. Louder this time. Then he heard her voice.

"Over here Gabe," she answered, disconsolately. She was sitting on a log under one of the big red gums she had admired the day before.

Gabe rushed to her side, fearing something terrible had happened to her. "Katie? Oh shit! We were worried sick. Are you alright?"

She didn't answer. Focused on the ground, she nodded.

"Aunty Betsy called and said you just took off down the paddock. Hell I didn't know what to do. The only thing I could think of was maybe you'd come back here to the trees. You sure you're alright?"

Katie again nodded. Gabe was enormously relieved. He wiped the nervous perspiration from his brow. "Well, alright then. Shit! You frightened hell out of all of us. I better get back and tell Aunty Betsy you're okay. Guess we didn't think you might have wanted to be on your own for awhile. It's been quite a week for you hasn't it? I'll be up at the house if you need anything."

Gabe turned to leave but Katie's words halted his stride. "Don't go," she murmured.

Gabe turned to face her. Tears flowed freely from her eyes. Immediately he sprung to conclusions. "Have those mongrels from Adelaide done this to you?" he said, handing her his handkerchief.

Katie shook her head. "It's not what you think Gabe. Absolutely nothing like that at all," she sobbed.

Gabe sat down next to her. Joker came over and lay at Katie's feet, his head tilted to one side and his ears pricked as if he too sensed something didn't seem right.

"Gabe," she began. "When you dragged me out of my car, I was on my way to Melbourne to start a new life. My mum and dad had been killed in a car accident and the man I was going to marry had died in a plane crash. His name was Paul. Paul Redman. It turned out he was very wealthy. He had his own architecture business in Adelaide and he also owned a place in Mildura called The Oakdale Country Club." She dabbed at her eyes, cleared her nose and continued. "Oh boy!" she went on, forcing a smile. "You should see that place. He had spent a fortune on it. It was so grand. Paul died the day he was going to propose to me. A few days earlier he changed his will. God I can't believe this! He changed his will leaving everything to me."

"You serious?" Gabe gasped.

Katie nodded. "And I know it's true, because he did it on video and this morning I was shown the tape."

"Well bugger me! So does that mean you're now very wealthy?"

Again Katie nodded. "It appears that way. But Gabe I can't accept that," she added. "He's left me his car, his inheritance, his club...oh God, what am I going to do?"

Gabe smiled. "Hell I don't see the problem..."

"But Gabe, I can't take any of that! He has brothers and sisters. His parents are still alive. And it's old money. Money that's been in his family. What do you think those people will think of me?"

"So that's what this is all about?" Katie didn't answer. She mopped more tears from her eyes. Gabe knew it was. He rose from the log and walked a few steps. "Who were the people who came to see you?"

"Paul's mum and dad and my solicitor."

"What have they had to say?"

"They've been wonderful. Mr and Mrs Redman bear no malice whatsoever. They say if it was Paul's wish, then so be it. They said the situation has been discussed with the whole family and they're more than happy to abide by Paul's wishes too."

"So what's the problem?"

"The problem is I don't know what to do. I am still very much in love with Paul. Having his car, his money and his club surely will only be a constant reminder of someone I wanted to grow old with, but who was taken from me. I don't think I could live with the daily pain of having everything about him around me and never being able to see him again. Besides, I'm a simple, working girl. What on earth am I going to do with a million dollars?"

"A million bucks! Jesus Christ! A million bucks!" Gabe shook his head in disbelief. "So what are you going to do?"

"I've asked Mr and Mrs Redman and my solicitor to stay in Naracoorte for the rest of the day and to ring me in the morning. But I'll probably go back to Adelaide with them. But right now I need to think it through."

Suddenly his expression became mournful. Katie went to him. He turned away from her, but she followed. She could see tears in his eyes. "What's wrong?"

"So if you leave here tomorrow, we'll probably never see you again."

"That's not true," she protested, trying to console him. "I can come back and visit."

"But it seems you've already made up your mind?"

"Do I have a choice? Do I close the club? Give the money to a charity? Sell the car? Paul wouldn't have wanted that. If he did, he would've said so in his will. Gabe, please don't be sad. You are a very special person to me. Heaven forbid, you saved my life for goodness sakes. I'm not going to forget that. Besides," she added, trying to lighten the moment, "they say if you save someone's life, you then become responsible for them. Imagine how many pet lambs you'd have to look after then."

Gabe forced a smile. "I wouldn't give a stuff if it was a thousand, I just don't want to see you go."

He knew Katie wouldn't be staying at Mrs Cropp's long, but to leave. Now? In getting to know her, he was experiencing moments and emotions that left him hungry for more. The touch of her skin, the look in her eyes. Her walk. Her smell. Her smile. The thought of her leaving in a few short hours ripped through his gut like a blowtorch.

Katie raised her hand and lightly brushed a tear from his face. "Oh Gabe, please don't be sad. Think of us as two people whose paths crossed for a moment and we're both much richer for the experience."

Katie's words caused a stronger flow of tears from the big man. "Jesus girl! I don't believe I'm doing this," he said, walking away from Katie. "Bloody hell! Blokes don't cry...and what the fuck am I crying about? I don't even know you," he blurted, knowing full well the reason.

Katie watched from a few feet away as he tried to get a hold of himself. A gentle breeze rustled the leaves of the giant red gums on the river bank. She went to Gabe. "Please don't be sad," she told him, as she put her arms around his waist and rested her head against his chest. "I promise I'll come back and see you. Right now I don't have too many special people in my life and I'd say you'd have to be right up there."

Gabe heard her words and knew they were the consolation prize. He wanted to put his arms around her, but his body had again become a stringless puppet in her presence.

Katie could hear his heart pounding in his chest. Suddenly she heard Mrs Cropp's words, that he'd never been out with a girl in his life. *I'm not being very fair on him am I?* she thought, easing herself away.

She convinced Gabe she needed time on her own, so with reluctance he drove back to Mrs Cropp's alone. But only after she conceded to allow Joker to stay with her.

Mrs Cropp heard Gabe's approach to the house. She went quickly to meet him. "Oh Lord, have you found her?" she blurted.

Gabe told his Aunty Betsy the story and they sat well into the afternoon discussing Katie McFarlane's inheritance.

"What do you think she should do?" Gabe wanted to know.

Mrs Cropp looked puzzled. "It's a tough one isn't it? At least Cyril and I were married, which made it easier I guess. But this poor girl. She obviously had no idea she would cop the lot. I think she's very frightened by it all. I think now, more than ever, she desperately needs to be loved and by someone who has a broad shoulder and a very smart financial brain. No. I can't answer that. I don't know what I'd do. What about you?"

"Bloody hell Aunty Betsy, it's a million bucks. Shouldn't take too much thinking about..."

"Ah, but you're wrong you see. She hasn't physically earned it. She hasn't won it in a lottery. It's not a superannuation policy. It didn't come from her own family. That in itself would be a burden. If she spends it, she'll always have that man of hers counter-signing the cheques. In her mind, sure, but he'll be there. I don't think she'll ever enjoy that sort of inheritance because it will carry enormous responsibilities."

"Like what?"

"Well the Redmans are lovely people. But you don't think they'll want to keep an eye on her? Of course they will. And what on earth is that poor girl going to do with a country club and all those poker machines? Oh dear, I feel so sorry for her. She should walk away from it. But she won't. Human nature's a funny thing you know."

Chapter 22

The Oakdale Country Club was abuzz. Word had spread that Katie McFarlane was the new owner and managing director. General manager Peter Lidcombe looked across his desk at accountant Jill Lawson, opening his arms in a gesture of dismay. "Do you reckon she'll keep the place?"

Jill Lawson, equally dismayed that Paul Redman left the complex entirely to Katie McFarlane, met Peter's gaze and shrugged. "Can't imagine so myself. I mean she's an Adelaide girl. She's a nursing sister, so her background is medical not office administration or clubs. No, I think she'll sell."

"Be interesting if she does keep it. We've both met her. She appears to be a good type of person. And on all her visits here, she was always damned immaculate, I know that."

"Yes, but you need more than a pretty face to run a club..."

"We could help her. Do you see a problem in that?" Peter Lidcombe cut in.

Jill Lawson's face became a little animated. "No, no, God no! I think it would be great to have her. I just don't feel she'll want to do it." Silence fell between the two for a few moments, then Jill continued. "Too many memories Peter. Everywhere the poor girl will turn will have Paul Redman written all over it. You have to remember they weren't married. They were about to be, so everything's going to be pretty raw.

"The first time Paul brought her here will always be in the back of her mind. When she walks into the foyer, restaurant, climbs the stairs, Paul's going to be there. If she does decide to take it on, then it's you and me she'll turn to. I can handle that. As for running the place, we've been doing that since Paul died anyway. But people do change with a sudden and dramatic change in their circumstances. Time will tell if Katie McFarlane remains the delightful young woman we met on those few occasions, or she turns into some capitalist monster. It's hard to say which way she'll go."

Peter Lidcombe bit on his bottom lip, creasing his eyes a little. "My betting is she won't change, until she discovers the power of the cheque book."

Jill Lawson forced a concerned smile. "I think I can see the cogs turning over?"

He offered a wry grin. "Stranger things have happened."

They were interrupted by Kazumi's knock on his door. Jill and Peter looked up. "Excuse me Mr Peter, Miss Jill. Miss Katie, she arrive today? Yes?"

Jill checked her watch, glanced at Peter and told her Katie McFarlane was expected at the club within the hour.

"She stay in Mildura too, yes?"

Jill Lawson told her a fully furnished two-bedroom unit had been acquired a few minutes drive from the club, and, "Yes, Miss Katie will be staying up here for awhile."

Kazumi was thrilled with the news. She thanked Jill Lawson and Peter Lidcombe and quickly left. She had much to do.

"I'm wondering whether you shouldn't have let Katie have your office and you moved into the one where you're putting her?" Jill mentioned, a note of concern in her tone.

Peter dismissed the suggestion, telling her Katie would probably be better off tucked away, out of public view. "At least until she settles in, that is, if she stays that long." Jill Lawson wasn't convinced and Peter Lidcombe sensed it. "You're not seriously suggesting she have this one are you?"

"Well she is the managing director."

Peter scoffed. "Oh God, in title only. It'll still be you and me who run the place. No, she'll be alright. I'll humour her," he added.

* * *

It was the day Katie McFarlane had been dreading. The day when she was to take over as managing director of The Oakdale Country Club. The local press had made much of Paul Redman's death and speculated about the club's future. She was pondering over the newspaper stories when Jim Duncan turned off the main highway and headed in towards Oakdale. "Pull over for a moment will you?" she asked.

Jim slowed and brought his car to a halt. "Look, you don't have to do this. I've been telling you for weeks, walk away. Just walk away. We can sell the club. You don't even have to be here. You can oversee the sale from a distance, pick up your cheque and walk off into the sunset. Katie, do you hear me?"

Katie barely acknowledged her solicitor. She was looking out the car's window at nothing in particular. Thinking. Pondering. Worrying. For the entire journey from Adelaide to Mildura, Katie had hardly spoken. She was too absorbed in what she was about to do. Taking over the running of a club she knew would not be a pushover. A thousand questions continuously raced through her mind ever since she made her mind up to accept Paul Redman's decision that she be given the club, lock, stock and barrel.

"Katie. Katie!" Jim Duncan repeated himself.

There were no tears in her eyes, but her stomach was as tight as a drum. "Jim, I'm going to have to learn who I can trust at the club. I'm fully aware of Paul's faith in Peter Lidcombe and Jill Lawson, but they worked for him. Now they're going to be working for me. I'm going to instruct Peter he is to provide you with the figures each week. Debits and credits. And each month I want you to have them audited independently. But I want you to choose a different auditor each month. I will need to speak to you on the phone every Monday morning, and for you to explain to me in simple terms how I'm going. Every three months I want you to send an audited report to the Redman family. It's important to me they be kept informed of what's going on."

"But you don't have to do that!" Jim protested. "The Redman family has nothing to do with the club anymore. The Oakdale Country Club now belongs entirely to you."

"Paul was their son and brother. I will not be seen as some gold-digger from the city honing in on their wealth."

"Oh Katie, really. We've been through all this. You know how they feel about it. They've all given you their blessing. Remember?"

Katie was lost in thought for a moment. "And one more thing too, Jim," she said. "I am going to destroy the rubber stamp of my signature the club has been using to operate. From now on I will personally sign all cheques. If for some reason I can't, then I want you to counter-sign with Peter."

Jim Duncan grinned. "He's not going to like that very much."

"Well that's too bad for him. If I am to make this club work, then I am going to need your support, and I'm going to need to know exactly what money is coming in and most certainly what money is going out. If you have any doubts whatsoever about a cheque Peter wants you to sign, then wait until you can speak with me. If that's not possible, then speak with Jill Lawson. I must be careful."

"Hey, it's your club. If that's what's going to make you feel comfortable, then that's what we'll do."

"Okay. If I'm going to do this thing, then let's do it."

As Jim Duncan slowly proceeded towards The Oakdale Country Club, a look of startled amazement fell across their faces.

"Good God!" he exclaimed.

"Oh for goodness sakes!" uttered Katie.

As they got closer, masses of balloons came into view. A large banner over the club's front entrance read WELCOME MISS KATIE. Gathered outside the front doors was the entire staff of The Oakdale Country Club. Jim Duncan halted his car about thirty feet from them. Paul's chauffeur, George Raisin, quickly stepped forward and opened her door.

"George Raisin, Miss McFarlane, welcome to Oakdale," he said offering his hand. She took it. "Oh George, this is unbelievable!" she told him hesitantly, trying to find the words as she climbed from the vehicle.

Immediately, spontaneous and very loud applause erupted from within the ranks of those gathered. Kazumi emerged from the group carrying a large sheath of flowers. She went to Katie. There were tears in her eyes. "Miss Katie, this very special day for you, yes. You now Miss Boss Lady. Please, we welcome you."

It's like Paul told them I was coming, was a thought that flashed through her mind. After a moment, words came. She accepted the flowers from Kazumi and put her arms around her. "You are so good to me. Thank you. Thank you."

Peter Lidcombe stepped forward and held out his hand. "Hi Katie. As Kazumi has said, you're now the new boss lady. Please understand we all loved Paul Redman dearly and gave him our full support. We'd like you to know, in welcoming you here today, every single one of us is overjoyed that you have decided to take over the place and keep it running and, in turn, you also have our utmost support."

Katie smiled. *Now tell me what you really think,* she thought. She thanked Peter Lidcombe for his words of welcome then went on to shake hands with every staff member.

Welcomes completed, staff members returned to their duties and Katie entered the club. Peter Lidcombe led the way. "Many in today?" she asked Jill Lawson.

"Not many this morning, but there'll be three buses this afternoon."

"And it's just down here a little Katie," Peter said, walking a couple of paces in front.

Moments later he stood at a door leading to an office. Inside, a glass-topped coffee table decorated with a small bunch of flowers. Two chrome chairs with leather seat and back supports sat in front of the desk. Katie noticed a couple of pictures on the wall. A lampshade on a corner, glass-topped table. Behind the desk, a standard, five-wheeled office chair. On the desk, a telephone and intercom.

"Welcome to your new home," Peter Lidcombe beamed.

Katie entered the office, and immediately felt belittled. She was mortified. *Plain and nice and probably comfortable. God I hate it. It's so sterile. Oh no, this is not on. This is just not on!* But she decided to let it ride for the moment. She placed her brand new leather Condotti briefcase she'd bought specially for her new role on the top of the desk. "And you're just around the corner?"

"Yes," Peter said. "Jill's two doors down. So, what do you think?"

Katie was more hurt than angry. It was obvious her role at the club was being looked upon as one of tokenism. She wanted to lash out. But she remained calm. "Oh it's fine, thank you," she said, and walked behind the desk and sat down, placing her arms on the glass top in front of her. "So," she began, "how many staff in total?"

"Fifteen," Peter told her, "but on weekends, we add another five to the numbers to help in the restaurant and pokies room."

"Wages bill?"

Peter sat in one of the chrome chairs. "Oh, it varies Katie. But don't you worry yourself. Jill and I look after that?"

"Weekly food bill for the restaurant?"

Peter Lidcombe smiled, "It varies, depending on the numbers," he told her, avoiding a direct answer.

Katie showed no emotion. Jill Lawson had chosen to remain standing. "So how much a week is spent on alcohol?"

Again Peter Lidcombe chose to brush aside the question. He rose from his chair. "Oh Katie, really, come now, you've only just arrived. You don't have to bother yourself with all this..."

A knock on the door interrupted Peter's answer. It was Kazumi telling Katie that lunch had now been served in the restaurant.

"Thank you Kazumi," Katie replied returning to Peter Lidcombe. But Kazumi was persistent.

"Miss Boss Lady can come now please, yes?"

Katie could not refuse her chef's inviting smile. She rose from her desk and followed Kazumi. "Jill," she said, suddenly remembering. "Would you mind seeing what's happened to Jim, my solicitor. He may be still sitting outside in the car. Would you please find him and invite him in for lunch?"

When Katie walked into the restaurant, again it was to the smiles of the entire staff and a table especially laid for her. Over the top of the table was a small arch of flowers creating the words WELCOME MISS BOSS LADY. Katie's glance shot to Kazumi. "You are determined to spoil me aren't you?"

George Raisin made his way towards her. "It seems I'm to do the honours," he smiled. "Miss McFarlane," he began, "you don't need us to tell you the affection we held for Paul. And it was always a joy whenever he brought you up to visit. When we heard you decided to keep the club, it meant, with your assurance, we could keep our jobs. That meant a lot to all of us. And of course Kazumi being Kazumi, well she wanted to do something special for you on your first day. When she asked the staff about a special lunch for you, everyone kicked in, so the present you see wrapped on the table is a token of our appreciation and just our way of saying thank you. We hope you will be very happy here and we'll do our darndest to make sure we run a very special outfit. Won't we folks?"

George Raisin's comments were met with warm applause. Kazumi stepped forward. "You open yes, and then eat, okay?"

Katie smiled. "Okay," then turned her attentions to the parcel. As she peeled back the paper and lifted the lid from the box, she could see it was an Oroton writing case in hand-made Italian leather. She picked it up, and immediately pressed it to her face. "It smells wonderful. I just love leather. Thank you every one, very much. This is all most unexpected. In fact, my being here is probably a bigger shock to me than to you. Obviously none of us expected to lose Paul like we did. But from what I knew of him and loved of him, his one big obsession in life was this club. I agonised over whether I could do justice to his memory in keeping it. On meeting you all again today, and hearing the words of encouragement from Peter and of course you, George, I am sure we can continue to run a very successful club. Please be patient with me. I have a lot to learn, but I am going to learn. And all of you, remember, my door is always open. If you have a problem, I want you all to feel free to talk to me about it."

Peter Lidcombe shifted uneasily and mumbled something under his breath only Jill seemed to hear.

"Not while I'm in the driving seat," Katie continued. "We're in this together. When people visit us I want them to go away with happy memories. Again, thank you Kazumi. I'm famished."

* * *

For the next ten weeks, Katie McFarlane spent most of her time between the club and setting up her home. She worked diligently in getting to know her staff. She regularly conferred with Kazumi. Had long meetings with Jill Lawson and the two had become firm friends. But meetings she set down with Peter Lidcombe almost always resulted in brief sessions. And this bothered her. It also bothered her how he skimmed over bottom-line figures, making light of them with spur-of-the-moment, trite comments. She didn't enjoy the vibe she was receiving from her general manager, but seemed powerless to do anything about it.

Even if I raise it with Jim Duncan, what am I going to say? she asked herself. She couldn't fault his ethics as a manager, but she resented greatly his patronising attitude towards her. He baulked at having to provide Jim Duncan with the figures, and it was obvious he resented the new restrictions she had placed on who wrote the cheques. But what really bothered her was his attempt to get her out of the place.

Why does my being here bother him so much? Everything seems to be above board. No, no, something's not right! Peter Lidcombe is up to something, I just know he is. But what? How on earth do I find out? Jill hasn't said anything and I'm sure she would have if she suspected something. Paul never gave me any indication he was worried about his general manager. Maybe it's me! Maybe he just resents the intrusion of an outsider into his patch?

She decided to challenge him at their next predictably brief session together. "Peter, why is it that whenever I want to sit down with you, you've got more pressing matters to attend to?" Katie asked.

"Maybe we should do it after hours and I wouldn't have so many distractions," he answered.

"So what do you have in mind?" she replied, going along with him to see where the conversation led.

He moved around from behind his desk and sat down next to her. "Look, I know you've jumped in at the deep end on this," he began, placing his hand on top of hers. "Why don't you leave all this to the experts and put your feet up?"

"You want me to go back to Adelaide and let you run the club?"

"Well not in as many words but, if you like, yes. I can come down once a week and see you, show you the figures. We could have dinner..."

Katie withdrew her hand. "Are you moving in on me Peter?"

"Obviously I find you attractive. We're all human. I have needs. You have needs. I think in each other we could probably satisfy them."

Katie got to her feet. "I'll think about it," she told him, and left his office. Quickly she went to the ladies toilets and ran her hand under the tap. *Oh yuk! Who does he think he is? God I feel sick!* And she was slightly. *That man wants me out of the club, into his bed and a thousand miles away! The outright bloody gall of him!*

For the remainder of the day, Katie gave Peter Lidcombe a wide berth. She didn't want to even set eyes on him. She had a problem and she knew it.

Later that evening, Katie was in the kitchen with Kazumi checking menus and pricing. She excused herself to go to the toilet. When she opened the door, the room was in darkness. She flicked the switch and discovered the bulb had blown. On the spur of the moment she decided to use the men's toilet. She chose the cubicle at the far end. That way, if someone did come in he wouldn't know she was there, thus avoiding any embarrassment for either party.

Moments later she heard footsteps enter the toilet, then two voices. One of them familiar. It was Peter Lidcombe's. As they stood at the urinal she clearly heard the conversation.

"And how are you Peter."

"Good mate."

"What's with the new chick?"

"Katie?"

"Yeah, top sort eh...been there yet?"

Peter laughed, "Working on it mate, working on it."

"Listen, the boys are getting a bit worried about their discount piss. What if she finds out not every carton of grog hits the club and not every bottle of Jack gets sold?"

"Mate, trust me. She'll never know. I'm working on getting her the fuck out of here. She's only some bimbo who happened to inherit the joint from a fucking playboy who didn't know piss from popcorn!"

"What are you gonna do?"

"Mate, fuck the arse off her, then get her back to Adelaide and blind her with bullshit whenever I see her. Don't worry, things will go on the same."

Katie sat in the cubicle, mortified at what she'd just heard. Anger built up inside her. She waited a few minutes, then quietly sneaked from the toilet, careful not to be seen as she left. She went to the reception desk and picked up the phone.

Within minutes George Raisin had arrived and the two drove off into the night.

* * *

The next morning, Katie McFarlane was sitting in Peter Lidcombe's office when he arrived for work. Seeing Katie McFarlane sitting in his leather-bound chair made the hair stand up on the back of his neck.

"Katie?" he said, cautiously walking into his office, his attention flashing immediately to the man sitting across from her.

"Good morning Peter," she replied curtly.

"What's going on?"

"Sit down Peter, this is Inspector David Reyne from the Mildura Police. I don't believe you've met?"

Peter Lidcombe glanced at the policeman and then shot back to Katie. Katie opened her briefcase and threw a folder onto the desk. "I was wondering if you'd like to have a look at that and explain to me just what is going on?"

Peter snatched the folder and opened it. Before him was the monetary value of the amount of alcohol missing from the club in the past twelve months. It came to fifteen thousand dollars. The next page contained an approximate value of food that had disappeared from the kitchen. That amount came to ten thousand dollars. Peter Lidcombe looked at the figures then glared at Katie.

"What's that got to do with me?"

"So you don't know anything about it?"

"Come on Katie, of course I don't. Good God I've got more to do with my time than to knock off the bloody booze cupboard?"

"Peter," Katie said, "before you get yourself in any deeper, let me tell you I had, for me the good fortune, for you the misfortune, of having to use the men's toilet last night. It was getting late and you'd obviously thought I'd left for the night. Shall I go on?"

Peter Lidcombe to this point remained solid. "Please do."

"To avoid any embarrassment should anyone come in, I chose to use the cubicle right down the end. In fact, two men did come in. One of them was you. Do you still want me to go on."

"Suit yourself," he replied.

Katie stood up from behind his desk, steeled herself, walked over, closed the door, and turned on him with the venom of a thousand vipers. "So, to use your words, I am nothing but a bimbo you are going to fuck the arse off and send back to Adelaide. And Paul Redman was nothing but a fucking playboy who didn't know piss from popcorn? Oh, and what about the discount piss mate? The boys are getting worried about it. Shall I continue? she yelled.

Peter Lidcombe sprang to his feet. "Why you dirty, lowdown, little fucking trollop."

Inspector Reyne leapt forward, his arms latching onto Peter Lidcombe. "Sit down please sir."

"Piss off copper!"

Quicker than the blink of an eye, Inspector Reyne drove a thunderbolt jab into the solar plexus of Peter Lidcombe. His eyes bulged and his knees buckled. Inspector Reyne caught his body weight and eased him down into his chair. "There you go," he told him. "You be a good boy and listen to what Miss McFarlane has to tell you."

As Peter gasped and fought to regain his breath, Katie McFarlane pointed out the state of play. She told him staff members were already at his house waiting for him to return home whereby he would allow them to collect the many dozens of cases of alcohol that didn't belong to him. She then presented him with a document which he could sign. It meant him forgoing any financial claims on The Oakdale Country Club for any wages or holiday pay, superannuation entitlements or severance pay. If he refused to sign, then Inspector Reyne would place him under arrest for fraudulent activities and he could take his chances before the court.

"Sign that and you're free to go Peter. If you don't sign it, I'll hand everything over to Inspector Reyne."

Peter Lidcombe struggled to get to his feet. Angrily, he grabbed for a pen, walked to the door and turned back to Katie. "Fuck you bitch! And fuck that bastard right along with you!"

"Nice man," Katie said, as she watched her former general manager leave the premises. Although she appeared calm on the outside, the incident left her traumatized.

"I think you better let me take you home," Inspector Reyne said.

Katie offered no protest. "Just a quick call first." She leaned over the desk and buzzed Jill Lawson. "Can you pop in for a moment. I'm in Peter's office."

She was there in an instant. "Close the door Jill. I'd like you to meet Inspector Reyne. I'll explain later," she added quickly, seeing Jill's puzzled expression. "Inspector, this is my accountant Jill Lawson and, as from this moment, the new general manager of The Oakdale Country Club."

* * *

The moment she walked inside, Katie McFarlane closed her front door and began to undress all the way to the bathroom. She stood naked as she ran the bath. When the tub was half full, she tested the water with her toe, then gently eased herself in. As she lay there, feeling the heat do its job on her stressed muscles and aching body, she went over in her mind the events which led to the downfall of Peter Lidcombe.

Having George Raisin drive her to barman's home. Keeping him up half the night going over the figures of liquor sales. Getting Kazumi out of bed at two a.m. to do the same spot check on food purchases and sales. By five a.m. she knew she had him. An hour later she was sitting in the waiting room of the Mildura police station waiting for Inspector Reyne to arrive for work. One-and-a-half hours later, the two of them were waiting in Peter Lidcombe's office. It was only then she realised she hadn't been to bed. She had been running on pure adrenaline.

Katie felt she was beginning to drift off, so she quickly dried herself and climbed into bed. It had been a long day.

Chapter 23

Seven weeks later, Katie McFarlane stood outside her office door, the office previously occupied by Peter Lidcombe, and cast an admiring glance around her handiwork. She entered and quietly closed her door. As she leaned back against it, her eyes took her round a room she had turned into her own private sanctuary. She walked a few steps and sat in the armchair she had ordered especially. It was similar to the one she spent so many hours sitting in at Mrs Cropp's: wide arms, deep cushioning, mahogany inserts to hold a drink or an ashtray. A coffee table with a telephone on top sat next to it. She thought it may not be in keeping with the mood she had created, but she didn't care. She loved the chair at Mrs Cropp's and she wanted one just like it. Probably because she could sit in it, curl her legs under herself and feel the security of something big and strong surrounding her. She wondered if that wasn't the same sort of faint attraction she also felt for Gabe Caplin. From her chair she looked at the trompel'eoil on the largest wall in her office. She had gone to the trouble to hire a photographer to take a wide shot of the driveway leading into Mrs Cropp's farm. She had Casey track down the artist who painted the one behind the reception desk and commissioned him to recreate the scene in the photo, which he had done so magnificently.

In redecorating the office, Katie McFarlane was always very conscious of the fact she was a woman working in what was always described to her as a man's world. Not only that, she was young, wealthy, available and regarded as a 'good sort' by the locals. All this she knew could work against her, if she let it. At this stage in her life, her ownership of the club was the be-all to end-all, as was the professional image she portrayed. Everything she did, and the way she did it, annulled the fact she was only learning. So efficient was the professional package she presented, her abilities were never questioned. As a further enhancement, she tailored her wardrobe, her looks, her office and her behavior accordingly. When she made the decision to move into Peter Lidcombe's vacated office, she couldn't see one thing he had placed around him she wanted to keep. So with a wave of her hand, she had the room brought back to four walls in a couple of hours. She remembered the Salvation Army ringing to thank her for such 'a generous donation'.

The first thing to go in was the trompel'eoil. Then the painters blended colour tonings of soft creams and pale greens to transform the walls and ceiling. She particularly liked the eight-inch border print, chosen in shades totally compatible with the other colours of the room. The off-white, pure wool, ultra-thick, luxurious carpet was next, followed by her specially chosen light fittings. In the back of her mind she wanted to create an atmosphere of a clutter-free office, but allowed herself the indulgence of the old fashioned arm chair.

To the left of the entrance and just near the door, she had placed a formal, three-seater leather lounge with a small coffee table in front of it. Behind the lounge she hung the ornately framed original depiction of the building when it was actually the local golf clubrooms. And, because she enjoyed the feeling of being close to Mrs Cropp's farm, she placed her desk on the other side of the room, directly in front of it. Katie particularly liked her desk. She had seen it sitting in an auction room, discarded, with the appearance of being kicked from pillar to post over thousands of meetings. She bought it for a song, had it transported to Adelaide where she commissioned two french polishers to work on it full time for a month. As it sat across from her, new life oozed from its revitalized mahogany. A green-leather inlay adding to its opulence. She knew it wasn't very feminine, but it exuded a masculine strength with a touch of historical presence. And it was big enough for her to lay out papers without looking disorganised or messy. From behind its protective dimensions, she had, by chance, acquired a dark-green, leather, high-backed swivel chair. She thought it would give her the required 'presence' when needed.

In the front of her desk, but off to each side so as not to inhibit her view of the trompel'eoil, two further executive office chairs. To her right and sitting in the corner over from her desk, a crystal and mahogany made-to-order drinks cabinet. On the top, a framed photograph of Paul Redman and her parents. Sitting in the big, old-fashioned arm chair, she allowed herself a smile of contentment. She kicked off her shoes and dug her toes into the lush wool carpet.

She had sought advice from Jack Redman before she renovated and thought he'd be pleased with the results. "Always create the presence of power," he had told her. "People respond to power. People respect power. And if you're a woman wielding that power, then create your power base straight from the men's locker room. Use the greens and creams and leather and mahogany. That will confuse the hell out of them. And while they're sitting there thinking about it, trying to pigeon-hole you, go for the jugular. You won't always win, but you'll win more than you lose."

As she focused on the far wall, she found herself in Mrs Cropp's front yard. The weeks had rolled by and this was really the first opportunity she had allowed herself to sit and relax and reflect upon the most recent events in her life. She reached for the phone.

"Mrs Cropp?"

"Yes...oh, is that you Katie?"

"Yes it is, how are you? Did you get my letter?"

"Well yes I did. I'm fine. But how are you?"

"If I stop and think about it, I guess I'm still very sad. So I keep myself busy. How's Gabe?"

Mrs Cropp's voice dropped. "Yes, he's good," she answered.

"Not by the sound of that he's not?"

"Oh Katie, he misses you. I miss you. God, I think even old Stanley wanders around the place trying to find you. Did Gabe fix up about your car alright?"

"Yes, yes, I got the cheque a few weeks ago actually, so I had to go out and get myself another one."

"But haven't you got that Mercedes?"

"I couldn't Mrs Cropp. That was Paul's car. The first time I got behind the wheel everything came flooding back, so I asked his dad if I could give it to his family. They didn't want to accept it. Wanted to pay me for it. But I put the keys in Mr Redman's pocket and left it at the family home in Adelaide. Mr Redman said it now had added meaning and he was going to build a special garage to house it."

"Well, when you can, you better pop back through this way. There's a couple of people here who think and talk about you quite a bit."

"You're wonderful. Does Gabe still have the pet lambs?"

"Are you kidding?" she shrieked. "He hardly lets them out of his sight. He even goes down to the shed after dark to check on them. That's not bad from a man who used to say keeping pet lambs was a lot of tommy-rot. He asks me all the time if I've heard from you. Anything you want me to tell him?"

Katie laughed. "No, I'll tell him. I'll ring him when I get off the phone from you."

"Oh he'll love that. So, any plans to drop by?"

"Well there are actually. It won't be for a few weeks, but I thought I'd like to come and spend a few days with you again."

Mrs Cropp was delighted. "Katie that's wonderful."

"But don't tell Gabe. When I do come, I want it to be a surprise."

"I won't tell him. Sweetheart, please take care of yourself. Anytime. Anytime at all. You know that."

Katie flicked the pages of her notebook for Gabe's number. "Gabe?" she asked softly.

"Katie! Hi. Where are you? Are you here? Are you coming over?"

Katie laughed out loud. "Hang on, hang on, no, I'm not down there. I'm up here. In Mildura. How are you?"

"Great...that's not true. Shithouse!"

"Whatever's the matter?"

"Well you're not here for starters! The bloody pet lambs are miserable. The dog's crook, the car won't start and the bore's run dry."

"All because I'm not there?"

"Absolutely!"

She chuckled. "Oh Gabe. How are you really?"

"Hell, I don't know. Nothing seems to be the same around here with you gone. We all miss you. Aunty Betsy misses you. Joker misses you and I miss you. But what about you? How are things going up there in fancy club land?"

"You'll have to come up and see."

Gabe scoffed a little. "I wouldn't know what to do with myself..."

"But I'll show you around. Find you a place to stay. If you don't like it, then you can come and stay with me. What do you think?"

It was a hugely tempting offer. But suddenly he felt inadequate. "No, that sort of stuff's not me Katie."

"Oh Gabe, won't you come?"

"I'll think about it."

When Katie hung up the phone, she knew Gabe would think about it. But she also knew there was no way he would get in the car and come to visit her at The Oakdale Country Club.

* * *

When she took over the complex, Katie McFarlane knew she had to promote the club's existence. She spoke with Archibald Design and listened long and hard to the advice she was given. Especially in the area that dealt with the media. Archibald Design in turn referred her to Scott and Martin's Advertising Agency in Melbourne. Using the advice, she insisted its creative director visit the club before one word of commercial copy was written and aired about the place. With specifically targeted advertising campaigns in both city and the country, the results were immediate. Almost overnight more tour buses began to drop by. Couples on holidays. Even more of the locals. Pleased with the results and the increased turnover, Katie became alarmed one afternoon to discover Kazumi in her storeroom, drenched with tears.

Ashamed at being discovered, she tried to hide her face. "No! No! Miss Katie. You not see me like this please. You go away please."

Katie ignored her pleas. "Kazumi, what's wrong?" she asked. But Kazumi refused to say. Instead, she kept pleading with Katie to be left alone. But Katie was equally as persistent. "If you think I'm leaving you like this, you've got another think coming. Are you feeling sick?"

Kazumi shook her head.

"Has someone done something terrible to you?"

"Oh no Miss Katie!" she said, "it be nothing like that."

Katie noticed a high stool next to where she was standing. She climbed up on it. "Okay, young lady, your Miss Katie is not moving until you tell her the problem!"

Silence fell between them. Kazumi was still standing with her back to Katie. She thought if she waited long enough, her boss would accept defeat and leave. But she was wrong. After a couple of minutes, Kazumi's tears had stopped and she hesitantly moved her head sideways. Just enough to allow her to peer back over her shoulder. Katie was still there. She climbed off the stool and put her arms around her.

"Kazumi, you are one of the most important people in this place. In fact, without you, I don't have a restaurant. If something has upset you, then it's upset me. Is it something I've done or haven't done?"

Kazumi slowly responded to Katie's coaxing. As she began to speak, her eyes again welled with tears. Katie reached for her own handkerchief and dabbed at her eyes.

"I think sometimes I disappoint you because I not cope Miss Katie."

"You not cope? What on earth do you mean? I don't know of anyone who could possibly cope better."

"Lately, so many people. All the time in the kitchen, yes. All the time, night time, day time, early morning time, before sun even come up, I in kitchen, because I have much trouble to cope."

Suddenly, Katie realised the problem. With the increased traffic flow, the extra demands placed on The Oakdale's kitchen was enormous. She had failed to recognise the fact. Kazumi was busting her gut working to the point where she had broken down. But she was much too proud to ask for help.

"Oh my God Kazumi. I'm sorry. I'm so terribly sorry. I never realised. No, it's worse than that. I didn't stop to think of the extra work load I had placed on you. I will get you some help, alright?"

Kazumi's eyes brightened, then went sad. "You hire another cook yes?"

Katie laughed. "No, I not hire another cook. You are the cook. I hire someone to help you, not someone to replace you. Okay?"

Back in her office, Katie felt wretched. She buzzed Jill Lawson. After explaining the situation, the general manager suggested a newspaper ad be placed.

Then a thought struck Katie. "Hold off on that a moment will you."

She buzzed reception. "Casey, get me the Royal Adelaide Hospital will you please."

After being put through from one department to another on three occasions, finally the familiar voice of nurse Sally Isaacs came on the line. "Hi Katie, wow, how are you?"

For the first real time since she left, she missed her old job. Hearing Sally Isaacs carrying on and fooling around made her realise just what a great bunch of mates she left behind. It took awhile, but she was finally able to get Sally to be serious for a few moments. "Do you remember the time a little girl was brought in? Her name was Emma Downs. Her mother's name is Lorry. Can you check for me and get me their address?"

"I remember her. She turned up at Paul's funeral."

"Would you mind? It's Emma's birthday and I remember promising to send her a card," she said, not wanting to disclose her true intentions.

True to her word, Nurse Sally Isaacs retrieved the information Katie needed. Katie then buzzed reception. "Casey, ask George to bring the car around will you. And tell him to fill the tank. I need to go to Adelaide."

Four hours later, Katie McFarlane was knocking on the door of Lorry Downs' third-floor flat. After waiting for what she considered a fairly lengthy period, slowly the door opened. It was on a chain.

"Who is it?" came a feeble voice.

Katie thought she must be in the wrong place. "Oh. Hello, My name's Katie and I'm looking for Lorry Downs. I guess I must have the wrong place." She was about to turn and leave when the voice brightened a little.

"Katie? No, you're right. I'm Lorry. Hang on a moment and I'll open the door." Quickly Lorry closed the door, released the chain then opened it again.

"Lorry?" Katie asked, unable to disguise the shock in her tone. Standing before her was a woman with black rings under her eyes, straggly, unwashed and unkempt hair. She also looked filthy and desperately malnourished.

"Hi. Sorry to be a little evasive," she offered. "You never know whose around these days knocking on your door. There's so much bad stuff going on." As she spoke, she was too embarrassed to look her visitor in the eye.

Katie was almost too shocked by what greeted her to carry on any sort of conversation. Overflowing ashtrays, discarded pizza boxes, a big pile of empty beer cans in one corner of what she assumed must be the lounge room. Others strewn about the floor. The television set's fourth leg replaced by an old fruit box. The curtains and blinds were drawn. A solitary globe dangling from loose flex provided the only light. She noticed the doors to the other rooms were closed.

Lorry finally looked at Katie. "Not much to show for one's life is it?"

She was aghast. "My God, what has happened to you? Lorry this is awful. How come you're living like this? Where's Emma?"

"In the other room. She's alright. Thanks to you that time. What do you want?"

"I'll get to that. What's going on here? Are you still with that man who threatened you? Have you got a job?"

Lorry shook her head. "Don't have a choice. He said if ever I left him, he'd track me down and cut Emma's throat. And the thing is I believe he would."

"Can't you go to the police?"

"Don't you understand? I told you about this guy. He brutalises me, bashes me, rapes me and all the time keeps threatening my kid. He forbids me to get a job. And he's ordered me not to leave the flat." The tears began to flow. Lorry's trembling fingers had three separate attempts to light a cigarette until she finally gave up. Katie picked up the packet, lit a fresh one and handed it to her.

"But you can't go on like this. You'll die for God's sakes!"

Nervously Lorry Downs looked at the clock on the wall. "Scarfe will be home in a minute. It's best he doesn't find you here. Can you tell me what you want?"

"Alright. Listen to me. I'll come back and see you in the morning. What time?"

"Anytime after seven-thirty. Scarfe leaves here at about seven...but tell me what you want."

"In the morning," Katie promised, offering her a reassuring smile.

* * *

It was just after seven-forty-five when Katie McFarlane climbed the steps to Lorry Down's flat the following morning. Katie didn't get the chance to knock. Lorry already had the door open. She had made a serious attempt to clean herself up, but could not disguise the hurt and pain in her eyes. Emma, thumb in mouth, clung to her mother's thigh. She didn't take her eyes off the visitor.

Katie greeted the two of them. Seeing Emma, she immediately leaned down. "And you must be Emma. Hello. I'm Katie. Do you remember me?" she asked, taking hold of her hand. She immediately felt a roughness on her palm. Casually she turned it up and a sickening feeling gripped her stomach. It was the scarring which resulted from her hands being pressed onto a hot plate. She could not believe how badly she'd been brutalised. The child looked at Katie and, quick as a flash, sprang from her mother's thigh and threw her arms around Katie's neck. Katie craned her head back to look at Lorry.

"I think she does."

Katie withdrew the child's arms and stood to her feet. "Okay, let me tell you what this is all about."

Lorry invited her in and pulled out a kitchen chair for her to sit on. Katie McFarlane explained how she had taken over the club since Paul's death and of her head chef's need for help in the kitchen. "Would you like the job?" she asked her.

Lorry Downs was flabbergasted. "You mean you've driven all the way down here just to offer me a job? But why?"

"Because I think you need a break."

"Shit Katie, you don't even know me. And why would you want to? Look at me. Look how I live. I'm a nervous, fucking wreck. And besides, where would I live? The kid's got to go to school. And how would you suggest I get away from Scarfe?"

"Lorry," she said determinedly, "you showed me great kindness and compassion at Paul's funeral. For some reason I've always remembered the both of you. Probably because in all my years of nursing, I had never seen a woman and child so brutalised. Will you come? Don't worry about the money, I'll fix that. What do you say?"

"You're offering me a job in the kitchen?"

"And a school for Emma plus a place to live. Why, we'll even pay you," she smiled.

Lorry Downs became visibly excited at the prospect of a new life. Then she began to tremble with fear. What would Scarfe do to her if he found her? Maybe she could escape. But even the thought terrified her. Lorry looked at Katie with saddened eyes. "I'm sorry you went to so much trouble to find me. But I can't. I truly can't."

Katie bit on her bottom lip. She could see how Lorry Downs was trapped. The hopeless situation she was in. She thought of going to the police herself, but decided against it. *If something happened to Emma because of it, I'd never forgive myself.* She opened her handbag and took out several twenty dollar notes and pressed them into Lorry's hand. "This will pay for your petrol. I'll keep the job open for three days. If you change your mind, just arrive. I'll take care of the rest."

Lorry Downs looked at the money in stunned amazement.

"Three days," she repeated as she went to the door.

* * *

Lorry watched Katie walk down the steps and across the street to the chauffeur-driven car. As it drove away, she looked at the money in her hand. *A new life*, she thought. She paced the room with a renewed enthusiasm. *A new life*, she kept saying over and over. On the spur of the moment she changed her mind. She would take the job. She decided this was her one big chance to escape Scarfe Olsen. But how?

Oh God, how am I going to do it? She dare not try and leave now as Scarfe has the habit of sometimes slipping home from his work to check on her. What if he saw her driving down the street? *Plan it. I've got to plan it*, she told herself.

Lighting one cigarette after another, she moved from one room through to another, a slight panic in her stride. *Plan it. I've got to plan it.*

She sat Emma down and told her mummy was going to take her on a long drive, but it was important that Scarfe not know they were going away. "Will you watch at the window for mummy and tell her immediately if you see Scarfe arrive home?"

Emma said she would. Lorry didn't own a suitcase. The closest she could come to anything of a carrying nature were garbage bags. She hurriedly filled several with as many possessions as she could. Nearly frightened out of her wits, she cautiously left the flat and piled the bags into her old Holden car. All the time, looking around to make sure Scarfe wasn't standing behind her.

By late afternoon she had completed her task. Within an hour Scarfe would be home. She steeled herself for the next part of her plan. She went into the kitchen and took Scarfe's baseball bat from the broom cupboard. It was something that always puzzled her. He never played the sport or even spoke about it. Satisfied it would do the job she wanted it for, she put Emma in her room and told her under no circumstances was she to come out.

"Mummy will come and get you when it's time to leave, alright?"

Lorry checked her watch. Fifteen minutes before Scarfe walked in the door. Ten minutes. Five. She heard his car arrive. She felt her bowels loosening and squeezed hard on the cheeks of her bottom. Her stomach was churning. Scarfe made his way to the steps. Half way up he stopped and turned around. Almost suspecting something wasn't right. Lorry heard the footsteps stop.

Oh fuck! What? she screamed inside. Then they continued.

Moments later she heard his key in the door. She raised the baseball bat over her head. As Scarfe walked in Lorry swung the bat with every ounce of strength in her body and smashed it down on his head. Scarfe dropped to the floor without uttering a sound. To make sure she'd knocked him out, she crashed the bat into his skull a second time, then flung it to the end of the room. She stood with her hands to her mouth, horrified at her own actions. Terrified, she bent down and hesitantly placed her fingers against his neck to be sure he still had a pulse. Satisfied he was still alive, she raced into the bedroom, grabbed Emma's hand and scrambled out the front door, slamming it shut as she went.

At nine o'clock the next morning, holding on to her daughter's hand, Lorry Downs walked into The Oakdale Country club and asked to speak to Katie McFarlane.

Chapter 24

When Paul Redman carried out the renovations and re-building of The Oakdale Country Club, he incorporated in the design a fully self-contained two-bedroom unit at the rear of the complex. Although the key to its front door sat in a tray at the reception desk, Katie had never been able to bring herself to enter it. Instead, she had Jill Lawson arrange for removalists to pack up everything in the place and send it back to Adelaide. Even knowing it was empty, Katie still couldn't face walking in the front door, knowing it belonged to the man so tragically taken from her. She decided she would allow it to be used as the new home for Lorry Downs and her daughter Emma. Basically because it offered a safe haven for two people who, for years now, had been terrified and brutalised by Scarfe Olsen.

One thing's for sure, she consoled herself, *that bastard won't find them here.*

* * *

It had been three months since Katie McFarlane spoke to Betsy Cropp on the phone. As she leaned back in her green leather chair and rested one knee against the edge of the mahogany desk, she took time to reflect. She was pleased with how the club had progressed. The advertising campaign was working, and her decision to employ Lorry Downs, and provide a home for two people who had been dealt a vicious blow in life, pleased her. Emma had settled well into school. To be sure she faced no dangers in travelling to and from the classroom; Katie had George Raisin pick her up and bring her home each day.

To avoid undue criticism of the 'chauffeur-driven school kid,' the decision was made that George take a different route each day, and stop a short distance from the schoolyard, away from 'prying eyes.' No one, apart from Katie McFarlane and Lorry Downs, knew the real reason for the protection. Even George Raisin wasn't told. Lorry, who seemed to be living in constant fear that Scarfe Olsen would 'just turn up,' told Katie she was overwhelmed by such a display of selflessness and compassion. Katie too relished her daily visits from Emma. It mattered little where she was or what she was involved in, Emma Downs would seek her out for a cuddle and to pass on all the schoolyard gossip. As a treat, once a week, Katie would take her into the kitchen and Kazumi would let her have her pick of the desserts or icecreams in her fridge. Katie wondered if Lorry ever became a little miffed that her daughter always ran to her first. Lorry dismissed her concerns.

"Wait till she starts calling you Aunty Katie," she laughed.

She looked around her office, still thinking. Jill Lawson had taken to being the new boss with great flair and efficiency. Paul's best friend, Michael Knight, had dropped by and they had lunch. Jill Lawson joined them and the attraction was immediate. Michael had only intended popping up from Renmark to see Katie for a couple of hours. Three days later, he was still in Mildura.

Suddenly Katie felt the pangs of jealousy. She envied her general manager's good fortune, and her mind went back to when she was swept off her feet by Paul Redman. The pain of his loss seemed a little easier to bear with the passing of the weeks and the months, but she missed him terribly. She also knew that, because she kept herself so busy, she had little time to think about the frailties of love and destroyed opportunity. But now as she sat, reflecting, she suddenly felt desperately lonely. She also felt she had become a little jaded.

Then, as if being jolted into doing it, she picked up the phone and called Betsy Cropp.

* * *

Later that evening, Betsy Cropp fiddled and fussed about her room, making sure it was perfect for when her house-guest arrived. Shortly before nine, Katie's car headlights shone into the driveway. The two greeted each other warmly and for the next two hours conversation between the two didn't stop.

"So. Now you own that magnificent club. That must have been the most daunting of tasks to accept.," said Mrs Cropp.

"It was, and is. But I've had some wonderful help. The Redmans have been marvellous, but I guess most of all it's been a lesson in human nature."

"So do you miss being a nurse?"

"I miss my mates at the Royal Adelaide," she replied thoughtfully. "But then again I miss a lot of things. I miss my mum and dad dreadfully. And Paul of course. But I've been really busy and sometimes when I stop to think, I begin to feel guilty that Paul hasn't taken up more of my thoughts. But I can't dwell on that. Sometimes I become so swept away with loneliness, thoughts of a love gone forever no longer console me. I need to love again Mrs Cropp. I just need to love again. Is that so wrong?"

Betsy Cropp sat down next to Katie and held her hand.

"There are no rules," she told her, "no text books, no sacred psalms which say the grieving period shall be this length of time. It's a very individual, very personal thing. I learned to combat my loneliness because there was a warmth in my heart not even the coldest winter could destroy. My greatest wish is to see you find another man. A man worthy of your beauty, your love and your loyalty."

Katie turned over Mrs Cropp's words in her mind. Then, "How's Gabe?" she asked, casually.

Mrs Cropp laughed lightly. "He's good, but of course he misses you, as I told you over the phone. So I've had to tell him straight that he is only to think of you as someone very special he had the good fortune to meet. I've had to try and make him understand city girls like Katie McFarlane don't fall for country fellows like Gabe Caplin. Girls these days expect more than windmills, tractors and a mob of sheep."

"Oh, maybe...maybe not," Katie replied.

"Anyway, I haven't told him you were coming, so he'll get the shock of his life tomorrow when he sees you."

* * *

Gabe Caplin was putting in a new strainer post on his boundary fence when he glanced up to see a vehicle travelling slowly towards him. He didn't give it more than a moment's attention as he continued on the back-breaking task of digging a large post-hole for a seven-foot length of solid redgum. As he battled with the clay in the base of the hole with a crowbar, Joker began getting edgy. He started to whine and frantically wave his tail.

"What the fuck's up with you?" he cursed. "Siddown." But Joker only became more excited. "You're a crazy bastard sometimes!" Gabe said to him, but his words meant little. The dog was almost beckoning his master to turn around. Finally he did. Walking towards him was Katie McFarlane carrying a picnic basket and a thermos.

He wiped the sweat from his brow, then pushed his hat back with one hand and scratched his head in dismay. Joker ran to greet her.

"Mrs Cropp said she thought there might be someone down here in need of a cup of tea and a bit of lunch!" she said, patting Gabe's dog affectionately.

"I don't believe this! Katie!" he yelled. "Oh God, this is incredible!" he blurted, rushing to her. She placed the basket and thermos on the ground and the two embraced for a moment. "Aunty Betsy know you're here?"

"I've just come from there. She packed your lunch for you."

"You mean she knew you were coming and she didn't tell me?"

"I asked her not to. I wanted to surprise you."

"By hell you certainly did that! Can you stay long?"

"A few days. I really needed to get away."

"Those bright lights get a bit much do they?"

"Oh Gabe, they're hardly bright lights! If you'd only bother to drag yourself away from here and come and have a look. It's hardly Las Vegas you know. It's a very nice, very professionally run, very friendly country club where people like to come and spend a few hours. Why won't you come up?"

"I might surprise you one day."

"Yes, and the ground might swallow me up too, just like it is that black thing you've got stuck in that hole over there."

Gabe turned to see his crowbar slowly starting to disappear in the hole he was digging for the strainer post. He bounded over to it, barely managing to grab it before it slid out of sight.

"Good God!" he exclaimed. "Looks like we've struck a water table." He paused. "I reckon if I open that hole up, wider and deeper, I'll find a spring a few feet down. But that's for another day."

"Would it take long to dig down and find out?"

"You're not interested in this sort of stuff," he told her. "Pour a cup of tea and tell me everything that's been going on."

"No, no, really! Would it take long?"

Gabe looked at her. "You serious?" The look on her face told him she was. "I'd have to get the tractor and put the post-hole digger on the back. Oh I don't know, a couple of hours."

"Do you think we could give it a go?"

"What, now?"

"Might be fun."

"Digging for water is hardly fun, but if you insist," he told her. "But not until I've had a sandwich and a cup of tea."

As Gabe spoke of the latest happenings from the district, Katie sat cross-legged on the ground, taking it all in, and watching him closely. She didn't know how she would feel seeing him again. But she found as she got closer to Mrs Cropp's house on the drive down from Mildura, she became increasingly anxious about seeing Gabe. She felt there was 'something' about him before, but she was so strung out emotionally, she thought little more about it. But in the months she had been away, she began to think more and more about him. As he kept chatting, she took in little of what he was saying. She was concentrating more on his mouth, his eyes, his lips, his muscled, rugged torso and his massive arms. She wondered what it would be like to lay with such a big man. Especially a man she remembered Mrs Cropp telling her had never even had a girl friend. Then she cursed herself for allowing loneliness to over-ride her emotions. But all of a sudden, on seeing him again, she wanted to get to know him.

Katie poured him a cup of tea from the thermos, and as he

accepted it from her, the tips of their fingers touched. Instantly their eyes met, then darted away from each other. Then a temporary stand-off developed between them, each not quite knowing how to react. Further comments were scattered with polite anecdotes, each a little wary of the other.

Katie enjoyed riding back to the house with Gabe on the tractor. She helped him hitch up the post-hole digger, then stood back and watched him attach the bucket to the front end loader. She had sought out her old position, the battery case, and had remembered to tuck her legs in under herself. The wind blew in her hair and she revelled in it blowing on her face.

Back at the excavation, she leaned against the mudguard of her vehicle as Gabe drilled a series of holes on his side of the boundary fence. Each hole was about four feet deep and a few inches apart. He then turned the machine around and began to dig them out with the front end loader. He had only deposited a few bucket-loads away from the area when he jumped off the tractor and looked down into the excavation. Water was beginning to rapidly seep in. He grabbed his spade, then a rope off the back of the tractor. He tied one end to the machine and the other around his waist. He gathered the slack and slowly eased his way down into the excavation.

"Have a look at this," he called to Katie. "It's a bloody spring for God's sakes." He drove his spade into the sidewall and began to dig. The further he moved around the wall, digging as he went, the more the water began to seep in. Soon, he was up to his knees in it.

"This is unbelievable!" he called to Katie, who was now standing at the edge of the excavation. Gabe leaned down and let some water run into the palm of his hand then sipped it. "Unbelievable! Bloody unbelievable! It's pure, spring water. No salt. Like a taste?"

"Hang on, I'll grab the lid off the thermos," she said.

As she leaned over the edge of the excavation to hand it to Gabe, the dirt gave way and she slid on her bottom into the muddy water. She squealed as she plunged into the mud, now about a foot deep. When she regained her feet, it was to Gabe's thunderous laughter. For an instant she was as mad as hell, but then she realised how ridiculous she must have looked sliding on her backside into a pool of muddy water.

"You want to take that drink now?" Gabe asked, trying to get the words out amongst howls of laughter.

She leaned down, scooped her hands and splashed a large amount of brown water over Gabe then lunged at him, pushing him off his feet. They both fell together and became submerged momentarily in muddy spring water. Katie got herself tangled in the rope Gabe had tied around his waist as each threw mud and water at each other. They laughed hysterically. Joker stood up top, barking excitedly and running around the edge of the excavation. Then Katie stood in the one spot and jumped up and down several times, squealing and screeching with delight. She slapped her hands on top of the water, then began to scoop it up over herself. It was as though her release valve had finally been tapped. Gabe, standing up to his knees in muddy water, stood mesmerised by her actions. Then he realised she was letting off steam, venting her spleen, purging her grief. He let her go. Finally, exhausted, she threw her arms in the air.

"More?" Gabe put in, pretending to make a grab for her.

"Oh God no! Gabe. Please. I'm pooped."

They stood looking at each other, not ever having remembered engaging in such activities before. Gabe reached over and held out his hand. Katie took it. "Hang on to the rope and pull yourself back up to the top. Can you do that?"

"You might have to give me a shove."

But he could see she would need quite a breather before she could undertake such a task. So he turned around and half bent over.

"Climb up on my back and I'll lift you out."

"Oh Gabe!"

"Come on, get on."

Again they started giggling like infants in a schoolyard.

"Put your arms around my neck."

She did, and Gabe took the three or four large strides needed to climb clear of the excavation. She lowered herself to the ground and the two stood looking at each other, covered in mud from head to toe.

"My clothes will be ruined!" she said, casting her eyes over herself.

"Hop on the tractor and we'll go back to the house."

"My clothes are over at Mrs Cropp's."

Aunty Betsy saw Gabe coming down her driveway from her kitchen window and hurried outside as Gabe brought the tractor to a halt. "Well I do declare," she laughed. "What on Earth? Katie look at you."

"Looks like we're going to need the hose, Aunty Betsy," Gabe said as they both began to laugh again. Gabe helped Katie off the tractor, then walked across the front lawn to pick up the hose, telling Mrs Cropp as he went of his good fortune in stumbling across the spring.

"Gabe that's marvellous. Does it look to be very much?"

He turned on the hose and began to squirt the mud off Katie who huffed and puffed and squealed as the cold water hit her body. "I reckon I counted about eight to ten inlets into the excavation. If it's as good as I think it is, it'll be enough to irrigate that bottom thirty acres and your twenty-five of strawberry clover."

Mrs Cropp couldn't hide her delight. Discovering a water-table close to the surface was a God-send.

Satisfied all the mud had been washed off her, Katie reached for the hose. "My turn! My turn!"

An hour later, both had dried and got themselves into clean gear while Betsy Cropp ran their soiled clothes through the washing machine and hung them out to dry. "So you two, what now?"

"Better go back and finish putting in that new strainer I guess. What about you Katie, want to see your pet lambs?"

Her face lit up. "You still have them?"

"Part of the family," he told her.

"Oh yes please! Mrs Cropp, you coming too?"

"You go ahead, I'll come over in a minute."

* * *

Gabe took Katie to the rear of his house, to a small area he had fenced off. "Here we go," he said, helping her off the tractor. "Have a look over there. Come on," he called. "Come on." Instantly, thinking it was feed time, six very large lambs appeared. "What do you think?"

"Oh wow! That's them? They were so tiny and helpless. That's wonderful," she said. "Thank you for looking after them," she told him warmly.

"It's the only memory of you I have on the place, so I wasn't likely to let them go or have anything happen to them."

Katie smiled and put her hand to his face. "I've thought about you a lot Gabe. I don't know why, I just have. It's not everyday in her life a girl gets saved from death's door by a handsome stranger."

He sniggered. "And I'm really a handsome bloody stranger too, aren't I?"

"Well I've come back to see you, haven't I?"

"Mrs Cropp you mean," he came back.

Gabe's comment hurt her a little. "No Gabe, not only Mrs Cropp. You too. Why do you have such a low opinion of yourself? Don't you think women could find you attractive?"

Pangs of embarrassment swept through him. He didn't know where to look. He found the pluck. "Not women Katie. One woman. You."

"Oh Gabe, you flatter me. I never thought you'd even think of me in that way."

"I haven't been able to think of anything else for months. And now you're here, I'm that happy I could burst."

"I wasn't sure how you'd react to seeing me again?"

"Oh, what about the happiest man in the world?" he told her, moving across to help her back on the tractor.

When they arrived back at the excavation, the water had already filled the hole Gabe had dug and begun to overflow on the ground.

"How can you use that?" Katie asked.

"I'll have to get a few blokes to come and dig it out. Then we'll cap it somehow. What it means is that this paddock we're in and that one over there," pointing to Mrs Cropp's patch of strawberry clover, "can now be irrigated with no outlay apart from the setting up cost. What will probably happen is that we'll dig down about eight to ten feet. Make the hole about twelve feet across. The next time you see it, I'll have a pump on it and all around the inside of the excavation you'll see about eight inlets which will have widened to about a foot and the water will be pouring in. There's one like this out at Keppock, about twenty-five miles the other side of Naracoorte. The same thing happened there. Unbelievable thing to see. The water pours in there at the rate of thousands of gallons an hour."

Back at the house, Gabe busied himself on the phone speaking to various drilling contractors in a bid to get the excavation dug and capped. Katie sat making small talk to Joker, then she casually began to walk around the kitchen. She ran her fingers across the old leather couch which ran the length of the kitchen window. The big old oak table with the scarred and pitted surface. A couple of very old, wooden chairs pulled in against it on the other side. A linoleum floor, covered in places with old mats to cover up wear marks. Honey-coloured sticky fly strips hanging from the ceiling. A lead-light kitchen cabinet with a meat safe on one end. A set of dust-covered, canisters on top. And like Mrs Cropp, a Charles Hope kerosene refrigerator. A jug-and-bowl set sat on the kitchen sideboard. On the end wall, the stove and a fully stacked woodbox. She looked at the clock, checked her watch, then looked at the clock again.

"Must have stopped," she thought, moving her eyes to the right of the framed photograph of a woman. She stepped forward to take a closer look.

Half turning and placing his hand over the mouthpiece of the phone, "That's her. That's mum," Gabe said, continuing his conversation.

Katie took the frame in her hand and studied the photograph more closely. She glanced at Gabe then back to his mother, returning it to its position.

Gabe hung up the phone. "Reckon they can be here in about a week. What do you think of me mum?"

"You're a lot like her. You have her nose."

"Better hers than the mongrel she married!" he said. "You won't find any pictures of him around here."

She felt sad. "I don't suppose you'll tell me will you?"

Gabe gestured with his hand. "Oh, maybe one day." He thought for a moment and looked at her. "You know, as a kid, all you really know are your parents. Other kids at school of course, but it really comes down to your parents. What they're like. How they treat you. When I was growing up I thought it was natural for the woman to be kind, loving and gracious and the man to be a tough mongrel. That was how it was. I knew he was neither kind nor seemed to have a hell of a lot of good in him towards me but, for some strange reason, I never stopped trying to please him and win his acceptance. No Katie, you won't find any pictures of that bastard in this place."

Katie was about to speak when the phone rang. It was Aunty Betsy telling them dinner was on the table. "You have anything special you'd like to do tomorrow? You want to stay over at her place, come back here. What do you think?" he asked her, preparing to leave.

"I'll tell you after tea," she smiled.

Conversation flowed freely over Betsy Cropp's dining-room table. Both were overjoyed at Katie's decision to visit and it wasn't long after the dishes were done that Betsy Cropp found herself seated at her piano playing her house guest's two favorite songs. As the evening wore on, Betsy Cropp decided her day had been long enough, said goodnight and took herself off to bed. Gabe and Katie continued talking until well after midnight.

"So what do you think about tomorrow," he asked her.

She climbed out of her armchair and went and sat next to him on Mrs Cropp's three-seater lounge. "You're the one who says it's not safe for me to be out of your sight," she told him in a mock tone. "What would you suggest?" her eyes softening as she drew little circles with her index finger on his thigh.

Gabe failed to recognise the signals. He twisted in his seat and turned his head away. "Could go for a drive I suppose," he shrugged.

"Is that what you'd like to do?"

"Yes it is," he told her. "I've never seen the sea, why don't we head off to Robe? Apparently it's quite nice. We could have lunch at a pub."

"You've never seen the sea?" Katie exclaimed.

"Amazing isn't it! Learn something new everyday don't we? No! Never had cause to make the trip I suppose. But your being here makes me think it's time I had. What do you think?"

"I think it sounds wonderful," she told him.

"What time would you like to go?"

"You're the boss. I'll be ready whenever you say."

He moved to climb out of the lounge when his arm accidentally dropped across Katie's shoulder. Their eyes met. Their lips were only inches apart. Gabe's heart started to race and he felt his mouth go dry. Katie began to tremble slightly. Their heads only a breath apart. Ever so slightly, she edged towards him. Gabe gently touched his lips against hers. The sensation he felt was electric. As he pulled away slightly, Katie went to him, and ran her tongue along the inside of his top lip. Both were fully aware of the effect they were having on each other, but Gabe couldn't come to terms with his own self-consciousness. He made an excuse and eased himself away from Katie. He climbed to his feet, keeping his back to her.

What the hell is she going to think if she sees me like this? he cussed, walking out to the kitchen. As he went behind the door he knew he couldn't be seen by her, so he quickly adjusted his clothing to prevent her seeing how aroused he'd become. He went to the sink and ran himself a glass of water then returned to the lounge room.

"If I have to be up with the birds, then I guess I better make a move," he said awkwardly.

Katie could see how tense he'd become and threw him a warm, enticing smile. "So nothing I could say or do would keep you here any longer?"

Gabe's face took on full colour. "Shit, Katie! Aunty Betsy has read me the riot act about you..."

His words stopped mid sentence when she walked over to him, put her arms around his waist and looked up at him. "I won't break you know." Then she smiled. "I'll see you in the morning."

As Gabe drove away from Betsy Cropp's house, he yelled and roared like never before. "Holy shit! You stupid, dumb, bloody dork, why the fuck don't you do something? She's been giving you the green light all night, but no! not you! you dumb bastard! What is wrong with me? What is wrong with me?" he screamed into the night.

* * *

Gabe rose early, fed the pet lambs and hurried back to the house. "Oh shit!' he cussed, "I still haven't sunk that bloody strainer post." Giving his oversight fully two seconds thought, he then dismissed it. "Buggar the strainer post. This bloke's gonna take that blonde sheila for a drive. And today I'm gonna make my move. No more of that self-conscious bullshit! Today's the day!"

By the time he pulled up in Betsy Cropp's driveway, Katie was already standing at the gate. Her long, blonde hair shining in the early morning sun framed her face and painted a portrait of delicate beauty. Gabe's first-up, quick glance at her, totally dissipated his earlier rantings of his self-promised bravery. He shook his head in dismay.

She looks more sensational every time I see her.

He tried desperately not to let it affect him. He bounced out of the front seat of his old ute with Joker following at his heels. "Mornin' sweet girl, did you have a good sleep?"

"The whole six hours, yes thank you. And you?"

"Never better!" he lied. He certainly wasn't going to let on he spent the night tossing and turning in wondrous anticipation of spending the day with her at the beach.

Betsy Cropp came to her front door. "You feeling alright Gabe? Katie tells me you're off to Robe? I don't ever remember you going for a drive for the sake of it in your life!"

"Would you like to come too?"

"And be a wet blanket? No thank you! You go and have fun. Don't worry about Joker, I'll look after him. I think it's wonderful you've been able to get this man to actually leave the place for a day."

Katie made her way to the utility and Gabe held her door open. As she climbed in, she casually glanced in the back. It was empty. "You've had a bit of a clean out."

Gabe laughed. "The old girl's about a half a ton lighter now. I couldn't believe how much junk I had lying around in there. Didn't seem much sense in carting drums of diesel and petrol and all the other crap all the way down to Robe and back. Park the bloody thing and some bugger might pinch it," he said a matter-of-factly.

Joker followed Gabe's ute all the way down the driveway and sat down, watching as they drove onto the road. Then they were gone.

Chapter 25

Silence fell between them for a few miles. Katie was contented to look out the window and, although she promised herself she wouldn't, she began to compare the Mercedes with the Holden ute, Paul with Gabe. She found herself attracted to Gabe, and she thought he was attracted to her. But she had to break down the barriers. She had to rid him of his nervousness, his self-consciousness. She knew it wouldn't be easy, especially as he'd never been out with a woman on a date in his life.

I want to get to know him. I need to get to know him. I don't know if he's the sort of man I want, but at least you know where you stand with him. Perhaps it's his naivety I find so appealing.

As they passed through the small country town of Lucindale, Katie looked over at him. "What sorts of things did you dream about when you were a small boy?" she asked.

"Good God, I don't know! Never really thought about it I guess. And you?"

"Oh, I always dreamed of becoming a nurse."

"And you did. Did you ever play any sport?"

"Tennis sometimes. Basketball. But not very much. You?"

"Never allowed to. Played a bit of footy at school. Cricket in the summer. Never seemed to be a lot of point to it, because the school also wanted you to play on Saturdays and I was never allowed to. The old man always made me stay home."

"What about when you got older?"

He shook his head. "You didn't know the old man. Mum wanted to let me go, but he wouldn't hear of it."

"Gee I think I would've rebelled if my parents had've treated me like that. But they were wonderful. I was involved in everything, and they were right by my side all the time. Weren't you allowed out at all?"

"No, never. That's why I'm so bloody awkward with you. Never really had a lot of contact with other folk. The opportunity was there after the old man died. Before then too. I suppose as I got old enough to please myself a bit, but you don't. You just don't. You become so enclosed in your own little world, you don't know how to react if you're taken away from it."

"But you haven't left the place in years. Going by what Mrs Cropp said, this is probably the first time you've ever been driving for the pleasure of it."

"Never been anywhere Katie. Even had to check the map for Robe."

"Do you read books?"

"No. The paper when I get one. I suppose knowledge-wise I'm not too clued up about the world but, farm-wise, I get by. And that too is another reason I find it awkward being around other people. I can't compete. I can't talk about the things they talk about because I haven't done anything. Since meeting you I've tried to take stock of myself and smarten up a bit. For example I now know Mount Everest takes its name from the surveyor-general of India, Sir George Everest, and is twenty-nine thousand and twenty-eight feet high. The Garganey are a breed of duck which migrate three thousand miles from Africa to Europe to breed. Dreep is Scottish for a useless or dismal person. And especially for you, seeing you're a nurse, when we frown, we use forty-three muscles. In contrast it takes only seventeen muscles to smile. How about that?" he said. "And those clouds we can see off in the distance are called cumulo-nimbus. They're up pretty high but often indicate there's rain and thunderstorms on the way. How am I doing? You impressed?" he grinned.

Katie was surprised. "Well yes, indeed I am."

"And cheese? Do you know the history of cheese?"

She giggled. "No I don't know the history of cheese."

"All cheese begins as milk. Mostly cows milk, although it can be the milk of sheep or goats. Earliest records show it hit the tables in Mesopotamia three thousand B.C. It's made by adding rennet, the inner lining of the fourth stomach of calves. A dried extract of this is used to curdle milk. This is called curds and whey. Whey is the watery part of milk. The curds are drained of whey, heated, salted, and pressed into drum shaped moulds. These are then ripened, sometimes for years. And depending on how much fermentation takes places determines the flavor. For example, that stinking, mouldy rubbish called blue vein gets its veining from bacteria that's allowed to grow on and into it. Dreadful stuff."

"I quite like it actually. Especially on toast."

"Well that just indicates to me you have absolutely no respect for your stomach..."

And so they continued to question and comment to each other on general knowledge as they made their way towards the beachside resort. There was much laughter and both were revelling in each other's company. But more than that, Katie was having fun and Gabe could see she was. He was thrilled that for a few hours at least, she could cast her past to the wind and all her grief along with it.

Bringing the conversation back to a serious level, she asked him if he ever at any stage in his life thought he'd like to be in love.

"Maybe when I was younger and you saw others you went to school with tying the knot. But it was also a case of availability. I mean, I'm not exactly the sort of bloke I can imagine many young women would've had in mind."

"What if you fell in love now?"

"I have."

"No, seriously."

"I am serious."

"But you don't even know me."

"I know I've seen you at your low points and high points, and if that's as rough as it gets, then hell, you're a pushover."

"OK. Seeing you're so determined to be in love with me, then why did you walk away from me last night?"

He felt his face become flushed. He twisted his hands on the steering wheel. "Be...Because I didn't know what to do," he told her.

"Well it's not that difficult...pull over."

He shot his glance at her. "Go on, pull over!"

Gabe stopped his vehicle.

"Now put your arms around me." She could tell she was embarrassing him, but was determined to see it through. "Come on, put your arms around me."

Gabe did. "Now kiss me...come on, kiss me."

He needed no further encouragement. They held their embrace for a lengthy moment. Slowly they came away from each other.

"You see?" Katie whispered, "I told you I won't break."

Slowly he drove on, his mind racing from the encounter.

"So let me ask you this," Katie continued. "Let's say, hypothetically, you do meet a girl and want to make something of it. What if finding the love of your life meant changing the life you loved?"

"You mean leave the farm?"

"If you like."

"What the hell would I do?"

"So you wouldn't leave?"

"I couldn't leave!"

"What if she asked you to?"

"I'd have to say no."

"What if I asked you to?"

"You won't."

"You don't know that!"

"That's not fair."

"You say you love me."

"But you wouldn't come here."

"And you wouldn't leave."

"You're tormenting me. There's no way you would want someone like me in your life."

"I'm in your life today."

"But this is just one day."

"Okay, let's make it three days."

"Three days?"

"Why not? The shops in Robe are still open. Let's buy what necessities we need and stay a few days."

"Where?"

"Ever heard of motels?"

Gabe became excited. "You mean it?"

"Absolutely."

As they drove into the town, they stopped and bought a change of clothes and toiletries, then found a motel and booked adjoining rooms. Katie thought the best place for him to get his first experience of the ocean would be Long Beach. She'd not been there, but knew about it from friends. As she drew the utility to a standstill, she felt the look on Gabe's face would be indelibly printed on her mind forever. His eyes opened as wide as saucers as he gasped in disbelief. Long Beach, a long, sweeping stretch of silver-white sand, seemed to run forever in both directions.

"My God!" he gushed. "Have a look at that! Oh Katie, I would never have imagined. It's bloody sensational!"

Quickly he took off his shoes and socks, rolled his trousers up and ran down to the water's edge. Small waves lapped over his feet. He called to her. Moments later she joined him.

"I don't know what to say," he told her, throwing his arms around and spinning himself in a circle. "God if I had known this was what I was missing out on, I'd have been here all my life. Fuck my old man and all his fucked-up values! That prick told me the beach was no big deal and couldn't understand why anyone would want to go there. Fuck you Garth!" he screamed at the sky. "Something else you deprived me of. Fuck you, you bastard!"

Katie watched him enjoy what she figured most of us took for granted. She too felt bitter towards his father for never allowing his son the truth of such a wonderful experience. Katie stood off silently, allowing him the solitude to savor the moment. Gradually, he began to collect himself.

"Oh God, this is so exhilarating! Katie I love it! I love it! I love it!, I love it!," he cried out over and over again spinning himself in a circle. "Can we spend the rest of the day here?"

"I can't think of a better place," she told him.

As it was off-season, they had Long Beach pretty much to themselves. One or two people out for a walk a good distance ahead. The ocean was calm, the sun was out. The day was warm. But Gabe still kept an eye on the cumulo-nimbus clouds way off in the distance.

"I reckon in less than two days we'll be in for a drenching," he said.

Swept away from the exhilaration and emotion of his first experience with the sea, he walked up and back, dragging his toes through the sand and allowing the waves to lap at his feet for two hours. Katie had made her way up the beach, content to sit and watch him. When they returned to his vehicle, he sat down, stared at the ocean and just shook his head. "To think it's taken me half a lifetime to experience this. I am so pissed off about that, you can't begin to imagine."

"Well we don't have anything else to do except enjoy it. So why don't we do just that?"

Back at the motel, Gabe rang Betsy Cropp and told her they'd decided to stay in Robe for a day or two. She offered the usual motherly concerns. Gabe tried to put her mind at rest, but she was still concerned. "Aunty Betsy," Gabe said finally, "we'll be alright...really!"

That night, Gabe desperately wanted to be with Katie. Katie was entertaining the prospect that he may ask her to. But he didn't. They both had a restless night in their separate rooms and only began to feel like sleeping when it became time to get up. They joined each other for breakfast and, after a brief walk around the streets of Robe, returned to Long Beach.

"What would you say to spending the night right here, on the beach with just a rug between us, and watch the sunrise in the morning?" Katie asked him. "Might be fun. We could have a bit of lunch in town, go back to our rooms for a nap, then come back tonight and wait for the sun to rise."

When Katie applied her charm with him, he found himself looking into her deep, blue eyes and any resistance he was conjuring up was immediately annulled. "How come you can get around me so bloody easily?" he said.

Katie giggled, and Gabe just revelled in the attention she was giving him. He took her in his arms, and with the waves washing over their feet, kissed her gently, lovingly. Then with their arms wrapped around each other, proceeded to walk as far up Long Beach as they could before turning round to walk back.

If the age difference was a factor to either of them, it bore no comment as they strolled together along the silver sands of Robe's Long Beach.

* * *

The sun was just beginning to creep across the horizon. Katie inched her body in closer to Gabe. They sat nestled into the sand, peering out from under the travel rug they'd pulled up over themselves to keep off the chilly ocean breeze. It was nearly six a.m. under a brightly moonlit sky. The ocean had spent the night lying dormant, its surface as flat as the shiny finish of a wall mirror. Gradually it began to change as the sun's rays penetrated, as if telling it to awaken to a brand-new day. Gabe dug his feet into the sand and wriggled his toes. The sandpapery roughness of the granules felt good against his skin. He wondered at the awesomeness he saw before him. As the sun continued to rise above the horizon, Gabe felt Katie's skin quiver a little and pulled her in closer under his protective arm. The breeze began to stiffen as clouds swept in from the north. They watched them swirling overhead, their colours changing from white to grey to black. White caps appeared on the water, as though in protest at the rumblings and churning of the atmospheric activities.

"Ever seen anything quite so stunning," she asked Gabe, "watching the sun creep above the ocean?"

"Just blows me away, but the clouds are a worry. Do you want to go back to the car?"

Katie shook her head against the crook in his shoulder. "This is such a wonderful, wonderful moment," she said softly. "The breeze, the sunrise, the sea changing as we watch. I'm so happy I'm trembling inside."

Gabe's eyes were beginning to water. He didn't know if it was from the chilly wind blowing against them or the result of the continuous thrill running through his body. For he too was shivering inside, from the sheer exaltation of the moment.

"Katie, I don't know what a man is supposed to say when he finds himself wound up tighter than a drum. It's, it's a sort of feeling of anxiety, of wanting to explode."

"Is that how you feel right now?" she whispered, moving up on him a little so her forehead touched the bottom of his jaw.

He didn't know what to say, instead he gestured with a slight nod.

Katie ran her fingers along his left hand which had fallen between her breasts. She lifted it and pushed it inside her bra. "Touch me Gabe."

"I don't know how. I want to. All over, but I'm scared to."

Katie moved up higher, so her mouth was even with his. She kissed his top lip. "I'm not going to push you away."

Gabe felt powerless against the scent and closeness of Katie McFarlane. He liked the feel of her hair blowing against his face. He cursed himself for never having lived before. For not knowing what to do. For not knowing what was expected of him. He always believed in courtship, the man led the way. But he was so overpowered by her presence, he could do little except be led along by her. Yet despite Katie's encouragement, Gabe was too apprehensive to move. Too tense to pursue her request.

"For weeks, months...damn it from the first time I ever set eyes on you, my heart has done nothing else but call to you. This moment is everything I could ever have wished for, yet I feel I'm the only one who knows it. Right now, right at this instant, I think I could love you for a thousand years, but I guess I'm just a simple country bloke who's not very good at explaining himself."

Suddenly he was aware he was holding Katie's breast and became aroused like never before. As it lay in the palm of his hand, he swore to God he'd never before felt anything so erotic or sensual. This was the closest he'd ever been to her heartbeat. He'd saved her from death and held her in his arms. But this was different. She was allowing him to hold her very mortality. He felt the blood run to the tops of his ears and they began to throb. Katie withdrew Gabe's hand then twisted her body so she lay facing him. Both Gabe's arms were now wrapped around her as she found his mouth.

"I never knew until this moment the warm of your breathing could be so intoxicating," she whispered, before hungrily returning to his lips. Like a giant explosion erupting inside himself, Gabe could hold back no more. He didn't know what he was supposed to do. Instead, he allowed instinct to be his guide. He rolled Katie over on her back and began to kiss her forehead, the bridge of her nose, then her lips. Quickly. Frantically. He ran his tongue in a circle around her mouth and smiled at her.

"I love your mouth, it says so much," he whispered as she joined her lips to his. Suddenly the sounds of the waves became louder. His heart was throbbing so strongly in his ear drums he knew he needed a release. Katie placed her hand upon him and he rolled her in his arms.

"Make love to me Gabe." Quickly she helped him to slip her out of her jeans. Moments later, he was lying on top of her as light rain began to fall. She raised her legs and he placed his massive arms around her shoulders and under her back. She wrapped her fingers around him to guide him.

"Oh God!" she gasped.

He drove himself into her. At the full length of his thrust, Katie groaned as she sucked in a lung full of air then began to frantically jerk her body against his. It was too much for Gabe to contend with. Too much to control and she felt him explode inside her as he brought her to a climax. So intense was the moment, Gabe's head felt it was going to shatter from the pain of unbearable throbbing and rushes of blood. Only then did the two realise their naked bodies were drenched with perspiration and rain. As they lay together as one, Katie spoke softly to Gabe. Her voice almost child-like.

"When I lost Paul, I never thought I would ever be able to make love again. At least not in a situation where it really meant something. Thank you for rescuing me from my darkness."

Gabe moved onto his side and rested his head in his hand. He couldn't believe how relaxed he felt. How drained. How spent. The throbbing had cleared in his brain. He raised his hand and gently stroked her face.

"I'm always in a situation where I'm never sure what to say to you," he said. "I only know that right now I never want to be anywhere else, ever, than entirely with you." His face took on a sad and disappointed look. "And I know too, someone like you was never meant to spend more than a brief interlude with someone like me. You have your life filling up with other events, but I want you to know what I experienced with you, if it never happens again, will last me a lifetime. I needed the memory Katie...I needed the memory. Frankly, I need a lifetime with you, but I know it can't be. That memory will be your gift to my life and I thank you for that."

As the cold rain continued to fall on their fully exposed bodies, neither seemed to care.

"Please don't say that Gabe. You make it sound so final. It's not final. I'm not going to run away. I'm not going to break if you put me down. You are truly a most amazing man. So gentle. So considerate. From our very first meeting. I am so thankful for your kindness. And, apart from that, I also happen to think you're a great lover."

Gabe blushed at the compliment then felt terribly self-conscious. "Some great lover," he scoffed. "When I had to be shown what to do!"

"We both know that's not true," she countered. "I helped you find me. Did it ever occur to you I couldn't get to you quick enough? So, seeing you are so intent in believing what we did was a once-only, that you think I'm somehow going to spread my wings and fly away, then you're going to need more than one memory of me to live on for the rest of your life."

Katie then reached up and kissed Gabe long and hard, at the same time, placing her hand around him once more. Instantly Gabe felt himself stir with all the feelings and emotions of a few minutes previous. Seconds later, they were again drowning in each other's perspiration and emotions as the rain beat down harder. Exhausted and laying spent in each other's arms, Katie eased herself onto her feet and ran towards the water's edge.

"Come on!" she called. "Last one in has to drive home."

Gabe watched as she ran and ran. *This girl could laugh the rain away*, he thought, as her carefree laughter drifted in the breeze towards him. Quickly he joined her. Together they giggled and shivered as they bounced and bobbed in the water. Although Gabe had never seen the sea before, or the sand or the seagulls or anything else with the shore line, there was nothing more glorious to him than the sight of Katie McFarlane's naked body. Even drenched to the bone by the rain and the sea, she portrayed an image in his mind of a china doll. So pure. So innocent. So perfectly proportioned. He told himself if ever he did get to see her in her old age, she would never be a moment older than she was right now. As he watched her threshing about in the sea, he glanced around himself, thankful she had chosen a very deserted section of the beach to spend the night. He went to her.

"You better tell me this is really happening," he said, taking her in his arms.

Katie clung to Gabe's neck. "You make me feel so safe, so protected," she told him, then dropped her eyes.

"This Paul fellow never seems to be too far away from you, does he?" he asked.

"But I have to get on with my life Gabe. You have helped me do that. But no, Paul's never very far away. Maybe it's because he loved me so intensely, so entirely, that it's now impossible for me to continue in life without that very special emotion."

* * *

The breakfast trays were being delivered to the other motel rooms when Gabe pulled his vehicle into the car space at the front door.

"Look at that, this must be ours coming now," Gabe said. He quickly opened the door to the unit and the lady with the breakfasts placed a very heavily laden tray onto a small coffee table. Under two stainless steel covers were bacon and eggs. Under another two, two bowls of porridge. Under another, several rounds of toast, butter, jams and honey. In the stainless-steel pots were tea and coffee and a spare pot of boiling water. The local newspaper was also delivered, much to Gabe's surprise.

"Good God, the only time I ever see a paper is when Aunty Betsy remembers to buy one when she goes to town."

Gabe and Katie devoured all that was on the tray. Then, just to tease Gabe a little, she stood up in front of him as he was finishing his cup of coffee and began to undress. "I think I'll take a shower now," she said, leaning over at him, giggling a little, and shaking her shoulders, which in turn shook her breasts.

"Jesus you're amazing! How the hell am I supposed to turn my back on you and all you've become to me after you leave tomorrow?"

Katie cradled his head against her stomach. "I don't know what will happen after tomorrow," she answered, mournfully, casually focusing on Gabe's back. "Oh Lord!" she exclaimed, horrified. "What on Earth have you done to your back? Did you burn yourself or something?"

He grimaced a little, raised his eyebrows and threw his head to one side in a dismissive action. "I told you the old man was a mongrel," he told her.

Katie moved around behind Gabe, her fingers gently following the scarred ridges, the legacy of his father's stockwhip. She could tell the scarring was years old from the way the skin had regrown. "Oh for heaven's sakes, what did he use on you, a horse-whip?"

"Close."

"You're kidding!," she said, moving back to face him. "Why that's disgraceful. Your back's a mess."

"The bastard really lay into me."

"You're not serious are you?"

"He sure did. The bloody thing was nine feet long too. They call them stockwhips to be precise," he told her.

"How often?"

"Just the once with the whip, but he didn't know when to stop. But mostly it was anything he could lay his hands on."

Katie leaned over to the bed and pulled on a bath robe. "Didn't you go to the police?" she asked. "What about your mother? Did she just let it happen?"

Gabe got up and wrapped a towel around himself. "My father was a vicious,mongrel bastard Katie. He had mum shit-scared of him. One day the prick even knocked her to the ground. I was only a kid at the time, but I vowed there and then one day he'd have to answer to me. And that day eventually came. It took awhile and several more years, but it came pretty quick when I was on the wrong end of his fucking stockwhip. Mum had already passed on when it happened."

Katie didn't know what to say. She recalled Mrs Cropp referring to Gabe's father as a vicious, mongrel bastard who used to beat up on the boy, but never in her wildest dreams imagined the severity of the beatings. She went to him. "Some of that scarring is very deep?"

"It sure is! Sometimes he'd lay into me so much I had to stay home from school for days because I couldn't even get out of bed."

"So when did they cease?"

Gabe hesitated for a moment, then he said, "You wouldn't enjoy the story."

"I'm a big girl Gabe. You can tell me if you wish. But if it's still too painful to talk about, I'll understand."

Gabe sat on the end of the bed. He thought for a moment. He decided to tell her, briefly.

"He'd deliberately stuffed up my birthday party, so the next day I took him to task and called him a few names. Next thing, I'm on the end of that bloody stockwhip. He was laying into me like there was no tomorrow, and I knew at the time if I didn't do something, the bastard was going to kill me. So I lunged at him. Knocked him off his feet, then raced into the shed and grabbed the shotgun. He wouldn't believe me when I told him it was loaded, so I blew a hole in the shed roof," he said, laughing sourly. "He bloody believed me then, alright! Anyway, a few more things happened. Finally, I made him give in. Made him promise he'd never touch me again. Then I drove like buggery over to Aunty Betsy's and she took care of me. She wanted to call the cops and all that stuff, but I convinced her not to in the end. I think I must have stayed there for quite a few days. When I finally went back home, I was always on tenterhooks. Never knew if I could trust the bastard to keep his word, which is why I never strayed too far from the the shotgun. But things became pretty strained. We hardly spoke. I finally found the prick dead in the paddock. I remember wondering at the time why I didn't cry. I guess when you look at my back, the answer's there."

"I had no idea. Oh Gabe, you poor man. Do they still hurt?"

He sniggered a little. "No Katie, they don't hurt. In fact I even forgot they were there. If I'd remembered, I'd have left my shirt on. You don't need to see things like that or hear those stories."

"But it happened to you. Of course I want to know. And you've never sought revenge for all that pain you suffered?"

He looked at her questionably, then shook his head. "No. No revenge. It's been and gone now. But I got my revenge. That day with the shotgun."

Katie gently rubbed her fingers over his scars. "Would you have killed him?"

"It got that close," he told her, holding up a finger and thumb showing the tiniest distance between the two. "I've often asked myself that question over the years. It actually came down to just a few seconds.

I was buggered. I was in agony. I was covered in blood. I had the barrel of the shotgun jammed in his mouth but he wouldn't submit. He must have known he was going to die, because he only conceded when he saw my finger tighten on the trigger. Not a pretty story, and not one I'm proud to tell. Apart from Aunty Betsy, I've never told anyone. It's over thirty years ago now, but in answer to your question, yes, I'd have killed the bastard."

Katie rested her face against Gabe's back, and ran her fingers lightly over his skin. "My God, he really made you suffer didn't he? I don't think I'd have had your willpower. If I had suffered like you had, I think I would most certainly have pulled the trigger."

"Not a nice man, my father."

She could tell from Gabe's tone of voice, the subject was now closed. "And your mother? Mrs Cropp told me she was lovely? She certainly looks to be in her photo."

Gabe's face lit up. He thought for a moment recalling his mother's magical smile and gentle nature. "She was special Katie. You would have loved her. My memories of her are those of a boy. I wished she could have lived longer so I could have got to know her." He reminisced in his thoughts. "Yes, I sure would liked to have got to know her. So," he said, a brighter tone in his voice, "you were saying?"

"Come and lay on the bed with me," she half whispered. "I'd just like to feel close to you."

Within minutes, Gabe heard Katie's breathing slow. He placed the side of his head on top of hers. As he lay there listening to the life within her, he buried his hand in her long, blonde hair, pushing it into his face. *This must have been what Aunty Betsy was talking about*, he thought. *You won't know when it'll happen, but you'll know when it does.* He pushed more of her hair into his face, gourmandising on the aroma of what he convinced himself must be someone else's dream. This couldn't be him laying there. Life's not like that.

He let Katie sleep, allowing her to wake in her own time. About an hour later she did. "Oh I'm sorry," she said, raising her head with a start, "I didn't mean to go to sleep on you."

Gabe smiled and handed her a cup of tea. "When I saw you beginning to stir, I boiled the kettle. This time tomorrow morning I know I'm going to think back to these few days and just know they didn't happen."

"Oh Gabe, don't think like that. You have your farm. And I have a farm of a different sort. Please understand you are very, very special to me. Try and look past the sheer pleasure we gave each other and be guided by our brain, not by our heart. I excite you because I'm new to you. These experiences are new to you. You excite me because you are so strong and gentle and caring. And I am grateful to you. Not grateful in the sense that I'm paying you back with my body. I made love to you because I loved making love with you. And I'll love it even more if you come and wash my back in the shower," she told him, placing her cup of tea on the coffee table.

Gabe followed Katie into the bathroom. Never in his wildest dreams did he ever think he would ever be able to hold the young woman's hand. Then to make love to her, over and over, and now to shower with her. He was in fantasyland. He knew she was leaving in a few short hours, but that was tomorrow. He'd try and face that, then. As he ran a sponge over her back, she took hold of his hand and brought it round the front of herself so he washed between her breasts then between her legs, then let the sponge drop to the floor. He turned her round to face himself. Katie and Gabe embraced as the water from the shower rained down upon them. They held each other closely. Tightly. For how long, they didn't know, neither did they care.

* * *

Later that afternoon, Gabe and Katie left their motel and went for a drive around the area. Gabe was still intensely fascinated by the sea and, for a couple of hours, looked out over it from a high vantage point. They stood at the front of his vehicle, holding on to each other, facing the massive expanse of ocean. Neither spoke very much, being content to savour the moment. Then, as if reading each other's mind's, they returned to the vehicle and continued to drive. As they approached the seaside town of Beachport, Katie asked Gabe to stop by at the local hotel so she could use its bathroom. He pulled into the kerb and left the engine running and watched her as she walked through the door to the saloon bar. Gabe's thoughts took him back over the past few hours of his life, until he blinked hard, bringing himself back. *She's been gone awhile*, he thought, noticing the temperature gauge on the engine had crept up. *Better see if she's alright.*

Casually he cut the motor, took the keys from the ignition and went to the saloon. As he approached, he noticed a line of six Harley Davidson motor cycles lined up along the street, close to the hotel's front entrance. He stepped into the saloon and became immediately consumed with rage. Six leather clad figures had formed a circle around Katie and were taunting her.

"Where did you come from baby?" "How would you like to suck my cock blondie?" "Show us your tits babe." With the taunts came the pushing, probing and pulling of her hair. Other hotel patrons sat along the front bar, trying to ignore what was going on. They knew only too well what would happen to them if they mixed it with the tattooed, leather-clad bikies with their steel knuckle-dusters, belt buckles and bike chains.

Katie had formed herself into a standing cowering position, with her arms clenched tightly to her chest. "Please leave me alone!" she pleaded, tears now beginning to run down her face. Seeing her distress only egged her tormentors on.

Unnoticed as he entered, Gabe scanned quickly around the area. He spotted a billiard cue. He grabbed it, smashed it across the leg of a nearby pool table to break it in two, roared like a bull and charged into the group of six. Katie saw him coming.

"Hit the floor Katie!" he yelled as the first blow from the cue took one of her tormentors on the side of the neck with such force, he dropped like a sack of potatoes. By the time the others realised they had a war on their hands, two of them were on the end of a left and right thunderbolt. They too hit the floor with such impact Gabe knew he wouldn't need to bother with them again, especially the first one. He crashed so heavily, Gabe heard the bone in his arm break. The fourth let fly with a roundhouse right which Gabe saw coming. He threw up his arm and blocked it, then unleashed a powerhouse right cross. The blow caught the bikie on the point of the chin and sent him sprawling across the bar-room floor. He came to rest against the brass footrail running the length of the bar. The fifth attacker lunged at Gabe and grabbed him round the neck. At the same time, the last of the six let go a powerful punch to Gabe's midriff.

"You fucking, mongrel bastards!" he roared. "You ever touch this woman again I'll kill the fucking lot of you." Foaming at the mouth with untamed rage, Gabe jammed his elbow into the face of the bikie who had him round the neck, sending him back several feet. He then grabbed the hair of the sixth bikie and jammed his face into his knee. As he went backwards, spitting teeth and blood, Gabe lashed out with his boot and caught him plum in the groin. He screamed in agony. Gabe then dragged him up by the hair, took a few steps and hauled the fifth attacker to his feet, also by the hair and smashed their heads together. With no one left standing, he scrambled to Katie's side.

"Sweetheart! Jesus Christ, are you alright? Did they hurt you?"

Katie pointed to the fourth bikie laying sprawled on the floor who was just beginning to stir. "He grabbed my breast Gabe and it really hurt, bu...but I'll be alright."

Gabe shot his glance around. "What, this mongrel?"

Katie nodded. "But leave him," she offered weakly.

Gabe ignored her plea. He sprang to his feet and went to the half-senseless bikie. He leaned down, picked him up by his shirt front and slammed him into the bar. "So you like to grab sheilas by the tits do you?" Gabe smacked him hard. He got no response. "You fucking hear me?" Gabe slapped him again. Harder. Blood began to stream from his lip. Still no response. "I'll make you fucking talk you mongrel!" Gabe grabbed the bikie's testicles, squeezed, twisted and yanked hard. The bikie's eyes nearly popped their sockets as he let out an ear-piercing, agonising scream. "Fuuuck Yo...!" he tried to say, but the last syllables were cut short as Gabe's thunderous right hand crashed into his face.

He spun back to Katie and helped her to her feet. "Why didn't some of you bastards help her?" he called to those stunned and doubly startled at the bar. "Weak as piss the lot of you!" he cussed.

Katie was more frightened than hurt. As they side stepped the fallen bodies, the local drinkers were still too shocked to open their mouths. As Gabe helped Katie towards the car, she stopped a short distance from the passenger-side door.

"Hang on a minute," she said. She walked over to the row of motor cycles. She grabbed the handle bars of the first machine, and with all her strength heaved it upright off its stand and let it drop to the ground on the other side. She went to the next motor cycle and did the same, then continued along the line until all the Harleys had been tipped over. Many had their mirrors and other accessories broken in the action. Gabe stood by the side of his car, laughing loudly.

"Come on!" he called to her. "There might be more of the mongrels around the corner. I don't want to go through all that again."

Katie had a look of great accomplishment and satisfaction on her face as she climbed into the utility alongside Gabe. "I don't know what to say," she said. "You've now had to come to my rescue again. Are you hurt?" she asked, sitting forward in her seat and turning to him.

Gabe shook his head. "No, I'm alright," he assured her. "They're not too brave as individuals. But when I saw what they were doing to you, I just saw red. Jesus, I could have killed the bastards!"

"But they might come after us."

Gabe grinned. "Yes, they might. But it's going to be awhile before a few of them wake up. I know I broke one bloke's arm, and that last bastard, I felt his jaw go when I dropped him. No. I don't think they'll come after us. Besides, first they have to find us, and secondly, they know full well what'll happen to them if they do. So don't you worry. Anyway, were you able to use the bathroom?"

Katie told Gabe she had. "They grabbed me as I was coming out."

Back in the motel room, Gabe could tell Katie was still upset by her afternoon's experience. They had planned to find a hotel and have tea. Instead, Gabe suggested he order some takeaway. Later in the evening Gabe sensed Katie was holding him even closer as they lay on the bed in each other's arms.

"Gabe."

"Uh-huh."

"What are you thinking about?"

"I think I'm riding so high on you, I don't know that I have any thoughts. Maybe...maybe all the nights of my life I've spent without you. I read some lines once. For some reason they've always stayed with me.

"And down the empty corridor of my life
I heard a heartbeat in the distance.
As it drew closer to me,
it seemed to get further away.
Today I had a dream
that you stopped so I could catch up...
but it was only a dream."

"Gabe that's beautiful. Who wrote that?"

She felt him shrug his shoulders. "Don't know. Just something I read."

"Is that how you feel, that we're merely two lonely heartbeats, fading off into the distance?"

"I don't know," he answered. "I just know my life will never be the same after you leave tomorrow."

"Yes it will. I'm the first woman you've ever been out with. If nothing else, at least you've learned there's more to life than that jolly farm. Promise me you won't stay home all the time. Promise me you will start to get out a bit?"

"You know I won't do that," he told her.

"Will you try?"

Gabe didn't answer and Katie didn't push it. She knew it would take more than her coaxing to get him to become a little more social. As she began to draw imaginary circles around the watch on his arm, silence fell between them.

Chapter 26

Katie was sitting in her office when Lorry Downs knocked on her door. "You looking for me?" she smiled.

Lorry gazed at her, puzzled." Er, no," she smiled, "should I?"

"It's your anniversary," Katie told her. "It's six months ago today you started working here. Now look at you! No more rings around the eyes. There's colour in your cheeks, and Kazumi tells me she couldn't do without you. And Jill says you've been able to replace your car with something a little better. I think that's wonderful. But Lorry, tell me, are you alright? Do you feel safe here?"

"Oh God yes, Katie, thank you. The unit. The furniture you provided. I feel as though someone waved a magic wand over me. I was in a terrifying nightmare as you well know. Was that really me? I had become such a victim of that bastard. And I still have fears he'll try and find me. I don't know where I would've ended up if not for you. Probably dead I guess. Thank you for hauling me out it."

Katie leaned over to her. "You have to stop thinking about him. If he was going to hunt you down, he would've done it long ago."

"You don't know the prick," Lorry said, remembering.

"And what you don't know is that since you've been here, I've moonlighted the off-duty cops to have a presence in the place to protect you should that happen."

Lorry was dumbfounded. "You're doing that for me? Katie I don't know what to say."

"So no more talk or worrying over Scarfe Olsen okay? He's long gone." She then beamed a smile straight at Lorry. "And I'm so proud of you. I didn't make you what you are. You did. All I did was provide you with an opportunity. You're the one who took the initiative. And now look at you. No more straggly, unkempt-hair. You're vibrant, attractive and your work is excellent."

"You're far too complimentary for someone who's only the hired help..."

Katie got up from her desk, and closed her office door. "Now you stop that! You are a very vital cog in the workings of this place. Where the hell would I be if Oakdale's very nerve centre suffered a breakdown? Your job is crucial in that Oakdale is always presented in the finest manner possible. How many people do you think would come in here if the tables were grubby, there were dirty glasses and ashtrays all over the place and rubbish littering the floor? I see the pride you take in Oakdale, I see the pride you take in yourself, and that carries over to the confidence we're now seeing in Emma. So stop even thinking like that," she told her. "And apart from that, you've endeared yourself to everyone. But enough of all that." Katie pushed an envelope across her desk. It was addressed to Lorry Downs. "Thank you for all your wonderful work," Katie said.

Lorry felt a tinge of embarrassment as she opened the envelope. It was a cheque for two hundred and fifty dollars. "Oh shit!" she gushed, "I didn't expect anything like this. Believe me, I'm very glad to be here."

Katie smiled. "It's simply a personal thank you from me to you. Go and buy yourself something nice. You deserve it."

* * *

Scarfe Olsen was still angry six months after Lorry Downs had pole-axed him and run off. Despite cruising Adelaide's pubs and clubs, he had not been able to find any trace of her. It was no good his seeking out her friends to locate her whereabouts. Lorry didn't have any. He saw to that, keeping the bitch prisoner in her own home.

"She can't have disappeared off the face of the earth," he cussed almost on a daily basis. "Where the fuck is she? WHERE THE FUCK IS SHE?" he'd yell at the walls of his deserted flat.

In the months since she was gone, he still continued to pick up women, hurt them, violate them and dump them. But he couldn't shake the humiliation of allowing Lorry Downs to slip through his net.

Especially since he had brutalised her to the extent where he controlled her mind. At least he thought he did. *You fucking bitch! One day I'm gonna find you and when I do, you're gonna regret being born! You're gonna learn you don't walk out on the Scarfe babe. Oh boy, are you gonna learn that!*

One night after work, Scarfe decided to head home rather than the pub. His jerked open the fridge door to grab a beer then slammed it shut when he saw the shelf was empty. He stormed out and drove to a bottle shop. As he waited in line to be served, he casually glanced over at a car carrier loaded with vehicles. He hardly took more than a passing interest in it when suddenly he shot forward in his seat like he'd been hit with a cattle prod. "Well I'll be fucked! Have a look at that!" He reversed out of the bottle shop queue and accelerated wildly over to the car carrier. He bolted out the door and stood looking at an old green Holden Kingswood on the bottom tier. He looked at the registration and eyed the vehicle again.

"That's the bitch's car!" He looked around for the driver of the rig but there was no one in sight. He looked again at the old Kingswood. "Christ I can't believe it!" Scarfe immediately headed for the front bar of the hotel adjoining the bottle shop. He approached a group of four young men. All were dressed in football shorts, blue singlets and wearing thongs, the truckies' uniform.

"Any of you blokes driving the car carrier out there?"

One of them spoke. "Yeah mate, me. What's your problem?"

"No problem," he gestured lightly, wanting to avoid any kind of confrontation. "Just wondering where you might have picked up the green Kingswood you're carrying?"

"What'd some bastard pinch it from you?" The group laughed.

"No no, I reckon I used to own it myself, years ago," he lied. "Just wondering where the old girl ended up."

"Mate, they're all headed for the wreckers. This load comes in from up north. I loaded first in Mildura, and they went on the bottom, and the second tier came out of Renmark."

"Well I'll be buggered!" Scarfe said. "Thanks mate. Bloody Mildura! Fancy the old girl ending up there!"

* * *

Gabe Caplin was a morbid, moping mess. Katie McFarlane had been gone for months, and in that time the big man was like a tractor without a steering wheel.

Everywhere he went on the farm reminded him of her. He'd pick things up, knowing the last person to touch them was Katie. He'd stand at the door and recall their most intimate moments. The things she said. The way she'd smile. Her favorite cup and saucer stayed on the sink, exactly where she'd left it. Even her comb she accidentally left on his kitchen table. He'd pick it up and hold it gently in his hands, looking at the strands of her long, glorious, blonde hair. Joker too, Gabe thought, was acting strange.

"What the hell's the matter with you?" he'd cuss, knowing full well he missed her as much as he did. "She's gone boy! It's no bloody good crying about it," he'd say, raising his hands to his face, fighting his emotions. "Jesus, this is worse than somebody dying!" He continued to go about his daily routine, but his heart wasn't in it. He'd sleep late, which is what he never did. He'd only eat when he knew he had to. He'd forget to close gates, causing the stock to box. But he didn't care. All he could think of was the eleven days that Katie McFarlane had been part of his life.

Betsy Cropp was getting concerned. She hadn't seen Gabe for two weeks. So she drove over to his farm. Gabe was sitting on the front verandah. He hadn't shaved for days and, when she pulled up, he appeared to be staring vacantly into space. "Gabe?"

"Hi Aunty Betsy," he replied, glumly.

She walked over and sat down next to him. Joker immediately came to her side, seeking a pat as he waved his tail. Mrs Cropp obliged. She looked at Gabe. "For God sakes, did she really have that much effect on you?"

Gabe leaned over, picked up a stick, and walked away from the verandah. He threw it a few feet in front of himself. Joker darted off and immediately retrieved it. "Fraid so."

"Well you can't go on like this. How long since you've had a decent meal? And what are all the wethers doing boxed in with the ewes and lambs in the south paddock?"

"Couldn't care less," he uttered.

"I know it must be hard for you," Betsy Cropp began. "But you must understand, Katie is a city girl. You were there when she desperately needed your help. In fact, you saved her life. But you have to let her go. Katie now has her own life. I know we both loved her dearly. I guess she was a once in a lifetime experience for both of us. But you have to treat her as a snowgoose. You healed her broken wing, then you set her free. Maybe, as I've told you before, as she migrates through life, she will pass our way again."

Betsy's words caused tears to roll down Gabe's face. "You remember once telling me what love was? I still remember what you said like it was yesterday. One day it will happen, you said. You won't know where. You won't know when. Then out of the blue you'll feel your knees go weak, your mouth go dry and your stomach will tie itself into one big knot. Ever since I dragged her from that car wreck, my knees have been weak, my mouth's been dry and my guts have been tied in a knot. You also said that when you touch each other you'll feel the most wonderful sensation. Well, I can't shake that feeling." Gabe paused to collect himself. "And you also said love wounds cut the deepest and take the longest to heal. I didn't know what it meant then," he added, wiping his eyes with his sleeve. "I bloody do now."

Betsy Cropp looked up at Gabe. "Well I'm blessed..."

"I don't think I want to live without her."

"Oh Gabe, Gabe," she said as she put her arms around him. "Then you must go to her."

"I can't do that," he said. He shook his head, embarrassed.

"Tell you what. Get inside. Have a shower and a shave, then we'll go into Heards or Wisharts. And bring your cheque book. You'll need it."

* * *

Katie McFarlane picked up Paul Redman's picture she kept on the filing cabinet in her office and stood for a moment looking at it.

My darling, darling man. I miss you so much. But please understand I have to try and live my life. And if I am to preserve your memory forever, I need to be free. Darling, I have to let you go. There is not a man in the world who could ever replace you, but I'm lonely and I desperately need to love, and be loved, again. There is such a man, but I'm not sure if he thinks I would fit into his world. He's a wonderful man darling. He's not at all worldly like you, but he's a good man. He's kind and ever so gentle. In the eleven days we've spent together, he showed me more of me than I ever thought possible. He taught me it was fine to love, but to go on grieving would serve no further purpose. Paul darling, I don't know if he'll have me, but I'm going to call him. My only hope is I haven't left it too long. Please don't see this as a betrayal. With this man I think I can love again. He won't take your place. Thank you for us my dear. I promise your memory will only ever be a moment away.

Katie opened the bottom draw of her desk and placed the photograph in a specially made velvet box and closed the lid. "Goodbye my darling."

* * *

Scarfe Olsen felt the adrenalin charge through his body as he sped back to his flat. He was bellowing in excited rage. "You fucking bitch! You fucking bitch! So you're in Mil-bloody-dura. Jesus, tomorrow's gonna be a great day." He rushed inside, threw some clothes into an old airlines bag, grabbed his pump-action shotgun, which Lorry never knew he had, fed one cartridge into the chamber, put five more in the magazine and stuffed some loose shells into his pocket, double magnum two's. *These oughta open the bitch up*, he smiled to himself.

He also grabbed two five-gallon jerrycans and threw them in the boot of his old Holden. By eight p.m., Scarfe Olsen was heading for Mildura.

* * *

Katie was joined by the other staff members, when, as promised, she opened an expensive bottle of champagne in honour of Lorry Downs. Emma, as usual, had called in on her way home from school and was presented with the biggest icecream spider she'd ever set eyes on.

"You'll spoil your tea if you drink all that," her mother laughed.

"But mum, this is tea!"

* * *

Scarfe drove through the night, but was forced to pull over halfway between Renmark and Mildura. Twice he nearly hit kangaroos, so he decided he wouldn't push his luck. He dozed for a couple of hours and got going again shortly after sunrise. Mildura was barely stirring when he pulled into the Shell service station on the edge of the town. He filled the car and the two jerrycans, then wandered into the cafe and ordered breakfast. Waiting for his meal, he asked for the local phone book, a pen and paper. Carefully he listed the twenty-six caravan parks, seven bed and breakfasts, fifty motels, twenty houseboats, plus a wide variety of restaurants and hotels in the Mildura area.

"Gee you're having a busy time," the waitress commented as she delivered his steak and eggs.

Scarfe ignored her and kept writing. He was still copying names and phone numbers an hour after he'd finished his meal. He then paid at the counter and left. Opposite the service station was a caravan park. He drove in, paid for an on-site van a week in advance then drove into the town centre. He pulled up next to the post office. When the doors opened at nine, he cashed a number of notes for change to use in a public phone box and went to work.

"Hello, I'm looking for Lorry Downs..."

"Sorry sir, no one here by that name."

Again he dialled. Again the same response. For three hours he dialed telephone numbers. No-one had heard of her. *Maybe the bitch has changed her name.*

He dialled again. As he flicked through the phone book, more or less doodling while he waited for another call to answer, he spotted an ad for The Oakdale Country Club. *Bit bloody classy for her*, he thought, dialling the number just in case. "Hello, can I have a word to Lorry, please?"

"Lorry Downs sir?"

Scarfe felt his heart jump. "Yes, Lorry Downs,"

"One moment please."

Scarfe slammed the phone down.

"Bingo!" he yelled, throwing hands and phone lists into the air. "You fucking bitch, have I got a surprise for you!"

* * *

Gabe Caplin liked what Mrs Cropp had chosen for him at Heard's menswear. Dark, blue pin-stripe, a pale, blue shirt and a tie with soft red, blue and grey tonings. Matching belt, socks and handkerchief. Up to Max Brown's shoes and Mrs Cropp saw to it Gabe chose something classy and expensive. He walked out with a pair of English imported Crochet and Jones blue-coloured moccasin-style slip-ons.

When Gabe arrived home he lay his outfit on the bed, then stood back and looked at it. "Good God! I've never had clobber like that in my life."

He checked his watch. *Better get to bed. Got an early start in the morning, not that a man's gonna sleep anyway. Jesus, is this the right thing to do?* He began to doubt his actions. *What if she tells me to piss off? What if she won't see me?* Gabe's mind was churning. Suddenly he felt excited at the prospect of seeing Katie again, but scared witless of what he was putting himself through in order to do it.

Joker's barking woke him at dawn. "What the hell are you on about boy?" Gabe climbed out of bed and went to the kitchen window. "Oh shit, of all bloody days!" he cussed.

He hadn't closed the gate by the shed properly so about fifteen-hundred sheep decided to take an early morning stroll up the main road. He flung open the kitchen door. "Get out there boy and bring those bastards home," he yelled at Joker. Instantly the dog was gone. Still hitching up his pants, he climbed into his old ute and raced off after them. "Bugger the bloody sheep!" he cursed. "Christ I'm gonna be nice and late getting away."

The sheep had stretched themselves a long way up the main road straight past his front gate and down towards Mrs Cropp's. By the time Gabe had them back in the home paddock, he was wet through with perspiration and as mad as a March fly in a heat wave. It was after nine a.m. before he finally showered, dressed in his new clothes and set off to Mildura. He thought he would arrive around three thirty, compensating for the half hour time difference between South Australia and Victoria. As he continued to toss around the pros and cons of making the trip, he found he was also enjoying the long drive.

Not long after an almighty bang came from the engine. "What the fuck was that?" he yelled, as a massive cloud of blue smoke popped up in his rear-view mirror. Slowly the old ute rolled to a standstill. The air was double blue as Gabe jerked himself from the cabin and reefed open the bonnet. He looked down at the engine, steaming, belching smoke, with oil everywhere.

"You rotten, mongrel bastard!" he roared. "Jesus Christ! First it's the bloody sheep, then you go and drop your guts! Now what the fuck am I gonna do?" A short distance ahead he saw a service station and set off towards it. He explained who he was to the service station owner, a kindly fellow. He then pointed out his urgency to get to Mildura.

"What do you wanna do?" the station owner said. "You got any money?"

Gabe glared at him.

"Meaning can you afford to hire a car?"

Gabe eased off. "Christ yes! The whole bloody fleet if I have to."

"Tell you what," he said. "Leave the old bus here with us and I'll see what needs to be done to get her back on the road. Meantime we'll get you fixed up with a hire car and you can get crackin'."

Twenty minutes later, a sparkling new Ford Falcon pulled up in the driveway. Ten minutes later, after fixing up the paper work, Gabe climbed behind the wheel.

"You'll be there in no time," the station owner said. "See you when I see you."

Gabe gloated over the newness of the vehicle, captivated with the smell and the amount of power under the accelerator. He wondered about the cost of getting his car fixed. It probably needed a new engine. He also knew he was now going to be an hour later getting into Mildura.

At ten past five, Gabe pulled into the Shell service station on the edge of the town, filled up and asked for directions to The Oakdale Country Club. A short time later, he pulled into its car park, but a good distance from the front entrance.

"What if I make a fool of myself?" Gabe said aloud, steering closer to the front entrance.

Then he saw a familiar face and knew something bad was up.

Chapter 27

Earlier that day, Scarfe got directions to the club and drove to it. He saw only a smattering of vehicles in the car park. With the engine running, he cast his eyes over the complex. He checked his watch, figuring he'd come back around five, when the place got busier. With what he had in mind, he needed people about to avoid unnecessary attention being focused on himself.

* * *

Gabe steered his vehicle closer towards the club. He figured he was now about fifty yards from the front door. *Jesus I'm bloody scared shitless,* he thought.

Then he saw a figure clad in black, walking round the perimeter of the building pouring liquid from a jerrycan. *That's strange*, he thought, not taking a lot of notice. He was more intent on concentrating his thoughts on how he would be greeted by Katie McFarlane. The black-clad figure then looked up and Gabe saw his face.

"Jesus that's that bloody Slick Bennedict!" he said aloud, wondering what he was up to. *That mongrel bastard. Surely Katie wouldn't have given him a job? Maybe he works for some pesticide mob. Maybe they've got rats or something and he's putting some poison down.*

As Gabe watched Slick, he saw him return to the boot of his car, replace the jerry can with another, take out a large, long box and walk in the front entrance of the club. *Doesn't look right to me*, he thought. He opened his car door and walked over to where he saw Slick pouring the liquid. He leaned down, scooped up some dirt in his fingers and raised them to his nose. *Oh Jesus! Bloody petrol. What the fuck is he up to?.*

Slick Bennedict ambled through the front entrance of The Oakdale Country Club and went to the top of the stairs. Patrons noticed him but kept on about their business. Casually, Slick opened the top of the jerrycan and fitted a special pourer which enabled liquid to flow freely. He made his way down the stairs, pouring the liquid as he went. Quickly he moved to the bottom and raced around the inside walls of the reception area, pouring petrol as he went. Startled patrons looked on, wondering what was happening. He then hurried to the edge of the fountain and threw the empty drum in the water. Moments later he discarded the rectangular box and stood brandishing his twelve gauge shotgun. Gabe got to the front door as Slick was about to execute his violent plan.

"LORRY DOWNS!" he yelled, 'WHERE THE FUCK ARE YOU? LORRY DOWNS! CAN YOU HEAR ME? GET YOUR FUCKING ARSE OUT HERE!"

A massive blast filled the air. Slick fired a shot into the chain holding the eight-foot chandelier hanging over the centre of the reception area. It plummeted to the floor as though dropped by a crane. It exploded and shattered into a million fragments of smashed and broken glass. Shocked and startled patrons screamed and ran to the nearest exits. Gabe jammed himself back behind some panelling built behind the front doors. Casey screamed and dived for the phone on her reception desk. Slick spotted her and fired, almost point blank. The double magnum took off part of her face and opened her chest like a butchered sheep. She was dead before she hit the floor. Slick ejected the spent cartridge and chambered another.

"LORRY FUCKING DOWNS, GET YOUR ARSE OUT HERE!" Slick screamed.

Mass panic erupted within the club. Patrons downstairs scattered to the nearest exits, while those upstairs, witnessing what was happening, made for the rear stairs and fire escape. Staff with presence of mind grabbed for the phone and called the police before making their escape.

Downstairs, Katie McFarlane had been out the back in the kitchen talking with Lorry Downs when Slick made his move. The sound of the first shot and subsequent explosion had them race to investigate. When the second shot rang out, they were both running towards the reception area. As they approached, Slick Bennedict had his back to them. They saw the mangled chandelier, then the barrel of the gun. Terror stricken, they ducked in behind a doorway.

Lorry went stony white. "Oh Jesus, Katie it's him!" she blurted in a muffled voice, frightened out of her wits.

Katie glanced at Lorry. "Who?"

"Scarfe! Jesus he's found me. Katie what am I going to do?"

"COME ON BITCH, GET YOUR FUCKING ARSE OUT HERE! LORRY DOWNS! LORRY DOWNS! YOU'VE GOT TEN SECONDS TO GET OUT HERE OR EVERYONE'S GONNA FRY. DO YOU HEAR ME?" Slick bellowed.

Gabe was backed in hard against a wall. Slowly the petrol fumes wafted up. Katie and Lorry also smelled the fumes.

"He's calling for me!" Lorry panicked. "Katie, he's calling for me!"

Slowly the two began to edge forward. Katie was in front. As she peered around a corner of the ground-floor structure, she saw Casey's body lying crumpled on the floor with half her head missing. Katie gagged. As she ducked back, Slick heard a movement and fired, the pellets smashing into the plastered wall she was leaning against. Without thinking, she charged in the direction of the gunman.

"NOOOO!" she screamed as she lunged at him. Slick saw her coming and crashed the butt of the shotgun into her head. Katie collapsed in a dazed heap. Gabe saw what happened to Katie, but knew he was too far away to do anything. Blind rage tore through his body.

Slick bent down and hauled Katie up by the hair and stood with his arm around her throat. "YOU WANNA BE NEXT, YOU STUPID, FUCKING SLUT?"

Katie struggled to breath properly.

"Stop your bloody struggling bitch or I'll blow your fucking brains out. DOWNS, WHERE ARE YOU? WHERE ARE YOU, BABY?"

"Stay where you are!" Katie screamed.

Slick twisted Katie's neck at an awful angle. "You shut your bloody mouth or you're dead. You hear me?"

Lorry stood trembling as she hid from Slick. Slowly she edged forward, the petrol fumes now intense. Soon she was standing exactly where Katie had stood. Crowds of onlookers gathered outside, peering through the front glass doors to see what was happening. Still Slick continued his ravings. Then he changed his grip on Katie to hold her with his gunarm as he flicked the top over on his zippo lighter and lit it. Onlookers outside scattered in wild panic. Slick waved the lighter around, only feet from the petrol-soaked carpet.

"YOU HEAR ME, DOWNS? GET YOUR ARSE OUT HERE BABE, OR WE'RE ALL GONNA FRY."

Katie continued to struggle. "What do you want from her? She's done nothing to you."

"Whacky-do baby," he laughed. "Didn't think I'd find her did she? SHOULDN'T HAVE SOLD YOUR CAR, BABY. CARS CAN BE TRACED, RIGHT? NOW GET THE FUCK OUT HERE!"

"Let her go!" Katie blurted, struggling more for breath as Slick tightened his grip on her throat.

Gabe was seething with rage. But he knew to make a charge at Slick would see him dead. If he didn't, he'd kill Katie. He knew that most of all he had to stay calm. If he panicked, Katie would surely die.

Katie's pleading to Slick lasted several minutes. Long enough for the sounds of the first police siren to be heard. Lorry peered around the same edge of the building as Katie had previously and immediately saw Casey's blood-soaked body. Convulsive rage erupted within her body and with no thoughts for her own safety, she bolted from cover.

"MURDERER!" she screamed as she lunged at Slick. But her actions were doomed. The distance between her and the crazed killer was too great for her charge to have any effect. Slick saw her coming, swung the shotgun in her direction and pulled the trigger. The double magnum load caught Lorry Downs full on in the face and chest, the same as Casey. Part of her head was blown away, and her chest opened up exposing her heart and lungs. Lorry was dead before her knees began to buckle. Slick moved to chamber another round. Katie seized her chance. She drove a straight arm back into his groin.

As Slick doubled over in pain, Katie dived for cover behind one of the ornamental brass, cast-iron and wooden peacocks. Slick fired again. The blast disintegrated the peacock. Katie screamed in agony as several pellets tore into her upper arm.

Slick stood watching her, deciding whether to finish her, his back to Gabe. Like a raging bull, Gabe burst from the partition and lunged straight at Slick. He moved with the speed of a startled gazelle. Slick heard him coming. As he swung round, he worked the pump on the twelve-gauge but he didn't have time to aim and fire before the big man drove a vicious right hand square to the middle of his face. Slick dropped like he was pole-axed. Seeing him fall, Gabe thought he had knocked him out. He scrambled to Katie's side. He was kneeling to gather her in his arms when he felt the barrel of the shotgun rammed into his ear. Bleeding profusely from a busted nose and a near-severed top lip, Slick Bennedict sneered at him.

"I fucking thought it was you. You're that dickhead from Naracoorte aren't you?" he said, spitting blood and teeth, trying to shake off the effects of Gabe's right hand.

Gabe, white eyed with rage, turned to look at him. "You oughta know Slick, I saved your arse once."

"Yeah, yeah, years ago." He tried to grin, but the profuse bleeding and pain of his face made talking difficult enough, let alone any attempts to smile.

"Still belting the shit out of women?" Gabe asked.

"No man! I just shoot the bitches now. Like these two. This fucking blonde bitch right here is gonna end up just like 'er."

Gabe looked at Katie. She was bleeding profusely and trying to press her fingers against her wounds to stop the blood flow. Gabe knew he had to do something, but with a twelve-gauge jammed in his ear, he had few options.

"So what are you gonna do now Slick? The way I figure it, you've only got one shot left. That's if you started off with one up the spout plus the five in the magazine."

"Wrong Caplin!" he sneered, feeding a couple more rounds from his pocket into the magazine. "Still plenty up the spout to put your fucking brains in the fish pond. Get on your feet."

* * *

Out in front of The Oakdale Country Club, police, ambulances and TV crews began to arrive. When the first calls came in, police were told shots had been fired. Crack marksmen were rushed to the scene when it was learned someone had been shot. Two detectives, wearing bullet-proof vests, cleared the area of onlookers and scaled the front entrance using a workman's ladder.

Inside, while the marksmen took position above the gunman, one of the off duty cops hired by Katie McFarlane as security for Lorry Downs edged his way against the staircase toward Slick. He made his move. "Drop it arsehole!" he shouted.

Slick spun Gabe around, dropped the shotgun to his hip and fired. The off duty cop didn't know what hit him. Half the blast tore into the staircase, but the other half tore into his head and chest. He died instantly.

* * *

As Slick Bennedict had his shotgun jammed into Gabe's ear, Gabe's mind flashed back to how his father must have felt when he did the same to him all those years ago. *But the difference was*, he thought, *that incident centred on one of self-survival and bluff.*

His mind returned to the present. Slick Bennedict was on a thrill-kill lust for revenge. He had already killed three times, maybe even four. Another dead body wasn't going to matter. Gabe had heard the approaching police sirens and couldn't understand why a swarm of bullet-proof-vest-wearing coppers hadn't come charging through the door. Gabe turned his attacker side on as he was eased over to Lorry Down's body. Slick kicked her head and it flopped over, a brainless oozing mass.

"Fucking bitch!" he hissed. Then he laughed. "Fucking showed her you don't mess with Slick Bennedict!" Slick forced Gabe to look at her. "You see her, arsehole? That's you in thirty seconds."

"What about the others, Slick?" Gabe said, noticing a slight movement on the roof above the entrance. He hoped it was the police. *Show yourselves, you blokes, this bastard's playing for keeps.* Katie was bleeding and in severe pain. She needed him. He knew she did. His heart had never beat like it. Not even when he bailed his father up. Gabe was like an overheated pressure cooker with a jammed valve, on the verge of exploding.

Slick, sensing Gabe was planning a move, jammed the barrel in harder against his ear. "Don't even think about it, arsehole," he sneered. Then he laughed again. "That stupid bitch over there picked up the phone. Certainly fucked her day eh?"

"What about the copper?" Gabe said. "He might be still alive." Slick dropped the shotgun and fired into the policeman's motionless body, his lightning-quick action to reload preventing any movement from Gabe.

"You fucking sick bastard!" Gabe screamed.

Slick laughed even more. "That answer your question, arsehole?" again jamming the end of the barrel in his ear.

"What about the blonde? What did she do?"

"She come at me man, just like you fucking did. You next, then her. Just like that dopey, dumb, copper bastard!"

"Put the gun down. Me dead isn't going to get you out of here."

"You shut your damn face!" Slick flicked the lid again on his zippo lighter. He held it out at arm's length. "COME ON YOU COPPER BASTARDS! WHY THE FUCK DON'T YOU COME IN AND GET ME? YOU HEAR ME? COME AND FUCKING GET ME!"

Just then, the enormous crack of a four-one-six magnum filled the air. The glass roof sheeting shattered and Slick Bennedict's face took on an ugly twisted look of anguish and surprise as the soft nose catapulted him free of his hostage. The marksman's high-powered load, with over five-thousand pounds of energy, took Bennedict right on the point of the shoulder. Its awesome hitting power ripped the shoulder and the arm holding the gun completely from the body. The force of the impact spun Bennedict in a circle and sent him back five feet. His shoulder and arm, still holding the shotgun, reeled across the carpet, stopping at Katie McFarlane's feet.

As Bennedict hit the floor, another shot took off the top of his head at the hairline above his left ear. But the instant the shot was fired, Slick flicked his lighter. When the bullet struck him and spun him round, the cigarette lighter flew out of his hand and landed on the petrol-soaked carpet. There was an ear-splitting whoosh as the fumes and the petrol ignited instantaneously, sending flashes and flames thundering throughout the ground floor and staircase. In seconds, flames had snaked their way through the front entrance and around the perimeter of the complex.

Oakdale was burning.

* * *

Trapped inside, Gabe looked around, half dazed and in shock. Something more awesome than anything he'd ever seen or heard had wiped his attacker off the face of the Earth. His clothes were splattered with Slick's blood and bone fragments. A few feet away he saw the young hoodlum whose grip had been ripped from his body, almost headless. His shoulder and gun arm lay near Katie's feet, torn away by what he thought must have been from the horrific force of a high-powered bullet. Blood was running freely from Slick's body as Gabe found himself staring at the corpse. He vomited when his mind conceived the sight of Slick's shoulder and gun arm laying shattered, bleeding and pulsating.

The flames had now engulfed the entire reception area with a impenetrable wall raging right across the front entrance. The heat, searing through his clothing onto his skin, brought him back. "Katie. Jesus, KATIE!" He threw himself at her. He glanced at her wounds. "Katie, my darling Katie. Jesus Christ, what the fuck did he do to you?" he cried, attempting to touch her wounds, then withdrawing his hand quickly.

He looked up at the wall of flames. He became frantic as the heat and fire closed in. "HELP US! FOR CHRIST SAKE'S SOMEONE, HELP US!," he screamed.

Katie looked at him, her face, grimaced in pain and white with fear. "Go Gabe! Please go! Save yourself! I can't make it through there!" she cried in panic.

Gabe ignored her. He scooped her into his arms and stood amongst the shattered glass, the burning chesterfields and the flames creeping closer. He knew he only had seconds left. Glass tops, windows and partitions began to shatter and splinter. Gabe dropped Katie into the water fountain. Quickly he jumped in after her, rapidly thrashing his arms about to make himself as wet as possible. He leapt out and shoved his hand into his pocket for the pen knife he always carried. He dropped to the floor and frantically tore at the carpet. It seemed to take forever. Then he tore up a piece about four feet square. Gabe hauled Katie out of the water, knelt down and grabbed the carpet.

"Have you got a good arm?"

"W...what?" she cried.

"Come on sweetheart! Don't give up on me now. We're nearly home," he said. "Hold your good arm up. Come on! Hold your good arm up!" She did so. "Now hang on to this." Gabe put one end of the carpet square in her hand and turned it over so it wouldn't be exposed. He grabbed the other. He held it up in front of them creating a shield. "Hang on now!" he yelled. "We're gonna make a run for it!"

He bolted towards the fire-engulfed entrance with Katie in his arms. The carpet fell back across their heads and shielded their upper bodies down to Gabe's thighs. Katie was totally covered. As he entered the wall of flame, he'd only gone a few steps when he felt the intense heat on his back, cutting through his brand new suit.

He charged on. Each step a nightmare as he surged forward. He couldn't see where he was going. For all he knew he may have been racing into an even bigger inferno. He started to scream when he feared death was only moments away. Still he kept lunging forward, dropping his head and shoulders over Katie, to give what remaining protection he could. Suddenly he was through to the other side and clear of the building. He knew he had survived one of the most terrifying five-second periods of his life. He dropped to his knees and flung the burning carpet clear. Immediately he was surrounded by ambulance officers who quickly smothered him in a wet blanket. Gabe dropped his head to Katie's. Blackened by smoke and bleeding from shotgun-pellet wounds, she was otherwise unscathed, but in deep shock.

Gabe held her close. "We made it!" he blubbered. "Jesus Christ sweetheart, we made it! We made it, we bloody made it."

"Sir! Sir!" he heard. "We need to get to the lady. We need to get to the lady!" came an urgent voice.

Gradually he let her go and she was immediately placed on a stretcher. The next sound he heard was the disappearing, high-pitched wail of an ambulance siren.

Two police officers made their way towards him. Slowly he raised his eyes and looked back at the building. It was now a raging inferno. T.V. journos tried to jostle in, but were quickly herded away. "Sir, can you speak?" the sergeant asked.

Gabe slowly got to his feet. "Jesus Christ!, he cussed. "What the hell happened in there?" He looked at the sergeant and saw the scoped rifle in his hand. "Did you fire that shot?"

The sergeant nodded and worked the bolt action, ejecting the spent shell. He grabbed it in mid-air, held it up, and threw it to him. "A four-one-six Remington magnum. Elephant gun!" he smirked. "Keep it as a souvenir."

Gabe caught the spent shell and fixed his eyes upon it. He had never seen a cartridge so big. "And I thought the old three-o-three was a big bugger!" he gushed. "No wonder it took his bloody arm off!"

"That was the general idea," the sergeant said. "We needed to make sure we had enough fire power to shoot through the glass roof and still take him down. Do you have any idea who the bloke was?"

"Yeah, he used to live in Naracoorte. Name's Bennedict."

Next instant a giant explosion and a fireball blew into the sky. Gabe jumped back. "Jesus! what was that?"

"I'd say all the scotch," McLoughlin said, showing no emotion. "And the blonde woman you brought out with you?"

"Katie McFarlane. She owns the place."

"Used to!" he told Gabe as another fireball blew into the sky. "The smokies won't save this baby. She's gone. Sure hope she was insured. By the way, what's your name?"

"Caplin. Gabe Caplin."

"Where you from, Mr Caplin?"

"Naracoorte," he answered, feeling his body begin to shake.

"Well Mr Caplin, I gotta tell you I reckon you're the bravest bastard I've ever seen in my life. How the hell you got yourself and the lady out of there is beyond me. Our blokes had people running around out here like chooks with their heads cut off, but they couldn't get near the place. The bloody heat was a nightmare. Thank Christ everyone inside could make it out the back entrances. How long before that prick would've pulled the trigger on you?"

"About three seconds."

"Shit! That close? We had to wait till he was on an angle so I could take his shoulder off. Lucky he turned when he did." McLoughlin looked at him. Then he remembered how the gunman was turned side-on enabling him to get a clean shot. "Jesus! You turned that bastard didn't you?"

Trying to control his shaking body, Gabe looked squarely into the policeman's eyes. "I saw a flash of something up on the roof. I hoped like buggery it would be you blokes. I knew the angle I was facing wasn't helping much, so when he forced me across to the woman's body, I half turned so you could see him better."

"Jesus! You're too bloody good for me. I couldn't have been that brave," McLoughlin acknowledged. "Not with a twelve-gauge jammed in my face."

"An...and the...the others?" Gabe stammered.

"We don't know yet. One of 'em was ours."

Gabe shook his head. "Poor bastard was a sitting duck."

McLoughlin continued. "Don't know about the other two yet. From what we saw on the roof, they were two young women."

Gabe dropped his head. "How long do you want me for?"

"Well the ambos say you're okay but I reckon you should spend twenty-four hours in hospital. Christ, you've got to be in shock after what you've been through!"

"Forget about it," Gabe said firmly.

"We'll take you to the station, get you cleaned up, into some dry clothes and take your statement. Is there somewhere you gotta be?"

"I've got to be at the hospital with Katie," he said.

"The blonde woman? You know her?"

Gabe nodded. "Yeah, we've met."

By now, hundreds of people had gathered to watch The Oakdale Country Club being razed to the ground. Police had already cordoned off the entire area around the building, now a major crime scene. When the flames were finally extinguished, then would begin the task of recovering the bodies.

* * *

Katie McFarlane had been traumatized from the violence of being shot and then trapped in the blazing inferno of The Oakdale Country Club. As she was driven from the scene in an ambulance she became delirious, with one officer being forced to restrain her.

"My club!" she blubbered hysterically. "My club! What about the staff? Paul's possessions! Stanley! Lorry! Gabe, I have to save Lorry! Where's Emma? Save my desk! I want my pictures!"

After being admitted to hospital the delirium continued until doctors sedated her. But even in a deep sleep, she kept calling. Reliving the horror. All the time, trying to leave her bed, but she couldn't break free of the wide leather straps used to pin her body. Medical staff sat with her through the first six hours. When she finally began to come round, through sleepy, hazy eyes, she could see Gabe sitting only inches from her, holding her hand. She saw a drip in one arm and the heavy bandaging on the other. She could feel no pain, although she knew there would be, once the drugs wore off. She raised a hand to rub her eyes and, although terribly groggy, could make out other forms directly behind Gabe.

"Hello," she tried to say, but her lips and throat were so dry her voice could barely be heard.

"Oh God Katie, thank Christ you're okay," he said, tears of joy running down his face. "Are you in any pain?" He wanted to hold her. Desperately. But he couldn't.

She nodded her head slightly. "But I'm not sure about my arm." She strained to see who was with him. One by one they each identified themselves. Jill Lawson was first. She had been fighting her own demons. Earlier that day she had offered to take Emma to the doctor after the little girl complained of a sore throat. Lorry Downs was grateful for the offer because at the time of the appointment, Kazumi would be needing her. Jill and Emma only knew of the catastrophic events that had taken place when they drove into the club's car park. She was blaming herself for not being there.

"I didn't know it was happening," she cried. "I was in town with Emma. I'm so sorry Katie, I should have been there. Maybe I could have done something. God, we thought we'd lost you."

"You did do something," Katie whispered in her ear. "You saved the child a lifetime of trauma and nightmares by stopping her seeing what happened to her mother."

Emma Downs followed. She reached up and gently slid her little arms under Katie's head and cried like a baby. "They killed my mummy! They killed my mummy!" she blurted.

Katie raised her hand to the little girl's cheek. Tears rolled freely from her eyes. "I know baby, I know. Would you like me as your new mummy?"

Emma's answer was to cling even more tightly to Katie. Gabe, Jill Lawson and Kazumi also began to cry. Katie asked for her head chef. Gabe withdrew the little girl from her and Kazumi took her place. Clutching Katie's hand and putting her cheek against Katie's, she broke down and wept uncontrollably.

"Miss Katie. Oh Miss Katie! I...er...we..." She couldn't go on.

"Gabe," she whispered. He dropped his ear to Katie's mouth. "Is everything gone?"

He wanted to lie but he knew it would serve little purpose. He nodded his head.

"Everything? My office, upstairs, Lorry's unit? The piano?"

"Everything Katie. Absolutely every damn thing."

She closed her eyes, squeezing them tight. She began to whimper and throw her head from one side of the pillow to the other.

"Nurse!" Gabe called.

* * *

For the next two days Gabe only left her side to use the bathroom or grab a cup of coffee. He didn't eat. He didn't sleep. He refused to leave.

On the morning of the third day he opened the venetian blinds to let the sun's rays fill her room. Slowly Katie McFarlane opened her eyes. Gabe was right there with her as she did. He hadn't shaved. His face was drawn and gaunt from lack of sleep, his eye's like sandpaper. A faint smile passed her lips.

"What time is it?" Katie asked.

"Just after seven," he told her, placing his hand on her cheek.

"Is it the next day already?"

"Sweetheart, you've been out of it for two whole days. This is the morning of the third."

"But Kazumi and Emma...and...and Jill were just here?"

Gabe smiled. "That was two days ago," he told her.

Her senses were rapidly returning. She rubbed her eyes, eased herself up in the bed and looked at her arm.

"You were shot...do you remember?"

"I do now. God that hurt! How bad is it?"

Gabe gently placed his fingers on the bandage. "Flesh wounds. About seven little holes. Doctors say the pellets went straight through, so you won't be carrying any lead around. But by God you were lucky. Another six inches and it would've been your face."

"And you. Are you hurt?"

Gabe shook his head.

"You should have left me..."

Gabe pressed his fingers against her lips. "Like bloody hell! It's taken me all my life to find you. You don't think I'd have given that bastard the satisfaction of claiming you too? If you were going to die, then we'd have died together. By Christ! We damn near did too!"

"Oh Gabe," she murmured. "You are such a dear, dear man. I can remember the gun going off, and all the blood on my arm. That madman being cut in half. Then you scooping me out of the water, the intense heat and the flames...the club...What am I going to do?"

He shook his head. "Was it insured?"

"Fully...and then some. But that's not the problem. Darling Casey is gone." More tears came. "That policeman. God what about his wife and family? And Lorry! If I hadn't have brought her here, she would still be alive!"

"You can't blame yourself for that. If he wanted to get her as badly as he did, she wouldn't have been safe anywhere. Was that her daughter who came to see you?" Katie nodded. "You told her you would take her mother's place. You sure about that?"

"She has no-one else in the world Gabe. I'll probably keep Kazumi on to help look after her."

"Do you want to go back and see what's left?"

"I'll have to think about that. I remember not wanting to see my car that time. So I'm not exactly jumping out of my skin to see the smouldering ruins of Paul Redman's dream."

"Will you rebuild?"

"Oh Gabe, I have to. Yes of course."

"What the hell happened in there?" Gabe whispered, careful not to aggravate the severe traumatic shock she suffered. "Didn't you have prior warning? Phone calls? Threats?"

"Nothing."

"So the bastard just turned up and started screaming for Lorry Downs?"

"Seems that way. Lorry lived in fear Scarfe would find her."

"Well, that might have been the name he was using, but his real name was Slick Bennedict. He came from down home. I remember him from years back. Used to get his kicks from hurting women, even as a kid."

"How come I didn't die too Gabe?" she blurted. "It just seems I'm cursed."

Again Gabe pressed his fingers to her lips. "Shhh, shhh, no, no, no, come on. You are the most special person in the whole world."

Gabe sat with her for the entire third day. Reluctantly, he left in the evening, found a motel room and slept solidly for twenty-four hours. When he finally woke it was early morning, a day later than he thought, and he was completely disorientated. He grabbed for the phone and, after some convincing, finally accepted he'd been out of it for as long as he had.

Quickly he went to the hospital. Katie was sitting up in bed. She had showered and washed her hair. She brightened up considerably when Gabe walked in the door. She greeted him warmly. "I've missed you. I thought you must have gone home. Can I have a hug?"

He went to her and held her in his arms. "Jesus, I'm sorry Katie. I fell in a heap and was non-compus for a day-and-a-half. I can't believe I did that!"

"After what you went through, it's a wonder you didn't sleep for a week!" As he was about to draw away, Katie held him close. "Kiss me Gabe."

Nervously, he looked over his shoulder to see if anyone else had entered the room. He turned his face to her and pressed his lips against hers. He had only intended it to be a brief encounter, but Katie had other ideas. She held him close and darted her tongue in his mouth. "I want you," she murmured.

Gabe drew back slightly and smiled. "Looks like you're on the mend doesn't it?"

"I am in so much physical and emotional pain, you seem to be the only one who knows how to do anything about it. Take me home to my place and make love to me," she whispered.

Gabe felt a little embarrassed. His body began to stir. It only seemed hours ago they were both knocking on death's door. He couldn't understand how Katie could wake up from a deep sleep and then want to make love. Especially as it had been so long since she had seen him.

"When are you allowed out?" he asked, trying to hide his discomfort and self consciousness.

"Doctors have said in the morning, but I want to go now. I need to be with you now."

"But sweetheart, the police want to talk to you tomorrow and the funerals are the next day."

Katie looked at him and slid her fingers through his hand. "Gabe," she began. "When that gun was pointed to my head, I prayed for you to be there. It was just the most ridiculous thing. There was no just way you would be in Mildura, but you were. And when I was shot, I was thinking of you."

"But Katie, you're Paul's girl."

She closed her eyes and shook her head. "I've already faced that. I've made my peace with Paul and pleaded with him to free me so I can love again and be in love again. I don't know if I can, but I know in the months that have passed since I have seen you, my mind always went back to those wonderful moments we had together. When we sat up all night to watch the sunrise. How we made love on the beach. At the time I thought I was getting rid of stress, built-up emotions, heart-breaking loneliness, but it was more than that. When you took me in your arms, everything else seemed unimportant. I asked myself how it was possible. How could I love one man then, within a year, find myself in the arms of someone else? But you did it to me Gabe.

Whether it was because in your own mind I was the totally unreachable goal, I don't know, but I can tell you, in the eleven days from when you rescued me until you rolled me in your arms, you gave me a confidence I firmly believed I would never have again."

Gabe was struck dumb for a moment. "Are you telling me...?"

She interrupted. "I'm telling you I want to be with you."

"But Katie," he began to protest.

"Don't say anything. Please just kiss me again and hold me."

Chapter 28

"I think I'd like to take a long hot bath," Katie told Gabe back in her apartment. "I don't know how I'm going to get through all this. The police. The funerals. The media. Facing those poor people who've been left behind. Rebuilding. The insurance. You haven't said why you were in Mildura?" she called from the bathroom.

Gabe was standing at her lounge-room window, carefully looking round the edge of the blind to see if any reporters had followed them. They had been camped outside the hospital hoping for an interview. "I had to have a look at some sheep," he lied.

"They grow citrus up here, not wool," she replied.

The closeness of her voice spun him round. Katie was standing directly in front of him, her dressing gown hanging open, exposing her nudity. "Please help me forget my nightmares," she said.

Katie's lounge-room clock chimed away the two hours they spent drifting on a dream.

"You're like a magnet to me," he told her. "Not only that, but it's obvious you can't be trusted to be let out of my sight," he jested.

"Does that mean you'll sell up and come to live in Mildura?"

"Does that mean you pack up and come and live on the farm?"

Katie smiled, but sadly. "It's a problem isn't it?"

"I don't know what to say," Gabe told her. "I'm with you, but I don't feel as though I am. I can't feel that it's real."

She went to him. "But we are real. I'm with you now."

Gabe wrapped a towel around himself and sat on the side of the bed. "Katie, whenever we've been together it's been out of circumstance, rather than choice. The car accident. Then you came down to Mrs Cropp's for a few days...the most sensational few days I've ever spent in my life too, I might add, but again through circumstance. And now this...this absolute fucking tragedy!"

He paused a moment, remembering, then continued. "But never are we together by arrangement. I know I'm not too worldly, but I'm smart enough to know that, out of choice, you would never have chosen to spend time with me. I'm only a country hick. I don't know shit about life. I've never been anywhere, done anything. And look at you. You're the stuff dreams are made of. I just happened to have been there on a couple of occasions when you needed some help. I'm not what you want. I could never be what you want. Look at the age difference. Look what you do. Look what I do. And I mumble and stumble my way through conversation with you because I'm intimidated by you. Sure, I'm in love with you. If love is how Aunty Betsy described it, then when I'm with you or away from you, it's all of that. When things start to settle down a bit and I get you through the next few days, you'll probably want to continue on like you have been and I can accept that. Right now you need me and, believe me, it's no great imposition on my part being around someone like you."

Katie sat up in bed and ran her fingers over Gabe's scarred back. She pressed her cheek against his skin. "You don't understand do you? You just don't understand."

He lay back on the bed and she leaned over the top of him, her touch again seducing him.

* * *

Gabe had forgotten about the media until later in the day when he walked out of Katie's apartment and was immediately confronted by a barrage of cameras, microphones and journalists.

"Mr Caplin, tell us what happened in the club?" "Mr Caplin? How's the young woman?" "Mr Caplin, did you know the gunman?" "Mr Caplin, how did the fire start?" "Mr Caplin. Excuse me, Mr Caplin..."

The rudeness and invasion of his privacy shocked and bewildered him. He wanted to strike out. He wanted to scream at them. But the sheer intensity of the presence of so many strangers destroyed his defences. When he hadn't spoken, the cameras and tape recorders kept rolling as the questions from journalists dried up. They wanted his reaction. And they waited. A strange and eerie silence fell over everyone.

"Er," Gabe stammered. "Look folks, if you don't mind, I'd like you all to leave. I've got nothing to say to you."

Bad move. He was now caught in a crush with more rapid-fire questions coming at him from all directions. One reporter, a shortish man whose torso looked longer than his legs, was particularly annoying. His voice seemed louder than everyone else's. As the questions continued to be fired at him, he spun round on his heel and made for the front door of the unit. He jammed the key in the lock and threw himself inside slamming the door after himself. Katie, on hearing the commotion, hurried to his side. He quickly explained the situation to her and she became frightened.

"Don't worry sweetheart, I've told them to leave. I'm sure they will."

As he spoke to Katie, he again peered round the corner of the blind. The shortish reporter had climbed into the branches of a tree in a further bid to try and get a picture of them. Gabe was furious. He turned to Katie. "Is there a hardware shop in Mildura?"

"Several...why?"

Katie fetched the Yellow Pages for him and he dialled a number. Gabe explained what he wanted and hung up the phone. "I'll fix that little bastard!" he said.

Forty minutes later there was a knock on the door. Gabe answered it and the waiting media rushed him. He ignored their pleas and questions and pushed his way through them to get to the delivery man. He took possession of the box, gave him a cheque, then had to push his way through them again to get back inside. He slammed the door then peered round the edge of the blind. The shortish man was still in the tree.

Gabe was visibly shaken by what was happening. "Shit Katie! These bloody people are like rabid animals!" he cussed, opening the box he'd just had delivered.

"What on earth are you going to do?" Katie queried.

He smiled at her. "These bastards want a story, then I'll give 'em one," he told her ripping open the lid and taking out a small chainsaw.

"Good God! what are you going to do with that?"

Gabe flicked the petrol tap, opened the throttle and jerked the starter cord. The little machine immediately burst into life, deafening them in such a small and confined space. He flung open the front door, and bolted outside. The media again began to form its crush but halted in its stride when it saw Gabe wielding a chainsaw with its engine screaming.

He shot over to the tree and stood beneath the newsman. Gabe noticed that next to the tree was the next-door neighbour's garage. He gunned the trigger a few times and laid the base of the engine against the tree's small trunk. He looked up at the newsman. "You still say you're not gonna leave?" Gabe yelled over the top of the engine.

"Piss off arsehole!" came the reply.

The cameras whirred frantically as Gabe gunned the chainsaw and sunk the blade into the small trunk, chewing into the timber. Fearing a fall of about twenty feet, the reporter quickly began to make his way down to ground level. Gabe watched his little legs work overtime as he scrambled down the tree. Gabe cut the chainsaw and put it on the ground. At that moment, the newsman still had a few feet left to descend. Gabe reached up and grabbed him by the scruff of the neck and the seat of his pants and hauled him down. The newsman was huffing and puffing and screaming abuse. The media mass began laughing hysterically at his plight.

Gabe had him in an iron-clad grip and began to swing him back and forth, much like a seaman setting himself to hurl a coil of rope over a distance. "You pock-faced, mealy-mouthed, beady-eyed little creep. I told you to fuck off!" When he finally felt he had the momentum to launch him, he did. Right on to the roof of the neighbour's garage... to the howls of laughter of everyone gathered. Gabe turned to face the cameras.

"Okay, show's over. Please. Leave us alone." He walked over, picked up the chainsaw, gunned the motor and drove the blade back into the trunk of the small tree, felling it to the ground.

"Seeing you like it so much, you might like to take this with you when you leave," he called to the newsman, still trying to find his feet on the roof of the neighbour's garage. He went back inside and Katie was splitting her sides laughing. It was the first time she'd laughed for days. But mostly she'd enjoyed watching Gabe dispense his own special form of 'bush justice'.

"My God! Are you going to be on the six o'clock news or what?"

He looked at her. "Not me. Him!" he gestured towards the reporter on the roof.

"Both of you," she said, peering around the blind. "Looks like you've made your point. They're all leaving."

* * *

Officers from the Mildura C.I.B. called at Katie's apartment the next morning and, over a period of five hours, took her statement of the events which took place at The Oakdale Country Club. Later that afternoon she had Gabe take her into town, where she purchased a mourning outfit and hat to wear to the three funerals the next day. Aware too he also needed clothes, Katie went with Gabe to replace his new suit. She insisted on paying for it plus a number of other items she knew he would need. Leaving the store, she took hold of his hand.

"I think I should see Oakdale."

"You don't have to, you know."

"I know. But I think I'll always wonder if I don't."

About a hundred yards from the police lines, Gabe stopped his hire vehicle and they got out. He searched her face for a reaction.

Katie stared in disbelief of what lay in front of her. Suddenly she felt numb all over. "Will you hold my hand Gabe?"

The two crossed the police lines, after identifying themselves and being given permission to do so by a young constable standing guard. As they approached what was left of the front entrance, Gabe stopped and Katie proceeded on her own. She walked around, visualising what had previously been there. Twisted and charred facades, the partly burned but destroyed reception desk, the spot where Casey fell, Lorry and the police officer, the staircase. She looked to where her office once was and walked into the area. Her lovingly restored desk was now watersoaked, crushed by falling debris and partially burned. She looked to see if any of the drawers were intact but they weren't. She leaned down to see if anything at all could be salvaged. Even Paul's photo was gone. Turning her head, she looked to where her drink stand once stood. *And mum and dad too?* She walked slowly back to Gabe, glancing over to where she lay after being shot and at the fountain where Gabe soaked her before making a run for it. Her heart sank deeper and deeper.

I *must rebuild this place. I simply must...and quickly*, she thought.

* * *

For the next twenty-four hours Katie McFarlane battled heart-rending grief and sorrow. *My God, my life is filled with funerals. Please Lord, please, no more*, she pleaded.

When she walked inside following the events of the day, she asked Gabe to run her bath. When the tub was half full, he walked in to the bedroom and found her already sound asleep. He didn't wake her. Instead, he eased her out of her black mourning dress and slipped off her shoes. He kissed her forehead and gently covered her with a blanket. It was fifteen hours before she awoke.

* * *

Two days later Gabe was sitting with Katie at the breakfast table. Katie knew he would want to be getting back to his farm. She also knew that trying to combine his life with hers would be near impossible. After the club was rebuilt, again she would be looking down the barrel at fifty to sixty hours a week, seven days a week. There was no room in her life for love. But she also knew she was falling in love with Gabe. At first she thought it was gratitude, and it probably was. But this giant of a man had got under her skin. She liked his gentleness, his innocence, his brute strength. She found herself yearning for the security of being wrapped in his powerful arms. She desperately needed to be with him.

She cast her mind back over their long conversations. How she loved him making love to her. She also loved being the teacher. She also knew her dominance of him in this area would be temporary, and she enjoyed that thought even more. She had made her peace with Paul, because she knew she was falling in love with Gabe and, psychologically, she needed to be free to do so. Perhaps her desire to be with Gabe would fade away. Perhaps it was a flash-in-the-pan. *And he will go away*, she thought, *if I put time and distance between us.*

But it wasn't to be the case. She fought to control the on-going argument within herself that she could love, so completely, two different men in such a short space of time. Yet no matter what she said to Gabe, she wouldn't be able to convince him she was genuinely in love with him, that her show of affection towards him wasn't purely one of gratitude and loneliness. If she were able, where could it lead? She was now about to take on the role of mother to a young girl. Where could this man possibly fit in? *Maybe it's fate. Maybe it was fate he was up here when that bastard walked into the club.*

They looked at each other. It was Katie who spoke. "Why do I get the feeling you're leaving today?" she asked him.

He couldn't look at her.

"Gabe?"

He still couldn't raise his eyes from the table. She reached over and touched his hand.

"Gabe?"

"It tears my heart out to say it, but I have to start thinking about getting back...and carrying on my life without you."

"I don't want you to go."

He leaned over and cupped her face in the palm of his hand. "Sweetheart, I'm so in love with you I can't think straight. But we can't go anywhere. You don't love me. Sure I know you might like me a bit, but it's not that...that...stuff Aunty Betsy was on about, that feeling of gut-wrenching agony when we part and that knee-buckling, gut-wrenching joy when we're together. Sure I've enough of that for both of us, but I reckon it's got to be a two-way street."

"What do you feel when you touch me?"

"We both know the answer to that. That's not the question here. It's what do you feel when I touch you?"

Katie got up from her chair and walked a few steps and turned back to him. "When I feel your hand on me, your skin on my skin, my body totally possessed by your body, I feel I'm fulfilling every dream and every wish I had as a little girl."

"But Paul did that."

"Gabe for goodness sakes, Paul is dead. Okay! Paul is dead! I loved him, yes, but now I'm falling in love with you. It was you who made me come alive again. It was you who made me realise too much grief is self-destructive. When I look at you I think of how lucky I am to even know you. I know of no other man with such strong principles, such virtue, such honesty and compassion. All those qualities are very easy to love. You, my wonderful man, are very easy to love. Me? I don't think it would be easy to love me. I've been spoiled. I've been doted on, and chances are I have the capacity to make you as mad as hell, but if you say you love me, then I guess you'll just have to accept it comes with the package. I don't know where to from here for me. Yes I'm going to be a mother to Emma. Yes I am now wealthy. I will rebuild the club and if necessary make Jill Lawson a director and she can totally run the place. I won't even have to be here. But it doesn't make me want you any less. Oh Gabe," she pleaded, going to him and sitting on his lap, "please don't leave. Not yet anyway."

Katie's outpouring stunned Gabe. He was no longer in any doubt.

"Sweetheart," she continued softly. "When I left to come back here the last time, a piece of my heart stayed with you. When I saw you burst into the club to save me, the terror that was striking at my very soul turned to elation, not because you were tackling the gunman, but purely on seeing you again. God I know it's a line that gets thrown around a bit but, at that moment, you were my hero. When you picked me up, I knew if we got out alive, I would promise you my heart. And as terrified as I was, I just knew we were going to be alright. But if you had to die, I was quite prepared to die with you."

"So you'd be prepared to rebuild Oakdale and let Jill Lawson run it?"

"Would you be prepared to take on a little girl and an Asian chef?"

"Depends."

"On what?"

"On whether you'll let me grow old with you."

"Gabe, ever since you've known me, you've had me gift wrapped and placed on a shelf. Please. Take me down. Take me down and unwrap me."

THE END

About the Author

Graham Guy is an Award-Winning Journalist who has worked in radio and television in both Australia and the United States of America.

His background is very diversified having worked in shearing sheds, factories, driven trucks, and seen service in the Royal Australian Navy. He is also a lyricist with many of his songs being set to music and recorded by various artists. For many years he wrote and produced many radio and television commercials and ran his own all-night talk show on commercial radio.

Graham has written several novels. *Eleven Days* was his first. He lives in Adelaide, South Australia.